I0757899

WERTHER & GRAY EDITIONS

WEREWOLF TALES

An Anthology

Collected and Edited by Charles Harrigan

Featuring Stories From

CATHERINE CROWE
CLEMENCE HOUSMAN
ALGERNON BLACKWOOD
SAKI
EUGENE FIELD
HUGH WALPOLE
and more!

DARLEY PRESS

Published by
DARLEY PRESS,
Delaware, USA

First Darley Press Edition ©2021
ISBN 978-1-955741-03-3
Cat # DPWG07

A NOTE ON THE TEXT:
At the discretion of the editor, the copytext has been brought into conformity with modern standards of punctuation, capitalization and spelling.

Cover illustration by Henry Anelay
Interior illustration by Mort Sudbury

Book design and formatting by Edgar's Ghost ©2021

WWW.DARLEYPRESS.COM

CONTENTS

HUGUES, THE WER-WOLF

by Sutherland Menzies

I

ON THE CONFINES of that extensive forest tract formerly spreading over so large a portion of the county of Kent, a remnant of which, to this day, is known as the weald[1] of Kent, and where it stretched its almost impervious covert midway between Ashford and Canterbury during the prolonged reign of our second Henry, a family of Norman extraction by name Hugues (or Wulfric, as they were commonly called by the Saxon inhabitants of that district) had, under protection of the ancient forest laws, furtively erected for themselves alone and miserable habitation. And amidst those sylvan fastnesses, ostensibly following the occupation of woodcutters, the wretched outcasts, for such, from some cause or other, they evidently were, had for many years maintained a secluded and precarious existence. Whether from the rooted antipathy still actively cherished against all of that usurping nation from which they derived their origin, or from recorded malpractice by their superstitious Anglo-Saxon neighbours, they had long been looked upon as belonging to the accursed race of wer-wolves, and as such churlishly refused work on the domains of the surrounding franklins or proprietors, so thoroughly was accredited the descent of

---

1 That woody district, at the period to which our tale belongs, was an immense forest, desolate of inhabitants, and only occupied by wild swine and deer, and though it is now filled with towns and villages and well peopled, the woods that remain sufficiently indicate its former extent.

the original lycanthropic stain transmitted from father to son through several generations. That the Hugues Wulfric reckoned not a single friend among the adjacent homesteads of serf or freedman was not to be wondered at, possessing as they did so unenviable a reputation, for to them was invariably attributed even the misfortunes which chance alone might seem to have given birth. Did midnight fire consume the grange, did the time-decayed barn, over-stored with an abundant harvest, tumble into ruins, were the shocks of wheat lain prostrate over the fields by a tempest, did the smut destroy the grain, or the cattle perish, decimated by a murrain, a child sink under some wasting malady, or a woman give premature birth to her offspring, it was ever the Hugues Wulfric who were openly accused, eyed askance with mingled fear and detestation, the finger of young and old pointing them out with bitter execrations. In fine, they were almost as nearly classed feroe natura as their fabled prototype, and dealt with accordingly.[2]

Terrible, indeed, were the tales told of them round the glowing hearth at eventide, whilst spinning the flax, or plucking the geese, equally affirmed too, in broad daylight, whilst driving the cows to pasturage, and most circumstantially discussed on Sundays between mass and vespers, by the gossip groups collected within Ashford parvyse, with most seasonable admixture of anathema and devout crossings. Witchcraft, larceny, murder, and sacrilege, formed prominent features in the bloody and mysterious scenes of which the Hugues Wulfric were the alleged actors. Sometimes they were ascribed to the father, at others to

---

2   King Edgar is said to have been the first who attempted to rid England of these animals, criminals even being pardoned by producing a stated number of these creatures' tongues. Some centuries after they increased to such a degree as to become again the object of royal attention, and Edward I appointed persons to extirpate this obnoxious race. It is one of the principal bearings in armoury. Hugh, surnamed Lupus, the first Earl of Kent, bore for his crest a wolf's head.

the mother, and even the sister escaped not her share of vilification; fair would they have attributed an atrocious disposition to the unweaned babe, so great, so universal was the horror in which they held that race of Cain! The churchyard at Ashford, and the stone cross, from whence diverged the several roads to London, Canterbury, and Ashford, situated midway between the two latter places, served, so tradition avouched, as nocturnal theatres for the unhallowed deeds of the Wulfrics, who thither prowled by moonlight, it was said, to batten on the freshly buried dead, or drain the blood of any living wight who might be rash enough to venture among those solitary spots. True it was that the wolves had, during some of the severe winters, emerged from their forest lairs, and, entering the cemetery by a breach in its walls, goaded by famine, had actually disinterred the dead. True was it, also, that the Wolf's Cross, as the hinds commonly designated it, had been stained with gore on one occasion through the fall of a drunken mendicant, who chanced to fracture his skull against a pointed angle of its basement. But these accidents, as well as a multitude of others, were attributed to the guilty intervention of the Wulfrics, under their fiendish guise of wer-wolves.

These poor people, moreover, took no pains to justify themselves from a prejudice so monstrous. Full well apprised of what calumny they were the victims, but alike conscious of their impotence to contradict it, they tacitly suffered its infliction, and fled all contact with those to whom they knew themselves repulsive. Shunning the highways, and never venturing to pass through the town of Ashford in open day, they pursued such labour as might occupy them within doors, or in unfrequented places. They appeared not at Canterbury market, never numbered themselves amongst the pilgrims at Becket's far-famed shrine, or assisted at any sport, merry-making, hay-cutting, or harvest home. The priest had interdicted them from all communion with the church, the ale-bibbers from the hostelry.

The primitive cabin which they inhabited was built of chalk and clay, with a thatch of straw, in which the high winds had made huge rents and closed up by a rotten door, exhibiting wide gaps, through which the gusts had free ingress. As this wretched abode was situated at considerable distance from any other, if, perchance, any of the neighbouring serfs strayed within its precincts towards nightfall, their credulous fears made them shun near approach so soon as the vapours of the marsh were seen to blend their ghastly wreaths with the twilight, and as that darkling time drew on which explains the diabolical sense of the old saying, "'tween dog and wolf," "'twixt hawk and buzzard," at that hour the will-o'-wisps began to glimmer around the dwelling of the Wulfrics, who patriarchally supped, whenever they had a supper, and forthwith betook themselves to their rest.

Sorrow, misery, and the putrid exhalations of the steeped hemp, from which they manufactured a rude and scanty attire, combined eventually to bring sickness and death into the bosom of this wretched family, who, in their utmost extremity, could neither hope for pity or succour. The father was first attacked, and his corpse was scarce cold ere the mother rendered up her breath. Thus passed that fated couple to their account, unsolaced by the consolation of the confessor, or the medicaments of the leech. Hugues Wulfric, their eldest son, himself dug their grave, laid their bodies within it swathed with hempen shreds for grave cloths, and raised a few clods of earth to mark their last resting place. A hind, who chanced to see him fulfilling this pious duty in the dusk of evening, crossed himself, and fled as fast as his legs would carry him, fully believing that he had assisted at some hellish incantation. When the real event transpired, the neighbouring gossips congratulated one another upon the double mortality, which they looked upon as the tardy chastisement of heaven. They spoke of ringing the bells, and singing masses of thanks for such an action of grace.

It was All Souls' Eve, and the wind howled along the bleak

hillside, whistling drearily through the naked branches of the forest trees, whose last leaves it had long since stripped. The sun had disappeared. A dense and chilling fog spread through the air like the mourning veil of the widowed, whose day of love hath early fled. No star shone in the still and murky sky. In that lonely hut, through which death had so lately passed, the orphan survivors held their lonely vigil by the fitful blaze emitted by the reeking logs upon their hearth. Several days had elapsed since their lips had been imprinted for the last time upon the cold hands of their parents. Several dreary nights had passed since the sad hour in which their eternal farewell had left them desolate on earth.

Poor lone ones! Both, too, in the flower of their youth. How sad, yet how serene did they appear amid their grief! But what sudden and mysterious terror is it that seems to overcome them? It is not, alas, the first time since they were left alone upon earth that they have found themselves at this hour of the night by their deserted hearth, enlivened of old by the cheerful tales of their mother. Full often had they wept together over her memory, but never yet had their solitude proved so appalling, and, pallid as very spectres, they tremblingly gazed upon one another as the flickering ray from the wood-fire played over their features.

"Brother! Heard you not that loud shriek which every echo of the forest repeated? It sounds to me as if the ground were ringing with the tread of some gigantic phantom, and whose breath seems to have shaken the door of our hut. The breath of the dead they say is icy cold. A mortal shivering has come over me."

"And I, too, sister, thought I heard voices as it were at a distance, murmuring strange words. Tremble not thus, am I not beside you?"

"Oh, brother! Let us pray the Holy Virgin, to the end that she may restrain the departed from haunting our dwelling."

"But, perhaps, our mother is amongst them. She comes, unshrived and unshrouded, to visit her forlorn offspring, her well-beloved! For, knowest thou not, sister, 'tis the eve on which the dead forsake their tombs. Let us open the door, that our mother may enter and resume her wonted place by hearthstone."

"Oh, brother, how gloomy is all without doors, how damp and cold the gust sweeps by. Hearest thou, what groans the dead are uttering round our hut? Oh, close the door, in heaven's name!"

"Take courage, sister, I have thrown upon the fire that holy branch, plucked as it flowered on last palm Sunday, which thou knowest will drive away all evil spirits, and now our mother can enter alone."

"But how will she look, brother? They say the dead are horrible to gaze upon, that their hair has fallen away, their eyes become hollow, and that, in walking, their bones rattle hideously. Will our mother, then, be thus?"

"No, she will appear with the features we loved to behold, with the affectionate smile that welcomes us home from our perilous labours, with the voice which, in early youth, sought us when, belated, the closing night surprised its far from our dwelling."

The poor girl busied herself awhile in arranging a few platters of scanty fare upon the tottering board which served them for a table, and this last pious offering of filial love, as she deemed it, appeared accomplished only by the greatest and last effort, so enfeebled had her frame become.

"Let our dearly beloved mother enter then," she exclaimed, sinking exhausted upon the settle. "I have prepared her evening meal, that she may not be angry with me, and all is arranged as she was wont to have it. But what ails thee, my brother, for now thou tremblest as I did awhile agone?"

"See'st thou not, sister, those pale lights which are rising at a distance across the marsh? They are the dead coming to seat themselves before the repast prepared for them. Hark! Listen to the funeral tones of the Allhallowtide[3] bells, as they come upon the gale, blended with their hollow voices. Listen, listen!"

"Brother, this horror grows insupportable. This, I feel, of a verity, will be my last night upon earth! And is there no word of hope to cheer me, mingling with those fearful sounds? Oh, mother! Mother!"

"Hush, sister, hush I see'st thou now the ghastly lights which herald the dead, gleaming athwart the horizon? Hearest thou the prolonged tolling of the bell? They come! They come!"

"Eternal repose to their ashes!" exclaimed the bereaved ones, sinking upon their knees, and bowing down their heads in the extremity of terror and lamentation, and as they uttered the words, the door was at the same moment closed with violence, as though it had been slammed to by a vigorous hand. Hugues started to his feet, for the cracking of the timber which support-ed the roof seemed to announce the fall of the frail tenement. The fire was suddenly extinguished, and a plaintive groan min-gled itself with the blast that whistled through the crevices of the door. On raising his sister, Hugues found that she too was no longer to be numbered among the living.

II

Hugues, on becoming the head of his family, composed of two sisters younger than himself, saw them likewise descend into the grave in the short space of a fortnight, and when he had laid the last within her parent earth, he hesitated whether he should not extend himself beside them, and share their peaceful slumber. It was not by tears and sobs that grief so profound as his manifested itself, but in a mute and sullen contemplation over the supulture of his kindred and his own future happiness.

---

3   On this eve formally the Catholic church performed a most solemn office for the repose of the dead.

During three consecutive nights he wandered, pale and haggard, from his solitary hut, to prostrate himself and kneel by turns upon the funereal turf. For three days food had not passed his lips.

Winter had interrupted the labours of the woods and fields, and Hugues had presented himself in vain among the neighbouring domains to obtain a few days' employment to thresh grain, cut wood, or drive the plough. No one would employ him from fear of drawing upon himself the fatality attached to all bearing the name of Wulfric. He met with brutal denials at all hands, and not only were these accompanied by taunts and menace, but dogs were let loose upon him to rend his limbs. They deprived him even of the alms accorded to beggars by profession. In short, he found himself overwhelmed with injuries and scorn.

Was he, then, to expire of inanition or deliver himself from the tortures of hunger by suicide? He would have embraced that means, as a last and only consolation, had he not been retained earthward to struggle with his dark fate by a feeling of love. Yes, that abject being, forced in very desperation, against his better self, to abhor the human species in the abstract, and to feel a savage joy in waging war against it, that pariah who scarce longer felt confidence in that heaven which seemed an apathetic witness of his woes, that man so isolated from those social relations which alone compensate us for the toils and troubles of life, without other stay than that afforded by his conscience, with no other fortune in prospect than the bitter existence and miserable death of his departed kin. Worn to the bone by privation and sorrow, swelling with rage and resentment, he yet consented to live, to cling to life, for—strange—he loved! But for that heaven-sent ray gleaming across his thorny path, a pilgrimage so lone and wearisome would he have gladly exchanged for the peaceful slumber of the grave.

Hugues Wulfric would have been the finest youth in all that

part of Kent, were it not that the outrages with which he had so unceasingly to contend, and the privations he was forced to undergo, had effaced the colour from his cheeks, and sunk his eyes deep in their orbits. His brows were habitually contracted, and his glance oblique and fierce. Yet, despite that recklessness and anguish which clouded his features, one, incredulous of his atrocities, could not have failed to admire the savage beauty of his head, cast in nature's noblest mould, crowned with a profusion of waving hair, and set upon shoulders whose robust and harmonious proportions were discoverable through the tattered attire investing them. His carriage was firm and majestic, his motions were not without a species of rustic grace, and the tone of his naturally soft voice accorded admirably with the purity in which he spoke his ancestral language, the Norman-French. In short, he differed so widely from people of his imputed condition that one is constrained to believe that jealousy or prejudice must originally have been no stranger to the malicious persecution of which he was the object. The women alone ventured first to pity his forlorn condition, and endeavoured to think of him in a more favourable light.

Branda, niece of Willieblud, the flesher of Ashford, had, among other, of the town maidens, noticed Hugues with a not unfavouring eye, as she chanced to pass one day on horseback, through a coppice near the outskirts of the town, into which the latter had been led by the eager chase of a wild hog, and which animal, from the nature of the country was, single-handed, exceedingly difficult of capture. The malignant falsehoods of the ancient crones, continually buzzed in her ears, in nowise diminished the advantageous opinion she had conceived of this ill-treated and good-looking wer-wolf. She sometimes, indeed, went so far as to turn considerably out of her way, in order to meet and exchange his cordial greeting. For Hugues, recognizing the attention of which he had now become the object, had, in his turn, at last summoned up courage to survey more leisurely the pretty Branda, and the result was that he found her as buxom and pretty a lass as, in his hitherto restricted rambles out of the forest, his timorous gaze had ever encountered. His gratitude increased proportionally, and at the moment when his domestic losses came one after another to overwhelm him, he was actually on the eve of making Branda, on the first opportunity presenting itself, an avowal of the love he bore her.

It was chill winter, Christmas-tide, the distant roll of the curfew had long ceased, and all the inhabitants of Ashford were safe housed in their tenements for the night. Hugues, solitary, motionless, silent, his forehead grasped between his hands, his gaze dully faced upon the decaying brands that feebly glimmered upon his hearth, he heeded not the cutting north wind, whose sweeping gusts shook the crazy roof, and whistled through the chinks of the door. He started not at the harsh cries of the herons fighting for prey in the marsh, nor at the dismal croaking of the ravens perched over his smoke-vent. He thought of his departed kindred, and imagined that his hour to join them would soon be at hand, for the intense cold congealed the marrow of his bones, and fell hunger gnawed and twisted his entrails. Yet, at intervals, would a recollection of nascent love, of Branda, suddenly appease his else intolerable anguish, and cause a faint smile to gleam across his wan features.

"Oh, blessed Virgin! Grant that my sufferings may speedily cease!" murmured he, despairingly. "Oh, would I might be a wer-wolf, as they call me! I could then requite them for all the foul wrong done me. True, I could not nourish myself with their flesh. I would not shed their blood, but I would be able to terrify and torment those who have wrought my parents' and sisters' death, who have persecuted our family even to extermination! Why have I not the power to change my nature into that of a wolf, if, of a verity, my ancestors possessed it, as they avouch? I should at least find carrion to devour,[4] and not die thus horribly. Branda is the sole being in this world who cares for me, and that conviction alone reconciles me to life!"

Hugues gave free current to these gloomy reflections. The smouldering embers now emitted but a feeble and vacillating light, faintly struggling with the surrounding gloom, and Hugues felt the horror of darkness coming strong upon him. Frozen with the ague-fit one instant, and troubled the next by the hurried pulsation of his veins, he arose, at last, to seek some fuel, and threw upon the fire a heap of faggot-chips, heath and straw, which soon raised a clear and crackling flame. His stock of wood had become exhausted, and, seeking wherewith to replenish his dying hearth-light, whilst foraging under the rude oven amongst a pile of rubbish placed there by his mother wherewith to bake bread (handles of tools, fractured joint-stools, and cracked platters), he discovered a chest rudely covered with a dressed hide, and which he had never seen before, and seizing upon it as though he had discovered a treasure, broke open the lid, strongly secured by a string.

This chest, which had evidently remained long unopened, contained the complete disguise of a wer-wolf: a dyed sheepskin, with gloves in the form of paws, a tail, a mask with an elongated muzzle, and furnished with formidable rows of yellow horse-teeth.

Hugues started backwards, terrified at his discovery, so opportune that it seemed to him the work of sorcery, then, on recovering from his surprise, he drew forth one by one the several pieces of this strange envelope, which had evidently seen some service, and from long neglect had become somewhat damaged. Then rushed confusedly upon his mind the marvellous recitals made him by his grandfather as he nursed him upon his knees

---

4   Horseflesh was an article of food among our Saxon forefathers in England.

during earliest childhood: tales, during the narration of which his mother wept silently, as he laughed heartily. In his mind there was a mingled strife of feelings and purposes alike undefinable. He continued his silent examination of this criminal heritage, and by degrees his imagination grew bewildered with vague and extravagant projects.

Hunger and despair conjointly hurried him away. He saw objects no longer save through a bloody prism. He felt his very teeth on edge with an avidity for biting. He experienced an inconceivable desire to run. He set himself to howl as though he had practised wer-wolfery all his life, and began thoroughly to invest himself with the guise and attributes of his novel vocation. A more startling change could scarcely have been wrought in him, had that so horribly grotesque metamorphosis really been the effect of enchantment, aided, too, as it was, by the, fever which generated a temporary insanity in his frenzied brain.

Scarcely did he thus find himself travestied into a wer-wolf through the influence of his vestment, ere he darted forth from the hut, through the forest and into the open country, white with hoar frost, and across which the bitter north wind swept, howling in a frightful manner and traversing the meadows, fallows, plains, and marshes, like a shadow. But, at that hour, and during such a season, not a single belated wayfarer was there to encounter Hugues, whom the sharpness of the air, and the excitation of his course, had worked up to the highest pitch of extravagance and audacity. He howled the louder proportionally as his hunger increased.

Suddenly the heavy rumbling of an approaching vehicle arrested his attention. At first with indecision, then with a stupid fixity, he struggled with two suggestions, counselling him at one and the same time to fly and to advance. The carriage, or whatever it might be, continued, rolling towards him. The night was not so obscure but that he was enabled to distinguish the tower of Ashford church at a short distance off, and hard by which stood a pile of unhewn stone, destined either for the execution of some repair, or addition to the saintly edifice, in the shade of which he ran to crouch himself down, and so await the arrival of his prey.

It proved to be the covered cart of Willieblud, the Ashford flesher, who was wont twice a week to carry meat to Canterbury, and travelled by night in order that he might be among the first at market-opening. Of this Hugues was fully aware, and the departure of the flesher naturally suggested to him the inference that his niece must be keeping house by herself, for our lusty flesher had been long a widower. For an instant he hesitated whether he should introduce himself there, so favourable an opportunity thus presenting itself, or whether he should attack the uncle and seize upon his viands. Hunger got the better of love this once, and the monotonous whistle with which the driver was accustomed to urge forward his sorry jade warning him to be in readiness, he howled in a plaintive tone, and, rushing forward, seized the horse by the bit.

"Willieblud, flesher," said he, disguising his voice, and speaking to him in the lingua Franca of that period, "I hunger! Throw me two pounds of meat if thou would'st have me live."

"St. Willifred have mercy on me!" cried the terrified flesher, "is it thou, Hugues Wulfric, of Wealdmarsh, the born wer-wolf?"

"Thou say'st sooth, it is I," replied Hugues, who had sufficient address to avail himself of the credulous superstition of Willieblud. "I would rather have raw meat than eat of thy flesh, plump as thou art. Throw me, therefore, what I crave, and forget not to be ready with the like portion each time thou settest out for Canterbury market, or, failing thereof, I tear thee limb from limb."

Hugues, to display his attributes of a wer-wolf before the gaze of the confounded flesher, had mounted himself upon the spokes of the wheel, and placed his forepaw upon the edge of the cart, which he made semblance of snuffing at with his snout.

Willieblud, who believed in wer-wolves as devoutly as he did in his patron saint, had no sooner perceived this monstrous paw, than, uttering a fervent invocation to the latter, he seized upon his daintiest joint of meat, let it fall to the ground, and whilst Hugues sprung eagerly down to pick it up, the butcher at the same instant having bestowed a sudden and violent blow upon the flank of his beast, the latter set off at a round gallop without waiting for any reiterated invitation from the lash.

Hugues was so satisfied with a repast which had cost him far less trouble to procure than any he had long remembered, readily promised himself the renewal of an expedient, the execution of which was at once easy and diverting, for though smitten with the charms of the fair-haired Branda, he not the less found a malicious pleasure in augmenting the terror of her uncle Willieblud. The latter, for a long while, revealed not to a living being the tale of his terrible encounter and strange compact, which had varied according to circumstances, and he submitted unmurmuringly to the imposts levied each time the wer-wolf presented himself before him, without being very nice about either the weight or quality of the meat. He no longer even waited to be asked for it, anything to avoid the sight of that fiend-like form clinging to the side of his cart, or being brought into such immediate contact with that hideous misshapen paw stretched forth, as it were to strangle him, that paw too, which had once been a human hand. He had become dull and thoughtful of late. He set out to market unwillingly, and seemed to dread the hour of departure as it approached, and no longer beguiled the tedium of his nocturnal journey by whistling to his horse, or trolling snatches of ballads, as was his wont formerly. He now invariably returned in a melancholy and restless mood.

Branda, at loss to conceive what had given birth to this new and permanent depression which had taken possession of her uncle's mind, after in vain exhausting conjecture, proceeded to interrogate, importune, and supplicate him by turns, until the unhappy flesher, no longer proof against such continued appeals, at last disburthened himself of the load which he had at heart, by recounting the history of his adventure with the wer-wolf.

Branda listened to the whole of the recital without offering interruption or comment until its close. "Hugues is no more a wer-wolf than thou or I," exclaimed she, offended that such unjust suspicion should be cherished against one for whom she had long felt more than an interest. "'Tis an idle tale, or some juggling device. I fear me thou must needs dream these sorceries, uncle Willieblud, for Hugues of the Wealmarsh, or Wulfric, as the silly fools call him, is worth far more, I trow, than his reputation."

"Girl, it boots not saying me nay, in this matter," replied Willieblud, pertinaciously urging the truth of his story. "The family of Hugues, as everybody knows, were wer-wolves born, and, since they are all of late, by the blessing of heaven, defunct, save one, Hugues now inherits the wolf's paw."

"I tell thee, and will avouch it openly, uncle, that Hugues is of too gentle and seemly a nature to serve Satan, and turn himself into a wild beast, and that will I never believe until I have seen the like."

"Mass, and that thou shalt right speedily, if thou wilt but along with me. In very troth 'tis he, besides, he made confession of his name, and did I not recognize his voice, and am I not ever bethinking me of his knavish paw, which he places me on the shaft while he stays the horse. Girl, he is in league with the foul fiend."

Branda had, to a certain degree, imbibed the superstition in the abstract, equally with her uncle, and, excepting so far as it touched the hitherto, as she believed, traduced being on whom her affections, as if in feminine perversity, had so strangely lighted. Her woman's curiosity, in this instance, less determined her resolution to accompany the flesher on his next journey, than the desire to exculpate her lover, fully believing the strange tale of her kinsman's encounter with, and spoliation by the latter, to be the effect of some illusion, and of which to find him guilty, was the sole fear she experienced on mounting the rude vehicle laden with its ensanguined viands.

It was just midnight when they started from Ashford, the hour alike dear to wer-wolves as to spectres of every denomination. Hugues was punctual at the appointed spot. His howlings, as they drew nigh, though horrible enough, had still something human in them, and disconcerted not a little the doubts of Branda. Willieblud, however, trembled even more than she did, and sought for the wolf's portion. The latter raised himself upon his hind legs, and extended one of his forepaws to receive his pittance as soon as the cart stopped at the heap of stones.

"Uncle, I shall swoon with affright," exclaimed Branda, clinging closely to the flesher, and tremblingly pulling the coverchief over her eyes. "Loose rein and smite thy beast, or evil will surely betide us."

"Thou are not alone, gossip," cried Hugues, fearful of a snare. "If thou essay'st to play me false, thou art at once undone."

"Harm us not friend Hugues, thou know'st I weigh not my pounds of meat with thee. I shall take care to keep my troth. It is Branda, my niece, who goes with me tonight to buy wares at Canterbury."

"Branda with thee? By the mass 'tis she indeed, more buxom and rosy too, than ever. Come pretty one, descend and tarry awhile, that I may have speech with thee."

"I conjure thee, good Hugues, terrify not so cruelly my poor wench, who is wellnigh dead already with fear; suffer us to; hold our way, for we have far to go, and the morrow is early, market-day."

"Go thy ways then alone, uncle Willieblud, 'tis thy niece I would have speech with, in all courtesy and honour, the which, if thou permittest not readily, and of a good grace, I will rend thee both to death."

All in vain was it that Willieblud exhausted himself in prayers and lamentations in hopes of softening the bloodthirsty wer-wolf, as he believed him to be, refusing as the latter did, every sort of compromise in avoidance of his demand, and at last replying only by horrible threats, which froze the hearts of both. Branda, although especially interested in the debate, neither stirred foot, or opened her mouth, so greatly had terror and surprise overwhelmed her. She kept her eyes fixed upon the wolf, who peered at her likewise through his mask, and felt incapable of offering resistance when she found herself forcibly dragged out of the vehicle, and deposited by an invisible power, as it seemed to her, beside the piles of stones. She swooned without uttering a single scream.

The flesher was no less dumbfounded at the turn which the adventure had taken, and he, too, fell back among his meat as though stricken by a blinding blow. He fancied that the wolf had swept his bushy tail violently across his eyes, and on recovering the use of his senses found himself alone in the cart, which rolled joltingly at a swift pace towards Canterbury. At first he listened, but in vain, for the wind bringing him either the shrieks of his niece, or the howlings of the wolf, but stop his beast he could not, which, panic-stricken, kept trotting as though bewitched, or felt the spur of some fiend pricking her flanks.

Willieblud, however, reached his journey's end in safety, sold his meat, and returned to Ashford, reckoning full sure upon having to say a De Profundis for his niece, whose fate he had not ceased to bemoan during the whole night. But how great was his astonishment to find her safe at home, a little pale, from recent fright and want of sleep, but without a scratch. Still more was he astonished to hear that the wolf had done her no injury whatsoever, contenting himself, after she had recovered from her swoon, with conducting her back to their dwelling, and acting in every respect like a loyal suitor, rather than a sanguinary wer-wolf. Willieblud knew not what to think of it.

This nocturnal gallantry towards his niece had additionally irritated the burly Saxon against the wer-wolf, and although the fear of reprisals kept him from making a direct and public attack upon Hugues, he ruminated not the less upon taking some sure and secret revenge, but previous to putting his design into execution, it struck him that he could not do better than relate his misadventures to the ancient sacristan and parish grave-digger of St. Michael's, a worthy of profound sagacity in those sort of matters, endowed with a clerk-like erudition, and consulted as an oracle by all the old crones and lovelorn maidens throughout the township of Ashford and its vicinity.

"Slay a wer-wolf thou canst not," was the repeated rejoinder of the wiseacre to the earnest queries of the tormented flesher, "for his hide is proof against spear or arrow, though vulnerable to the edge of a cutting weapon of steel. I counsel thee to deal him a slight flesh wound, or cut him over the paw, in order to know of a surety whether it really be Hugues or no. Thou'lt run no danger, save thou strikest him a blow from which blood flows not therefrom, for, so soon as his skin is severed he taketh flight."

Resolving implicitly to follow the advice of the sacristan, Willieblud that same evening determined to know with what wer-wolf it was with whom he had to do, and with that view hid his cleaver, newly sharpened for the occasion, under the load in his cart, and resolutely prepared to make use of it as a preparatory step towards proving the identity of Hugues with the audacious spoiler of his meat, and eke his peace. The wolf presented himself as usual, and anxiously inquired after Branda, which stimulated the flesher the more firmly to follow out his design.

"Here, Wolf," said Willieblud, stooping down as if to choose a piece of meat, "I give thee double portion tonight. Up with thy paw, take toll, and be mindful of my frank alms."

"Sooth, I will remember me, gossip," rejoined our wer-wolf, "but when shall the marriage be solemnized for certain, betwixt the fair Branda and myself?"

Hugues believing he had nothing to fear from the flesher, whose meats he so readily appropriated to himself, and of whose fair niece he hoped shortly no less to make lawful possession; both that he really loved, and viewed his union with her as the surest means of placing him within the pale of that sociality from which he had been so unjustly exiled, could he but succeed in making intercession with the holy fathers of the church to remove their interdict. Hugues placed his extended paw upon the edge of the cart, but instead of handing him his joint of beef, or mutton, Willieblud raised his cleaver, and at a single blow lopped off the paw laid there as fittingly for the purpose as though upon a block. The flesher flung down his weapon, and belaboured his beast, the wer-wolf roared aloud with agony, and disappeared amid the dark shades of the forest, in which, aided by the wind, his howling was soon lost.

The next day, on his return, the flesher, chuckling and laughing, deposited a gory cloth upon the table, among the trenchers with which his niece was busied in preparing his noonday meal, and which, on being opened, displayed to her horrified gaze a freshly severed human hand enveloped in wolf-skin. Branda, comprehending what had occurred, shrieked aloud, shed a flood of tears, and then hurriedly throwing her mantle round her, whilst her uncle amused himself by turning and twitching the hand about with a ferocious delight, exclaiming, whilst he staunched the blood which still flowed: "The sacristan said sooth. The wer-wolf has his need I trow, at last, and now I wot of his nature, I fear no more his witchcraft."

Although the day was far advanced, Hugues lay writhing in torture upon his couch, his coverings drenched with blood, as well also the floor of his habitation. His countenance of a ghastly pallor, expressed as much moral, as physical pain. Tears gushed from beneath his reddened eyelids, and he listened to every noise without, with an increased inquietude, painfully visible upon his distorted features. Footsteps were heard rapidly approaching, the door was hurriedly flung open, and a female threw herself beside his couch, and with mingled sobs and imprecations sought tenderly for his mutilated arm, which, rudely bound round with hempen wrappings, no longer dissembled the absence of its wrist, and from which a crimson stream still trickled. At this piteous spectacle she grew loud in her denunciations against the sanguinary flesher, and sympathetically mingled her lamentations with those of his victim.

These effusions of love and dolour, however, were doomed to sudden interruption. Someone knocked at the door. Branda ran to the window that she might recognize who the visitor was that had dared to penetrate the lair of a wer-wolf, and on perceiving who it was, she raised her eyes and hands on high, in token of her extremity of despair, whilst the knocking momentarily grew louder.

"'Tis my uncle," faltered she. "Ah, woe's me, how shall I escape hence without his seeing me? Whither hide? Oh, here, here, nigh to thee, Hugues, and we will die together," and she crouched herself into an obscure recess behind his couch. "If Willieblud should raise his cleaver to slay thee, he shall first strike through his kinswoman's body."

Branda hastily concealed herself amidst a pile of hemp, whispering Hugues to summon all his courage, who, however, scarce found strength sufficient to raise himself to a sitting posture, whilst his eyes vainly sought around for some weapon of defence.

"A good morrow to thee, Wulfric!" exclaimed Willieblud, as he entered, holding in his hand a napkin tied in a knot, which he proceeded to place upon the coffer beside the sufferer. "I come to offer thee some work, to bind and stack me a faggot-pile, knowing that thou art no laggard at bill-hook and wattle. Wilt do it?"

"I am sick," replied Hugues, repressing the wrath which, despite of pain, sparkled in his wild glance; "I am not in fitting state to work."

"Sick, gossip, sick, art thou indeed? Or is it but a sloth fit? Come, what ails thee? Where lieth the evil? Your hand, that I may feel thy pulse."

Hugues reddened, and for an instant hesitated whether he should resist a solicitation, the bent of which he too readily comprehended, but in order to avoid exposing Branda to discovery, he thrust forth his left hand from beneath the coverlid, all imbrued in dried gore.

"Not that hand, Hugues, but the other, the right one. Alack, and well-a-day, hast thou lost thy hand, and I must find it for thee?"

Hugues, whose purpling flush of rage changed quickly to a death-like hue, replied not to this taunt, nor testified by the slightest gesture or movement that he was preparing to satisfy a request as cruel in its preconception as the object of it was slenderly cloaked. Willieblud laughed, and ground his teeth in savage glee, maliciously revelling in the tortures he had inflicted upon the sufferer. He seemed already disposed to use violence, rather than allow himself to be baffled in the attainment of the decisive proof he aimed at. Already had he commenced untying the napkin, giving vent all the while to his implacable taunts; one hand alone displaying itself upon the coverlid, and which Hugues, wellnigh senseless with anguish, thought not of withdrawing.

"Why tender me that hand?" continued his unrelenting persecutor, as he imagined himself on the eve of arriving at the conviction he so ardently desired — "That I should lop it off? quick, quick, Master Wulfric, and do my bidding. I demanded to see your right hand."

"Behold it then!" ejaculated a suppressed voice, which belonged to no supernatural being, however it might seem appertaining to such, and Willieblud to his utter confusion and dismay saw a second hand, sound and unmutilated, extend itself towards him as though in silent accusation. He started back. He stammered out a cry for mercy, bent his knees for an instant, and raising himself, palsied with terror, fled from the hut, which he firmly believed under the possession of the foul fiend.

He carried not with him the severed hand, which henceforward became a perpetual vision ever present before his eyes, and which all the potent exorcisms of the sacristan, at whose hands he continually sought council and consolation, signally failed to dispel.

"Oh, that hand! To whom then, belongs that accursed hand?" groaned he, continually. "Is it really the fiend's, or that of some wer-wolf? Certain 'tis, that Hugues is innocent, for have I not seen both his hands? But wherefore was one bloody? There's sorcery at bottom of it."

The next morning, early, the first object that struck his sight on entering his stall, was the severed hand that he had left the preceding night upon the coffer in the forest hut. It was stripped of its wolf's-skin covering, and lay among the viands. He dared no longer touch that hand, which now, he verily believed to be enchanted, but in hopes of getting rid of it for ever, he had it flung down a well, and it was with no small increase of despair that he found it shortly afterwards again lying upon his block. He buried it in his garden, but still without being able to rid himself of it, it returned livid and loathsome to infect his shop, and augment the remorse which was unceasingly revived by the reproaches of his niece.

At last, flattering himself to escape all further persecution from that fatal hand, it struck him that he would have it carried to the cemetery at Canterbury, and try whether exorcism, and supulture in holy ground would effectually bar its return to the light of day. This was also done, but lo! on the following morning he perceived it nailed to his shutter. Disheartened by these dumb, yet awful reproaches, which wholly robbed him of his peace, and impatient to annihilate all trace of an action with which heaven itself seemed to upbraid him, he quitted Ashford one morning without bidding adieu to his niece, and some days after was found drowned in the river Stour. They drew out his swollen and discoloured body, which was discovered floating on the surface among the sedge, and it was only by piecemeal that they succeeded in tearing away from his death-contracted clutch, the phantom hand, which, in his suicidal convulsions he had retained firmly grasped.

A year after this event, Hugues, although minus a hand, and consequently a confirmed wer-wolf, married Branda, sole heiress to the stock and chattels of the late unhappy flesher of Ashford.

A Story of a Weir-Wolf

by Catharine Crowe

IT WAS ON a fine bright summer's morning, in the year 1596, that two young girls were seen sitting at the door of a pretty cottage, in a small village that lay buried amidst the mountains of Auvergne. The house belonged to Ludovique Thierry, a tolerably prosperous builder. One of the girls was his daughter Manon, and the other his niece, Francoise, the daughter of his brother-in-law, Michael Thilouze, a physician.

The mother of Francoise had been some years dead, and Michael, a strange old man, learned in all the mystical lore of the middle ages, had educated his daughter after his own fancy, teaching her some things useless and futile, but others beautiful and true. He not only instructed her to glean information from books, but he led her into the fields, taught her to name each herb and flower, making her acquainted with their properties, and, directing her attention 'to the brave o'erhanging firmament,' he had told her all that was known of the golden spheres that were rolling above her head.

But Michael was also an alchemist, and he had for years been wasting his health in nightly vigils over crucibles, and his means in expensive experiments, and now, alas, he was nearly seventy years of age, and his lovely Francoise seventeen, and neither the elixir vitæ nor the philosopher's stone had yet rewarded his labours. It was just at this crisis, when his means were failing and his hopes expiring, that he received a letter from Paris, informing him that the grand secret was at length discovered by an Italian, who had lately arrived there. Upon this intelligence, Michael thought the most prudent thing he could do was to waste no more time and money by groping in the dark himself, but to have recourse to the fountain of light at once, so sending Francoise to spend the interval with her cousin Manon, he himself started for Paris to visit the successful philosopher.

Although she sincerely loved her father, the change was by no means unpleasant to Francoise. The village of Loques, in which Manon resided, humble as it was, was yet more cheerful than the lonely dwelling of the physician, and the conversation of the young girl more amusing than the dreamy speculations of the old alchemist. Manon, too, was rather a gainer by her cousin's arrival, for as she held her head a little high, on account of her father being the richest man in the village, she was somewhat nice about admitting the neighbouring damsels to her intimacy, and a visitor so unexceptionable as Francoise was by no means unwelcome. Thus both parties were pleased, and the young girls were anticipating a couple of months of pleasant companionship at the moment we have introduced them to our readers, seated at the front of the cottage.

"The heat of the sun is insupportable, Manon," said Francoise. "I really must go in."

"Do," said Manon.

"But wont you come in too?" asked Francoise.

"No, I don't mind the heat," replied the other.

Francoise took up her work and entered the house, but as Manon still remained without, the desire for conversation soon overcame the fear of the heat, and she approached the door again, where, standing partly in the shade, she could continue to discourse. As nobody appeared disposed to brave the heat but Manon, the little street was both empty and silent, so that the sound of a horse's foot crossing the drawbridge, which stood at the entrance of the village, was heard some time before the animal or his rider were in sight. Francoise put out her head to look in the direction of the sound, and, seeing no one, drew it in again, whilst Marion, after casting an almost imperceptible glance the same way, hung hers over her work, as if very intent on what she was doing, but could Francoise have seen her cousin's face, the blush that first overspread it, and the paleness that succeeded, might have awakened a suspicion that Manon was not exposing her complexion to the sun for nothing.

When the horse drew near, the rider was seen to be a gay and handsome cavalier, attired in the perfection of fashion, whilst the rich embroidery of the small cloak tint hung gracefully over his left shoulder, sparkling in the sun, testified no less than his distinguished air to his high rank and condition. Francoise, who had never seen anything so bright and beautiful before, was so entirely absorbed in contemplating the pleasing spectacle, that forgetting to be shy or to hide her own pretty face, she continued to gaze on him as he approached with dilated eyes and lips apart, wholly unconscious that the surprise was mutual. It was not till she saw him lift his bonnet from his head, and, with a reverential bow, do homage to her charms, that her eye fell and the blood rushed to her young cheek. Involuntarily, she made a step backward, into the passage, but when the horse and his rider had passed the door, she almost as involuntarily resumed her position, and protruded her head to look after him. He too had turned round on his horse and was 'riding with his eyes behind,' and the moment he beheld her he lifted his bonnet again, and then rode slowly forward.

"Upon my word, Mam'selle Francoise," said Manon, with flushed cheeks and angry eyes, "this is rather remarkable, I think! I was not aware of your acquaintance with Monsieur de Vardes!"

"With whom?" said Francoise. "Is that Monsieur de Vardes?"

"To be sure it is," replied Manon. "Do you pretend to say you did not know it?"

"Indeed, I did not," answered Francoise. "I never saw him in my life before."

"Oh, I dare say," responded Manon, with an incredulous

laugh. "Do you suppose I'm such a fool as to believe you?"

"What nonsense, Manon! How should I know Monsieur de Vardes? But do tell me about him. Does he live at the Chateau?"

"He has been living there lately," replied Manon, sulkily.

"And where did he live before?" inquired Francoise.

"He has been travelling, I believe," said Manon.

This was true. Victor de Vardes had been making the tour of Europe, visiting foreign courts, jousting in tournaments, and winning fair ladies' hearts, and was but now returned to inhabit his father's chateau, who, thinking it high time he should be married, had summoned him home for the purpose of paying his addresses to Clemence de Montmorenci, one of the richest heiresses in France.

Victor, who had left home very young, had been what is commonly called in love a dozen times, but his heart had in reality never been touched. His loves had been mere boyish fancies, 'dead ere they were born,' one putting out the fire of another before it had had time to hurt him or anybody else, so that when he heard that he was to marry Clemence de Montmorenci, he felt no aversion to the match, and prepared himself to obey his father's behest without a murmur. On being introduced to the lady, he was by no means struck with her. She appeared amiable, sensible, and gentle, but she was decidedly plain, and dressed ill. Victor felt no disposition whatever to love her, but, on the other hand, he had no dislike to her, and as his heart was unoccupied, he expressed himself perfectly ready to comply with the wishes of his family and hers, by whom this alliance had been arranged from motives of mutual interest and accommodation.

So he commenced his course of love, which consisted in riding daily to the chateau of his intended father-in-law, where, if there was company, and he found amusement, he frequently remained a great part of the morning. Now, it happened that his road lay through the village of Loques, where Manon lived, and happening one day to see her at the door, with the gallantry of a gay cavalier, he had saluted her. Manon, who was fully as vain as she was pretty, liked this homage to her beauty so well that she thereafter never neglected an opportunity of throwing herself in the way of enjoying it, and the salutation thus accidentally begun had, from almost daily repetition, ripened into a sort of silent flirtation. The young count smiled, she blushed and half smiled too, and whilst he in reality thought nothing about her, she had brought herself to believe he was actually in love with her, and that it was for her sake he so often appeared riding past her door.

But, on the present occasion, the sight of Francoise's beautiful face had startled the young man out of his good manners. It is difficult to say why a gentleman, who looks upon the features of one pretty girl with indifference, should be 'frightened from his propriety' by the sight of another, in whom the world in general sees nothing superior, but such is the case, and so it was with Victor. His heart seemed taken by storm. He could not drive the beautiful features from his brain, and although he laughed at himself for being thus enslaved by a low-born beauty, he could not laugh himself out of the impatience he felt to mount his horse and ride back again in the hope of once more beholding her. But this time Manon alone was visible, and although he lingered, and allowed his eyes to wander over the house and glance in at the windows, no vestige of the lovely vision could he descry.

Perhaps she did not live there. She was probably but a visiter to the other girl? He would have given the world to ask the question of Manon, but he had never spoken to her, and to commence with such an interrogation was impossible, at least Victor felt it so, for his consciousness already made him shrink from betraying the motives of the inquiry. So he saluted Manon and rode on, but the wandering anxious eyes, the relaxed pace, and the cold salutation, were not lost upon her. Besides, he had returned from the Chateau de Montmorenci before the usual time, and the mortified damsel did not fail to discern the motive of this deviation from his habits.

Manon was such a woman as you might live with well enough as long as you steered clear of her vanity, but once come in collision with that, the strongest passion of her nature, and you aroused a latent venom that was sure to make you smart. Without having ever 'vowed eternal friendship,' or pretending to any remarkable affection, the girls had been hitherto very good friends. Manon was aware that Francoise was possessed of a great deal of knowledge of which she was utterly destitute, but as she did not value the knowledge, and had not the slightest conception of what it was worth, she was not mortified by the want of it nor envious of the advantage; she did not consider that it was one. But in the matter of beauty the case was different. She had always persuaded herself that she was much the handsomer of the two. She had black shining hair and dark flashing eyes, and she honestly thought the soft blue eyes and auburn hair of her cousin tame and ineffective.

But the too evident saisissement of the young count had shown her a rival where she had not suspected one, and her vexation was as great as her surprise. Then she was so puzzled what to do. If she abstained from sitting at the door herself, she should not see Monsieur de Vardes, and if she did sit there her cousin would assuredly do the same. It was extremely perplexing, but Francoise settled the question by seating herself at the door of her own accord. Seeing this, Manon came too, to watch her, but she was sulky and snappish, and when Victor not only distinguished Francoise as before, but took an opportunity of alighting from his horse to tighten his girths, just opposite the door, she could scarcely control her passion.

It would be tedious to detail how, for the two months that ensued, this sort of silent courtship was carried on. Suffice it to say, that by the end of Francoise's visit to Loques she was in complete possession of Victor's heart, and he of hers, although they had never spoken a word to each other, and when she was summoned home to Cabanis to meet her father, she was completely divided betwixt the joy of once more seeing the dear old man and the grief of losing, as she supposed, all chance of beholding again the first love of her young heart.

But here her fears deceived her. Victor's passion had by this time overcome his diffidence, and he had contrived to learn all he required to know about her from the blacksmith of the village, one day when his horse very opportunely lost a shoe, and as Cabanis was not a great way from the Chateau de Montmorenci, he took an early opportunity of calling on the old physician, under pretence of needing his advice.

At first he did not succeed in seeing Francoise, but perseverance brought him better success, and when they became acquainted, he was as much charmed and surprised by the cultivation of her mind as he had been by the beauty of her person. It was not difficult for Victor to win the heart of the alchemist, for the young man really felt, without having occasion to feign, on interest and curiosity with respect to the occult researches so prevalent at that period, and thus, gradually, larger and larger portions of his time were subtracted from the Chateau de Montmorenci to be spent at the physician's. Then, in the green glades of that wide domain which extended many miles around, Victor and Francoise strolled together arm in arm, he vowing eternal affection, and declaring that this rich inheritance of the Montmorenci should never tempt him to forswear his love.

But though thus happy, 'the world forgetting,' they were not 'by the world forgot.' From the day of Victor's first salutation to Francoise, Manon had become her implacable enemy. Her pride made her conceal as much as possible the cause of her aversion, and Francoise, who learned from herself that she had no acquaintance with Victor, hardly knew how to attribute her daily increasing coldness to jealousy. But by the time they parted the alienation was complete, and as, after Francoise went home, all communication ceased between them, it was some time before Manon heard of Victor's visits to Cabanis. But this blissful ignorance was not destined to continue.

There was a young man in the service of the Montmorenci family called Jacques Renard. He was a great favourite with the marquis, who had undertaken to provide for him, when in his early years he was left destitute by the death of his parents, who were old tenants on the estate. Jacques, now filling the office of private secretary to his patron, was extremely in love with the alchemist's daughter, and Francoise, who had seen too little of the world to have much discrimination, had not wholly discouraged his advances. Her heart, in fact, was quite untouched, but very young girls do not know their own hearts, and when Francoise became acquainted with Victor de Vardes, she first learned what love is, and made the discovery that she entertained no such sentiment for Jacques Renard. The small encouragement she had given him was therefore withdrawn, to the extreme mortification of the disappointed suitor, who naturally suspected a rival, and was extremely curious to learn who that rival could be. Nor was it long before he obtained the information he desired.

Though Francoise and her lover cautiously kept far away from that part of the estate which was likely to be frequented by the Montmorenci family, and thus avoided any inconvenient reencounter with them, they could not with equal success elude the watchfulness of the foresters attached to the domain, and some time before the heiress or Manon suspected how Victor was passing his time, these men were well aware of the hours the young people spent together, either in the woods or at the alchemist's house, which was on their borders. Now the chief forester, Pierre Bloui, was a suitor for Manon's hand. He was an excellent huntsman, but being a weak, ignorant, ill-mannered fellow, she had a great contempt for him, and had repeatedly declined his proposals. But Pierre, whose dullness rendered his sensibilities little acute, had never been reduced to despair. He knew that his situation rendered him, in a pecuniary point of view, an excellent match, and that old Thierry, Manon's father, was his friend, so he persevered in his attentions, and seldom came into Loques without paying her a visit. It was from him she first learned what was going on at Cabanis.

"Ay," said Pierre, who had not the slightest suspicion of the jealous feelings he was exciting, "Ay, there'll be a precious blow up by and by, when it comes to the ears of the family! What will the Marquis and the old Count de Vardes say, when they find that, instead of making love to Mam'selle Clemence, he spends all his time with Francoise Thilouze?"

"But is not Mam'selle Clemence angry already that he is not more with her?" inquired Manon.

"I don't know," replied Pierre, "but that's what I was thinking of asking Jacques Renard, the first time he comes shooting with me."

"I'm sure I would not put up with it if I were she!" exclaimed Manon, with a toss of the head, "and I think you would do very right to mention it to Jacques Renard. Besides, it can come to no good for Francoise, for of course the count would never think of marrying her."

"I don't know that," answered Pierre. "Margot, their maid, told me another story."

"You don't mean that the count is going to marry Francoise Thilouze!" exclaimed Manon, with unfeigned astonishment.

"Margot says he is," answered Pierre.

"Well, then, all I can say is," cried Manon, her face crimsoning with passion, "all I can say is, that they must have bewitched him, between them. She and that old conjuror, my uncle!"

"Well, I should not wonder," said Pierre. "I've often thought old Michael knew more than he should do."

Now, Manon in reality entertained no such idea, but under the influence of the evil passions that were raging within her at the moment, she nodded her head as significantly as if she were thoroughly convinced of the fact—in short, as if she knew more than she chose to say, and thus sent away the weak superstitious Pierre possessed with a notion that he lost no time in communicating to his brother huntsmen. Nor was it long before Victor's attentions to Francoise were made known to Jacques Renard, accompanied with certain suggestions, that Michael Thilouze and his daughter were perhaps what the Scotch call, no canny, a persuasion that the foresters themselves found little difficulty in admitting.

In the meanwhile, Clemence de Montmorenci had not been unconscious of Victor's daily declining attentions. He had certainly never pressed his suit with great earnestness, but now he did not press it at all. Never was so lax a lover! But as the alliance was one planned by the parents of the young people, not by the election of their own hearts, she contemplated his alienation with more surprise than pain.

The elder members of the two families, however, were far from equally indifferent, and when they learned from the irritated, jealous Jacques Renard the cause of the dereliction, their indignation knew no bounds. It was particularly desirable that the estates of Montmorenci and De Vardes should be united, and that the lowly Francoise Thilouze, the daughter of a poor physician, who probably did not know who his grandfather was, should step in to the place designed for the heiress of a hundred quarterings, and mingle her blood with the pure stream that flowed through the veins of the proud De Vardes, was a thing not to be endured.

The strongest expostulations and representations were first tried with Victor, but in vain. He was "in love, and pleased with ruin." These failing, other measures must be resorted to, and as in those days, pride of blood, contempt for the rights of the people, ignorance, and superstition, were at their climax, there was little scruple as to the means, so that the end was accomplished.

It is highly probable that these great people themselves believed in witchcraft. The learned, as well as the ignorant, believed in it at that period, and so unaccountable a perversion of the senses as Victor's admiration of Francoise naturally appeared to persons who could discern no merit unadorned by rank, would seem to justify the worst suspicions, so that when Jacques hinted the notion prevailing amongst the foresters with respect to old Michael and his daughter, the idea was seized on with avidity.

Whether Jacques believed in his own allegation it is difficult to say. Most likely not, but it gratified his spite and served his turn, and his little scrupulous nature sought no further. The marquis shook his head ominously, looked very dignified and very grave, said that the thing must be investigated, and desired that the foresters, and those who had the best opportunities for observation, should keep an attentive eye on the alchemist and his daughter, and endeavour to obtain some proof of their malpractices, whilst he considered what was best to be done in such an emergency.

The wishes and opinions of the great have at all times a strange omnipotence, and this influence in 1588 was a great deal more potential than it is now. No sooner was it known that the Marquis de Montmorenci and the Count de Vardes entertained an ill will against Michael and Francoise, than everybody became suddenly aware of their delinquency, and proofs of it poured in from all quarters. Amongst other stories, there was one which sprung from nobody knew where—probably from some hasty word, or slight coincidence, which flew like wildfire amongst the people, and caused an immense sensation. It was asserted that the Montmorenci huntsmen had frequently met Victor and Francoise walking together, in remote parts of the domain, but that when they drew near, she suddenly changed herself into a wolf and ran off. It was a favourite trick of witches to transform themselves into wolves, cats, and hares, and weir-wolves were the terror of the rustics, and as just at that period there happened to be one particularly large wolf, that had almost miraculously escaped the forester's guns, she was fixed upon as the representative of the metamorphosed Francoise.

Whilst this storm had been brewing, the old man, absorbed in his studies, which had received a fresh impetus from his late journey to Paris, and the young girl, wrapt in the entrancing pleasures of a first love, remained wholly unconscious of the dangers that were gathering around them. Margot, the maid, had indeed not only heard, but had felt the effects of the rising prejudice against her employers. When she went to Loques for her weekly marketings, she found herself coldly received by some of her old familiars, whilst by those more friendly, she was seriously advised to separate her fortunes from that of persons addicted to such unholy arts. But Margot, who had nursed Francoise in her infancy, was deaf to their insinuations. She knew what they said was false, and feeling assured that if the young count married her mistress, the calumny would soon die away, she did not choose to disturb the peace of the family, and the smooth current of the courtship, by communicating those disagreeable rumours.

In the mean time, Pierre Bloui, who potently believed "the mischief that himself had made," was extremely eager to play some distinguished part in the drama of witch-finding. He knew that he should obtain the favour of his employers if he could bring about the conviction of Francoise, and he also thought that he should gratify his mistress. The source of her enmity he did not know, nor care to inquire, but enmity he perceived there was, and he concluded that the destruction of the object of it would be on agreeable sacrifice to the offended Manon. Moreover, he had no compunction, for the conscience of his superiors was his conscience, and Jacques Renard had so entirely confirmed his belief in the witch story, that his superstitious terrors, as well as his interests, prompted him to take an active part in the affair.

Still he felt some reluctance to shoot the wolf, even could he succeed in so doing, from the thorough conviction that it was in reality not a wolf, but a human being he would be aiming at, but he thought if he could entrap her, it would not only save his own feelings, but answer the purpose much better, and accordingly he placed numerous snares, well baited, in that part of the domain most frequented by the lovers, and expected every day, when he visited them, to find Francoise, either in one shape or the other, fast by the leg. He was for some time disappointed, but at length he found in one of the traps, not the wolf or Francoise, but a wolf's foot. An animal had evidently been caught, and in the violence of its struggles for freedom had left its foot behind it. Pierre carried away the foot and baited his trap again.

About a week had elapsed since the occurrence of this circumstance, when one of the servants of the chateau, having met with a slight accident, went to the apothecary's at Loques, for the purpose of purchasing some medicaments, and there met Margot, who had arrived from Cabanis for the same purpose. Mam'selle Francoise, it appeared, had so seriously hurt one of her hands, that her father had been under the necessity of amputating it. As all gossip about the Thilouze family was just then very acceptable at home, the man did not fail to relate what he had heard, and the news, ere long, reached the ears of Pierre Bloui.

It would have been difficult to decide whether horror or triumph prevailed in the countenance of the astonished huntsman at this communication. His face first flushed with joy, and then became pale with affright. It was thus all true! The thing was clear, and he the man destined to produce the proof! It had been Francoise that was caught in the trap, and she had released herself at the expense of one of her hands, which, divided from herself, was no longer under the power of her incantations, and had therefore retained the form she had given it, when she resumed her own.

Here was a discovery! Pierre Bloui actually felt himself so overwhelmed by its magnitude, that he was obliged to swallow a glass of cogniac to restore his equilibrium, before he could present himself before Jacques Renard to detail this stupendous mystery and exhibit the wolf's foot.

How much Jacques Renard, or the marquis, when he heard it, believed of this strange story, can never be known. Certain it is, however, that within a few hours after this communication had been made to them, the commissaire du quartier, followed by a mob from Loques, arrived at Cabanis, and straightway carried away Michael Thilouze and his daughter, on a charge of witchcraft. The influence of their powerful enemies hurried on the judicial process, by courtesy called a trial, where the advantages were all on one side, and the disadvantages all on the other, and poor, terrified, and unaided, the physician and his daughter were, with little delay, found guilty, and condemned to die at the stake. In vain they pleaded their innocence. The wolf's foot was produced in court, and, combined with the circumstance that Francoise Thilouze had really lost her left hand, was considered evidence incontrovertible.

But where was her lover the while? Alas, he was in Paris, where, shortly before these late events, his father had on some pretext sent him, the real object being to remove him from the neighbourhood of Cabanis.

Now, when Manon saw the fruits of her folly and spite, she became extremely sorry for what she had done, for she knew very well that it was with herself the report had originated. But though powerful to harm, she was weak to save. When she found that her uncle and cousin were to lose their lives and die a dreadful death on account of the idle words dropped from her own foolish tongue, her remorse became agonising. But what could she do? Where look for assistance? Nowhere, unless in Victor de Vardes, and he was far away. She had no jealousy now. Glad, glad would she have been, to be preparing to witness her cousin's wedding instead of her execution! But those were not the days of fleet posts. If they had been, Manon would have doubtless known how to write.

As it was, she could neither write a letter to the count, nor have sent it when written. And yet, in Victor lay her only hope. In this trait she summoned Pierre Bloui, and asked him if he would go to Paris for her, and inform the young count of the impending misfortune. But it was not easy to persuade Pierre to so rash an enterprise. He was afraid of bringing himself into trouble with the Montmorencis. But Manon's heart was in the cause. She represented to him, that if he lost one employer he would get another, for that the young count would assuredly become his best friend, and when she found that this was not enough to win him to her purpose, she bravely resolved to sacrifice herself to save her friends.

"If you will hasten to Paris," she said, "stopping neither night nor day, and tell Monsieur de Vardes of the danger my uncle and cousin are in, when you come back I will marry you."

The bribe succeeded, and Pierre consented to go, owning that he was the more willing to do so, because he had privately changed his own opinion with respect to the guilt of the accused parties. "For," said he, "I saw the wolf last night under the chestnut trees, and as she was very lame, I could have shot her, but I feared my lord and lady would be displeased."

"Then, how can you be foolish enough to think it's my cousin," said Manon, "when you know she is in prison?"

"That's what I said to Jacques Renard," replied Pierre, "but he bade me not meddle with what did not concern me."

In fine, love and conscience triumphed over fear and servility, and as soon as the sun set behind the hills, Pierre Bloui started for Paris.

How eagerly now did Manon reckon the days and hours that were to elapse before Victor could arrive. She had so imperfect an idea of the distance to be traversed, that after the third day she began hourly to expect him, but sun after sun rose and set, and no Victor appeared, and in the mean time, before the very windows of the house she dwelt in, she beheld preparations making day by day for the fatal ceremony. From early morn to dewy eve, the voices of the workmen, the hammering of the scaffolding, and the hum of the curious and excited spectators, who watched its progress, resounded in the ears of the unhappy Manon, for a witch-burning was a sort of auto da fe, like the burning of a heretic, and was anticipated as a grand spectacle, alike pleasing to gods and men, especially in the little town of Loques, where exciting scenes of any kind were very rare.

Thus time crept on, and still no signs of rescue, whilst the anguish and remorse of the repentant sinner became unbearable.

Now, Manon was not only a girl of strong passions but of a fearless spirit. Indeed the latter was somewhat the offspring of the former, for when her feelings were excited, not only justice and charity, as we have seen, were apt to be forgotten, but personal danger and feminine fears were equally overlooked in the tempest that assailed her. On the present occasion, her better feelings were in full activity. Her whole nature was aroused, self was not thought of, and to save the lives she had endangered by her folly, she would have gladly laid down her own. "For why live," thought she, "if my uncle and cousin die? I can never be happy again. Besides, I must keep my promise and marry Pierre Bloui, and I had better lose my life in trying to expiate my fault than live to be miserable."

Manon had a brother called Alexis, who was now at the wars. Often and often, in this great strait, she had wished him at home, for she knew that he would have undertaken the mission to Paris for her, and so have saved her the sacrifice she had made in order to win Pierre to her purpose. Now, when Alexis lived at home, and the feuds between the king and the grand seigneurs had brought the battle to the very doors of the peasants of Auvergne, Manon had many a time braved danger in order to bring this much loved brother refreshments on his night watch, and he had, moreover, as an accomplishment which might be some time needed for her own defence, taught her to carry a gun and shoot at a mark.

In those days of civil broil and bloodshed, country maidens were not unfrequently adept in such exercises. This acquirement she now determined to make available, and when the eve of the day appointed for the execution arrived without any tidings from Paris, she prepared to put her plan in practice. This was no other than to shoot the wolf herself, and, by producing it, to prove the falsity of the accusation. For this purpose, she provided herself with a young pig, which she slung in a sack over her shoulder, and with her brother's gun on the other, and disguised in his habiliments, when the shadows of twilight fell upon the earth, the brave girl went forth into the forest on her bold enterprise alone.

She knew that the moon would rise ere she reached her destination, and on this she reckoned for success. With a beating heart she traversed the broad glades, and crept through the narrow paths that intersected the wide woods till she reached the chestnut avenue where Pierre said he had seen the lame wolf. She was aware that old or disabled animals, who are rendered unfit to hunt their prey, will be attracted a long distance by the scent of food, so having hung her sack with the pig in it to the lower branch of a tree, she herself ascended another close to it, and then presenting the muzzle of her gun straight in the direction of the bag, she sat still as a statue, and there, for the present, we must leave her, whilst we take a peep into the prison of Loques, and see how the unfortunate victims of malice and superstition are supporting their captivity and prospect of approaching death.

Poor Michael Thilouze and his daughter had had a rude awakening from the joyous dreams in which they had both been wrapt. The old man's journey to Paris had led to what he believed would prove the most glorious results. It was true that report had as usual exaggerated the success of his fellow labourer there. The Italian Alascer had not actually found the philosopher's stone, but he was on the eve of finding it. One single obstacle stood in his way, and had for a considerable time arrested his progress, and as he was an old man, worn out by anxious thought and unremitting labour, who could scarcely hope to enjoy his own discovery, he consented to disclose to Michael not only all he knew, but also what was the insurmountable difficulty that had delayed his triumph. This precious stone, he had ascertained, which was not only to ensure to the fortunate possessor illimitable wealth, but perennial youth, could not be procured without the aid of a virgin, innocent, perfect, and pure, and, moreover, capable of inviolably keeping the secret which must necessarily be imparted to her.

"Now," said the Italian, "virgins are to be had in plenty, but the second condition I find it impossible to fulfill, for they invariably confide what I tell them to some friend or lover, and thus the whole process becomes vitiated, and I am arrested on the very threshold of success."

Great was the joy of Michael on hearing this, for he well knew that Francoise, his pure, innocent, beautiful Francoise, could keep a secret. He had often had occasion to prove her fidelity, so bidding the Italian keep himself alive but for a little space, when he, in gratitude for what he had taught him, would return with the long sought for treasure, and restore him to health, wealth, and vigorous youth, the glad old man hurried back to Cabanis, and "set himself about it like the sea."

It was in performing the operation required of her that Francoise had so injured her hand that amputation had become unavoidable, and great as had been the joy of Michael was now his grief. Not only had his beloved daughter lost her hand, but the hopes he had built on her co-operation were forever annihilated. Maimed and dismembered, she was no longer eligible to assist in the sublime process. But how much greater was his despair, when he learned the suspicions to which this strange coincidence had subjected her, and beheld the innocent, and till now happy girl, led by his side to a dungeon. For himself he cared nothing, for her everything. He was old and disappointed, and to die was little to him, but his Francoise, his young and beautiful Francoise, cut off in her bloom of years, and by so cruel and ignominious a death! And here they were in prison alone, helpless and forsaken! Absorbed in his studies, the poor physician had lived a solitary life, and his daughter, holding a rank a little above the peasantry and below the gentry, had had no companion but Manon, and she was now her bitterest foe, this at least they were told.

How sadly and slowly, and yet how much too fleetly, passed the days that were to intervene betwixt the sentence and the execution. And where was Victor? Where were his vows of love and eternal faith? All, all forgotten. So thought Francoise, who, ignorant of his absence from the Chateau de Vardes, supposed him well acquainted with her distress.

Thus believing themselves abandoned by the world, the poor father and daughter, in tears, and prayers, and attempts at mutual consolation, spent this sad interval, till at length the morning dawned that was to witness the accomplishment of their dreadful fate. During the preceding night old Michael had never closed his eyes, but Francoise had fallen asleep shortly before sunrise, and was dreaming that it was her wedding day, and that, followed by the cheers of the villagers, Victor, the still beloved Victor, was leading her to the altar. The cheers awoke her, and with the smile of joy still upon her lips, she turned her face to her father.

He was stretched upon the floor overcome by a burst of uncontrollable anguish at the sounds that had aroused her from her slumbers, for the sounds were real. The voices of the populace, crowding in from the adjacent country and villages to witness the spectacle, had pierced the thick walls of the prison and reached the ears and the hearts of the captives. Whilst the old man threw himself at her feet, and, pouring blessings on her fair young head, besought her pardon, Francoise almost forgot her own misery in his, and when the assistants came to lead them forth to execution, she not only exhorted him to patience, but supported with her arm the feeble frame that, wasted by age and grief, could furnish but little fuel for the flame that awaited them.

Nobody would have imagined that in this thinly peopled neighbourhood so many persons could have been brought together as were assembled in the marketplace of Loques to witness the deaths of Michael Thilouze and his daughter. A scaffolding had been erected all round the square for the spectators, that designed for the gentry being adorned with tapestry and garlands of flowers. There sat, amongst others, the families of Montmorenci and De Vardes—all except the Lady Clemence, whose heart recoiled from beholding the death of her rival. Although, no more enlightened than her age, she did not doubt the justice of the sentence that had condemned her. In the centre of the area was a pile of faggots, and near it stood the assistant executioners and several members of the church—priests and friars in their robes of black and grey.

The prisoners, accompanied by a procession which was headed by the judge and terminated by the chief executioner of the law, were first marched round the square several times, in order that the whole of the assembly might be gratified with the sight of them, and then being placed in front of the pile, the bishop of the district, who attended in his full canonicals, commenced a mass for the souls of the unhappy persons about to depart this life under such painful circumstances, after which he pronounced a somewhat lengthy oration on the enormity of their crime, ending with an exhortation to confession and repentance.

These, which constituted the whole of the preliminary ceremonies, being concluded, and the judge having read the sentence, to the effect, that, being found guilty of abominable and devilish magic arts, Michael and Francoise Thilouze were condemned to be burnt, especially for that the said Francoise, by her own arts, and those of her father, had bewitched the Count Victor de Vardes, and had sundry times visibly transformed herself into the shape of a wolf, and being caught in a trap, had thereby lost her hand, &c., the prisoners were delivered to the executioner, who prepared to bind them previously to their being placed on the pile.

Then Michael fell upon his knees, and crying aloud to the multitude, besought them to spare his daughter, and to let him die alone, and the hearts of some amongst the people were moved. But from that part of the area where the nobility were seated, there issued a voice of authority, bidding the executioner proceed, so the old man and the young girl were placed upon the pile, and the assistants, with torches in their hands, drew near to set it alight, when a murmur arose from afar, then a hum of voices, a movement in the assembled crowd, which began to sway to and fro like the awing of vast waters.

Then there was a cry of "Make way! Make way! Open a path! Let her advance!" and the crowd divided, and a path was opened, and there came forward, slowly and with difficulty, disheveled, with clothes torn and stained with blood, Manon Thierry, dragging behind her a dead wolf. The crowd closed in as she advanced, and when she reached the centre of the arena, there was straightway a dead silence. She stood for a moment looking around, and when she saw where the persons in authority sat, she fell upon her knees and essayed to speak, but her voice was choked by emotion, no word escaped her lips. She could only point to the wolf, and plead for mercy by her looks, where her present anguish of soul, and the danger and terror she had lately encountered, were legibly engraved.

The appeal was understood, and gradually the voices of the people rose again—there was a reaction. They who had been so eager for the spectacle, were now ready to supplicate for the victims. The young girl's heroism had conquered their sympathies. "Pardon! Pardon!" was the cry, and a hope awoke in the hearts of the captives. But the interest of the Montmorencis was too strong for that of the populace. The nobility stood by their order, and stern voices commanded silence, and that the ceremony should proceed, and once more the assistants brandished their torches and advanced to the pile, and then Manon, exhausted with grief, terror, and loss of blood, fell upon her face to the ground.

But now, again, there is a sound from afar, and all voices are hushed, and all ears are strained. It is the echo of a horse's foot galloping over the drawbridge; it approaches, and again, like the surface of a stormy sea, the dense crowd is in motion, and then a path is opened, and a horse, covered with foam, is seen advancing, and thousands of voices burst forth into "'Viva! Viva!" The air rings with acclamations. The rider was Victor de Vardes, bearing in his hand the king's order for arrest of execution.

Pierre Bloui had faithfully performed his embassy, and the brave Henry IV, moved by the prayers and representations of the ardent lover, had hastily furnished him with a mandate commanding respite till further investigation.

Kings were all-powerful in those days, and it was no sooner known that Henry was favourable to the lovers, than the harmlessness of Michael and his daughter was generally acknowledged. The production of the wolf wanting a foot being now considered as satisfactory a proof of their innocence, as the production of the foot wanting the wolf had formerly been of their guilt.

Strange human passions, subject to such excesses and to such revulsions! Michael Thilouze and his daughter happily escaped, and under the king's countenance and protection, the young couple were married, but we need not remind such of our readers as are learned in the annals of witchcraft, how many unfortunate persons have died at the stake for crimes imputed to them, on no better evidence than this.

As for the heiress of Montmorenci, she bore her loss with considerable philosophy. She would have married the young Count de Vardes without repugnance, but he had been too cold a lover to touch her heart or occasion regret, but poor Manon was the sacrifice for her own error. What manner of contest she had had with the wolf was never known, for she never sufficiently recovered from the state of exhaustion in which she had fallen to the earth, to be able to describe what had passed. Alone she had vanquished the savage animal, alone dragged it through the forest and the village, to the market square, where every human being able to stir, for miles round, was assembled, so that all other places were wholly deserted. The wolf had been shot, but not mortally; its death had evidently been accelerated by other wounds.

Manon herself was much torn and lacerated, and on the spot where the creature had apparently been slain, was found her gun, a knife, and a pool of blood, in which lay several fragments of her dress. Though unable to give any connected account of her own perilous adventure, she was conscious of the happy result of her generous devotion, and before she died received the heartfelt forgiveness and earnest thanks of her uncle and cousin, the former of whom soon followed her to the grave. Despairing now of ever succeeding in his darling object, what was the world to him! He loved his daughter tenderly, but he was possessed with an idea, which it had been the aim and hope of his life to work out. She was safe and happy, and needed him no more, and the hope being dead, life seemed to ooze out with it.

By the loss of that maiden's hand, who can tell what we have missed! For doubtless it is the difficulty of fulfilling the last condition named by the Italian, which has been the real impediment in the way of all philosophers who have been engaged in alchemical pursuits, and we may reasonably hope, that when women shall have learned to hold their tongues, the philosopher's stone will be discovered, and poverty and wrinkles thereafter cease to deform the earth.

For long years after these strange events, over the portcullis of the old chateau of the De Vardes, till it fell into utter ruin, might be discerned the figure of a wolf, carved in stone, wanting one of its fore-feet, and underneath it the following inscription: "In perpetuam rei memoriam."

THE MAN-WOLF

by Erckmann-Chatrain

CHAPTER I

ABOUT CHRISTMAS TIME in the year 18—, as I was lying fast asleep at the Cygne at Fribourg, my old friend Gideon Sperver broke abruptly into my room, crying, "Fritz, I have good news for you. I am going to take you to Nideck, two leagues from this place. You know Nideck, the finest baronial castle in the country, a grand monument of the glory of our forefathers?"

Now I had not seen Sperver, who was my foster father for sixteen years. He had grown a full beard in that time, a huge fox-skin cap covered his head, and he was holding his lantern close under my nose. It was, therefore, only natural that I should answer, "In the first place let us do things in order. Tell me who you are."

"Who I am? What! Don't you remember Gideon Sperver, the Schwartzwald huntsman? You would not be so ungrateful, would you? Was it not I who taught you to set a trap, to lay wait for the foxes along the skirts of the woods, to start the dogs after the wild birds? Do you remember me now? Look at my left ear, with a frostbite."

"Now I know you. That left ear of yours has done it. Shake hands."

Sperver, passing the back of his hand across his eyes, went on, "You know Nideck?"

"Of course I do, by reputation. What have you to do there?"

"I am the count's chief huntsman."

"And who has sent you?"

"The young Countess Odile."

"Very good. How soon are we to start?"

"This moment. The matter is urgent. The old count is very ill, and his daughter has begged me not to lose a moment. The horses are quite ready."

"But, Gideon, my dear fellow, just look out at the weather. It has been snowing three days without cessation."

"Oh, nonsense, we are not going out boar hunting. Put on your thick coat, buckle on your spurs, and let us prepare to start. I will order something to eat first." And he went out, first adding, "Be sure to put on your cape."

I could never refuse old Gideon anything. From my childhood he could do anything with me with a nod or a sign, so I equipped myself and came into the coffee room.

"I knew," he said, "that you would not let me go back without you. Eat every bit of this slice of ham, and let us drink a stirrup cup, for the horses are getting impatient. I have had your portmanteau put in."

"My portmanteau! What is that for?"

"Yes, it will be all right. You will have to stay a few days at Nideck, that is indispensable, and I will tell you why presently."

So we went down into the courtyard.

At that moment two horsemen arrived, evidently tired out with riding, their horses in a perfect lather of foam. Sperver, who had always been a great admirer of a fine horse, expressed his surprise and admiration at these splendid animals.

"What beauties! They are of the Wallachian breed, I can see, as finely formed as deer, and as swift. Nicholas, throw a cloth over them quickly, or they will take cold."

The travellers, muffled in Siberian furs, passed close by us just as we were going to mount. I could only discern the long brown moustache of one, and his singularly bright and sparkling eyes.

They entered the hotel.

The groom was holding our horses by the bridle. He wished us bon voyage, removed his hand, and we were off.

Sperver rode a pure Mecklemburg. I was mounted on a stout cob bred in the Ardennes, full of fire. We flew over the snowy ground. In ten minutes we had left Fribourg behind us.

The sky was beginning to clear up. As far as the eye could reach we could distinguish neither road, path, nor track. Our only company were the ravens of the Black Forest spreading their hollow wings wide over the banks of snow, trying one place after another unsuccessfully for food, and croaking, "Misery! Misery!"

Gideon, with his weather-beaten countenance, his fur cloak and cap, galloped on ahead, whistling airs from the Freyschütz. Sometimes as he turned I could see the sparkling drops of moisture hanging from his long moustache.

"Well, Fritz, my boy, this is a fine winter's morning."

"So it is, but it is rather severe, don't you think so?"

"I am fond of a clear hard frost," he replied, "it promotes circulation. If our old minister Tobias had but the courage to start out in weather like this he would soon put an end to his rheumatic pains."

I smiled, I am afraid, involuntarily.

After an hour of this rapid pace Sperver slackened his speed and let me come abreast of him.

"Fritz, I shall have to tell you the object of this journey at some time, I suppose?"

"I was beginning to think I ought to know what I am going about."

"A good many doctors have already been consulted."

"Indeed!"

"Yes, some came from Berlin in great wigs who only asked to see the patient's tongue. Others from Switzerland examined him another way. The doctors from Paris stared at their patient through magnifying glasses to learn something from his physiognomy. But all their learning was wasted, and they got large fees in reward of their ignorance."

"Is that the way you speak of us medical gentlemen?"

"I am not alluding to you at all. I have too much respect for you, and if I should happen to break my leg I don't know that there is another that I should prefer to yourself to treat me as a patient, but you have not discovered an optical instrument yet to tell what is going on inside of us."

"How do you know that?"

At this reply the worthy fellow looked at me doubtfully as if he thought me a quack like the rest, yet he replied, "Well, Fritz, if you have indeed such a glass it will be wanted now, for the count's complaint is internal. It is a terrible kind of illness, something like madness. You know that madness shows itself in either nine hours, nine days, or nine weeks?"

"So it is said, but not having noticed this myself, I cannot say that it is so."

"Still you know there are agues which return at periods of either three, six, or nine years. There are singular works in this machinery of ours. Whenever this human clockwork is wound up in some particular way, fever, or indigestion, or toothache returns at the very hour and day."

"Why, Gideon, I am quite aware of that. Those periodical complaints are the greatest trouble we have."

"I am sorry to hear it, for the count's complaint is periodical; it comes back every year, on the same day, at the same hour. His mouth runs over with foam, his eyes stand out white and staring, like great billiard balls. He shakes from head to foot, and he gnashes with his teeth."

"Perhaps this man has had serious troubles to go through?"

"No, he has not. If his daughter would but consent to be married he would be the happiest man alive. He is rich and powerful and full of honours. He possesses everything that the rest of the world is coveting. Unfortunately his daughter persists in refusing every offer of marriage. She consecrates her life to God, and it harasses him to think that the ancient house of Nideck will become extinct."

"How did his illness come on?" I asked.

"Suddenly, ten years ago," was the reply.

All at once the honest fellow seemed to be recollecting himself. He took from his pocket a short pipe, filled it, and having lighted it, said, "One evening I was sitting alone with the count in the armoury of the castle. It was about Christmas time. We had been hunting wild boars the whole day in the valleys of the Rhéthal, and had returned at night bringing home with us two of our boar-hounds ripped open from head to tail. It was just as cold as it is tonight, with snow and frost. The count was pacing up and down the room with his chin upon his breast and his hands crossed behind him, like a man in profound thought. From time to time he stopped to watch the gathering snow on the high windows, and I was warming myself in the chimney corner, bewailing my dead hounds, and bestowing maledictions on all the wild boars that infest the Schwartzwald. Everybody at Nideck had been asleep a couple of hours, and not a sound could be heard but the tread and the clank of the count's heavy spurred boots upon the flags. I remember well that a crow, no doubt driven by a gust of wind, came flapping its wings against the windowpanes, uttering a discordant shriek, and how the sheets of snow fell from the windows, and the windows suddenly changed from white to black—"

"But what has all this to do with your master's illness?" I interrupted.

"Let me go on, you will soon see. At that cry the count suddenly gathered himself together with a shuddering movement, his eyes became fixed with a glassy stare, his cheeks were bloodless, and he bent his head forward just like a hunter catching the sound of his approaching game. I went on warming myself, and I thought, 'Won't he soon go to bed now?' for, to tell you the truth, I was overcome with fatigue. All these details, Fritz, are still present in my memory. Scarcely had the bird of ill omen croaked its unearthly cry when the old clock struck eleven. At that moment the count turns on his heel, he listens, his lips tremble, I can see him staggering like a drunken man. He stretches out his hands, his jaws are tightly clenched, his eyes staring and white. I cried, 'My lord, what is the matter?' but he began to laugh discordantly like a madman, stumbled, and fell upon the stone floor, face downwards. I called for help, servants came round. Sébalt took the count by the shoulders. We removed him to a bed near the window, but just as I was loosening the count's neckerchief, for I was afraid it was apoplexy, the countess came and flung herself upon the body of her father, uttering such heartrending cries that the very remembrance of them makes me shudder."

Here Gideon took his pipe from his lips, knocked the ashes out upon the pommel of his saddle, and pursued his tale in a saddened voice.

"From that day, Fritz, none but evil days have come upon Nideck, and better times seem to be far off. Every year at the same day and hour the count has shuddering fits. The malady lasts from a week to a fortnight, during which he howls and yells so frightfully that it makes a man's blood run cold to hear him. Then he slowly recovers his usual health. He is still pale and weak, and moves trembling from one chair to another, starting at the least noise or movement, and fearful of his own shadow. The young countess, the sweetest creature in the world, never leaves his side, but he cannot endure her while the fit is upon him. He roars at her, 'Go, leave me this moment! I have enough to endure without seeing you hanging about me!' It is a horrible sight. I am always close at his heels in the chase, I who sound the horn when he has killed the forest beasts. I am at the head of all his retainers, and I would give my life for his sake, yet when he is at his worst I can hardly keep off my hands from his throat, I am so horrified at the way in which he treats his beautiful daughter."

Sperver looked dangerously wroth for a moment, clapped both his spurs to his mount, and we rode on at a hard gallop.

I had fallen into a reverie. The cure of a complaint of this description appeared to me more than doubtful, even impossible. It was evidently a mental disorder. To fight against it with any hope of success it would be needful to trace it back to its origin, and this would, no doubt, be too remote for successful investigation.

All these reflections perplexed me greatly. The old huntsman's story, far from strengthening my hopes, only depressed me—not a very favourable condition to insure success. At about three we came in sight of the ancient castle of Nideck on the verge of the horizon. In spite of the great distance we could distinguish the projecting turrets, apparently suspended from the angles of the edifice. It was but a dim outline barely distinguishable from the blue sky, but soon the red points of the Vosges became visible.

At that moment Sperver drew in his bridle and said, "Fritz, we shall have to get there before night. Onward!"

But it was in vain that he spurred and lashed. The horse stood rooted to the ground, his ears thrown back, his nostrils dilated, his sides panting, his legs firmly planted in an attitude of resistance.

"What is the matter with the beast?" cried Gideon in astonishment. "Do you see anything, Fritz? Surely—"

He broke off abruptly, pointing with his whip at a dark form in the snow fifty yards off, on the slope of the hill.

"The Black Plague!" he exclaimed with a voice of distress which almost robbed me of my self-possession.

Following the indication of his outstretched whip I discerned with astonishment an aged woman crouching on the snowy ground, with her arms clasped about her knees, and so tattered that her red elbows came through her tattered sleeves. A few ragged locks of grey hung about her long, scraggy, red, and vulture-like neck.

Strange to say, a bundle of some kind lay upon her knees, and her haggard eyes were directed upon distant objects in the white landscape.

Spencer drew off to the left, giving the hideous object as wide a berth as he could, and I had some difficulty in following him.

"Now," I cried, "what is all this for? Are you joking?"

"Joking? Assuredly not! I never joke about such serious matters. I am not given to superstition, but I confess that I am alarmed at this meeting!"

Then turning his head, and noticing that the old woman had not moved, and that her eyes were fixed upon the same one spot, he appeared to gather a little courage.

"Fritz," he said solemnly, "you are a man of learning. You know many things of which I know nothing at all. Well, I can tell you this, that a man is in the wrong who laughs at a thing because he can't understand it. I have good reasons for calling this woman the Black Plague. She is known by that name in the whole Black Forest, but here at Nideck she has earned that title by supreme right."

And the good man pursued his way without further observation.

"Now, Sperver, just explain what you mean," I asked, "for I don't understand you."

"That woman is the ruin of us all. She is a witch. She is the cause of it all. It is she who is killing the count by inches."

"How is that possible?" I exclaimed. "How could she exercise such a baneful influence?"

"I cannot tell how it is. All I know is, that on the very day that the attack comes on, at the very moment, if you will ascend the beacon tower, you will see the Black Plague squatting down like a dark speck on the snow just between the Tiefenbach and the castle of Nideck. She sits there alone, crouching close to the snow. Every day she comes a little nearer, and every day the attacks grow worse. You would think he hears her approach. Sometimes on the first day, when the fits of trembling have come over him, he has said to me, 'Gideon, I feel her coming.' I hold him by the arms and restrain the shuddering somewhat, but he still repeats, stammering and struggling with his agony, and his eyes staring and fixed, 'She is coming—nearer—oh—oh—she comes!' Then I go up Hugh Lupus's tower. I survey the country. You know I have a keen eye for distant objects. At last, amidst the grey mists afar off, between sky and earth, I can just make out a dark speck. The next morning that black spot has grown larger. The Count of Nideck goes to bed with chattering teeth. The next day again we can make out the figure of the old hag, the fierce attacks begin, the count cries out. The day after, the witch is at the foot of the mountain, and the consequence is that the count's jaws are set like a vice, his mouth foams, his eyes turn in his head. Vile creature! Twenty times I have had her within gunshot, and the count has bid me shed no blood. 'No, Sperver, no. Let us have no bloodshed.' Poor man, he is sparing the life of the wretch who is draining his life from him, for she is killing him, Fritz. He is reduced to skin and bone."

My good friend Gideon was in too great a rage with the unhappy woman to make it possible to bring him back to calm reason. Besides, who can draw the limits around the region of possibility? Every day we see the range of reality extending more widely. Unseen and unknown influences, marvellous correspondences, invisible bonds, some kind of mysterious magnetism, are, on the one hand, proclaimed as undoubted facts, and denied on the other with irony and scepticism, and yet who can say that after a while there will not be some astonishing revelations breaking in in the midst of us all when we least expect it? In the midst of so much ignorance it seems easy to lay a claim to wisdom and shrewdness.

I therefore only begged Sperver to moderate his anger, and by no means to fire upon the Black Plague, warning him that such a proceeding would bring serious misfortune upon him.

"Pooh!" he cried. "At the very worst they could but hang me."

But that, I remarked, was a good deal for an honest man to suffer.

"Not at all," he cried, "it is but one kind of death out of many. You are suffocated, that is all. I would just as soon die of that as of a hammer falling on my head, as in apoplexy, or not to be able to sleep, or smoke, or swallow, or digest my food."

"You, Gideon, with your grey beard, you have learnt a peculiar mode of reasoning."

"Grey beard or not, that is my way of seeing things. I always keep a ball in my double-barrelled gun at the witch's service. From time to time I put in a fresh charge, and if I get the chance—"

He only added an expressive gesture.

"Quite wrong, Sperver, quite wrong. I agree with the Count of Nideck, and I say no bloodshed. Oceans cannot wipe away blood shed in anger. Think of that, and discharge that barrel against the first boar you meet."

These words seemed to make some impression upon the old huntsman. He hung down his head and looked thoughtful.

We were then climbing the wooded steeps which separate the poor village of Tiefenbach from the Castle of Nideck.

Night had closed in. As it always happens with us after a bright clear winter's day, snow was again beginning to fall, heavy flakes dropped and melted upon our horses' manes, who were beginning now to pluck up their spirits at the near prospect of the comfortable stable.

Now and then Sperver looked over his shoulder with evident uneasiness, and I myself was not altogether free from a feeling of apprehension in thinking of the strange account which the huntsman had given me of his master's complaint.

Besides all this, there is a certain harmony between external nature and the spirit of a man, and I know of nothing more depressing than a gloomy forest loaded in every branch with thick snow and hoar frost, and moaning in the north wind. The gaunt and weird-looking trunks of the tall pines and the gnarled and massive oaks look mournfully upon you, and fill you with melancholy thoughts.

As we ascended the rocky eminence the oaks became fewer, and scattered birches, straight and white as marble pillars, divided the dark green of the forest pines, when in a moment, as we issued from a thicket, the ancient stronghold stood before us in a heavy mass, its dark surface studded with brilliant points of light.

Sperver had pulled up before a deep gateway between two towers, barred in by an iron grating.

"Here we are," he cried, throwing the reins on the horses' necks.

He laid hold of the deer's-foot bell-handle, and the clear sound of a bell broke the stillness.

After waiting a few minutes, the light of a lantern flickered in the deep archway, showing us in its semicircular frame of ruddy light the figure of a humpbacked dwarf, yellow-bearded, broad-shouldered, and wrapped in furs from head to foot.

You might have thought him, in the deep shadow, some gnome or evil spirit of earth realised out of the dreams of the Niebelungen Lieder.

He came towards us at a very leisurely pace, and laid his great flat features close against the massive grating, straining his eyes, and trying to make us out in the darkness in which we were standing.

"Is that you, Sperver?" he asked in a hoarse voice.

"Open at once, Knapwurst," was the quick reply. "Don't you know how cold it is?"

"Oh! I know you now," cried the little man, "there's no mistaking you. You always speak as if you were going to gobble people up."

The door opened, and the dwarf, examining me with his lantern, with an odd expression in his face, received me with "Willkommen, herr doctor," but which seemed to say besides, "Here is another who will have to go away again as others have done." Then he quietly closed the door, whilst we alighted, and came to take our horses by the bridle.

CHAPTER II

Following Sperver, who ascended the staircase with rapid steps, I was still able to convince myself that the Castle of Nideck had not an undeserved reputation.

It was a true stronghold, partly cut out of the rock, such as used formerly to be called a château d'ambuscade. Its lofty vaulted arches re-echoed afar with our steps, and the outside air blowing with sharp gusts through the loopholes—narrow slits made for the archers of former days—caused our torches to flare and flicker from space to space over the faintly illuminated protruding lines of the arches as they caught the uncertain light.

Sperver knew every nook and corner of this vast place. He turned now to the right and now to the left, and I followed him breathless. At last he stopped on a spacious landing, and said to me, "Now, Fritz, I will leave you for a minute with the people of the castle to inform the young Countess Odile of your arrival."

"Do just what you think right."

"Then you will find the head butler, Tobias Offenloch, an old soldier of the regiment of Nideck. He campaigned in France under the count, and you will see his wife, a Frenchwoman, Marie Lagoutte, who pretends that she comes of a high family."

"And why should she not?"

"Of course she might, but, between ourselves, she was nothing but a cantinière in the Grande Armée. She brought in Tobias Offenloch upon her cart, with one of his legs gone, and he has married her out of gratitude. You understand?"

"That will do, but open, for I am numb with cold."

And I was about to push on, but Sperver, as obstinate as any other good German, was not going to let me off without edifying me upon the history of the people with whom my lot was going to be cast for awhile, and holding me by the frogs of my fur coat he went on.

"There's, besides, Sébalt Kraft, the master of the hounds. He is rather a dismal fellow, but he has not his equal at sounding the horn, and there will be Karl Trumpf, the butler, and Christian Becker, and everybody, unless they have all gone to bed."

Thereupon Sperver pushed open the door, and I stood in some surprise on the threshold of a high, dark hall, the guard room of the old lords of Nideck.

My eyes fell at first upon the three windows at the farther end, looking out upon the sheer rocky precipice. On the right stood an old sideboard in dark oak, and upon it a cask, glasses, and bottles, on the left a Gothic chimney overhung with its heavy massive mantelpiece, empurpled by the brilliant roaring fire underneath, and ornamented on both front and sides with wood-carvings representing scenes from boar-hunts in the Middle Ages, and along the centre of the apartment a long table, upon which stood a huge lamp throwing its light upon a dozen pewter tankards.

At one glance I saw all this, but the human portion of the scene interested me most.

I recognised the major-domo, or head butler, by his wooden leg, of which I had already heard. He was of low stature, round, fat, and rosy, and his knees seldom coming within an easy range of his eyesight, a nose red and bulbous like a ripe raspberry. On his head he wore a huge hemp-coloured wig, bulging out over his fat poll, a coat of light green plush, with steel buttons as large as a five-franc piece, velvet breeches, silk stockings, and shoes garnished with silver buckles. He was just with his hand upon the top of the cask, with an air of inexpressible satisfaction beaming upon his ruddy features, and his eyes glowing in profile, from the reflection of the fire, like a couple of watch-glasses.

His wife, the worthy Marie Lagoutte, her spare figure draped in voluminous folds, her long and sallow face like a skin of chamois leather, was playing at cards with two servants who were gravely seated on straight-backed armchairs. Certain small split pegs were seated astride across the nose of the old woman and that of another player, whilst the third was significantly and cunningly winking his eye and seeming to enjoy seeing them victimised upon these new Caudine Forks.

"How many cards?" he was asking.

"Two," answered the old woman.

"And you, Christian?"

"Two."

"Aha! Now I have got you, then. Cut the king, now the ace, here's one, here's another. Another peg, mother! This will teach you once more not to brag about French games."

"Monsieur Christian, you don't treat the fair sex with proper respect."

"At cards you respect nobody."

"But you see I have no room left!"

"Pooh, on a nose like yours there's always room for more!"

At that moment Sperver cried, "Mates, here I am!"

"Ha! Gideon, back already?"

Marie Lagoutte shook off her numerous pegs with a jerk of her head. The big butler drank off his glass. Everybody turned our way.

"Is monseigneur better?"

The butler answered with a doubtful ejaculation.

"Is he just the same?"

"Much about," answered Marie Lagoutte, who never took her eyes off me.

Sperver noticed this.

"Let me introduce to you my foster-son, Doctor Fritz, from

the Black Forest," he answered proudly. "Now we shall see a change, Master Tobie. Now that Fritz has come the abominable fits will be put an end to. If I had but been listened to earlier—but better late than never."

Marie Lagoutte was still watching us, and her scrutiny seemed satisfactory, for, addressing the major-domo, she said, "Now, Monsieur Offenloch, hand the doctor a chair, move about a little, do! There you stand with your mouth wide open, just like a fish. Ah, sir, these Germans!"

And the good man, jumping up as if moved by a spring, came to take off my cloak.

"Permit me, sir."

"You are very kind, my dear lady."

"Give it to me. What terrible weather! Ah, monsieur, what a dreadful country this is!"

"So monseigneur is neither better nor worse," said Sperver, shaking the snow off his cap. "We are not too late, then. Ho, Kasper! Kasper!"

A little man, who had one shoulder higher than the other, and his face spotted with innumerable freckles, came out of the chimney corner.

"Here I am!"

"Very good, now get ready for this gentleman the bedroom at the end of the long gallery—Hugh's room. You know which I mean."

"Yes, Sperver, in a minute."

"And you will take with you, as you go, the doctor's knapsack. Knapwurst will give it you. As for supper—"

"Never you mind. That is my business."

"Very well, then. I will depend upon you."

The little man went out, and Gideon, after taking off his cape, left us to go and inform the young countess of my arrival.

I was rather overpowered with the attentions of Marie Lagoutte.

"Give up that place of yours, Sébalt," she cried to the kennel-keeper. "You are roasted enough by this time. Sit near the fire, monsieur le docteur, you must have very cold feet. Stretch out your legs. That's the way."

Then, holding out her snuff-box to me, "Do you take snuff?"

"No, dear madam, with many thanks."

"That is a pity," she answered, filling both nostrils. "It is the most delightful habit."

She slipped her snuff-box back into her apron pocket, and went on. "You are come not a bit too soon. Monseigneur had his second attack yesterday. It was an awful attack, was it not, Monsieur Offenloch?"

"Furious indeed," answered the head butler gravely.

"It is not surprising," she continued, "when a man takes no nourishment. Fancy, monsieur, that for two days he has never tasted broth!"

"Nor a glass of wine," added the major-domo, crossing his hands over his portly, well-lined person.

As it seemed expected of me, I expressed my surprise, on which Tobias Offenloch came to sit at my right hand, and said, "Doctor, take my advice. Order him a bottle a day of Marcobrunner."

"And," chimed in Marie Lagoutte, "a wing of a chicken at every meal. The poor man is frightfully thin."

"We have got Marcobrunner sixty years in bottle," added the major-domo, "for it is a mistake of Madame Offenloch's to suppose that the French drank it all. And you had better order, while you are about it, now and then, a good bottle of Johannisberg. That is the best wine to set a man up again."

"Time was," remarked the master of the hounds in a dismal voice, "time was when monseigneur hunted twice a week. Then he was well. When he left off hunting, then he fell ill."

"Of course it could not be otherwise," observed Marie Lagoutte. "The open air gives you an appetite. The doctor had better order him to hunt three times a week to make up for lost time."

"Two would be enough," replied the man of dogs with the same gravity, "quite enough. The hounds must have their rest. Dogs have just as much right to rest as we have."

There was a few moments' silence, during which I could hear the wind beating against the windowpanes, and rush, sighing and wailing, through the loopholes into the towers.

Sébalt sat with legs across, and his elbow resting on his knee, gazing into the fire with unspeakable dolefulness. Marie Lagoutte, after having refreshed herself with a fresh pinch, was settling her snuff into shape in its box, while I sat thinking on the strange habit people indulge in of pressing their advice upon those who don't want it.

At this moment the major-domo rose.

"Will you have a glass of wine, doctor?" said he, leaning over the back of my armchair.

"Thank you, but I never drink before seeing a patient."

"What! Not even one little glass?"

"Not the smallest glass you could offer me."

He opened his eyes wide and looked with astonishment at his wife.

"The doctor is right," she said. "I am quite of his opinion. I prefer to drink with my meat, and to take a glass of cognac afterwards. That is what the ladies do in France. Cognac is more fashionable than kirschwasser!"

Marie Lagoutte had hardly finished with her dissertation when Sperver opened the door quietly and beckoned me to follow him.

I bowed to the "honourable company," and as I was entering the passage I could hear that lady saying to her husband, "That is a nice young man. He would have made a good-looking soldier."

Sperver looked uneasy, but said nothing. I was full of my own thoughts.

A few steps under the darkling vaults of Nideck completely effaced from my memory the queer figures of Tobias and Marie Lagoutte, poor harmless creatures, existing like bats under the mighty wing of the vulture.

Soon Gideon brought me into a sumptuous apartment hung with violet-coloured velvet, relieved with gold. A bronze lamp stood in a corner, its brightness toned down by a globe of ground crystal; thick carpets, soft as the turf on the hills, made our steps noiseless. It seemed a fit abode for silence and meditation.

On entering Sperver lifted the heavy draperies which fell around an ogee window. I observed him straining his eyes to discover something in the darkened distance. He was trying to make out whether the witch still lay there crouching down upon the snow in the midst of the plain, but he could see nothing, for there was deep darkness over all.

But I had gone on a few steps, and came in sight, by the faint rays of the lamp, of a pale, delicate figure seated in a Gothic chair not far from the sick man. It was Odile of Nideck. Her long black silk dress, her gentle expression of calm self-devotion and complete resignation, the ideal angel-like cast of her sweet features, recalled to one's mind those mysterious creations of the pencil in the Middle Ages when painting was pursued as a true art, but which modern imitators have found themselves obliged to give up in despair, while at the same time they never can forget them.

I cannot say what thoughts passed rapidly through my mind at the sight of this fair creature, but certainly much of devotion mingled with my sentiments. A sense of music and harmony swept sadly through my soul, with faint impressions of the old ballads of my childhood, of those pious songs with which the kind nurses of the Black Forest rock to peaceful sleep our infant sorrows.

At my approach Odile rose.

"You are very welcome, monsieur le docteur," she said with

touching kindness and simplicity, then, pointing with her finger to a recess where lay the count, she added, "There is my father."

I bowed respectfully and without answering, for I felt deeply affected, and drew near to my patient.

Sperver, standing at the head of the bed, held up the lamp with one hand, holding his fur cap in the other. Odile stood at my left hand. The light, softened by the subdued light of the globe of ground crystal, fell softly on the face of the count.

At once I was struck with a strangeness in the physiognomy of the Count of Nideck, and in spite of all the admiration which his lovely daughter had at once obtained from me, my first conclusion was, "What an old wolf!"

And such he seemed to be indeed. A grey head, covered with short, close hair, strangely full behind the ears, and drawn out in the face to a portentous length, the narrowness of his forehead up to its summit widening over the eyebrows, which were shaggy and met, pointing downwards over the bridge of the nose, imperfectly shading with their sable outline the cold and inexpressive eyes. The short, rough beard, irregularly spread over the angular and bony outline of the mouth. Every feature of this man's dreadful countenance made me shudder, and strange notions crossed my mind about the mysterious affinities between man and the lower creation.

But I resisted my first impressions and took the sick man's hand. It was dry and wiry, yet small and strong. I found the pulse quick, feverish, and denoting great irritability.

What was I to do?

I stood considering, on the one side stood the young lady, anxiously trying to read a little hope in my face, on the other Sperver, equally anxious and watching my every movement. A painful constraint lay, therefore, upon me, yet I saw that there was nothing definite that could be attempted yet.

I dropped the arm and listened to the breathing. From time to time a convulsive sob heaved the sick man's heart, after which followed a succession of quick, short respirations. A kind of nightmare was evidently weighing him down—epilepsy, perhaps, or tetanus. But what could be the cause or origin?

I turned round full of painful thoughts.

"Is there any hope, sir?" asked the young countess.

"Yesterday's crisis is drawing to its close," I answered. "We must see if we can prevent its recurrence."

"Is there any possibility of it, sir?"

I was about to answer in general medical terms, not daring to venture any positive assertions, when the distant sound of the bell at the gate fell upon our ears.

"Visitors," said Sperver.

There was a moment's silence.

"Go and see who it is," said Odile, whose brow was for a minute shaded with anxiety. "How can one be hospitable to strangers at such a time? It is hardly possible!"

But the door opened, and a rosy face, with golden hair, appeared in the shadow, and said in a whisper, "It is the Baron of Zimmer-Bluderich, with a servant, and he asks for shelter in the Nideck. He has lost his way among the mountains."

"Very well, Gretchen," answered the young countess, kindly, "go and tell the steward to attend to the Baron de Zimmer. Inform him that the count is very ill, and that this alone prevents him from doing the honours as he would wish. Wake up some of our people to wait on him, and let everything be done properly."

Nothing could exceed the sweet and noble simplicity of the young châtelaine in giving her orders. If an air of distinction seems hereditary in some families it is surely because the exercise of the duties conferred by the possession of wealth has a natural tendency to ennoble the whole character and bearing.

These thoughts passed through my mind whilst admiring the grace and gentleness in every movement of Odile of Nideck, and that clearness and purity of outline which is only found marked in the features of the higher aristocracy, and I could recall nothing to my recollection equal to this ideal beauty.

"Go now, Gretchen," said the young countess, "and make haste."

The attendant went out, and I stood a few seconds under the influence of the charm of her manner.

Odile turned round, and addressing me, "You see, sir," said she with a sad smile, "one may not indulge in grief without a pause. We must divide ourselves between our affection within and the world without."

"True, madam," I replied. "Souls of the highest order are for the common property and advantage of the unhappy, the lost wayfarer, the sick, the hungry poor, each has his claim for a share, for God has made them like the stars of heaven to give light and pleasure to all."

The deep-fringed eyelids veiled the blue eyes for a moment, while Sperver pressed my hand.

Presently she pursued, "Ah, if you could but restore my father's health!"

"As I have had the pleasure to inform you, madam, the crisis is past. The return must be anticipated, if possible."

"Do you hope that it may?"

"With God's help, madam, it is not impossible. I will think carefully over it."

Odile, much moved, came with me to the door. Sperver and I crossed the ante-room, where a few servants were waiting for the orders of their mistress. We had just entered the corridor when Gideon, who was walking first, turned quickly round, and, placing both his hands on my shoulders, said, "Come, Fritz. I am to be depended upon for keeping a secret. What is your opinion?"

"I think there is no cause of apprehension for tonight."

"I know that. So you told the countess, but how about tomorrow?"

"Tomorrow?"

"Yes, don't turn round. I suppose you cannot prevent the

return of the complaint. Do you think, Fritz, he will die of it?"

"It is possible, but hardly probable."

"Well done!" cried the good man, springing from the ground with joy. "If you don't think so, that means that you are sure."

And taking my arm, he drew me into the gallery. We had just reached it when the Baron of Zimmer-Bluderich and his groom appeared there also, marshalled by Sébalt with a lighted torch in his hand. They were on their way to their chambers, and those two figures, with their cloaks flung over their shoulders, their loose Hungarian boots up to the knees, the body closely girt with long dark-green laced and frogged tunics, and the bear-skin cap closely and warmly covering the head, were very picturesque objects by the flickering light of the pine-torch.

"There," whispered Sperver, "if I am not very much mistaken, those are our Fribourg friends. They have followed very close upon our heels."

"You are quite right. They are the men. I recognise the younger by his tall, slender figure, his aquiline nose, and his long, drooping moustache."

They disappeared through a side passage.

Gideon took a torch from the wall, and guided me through quite a maze of corridors, aisles, narrow and wide passages, under high vaulted roofs and under low-built arches. Who could remember? There seemed no end.

"Here is the hall of the margraves," said he. "Here is the portrait gallery, and this is the chapel, where no mass has been said since Louis the Bold became a Protestant."

All these particulars had very little interest for me.

After reaching the end we had again to go down steps. At last we happily came to the end of our journey before a low massive door. Sperver took a huge key out of his pocket, and handing me the torch, said, "Mind the light. Look out!"

At the same time he pushed open the door, and the cold outside air rushed into the narrow passage. The torch flared and sent out a volley of sparks in all directions. I thought I saw a dark abyss before me, and recoiled with fear.

"Ha, ha, ha!" cried the huntsman, opening his mouth from ear to ear, "you are surely not afraid, Fritz? Come on, don't be frightened! We are upon the parapet between the castle and the old tower."

And my friend advanced to set me the example.

The narrow granite-walled platform was deep in snow, swept in swirling banks by the angry winds. Anyone who had seen our flaring torch from below would have asked, "What are they doing up there in the clouds? What can they want at this time of the night?"

Perhaps, I thought within myself, the witch is looking up at us, and that idea gave me a fit of shuddering. I drew closer together the folds of my horseman's cloak, and with my hand upon my hat, I set off after Sperver at a run;. He was raising the light above his head to show me the road, and was moving forward rapidly.

We rushed into the tower and then into Hugh Lupus's chamber. A bright fire saluted us here with its cheerful rays. How delightful to be once more sheltered by thick walls!

I had stopped while Sperver closed the door, and contemplating this ancient abode, I cried, "Thank God! We shall rest now!"

"With a well-furnished table before us," added Gideon. "Don't stand there with your nose in the air, but rather consider what is before you—a leg of a kid, a couple of roast fowls, a fresh caught pike with parsley sauce, cold meats and hot wines, that's what I like. Kasper has attended to my orders like a real good fellow."

Gideon spoke the truth. The meats were cold and the wines were warm, for in front of the fire stood a row of small bottles under the gentle influence of the heat.

At the sight of these good things my appetite rose in me wonderfully. But Sperver, who understood what is comfortable, stopped me.

"Fritz," said he, "don't let us be in too great a hurry. We have plenty of time. The fowls won't fly away. Your boots must hurt you. After eight hours on horseback it is pleasant to take off one's boots, that's my principle. Now sit down, put your boot between my knees... There goes one off, now the other, that's the way... Now put your feet into these slippers, take off your cloak and throw this lighter coat over your shoulders. Now we are ready."

And with his cheery summons I sat down with him to work, one on each side of the table, remembering the German proverb "Thirst comes from the evil one, but good wine from the Powers above."

CHAPTER III

WE ATE with the vigorous appetite which ten hours in the snows of the Black Forest would be sure to provoke.

Sperver making indiscriminate attacks upon the kid, the fowls, and the fish, murmured with his mouth full, "The woods, the lakes and rivers, and the heathery hills are full of good things!"

Then he leaned over the back of his chair, and laying his hand on the first bottle that came to hand, he added, "And we have hills green in spring, purple in autumn when the grapes ripen. Your health, Fritz!"

"Yours, Gideon!"

We were a wonder to behold. We reciprocally admired each other.

The fire crackled, the forks rattled, teeth were in full activity, bottles gurgled, glasses jingled, while outside the wintry blast, the high moaning mountain winds, were mournfully chanting the dirge of the year, that strange wailing hymn with which they accompany the shock of the tempest and the swift rush of the grey clouds charged with snow and hail, while the pale moon lights up the grim and ghastly battle scene.

But we were snug under cover, and our appetite was fading away into history. Sperver had filled the "wieder komm," the "come again," with old wine of Brumberg. The sparkling froth fringed its ample borders. He presented it to me, saying, "Drink the health of Yeri-Hans, lord of Nideck. Drink to the last drop, and show them that you mean it!"

Which was done.

Then he filled it again, and repeating with a voice that re-echoed among the old walls, "To the recovery of my noble master, the high and mighty lord of Nideck," he drained it also.

Then a feeling of satisfied repletion stole gently over us, and we felt pleased with everything.

I fell back in my chair, with my face directed to the ceiling, and my arms hanging lazily down. I began dreamily to consider what sort of a place I had got into.

It was a low vaulted ceiling cut out of the live rock, almost oven-shaped, and hardly twelve feet high at the highest point. At the farther end I saw a sort of deep recess where lay my bed on the ground, and consisting, as I thought I could see, of a huge bear-skin above, and I could not tell what below, and within this yet another smaller niche with a figure of the Virgin Mary carved out of the same granite, and crowned with a bunch of withered grass.

"You are looking over your room," said Spencer. "Parbleu! It is none of the biggest or grandest, not quite like the rooms in the castle. We are now in Hugh Lupus's tower, a place as old as the mountain itself, going as far back as the days of Charlemagne. In those days, as you see, people had not yet learned to build arches high, round, or pointed. They worked right into the rock."

"Well, for all that, you have put me in strange lodgings."

"Don't be mistaken, Fritz. It is the place of honour. It is here that the count put all his most distinguished friends. Mind that: Hugh Lupus's tower is the most honourable accommodation we have."

"And who was Hugh Lupus?"

"Why, Hugh the Wolf, to be sure. He was the head of the family of Nideck, a rough-and-ready warrior, I can tell you. He came to settle up here with a score of horsemen and halberdiers of his following. They climbed up this rock, the highest rock amongst these mountains. You will see this tomorrow. They constructed this tower, and proclaimed, 'Now we are the masters! Woe befall the miserable wretches who shall pass without paying toll to us! We will tear the wool off their backs, and their hide too, if need be. From this watch-tower we shall command a view of the far distance all round. The passes of the Rhéthal, of Steinbach, Koche Plate, and of the whole line of the Black Forest are under our eye. Let the Jew pedlars and the dealers beware!' And the noble fellows did what they promised. Hugh the Wolf was at their head. Knapwurst told me all about it sitting up one night."

"Who is Knapwurst?"

"That little humpback who opened the gate for us. He is an odd fellow, Fritz, and almost lives in the library."

"So you have a man of learning at Nideck?"

"Yes, we have, the rascal! Instead of confining himself to the porter's lodge, his proper place, all the day over he is amongst the dusty books and parchments belonging to the family. He comes and goes along the shelves of the library just like a big cat. Knapwurst knows our story better than we know it ourselves. He would tell you the longest tales, Fritz, if you would only let him. He calls them chronicles—ha, ha!"

And Sperver, with the wine mounting a little into his head, began to laugh, he could hardly say why.

"So then, Gideon, you call this tower, Hugh's tower, the 'Hugh Lupus tower?'"

"Haven't I told you so already? What are you so astonished at?"

"Nothing particular."

"But you are. I can see it in your face. You are thinking of something strange. What is it?"

"Oh, nevermind! It is not the name of the tower which surprises me. What I am wondering at is, how it is that you, an old poacher, who had never lived anywhere since you were a boy but amongst the fir forests, between the snowy summits of the Wald Horn and the passes of the Rhéthal—you who, during all your prime of life, thought it the finest of fun to laugh at the count's gamekeepers, and to scour the mountain paths of the Schwartzwald, and boat the bushes there, and breathe the free air, and bask in the bright sunshine amongst the hills and valleys—here I find you, at the end of sixteen years of such a life, shut up in this red granite hole. That is what surprises me and what I cannot understand. Come, Sperver, light your pipe, and tell me all about it."

The old poacher took out of his leathern jacket a bit of a blackened pipe. He filled it at his leisure, gathered up in the hollow of his hand a live ember, which he placed upon the bowl of his pipe, then with his eyes dreamily cast up to the ceiling he answered meditatively.

"Old falcons, gerfalcons, and hawks, when they have long swept the plains, end their lives in a hole in a rock. Sure enough I am fond of the wide expanse of sky and land. I always was fond of it, but instead of perching by night upon a high branch of a tall tree, rocked by the wind, I now prefer to return to my cavern, to drink a glass, to pick a bone of venison, and dry my plumage before a warm fire. The Count of Nideck does not disdain Sperver, the old hawk, the true man of the woods. One evening, meeting me by moonlight, he frankly said to me, 'Old comrade, you hunt only by night. Come and hunt by day with me. You have a sharp beak and strong claws. Well, hunt away, if such is your nature, but hunt by my licence, for I am the eagle upon these mountains, and my name is Nideck!'"

Sperver was silent a few minutes, then he resumed.

"That was just what suited me, and now I hunt as I used to do, and I quietly drink along with a friend my bottle of Affenthal or—"

At that moment there was a shock that made the door vibrate. Sperver stopped and listened.

"It is a gust of wind," I said.

"No, it is something else. Don't you hear the scratching of claws? It is a dog that has escaped. Open, Lieverlé, open, Blitzen!" cried the huntsman, rising, but he had not gone a couple of steps when a formidable-looking hound of the Danish breed broke into the tower, and ran to lay his heavy paws on his master's shoulders, licking his beard and his cheeks with his long rose-coloured tongue, uttering all the while short barks and yelps expressive of his joy.

Sperver had passed his arm round the dog's neck, and, turning to me, said, "Fritz, what man could love me as this dog does? Do look at this head, these eyes, these teeth!"

He uncovered the animal's teeth, displaying a set of fangs that would have pulled down and rent a buffalo. Then repelling him with difficulty, for the dog was re-doubling his caresses—

"Down, Lieverlé. I know you love me. If you did not, who would?"

Never had I seen so tremendous a dog as this Lieverlé. His height attained two feet and a half. He would have been a most formidable creature in an attack. His forehead was broad, flat, and covered with fine soft hair; his eye was keen, his paws of great length, his sides and legs a woven mass of muscles and nerves, broad over the back and shoulders, slender and tapering towards the hind legs. But he had no scent. If such monstrous and powerful hounds were endowed with the scent of the terrier there would soon be an end of game.

Sperver had returned to his seat, and was passing his hand over Lieverlé's massive head with pride, and enumerating to me his excellent qualities.

Lieverlé seemed to understand him.

"See, Fritz, that dog will throttle a wolf with one snap of his jaws. For courage and strength, he is perfection. He is not five years old, but he is in his prime. I need not tell you that he is trained to hunt the boar. Every time we come across a herd of them I tremble for Lieverlé. His attack is too straightforward, he flies on the game as straight as an arrow. That is why I am afraid of the brutes' tusks. Lie down, Lieverlé, lie on your back!"

The dog obeyed, and presented to view his flesh-coloured sides.

"Look, Fritz, at that long white seam without any hair upon it from under the thigh right up to the chest. A boar did that. Poor creature! He was holding him fast by the ear and would not let go. We tracked the two by the blood. I was the first up with them. Seeing my Lieverlé I gave a shout, I jumped off my horse, I caught him between my arms, flung him into my cloak, and brought him home. I was almost beside myself. Happily the vital parts had not been wounded. I sewed up his belly in spite of his howling and yelling, for he suffered fearfully, but in three days he was already licking his wound, and a dog who licks himself is already saved. You remember that, Lieverlé, hey, and aren't we fonder of each other now than ever?"

I was quite moved with the affection of the man for that dog, and of the dog for his master; they seemed to look into the very depths of each other's souls. The dog wagged his tail, and the man had tears in his eyes.

Sperver went on, "What amazing strength! Do you see, Fritz, he has burst his cord to get to me, a rope of six strands. He found out my track and here he is! Here, Lieverlé, catch!"

And he threw to him the remains of the leg of kid. The jaws opened wide and closed again with a terrible crash, and Sperver, looking at me significantly, said, "Fritz, if he were to grip you by your breeches you would not get away so easily!"

"Nor any one else, I suppose."

The dog went to stretch himself at his ease full length under the mantelshelf with the leg fast between his mighty paws. He began to tear it into pieces. Sperver looked at him out of the corner of his eye with great satisfaction. The bone was fast falling into small fragments in the powerful mill that was crashing it. Lieverlé was partial to marrow!

"Aha! Fritz, if you were requested to fetch that bone away from him, what would you say?"

"I should think it a mission requiring extraordinary delicacy and tact."

Then we broke out into a hearty laugh, and Sperver, seated in his leathern easy chair, with his left arm thrown back over his head, one of his manly legs over a stool, and the other in front of a huge log, which was dripping at its end with the oozing sap, and darted volumes of light grey smoke to the roof.

I was still contemplating the dog, when, suddenly recollecting our broken conversation, I went on.

"Now, Sperver, you have not told me everything. When you left the mountain for the castle was it not on account of the death of Gertrude, your good, excellent wife?"

Gideon frowned, and a tear dimmed his eye. He drew himself up, and shaking out the ashes of his pipe upon his thumbnail, he said, "True, my wife is dead. That drove me from the woods. I could not look upon the valley of Roche Creuse without pain. I turned my flight in this direction: I hunt less in the woods, and I can see it all from higher up, and if by chance the pack tails off in that direction I let them go. I turn back and try to think of something else."

Sperver had grown taciturn. With his head drooped upon his breast, his eyes fixed on the stone floor, he sat silent. I felt sorry to have awoke these melancholy recollections in him. Then, my thoughts once more returning to the Black Plague grovelling in the snow, I felt a shivering of horror.

How strange! Just one word had sent us into a train of unhappy thoughts. A whole world of remembrances was called up by a chance.

I know not how long this silence lasted, when a growl, deep, long, and terrible, like distant thunder, made us start.

We looked at the dog. The half-gnawed bone was still between his forepaws, but with head raised high, ears cocked up, and flashing eye, he was listening intently—listening to the silence as it were, and an angry quivering ran down the length of his back.

Sperver and I fixed on each other anxious eyes, yet there was not a sound, not a breath outside, for the wind had gone down. Nothing could be heard but the deep protracted growl which came from deep down the chest of the noble hound.

Suddenly he sprang up and bounded impetuously against the wall with a hoarse, rough bark of fearful loudness. The walls re-echoed just as if a clap of thunder had rattled the casements.

Lieverlé, with his head low down, seemed to want to see through the granite, and his lips drawn back from his teeth discovered them to the very gums, displaying two close rows of fangs white as ivory. Still he growled. For a moment he would stop abruptly with his nose snuffing close to the wall, next the floor, with strong respirations, then he would rise again in a fresh rage, and with his forepaws seemed as if he would break through the granite.

We watched in silence without being able to understand what caused his excitement.

Another yell of rage more terrible than the first made us spring from our seats.

"Lieverlé! What possesses you? Are you going mad?"

He seized a log and began to sound the wall, which only returned the dead, hard sound of a wall of solid rock. There was no hollow in it, yet the dog stood in the posture of attack.

"Decidedly you must have been dreaming bad dreams," said the huntsman. "Come, lie down, and don't worry us any more with your nonsense."

At that moment a noise outside reached our ears. The door opened, and the fat honest countenance of Tobias Offenloch with his lantern in one hand and his stick in the other, his three-cornered hat on his head, appeared, smiling and jovial, in the opening.

"Salut! l'honorable compagnie!" he cried as he entered. "What are you doing here?"

"It was that rascal Lieverlé who made all that row. Just fancy—he set himself up against that wall as if he smelt a thief. What could he mean?"

"Why parbleu! He heard the dot, dot of my wooden leg, to be sure, stumping up the tower stairs," answered the jolly fellow, laughing.

Then setting his lantern on the table, "That will teach you, friend Gideon, to tie up your dogs. You are foolishly weak over your dogs—very foolishly. Those beasts of yours won't be satisfied till they have put us all out of doors. Just this minute I met Blitzen in the long gallery. He sprang at my leg—see there are the marks of his teeth in proof of what I say, and it is quite a new leg. A brute of a hound!"

"Tie up my dogs! That's rather a new idea," said the huntsman. "Dogs tied up are good for nothing at all. They grow too wild. Besides, was not Lieverlé tied up, after all? See his broken cord."

"What I tell you is not on my own account. When they come near me I always hold up my stick and put my wooden leg foremost—that is my discipline. I say, dogs in their kennels, cats on the roof, and the people in the castle."

Tobias sat down after thus delivering himself of his sentiments, and with both elbows on the table, his eyes expanding with delight, he confided to us that just now he was a bachelor.

"You don't mean that!"

"Yes, Marie Anne is sitting up with Gertrude in monseigneur's ante-room."

"Then you are in no hurry to go away?"

"No, none at all. I should like to stay in your company."

"How unfortunate that you should have come in so late!" remarked Sperver. "All the bottles are empty."

The disappointment of the discomfited major-domo excited my compassion. The poor man would so gladly have enjoyed his widowhood. But in spite of my endeavours to repress it a long yawn extended wide my mouth.

"Well, another time," said he, rising. "What is only put off is not given up."

And he took his lantern.

"Goodnight, gentlemen."

"Stop, wait for me," cried Gideon. "I can see Fritz is sleepy. We will go down together."

"Very gladly, Sperver. On our way we will have a word with Trumpf, the butler. He is downstairs with the rest, and Knap-wurst is telling them tales."

"All right. Goodnight, Fritz."

"Goodnight, Gideon. Don't forget to send for me if the count is taken worse."

"I will do as you wish. Lieverlé, come."

They went out, and as they were crossing the platform I could hear the Nideck clock strike eleven. I was tired out and soon fell asleep.

CHAPTER IV

DAYLIGHT WAS BEGINNING to tinge with bluish grey the only window in my dungeon tower when I was roused out of my niche in the granite by the prolonged distant notes of a hunting horn.

There is nothing more sad and melancholy than the wail of this instrument when the day begins to struggle with the night, when not a sigh nor a sound besides comes to molest the solitary reign of silence. It is especially the last long note which spreads in widening waves over the immensity of the plain beneath, awaking the distant, far-off echoes amongst the mountains, that has in it a poetic element that stirs up the depths of the soul.

Leaning upon my elbow in my bear-skin I lay listening to the plaintive sound, which suggested something of the feudal ages. The contemplation of my chamber, the ancient den of the Wolf of Nideck, with its low, dark arch, threatening almost to come down to crush the occupant, and further on that small leaden window, just touching the ceiling, more wide than high, and deeply recessed in the wall, added to the reality of the impression.

I arose quickly and ran to open the window wide.

Then presented itself to my astonished eyes such a wondrous spectacle as no mortal tongue, no pen of man, can describe—the wide prospect that the eagle, the denizen of the high Alps, sweeps with his far reaching ken every morning at the rising of the deep purple veil that overhung the horizon by night mountains farther off, mountains far away, and yet again in the blue distance—mountains still, blending with the grey mists of the morning in the shadowy horizon, motionless billows that sink into peace and stillness in the blue distance of the plains of Lorraine. Such is a faint idea of the mighty scenery of the Vosges, boundless forests, silver lakes, dazzling crests, ridges, and peaks projecting their clear outlines upon the steel-blue of the valleys clothed in snow. Beyond this, infinite space!

Could any enthusiasm of poet or skill of painter attain the sublime elevation of such a scene as that?

I stood mute with admiration. At every moment the details stood out more clearly in the advancing light of morning. Hamlets, farm-houses, villages, seemed to rise and peep out of every undulation of the land. A little more attention brought more and more numerous objects into view.

I had leaned out of my window rapt in contemplation for more than a quarter of an hour when a hand was laid lightly upon my shoulder. I turned round startled, when the calm figure and quiet smile of Gideon saluted me with—

"Guten Tag, Fritz! Good morning!"

Then he also rested his arms on the window, smoking his short pipe. He extended his hand and said, "Look, Fritz, and admire! You are a son of the Black Forest, and you must admire all that. Look there below, there is Roche Creuse. Do you see it? Don't you remember Gertrude? How far off those times seem now!"

Sperver brushed away a tear. What could I say?

We sat long contemplating and meditating over this grand spectacle. From time to time the old poacher, noticing me with my eyes fixed upon some distant object, would explain...

"That is the Wald Horn. This is the Tiefenthal, here's the fall of the Steinbach. It has stopped running now, it is hanging down in great fringed sheets, like the curtains over the shoulder of the Harberg—a cold winter's cloak! Down there is a path that leads to Fribourg. In a fortnight's time it will be difficult to trace it."

Thus our time passed away.

I could not tear myself away from so beautiful a prospect. A few birds of prey, with wings hollowed into a graceful curve sharp-pointed at each end, the fan-shaped tail spread out, were silently sweeping round the rock-hewn tower. Herons flew unscathed above them, owing their safety from the grasp of the sharp claws and the tearing beak to the elevation of their flight.

Not a cloud marred the beauty of the blue sky. All the snow had fallen to earth. Once more the huntsman's horn awoke the echoes.

"That is my friend Sébalt lamenting down there," said Sperver. "He knows everything about horses and dogs, and he sounds the hunter's horn better than any man in Germany. Listen, Fritz, how soft and mellow the notes are! Poor Sébalt! He is pining away over monseigneur's illness. He cannot hunt as he used to do. His only comfort is to get up every morning at sunrise on to the Altenberg and play the count's favourite airs. He thinks he shall be able to cure him that way!"

Sperver, with the good taste of a man who appreciates beautiful scenery, had offered no interruption to my contemplations, but when, my eyes dazzled and swimming with so much light, I turned round to the darkness of the tower, he said to me, "Fritz, it's all right. The count has had no fresh attack."

These words brought me back to a sense of the realities of life.

"Ah, I am very glad!"

"It is all owing to you, Fritz."

"What do you mean? I have not prescribed yet."

"What signifies? You were there, that was enough."

"You are only joking, Gideon! What is the use of my being present if I don't prescribe?"

"Why, you bring him good luck!"

I looked straight at him, but he was not even smiling!

"Yes, Fritz, you are just a messenger of good. The last two years the lord had another attack the next day after the first, then a third and a fourth. You have put an end to that. What can be clearer?"

"Well, to me it is not so very clear. On the contrary, it is very obscure."

"We are never too old to learn," the good man went on. "Fritz, there are messengers of evil and there are messengers of good. Now that rascal Knapwurst, he is a sure messenger of ill. If ever I meet him as I am going out hunting I am sure of some misadventure, my gun misses fire, or I sprain my ankle, or a dog gets ripped up—all sorts of mischief come. So, being quite aware of this, I always try and set off at early daybreak, before that author of mischief, who sleeps like a dormouse, has opened his eyes, or else I slip out by a back way by the postern gate. Don't you see?"

"I understand you very well, but your ideas seem to me very strange, Gideon."

"You, Fritz," he went on, without noticing my interruption, "you are a most excellent lad. Heaven has covered your head with innumerable blessings. Just one glance at your jolly countenance, your frank, clear eyes, your good-natured smile, is enough to make any one happy. You positively bring good luck with you. I have always said so, and now would you like to have a proof?"

"Yes, indeed I should. It would be worth while to know how much there is in me without my having any knowledge of it."

"Well," said he, grasping my wrist, "look down there!"

He pointed to a hillock at a couple of gunshots from the castle.

"Do you see there a rock half-buried in the snow, with a ragged bush by its side?"

"Quite well."

"Do you see anything near?"

"No."

"Well, there is a reason for that. You have driven away the Black Plague! Every year at the second attack there she was holding her feet between her hands. By night she lighted a fire, she warmed herself and boiled roots. She bore a curse with her. This morning the very first thing which I did was to get up here. I climbed up the beacon tower. I looked well all round, the old hag was nowhere to be seen. I shaded my eyes with my hand. I looked up and down, right and left, and everywhere. Not a sign of the creature anywhere. She had scented you evidently."

And the good fellow, in a fit of enthusiasm, shook me warmly by the hand, crying with unchecked emotion, "Ah, Fritz, how glad I am that I brought you here! The witch will be sold, eh?"

Well, I confess I felt a little ashamed that I had been all my life such a very well-deserving young man without knowing anything of the circumstance myself.

"So, Sperver," I said, "the count has spent a good night?"

"A very good one."

"Then I am very well pleased. Let us go down."

We again traversed the high parapet, and I was now better able to examine this way of access, the ramparts of which arose from a prodigious depth, and they were extended along the sharp narrow ridge of the rock down to the very bottom of the valley. It was a long flight of jagged precipitous steps descending from the wolf's den, or rather eagle's nest, down to the deep valley below.

Gazing down I felt giddy, and recoiling in alarm to the middle of the platform, I hastily descended down the path which led to the main building.

We had already traversed several great corridors when a great open door stood before us. I looked in, and descried, at the top of a double ladder, the little gnome Knapwurst, whose strange appearance had struck me the night before.

The hall itself attracted my attention by its imposing aspect. It was the receptacle of the archives of the house of Nideck, a high, dark, dusty apartment, with long Gothic windows, reaching from the angle of the ceiling to within a couple of yards from the floor.

There were collected along spacious shelves, by the care of the old abbots, not only all the documents, title-deeds, and family genealogies of the house of Nideck, establishing their rights and their alliances, and connections with all the great historic families of Germany, but besides these there were all the chronicles of the Black Forest, the collected works of the old Minnesinger, and great folio volumes from the presses of Gutenberg and Faust, entitled to equal veneration on account of their remarkable history and of the enduring solidity of their binding. The deep shadows of the groined vaults, their arches divided by massive ribs, and descending partly down the cold grey walls, reminded one of the gloomy cloisters of the Middle Ages. And amidst these characteristic surroundings sat an ugly dwarf on the top of his ladder, with a red-edged volume upon his bony knees, his head half-buried in a rough fur cap, small grey eyes, wide misshapen mouth, humps on back and shoulders, a most uninviting object, the familiar spirit—the rat, as Sperver would have it—of this last refuge of all the learning belonging to the princely race of Nideck.

But a truly historical importance belonged to this chamber in the long series of family portraits, filling almost entirely one side of the ancient library. All were there, men and women, from Hugh the Wolf to Yeri-Hans, the present owner, from the first rough daub of barbarous times to the perfect work of the best modern painters.

My attention was naturally drawn in that direction.

Hugh I., a bald-headed figure, seemed to glare upon you like a wolf stealing upon you round the corner of a wood. His grey bloodshot eyes, his red beard, and his large hairy ears gave him a fearful and ferocious aspect.

Next to him, like the lamb next to the wolf, was the portrait of a lady of youthful years, with gentle blue eyes, hands crossed on the breast over a book of devotions, and tresses of fair long silky hair encircling her sweet countenance with a glorious golden aureola. This picture struck me by its wonderful resemblance to Odile of Nideck.

I have never seen anything more lovely and more charming than this old painting on wood, which was stiff enough indeed in its outline, but delightfully refreshing and ingenuous.

I had examined this picture attentively for some minutes when another female portrait, hanging at its side, drew my attention reluctantly away. Here was a woman of the true Visigoth type, with a wide low forehead, yellowish eyes, prominent cheek-bones, red hair, and a nose hooked like an eagle's beak.

That woman must have been an excellent match for Hugh, thought I, and I began to consider the costume, which answered perfectly to the energy displayed in the head, for the right hand rested upon a sword, and an iron breastplate inclosed the figure.

I should have some difficulty in expressing the thoughts

which passed through my mind in the examination of these three portraits. My eye passed from the one to the other with singular curiosity.

Sperver, standing at the library door, had aroused the attention of Knapwurst with a sharp whistle, which made that worthy send a glance in his direction, though it did not succeed in fetching him down from his elevation.

"Is it me that you are whistling to like a dog?" said the dwarf.

"I am, you vermin! It is an honour you don't deserve."

"Just listen to me, Sperver," replied the little man with sublime scorn, "You cannot spit so high as my shoe!" which he contemptuously held out.

"Suppose I were to come up?"

"If you come up a single step I'll squash you flat with this volume!"

Gideon laughed, and replied, "Don't get angry, friend. I don't mean to do you any harm. On the contrary, I greatly respect you for your learning, but what I want to know is what you are doing here so early in the morning, by lamplight? You look as if you had spent the night here."

"So I have. I have been reading all night."

"Are not the days long enough for you to read in?"

"No. I am following out an important inquiry, and I don't mean to sleep until I am satisfied."

"Indeed, and what may this very important question be?"

"I have to ascertain under what circumstances Ludwig of Nideck discovered my ancestor, Otto the Dwarf, in the forests of Thuringia. You know, Sperver, that my ancestor Otto was only a cubit high, that is, a foot and a-half. He delighted the world with his wisdom, and made an honourable figure at the coronation of Duke Rudolphe. Count Ludwig had him inclosed in a cold roast peacock, served up in all his plumage. It was at that time one of the greatest delicacies, served up garnished all round with sucking pigs, gilded and silvered. During the banquet Otto kept spreading the peacock's tail, and all the lords, courtiers, and ladies of high birth were astonished and delighted at this wonderful piece of mechanism. At last he came out, sword in hand, and shouted with a loud voice, 'Long live Duke Rudolphe!' and the cry was repeated with acclamations by the whole table. Bernard Herzog makes mention of this event, but he has neglected to inform us where this dwarf came from, whether he was of lofty lineage or of base extraction, which latter, however, is very improbable, for the lower sort of people have not so much sense as that."

I was astounded at so much pride in so diminutive a being, yet my curiosity prevented me from showing too much of my feelings, for he alone could supply me with information upon the portraits that accompanied that of Hugh Lupus.

"Monsieur Knapwurst," I began very respectfully, "would you oblige me by enlightening me upon certain historic doubts?"

"Speak, sir, without any constraint. On the subject of family history and chronicles I am entirely at your service. Other matters don't interest me."

"I desire to learn some particulars respecting the two portraits on each side of the founder of this race."

"Aha!" cried Knapwurst with a glow of satisfaction lighting up his hideous features. "You mean Hedwige and Huldine, the two wives of Hugh Lupus."

And laying down his volume he descended from his ladder to speak more at his ease. His eyes glistened, and the delight of gratified vanity beamed from them as he displayed his vast erudition.

When he had arrived at my side he bowed to me with ceremonious gravity. Sperver stood behind us, very well satisfied that I was admiring the dwarf of Nideck. In spite of the ill luck which, in his opinion, accompanied the little monster's appearance, he respected and boasted of his superior knowledge.

"Sir," said Knapwurst, pointing with his yellow hand to the portraits, "Hugh of Nideck, the first of his illustrious race, married, in 832, Hedwige of Lutzelbourg, who brought to him in dowry the counties of Giromani and Haut Barr, the castles of Geroldseck, Teufelshorn, and others. Hugh Lupus had no issue by his first wife, who died young, in the year of our Lord 837. Then Hugh, having become lord and owner of the dowry, refused to give it up, and there were terrible battles between himself and his brothers-in-law. But his second wife, Huldine, whom you see there in a steel breastplate, aided him by her sage counsel. It is unknown whence or of what family she came, but for all that she saved Hugh's life, who had been made prisoner by Frantz of Lutzelbourg. He was to have been hanged that very day, and a gibbet had already been set up on the ramparts, when Huldine, at the head of her husband's vassals, whom she had armed and inspired with her own courage, bravely broke in, released Hugh, and hung Frantz in his place. Hugh had married his wife in 842, and had three children by her."

"So," I resumed pensively, "the first of these wives was called Hedwige, and the descendants of Nideck are not related to her?"

"Not at all."

"Are you quite sure?"

"I can show you our genealogical tree. Hedwige had no children. Huldine, the second wife, had three."

"That is surprising to me."

"Why so?"

"I thought I traced a resemblance."

"Oho! Resemblance! Rubbish!" cried Knapwurst with a discordant laugh. "See—look at this wooden snuff-box. In it you see a portrait of my great-grandfather, Hanswurst. His nose is as long and as pointed as an extinguisher, and his jaws like nutcrackers. How does that affect his being the grandfather of me, of a man with finely-formed features and an agreeable mouth?"

"Oh no, of course not."

"Well, so it is with the Nidecks. They may some of them be like Hedwige, but for all that Huldine is the head of their ancestry. See the genealogical tree. Now, sir, are you satisfied?"

Then we separated, Knapwurst and I, excellent friends.

CHAPTER V

"NEVERTHELESS," thought I, "there is the likeness. It is not chance. What is chance? There is no such thing. It is nonsense to talk of chance. It must be something higher!"

I was following my friend Sperver, deep in thought, who had now resumed his walk down the corridor. The portrait of Hedwige, in all its artless simplicity, mingled in my mind with the face of Odile.

Suddenly Gideon stopped, and, raising my eyes, I saw that we were standing before the count's door.

"Come in, Fritz," he said, "and I will give the dogs a feed. When the master's away the servants neglect their duty. I will come for you by-and-by."

I entered, more desirous of seeing the young lady than the count, her father. I was blaming myself for my remissness, but there is no controlling one's interest and affections. I was much surprised to see in the half-light of the alcove the reclining figure of the count leaning upon his elbow and observing me with profound attention. I was so little prepared for this examination that I stood rather dispossessed of self-command.

"Come nearer, monsieur le docteur," he said in a weak but firm voice, holding out his hand. "My faithful Sperver has often mentioned your name to me and I was anxious to make your acquaintance."

"Let us hope, my lord, that it will be continued under more favourable circumstances. A little patience, and we shall avert this attack."

"I think not," he replied. "I feel my time drawing near."

"You are mistaken, my lord."

"No. Nature grants us, as a last favour, to have a presentiment of our approaching end."

"How often I have seen such presentiments falsified!" I said with a smile.

He fixed his eyes searchingly upon me, as is usual with patients expressing anxiety about their prospects. It is a difficult moment for the doctor. The moral strength of his patient depends upon the expression of the firmness of his convictions. The eye of the sufferer penetrates into the innermost soul of his consciousness. If he believes that he can discover any hint or shade of doubt, his fate is sealed. Depression sets in, the secret springs that maintain the elasticity of the spirit give way, and the disorder has it all its own way.

I stood my examination firmly and successfully, and the count seemed to regain confidence;. He again pressed my hand, and resigned himself calmly and confidently to my treatment.

Not until then did I perceive Mademoiselle Odile and an old lady, no doubt her governess, seated by her bedside at the other end of the alcove.

They silently saluted me, and suddenly the picture in the library reappeared before me.

"It is she," I said, "Hugh's first wife. There is the fair and noble brow, there are the long lashes, and that sad, unfathomable smile. Oh, how much past telling lies in a woman's smile! Seek not, then, for unmixed joy and pleasure! Her smile serves but to veil untold sorrows, anxiety for the future, even heartrending cares. The maid, the wife, the mother, smile and smile, even when the heart is breaking and the abyss is opening. O woman! this is thy part in the mortal struggle of human life!"

I was pursuing these reflections when the lord of Nideck began to speak. "If my dear child Odile would but consult my wishes I believe my health would return."

I looked towards the young countess. She fixed her eyes on the floor, and seemed to be praying silently.

"Yes," the sick man went on, "I should then return to life.

The prospect of seeing myself surrounded by a young family, and of pressing grandchildren to my heart, and beholding the succession to my house, would revive me."

At the mild and gentle tone of entreaty in which this was said I felt deeply moved with compassion, but the young lady made no reply.

In a minute or two the count, who kept his watchful eyes upon her, went on. "Odile, you refuse to make your father a happy man? I only ask for a faint hope. I fix no time. I won't limit your choice. We will go to court. There you will have a hundred opportunities of marrying with distinction and with honour. Who would not be proud to win my daughter's hand? You shall be perfectly free to decide for yourself."

He paused.

There is nothing more painful to a stranger than these family quarrels. There are such contending interests, so many private motives, at work, that mere modesty should make it our duty to place ourselves out of hearing of such discussions. I felt pained, and would gladly have retired. But the circumstances of the case forbade this.

"My dear father," said Odile, as if to evade any further discussion, "you will get better. Heaven will not take you from those who love you. If you but knew the fervour with which I pray for you!"

"That is not an answer," said the count drily. "What objection can you make to my proposal? Is it not fair and natural? Am I to be deprived of the consolations vouchsafed to the neediest and most wretched? You know I have acted towards you openly and frankly."

"You have, my father."

"Then give me your reason for your refusal."

"My resolution is formed. I have consecrated myself to God."

So much firmness in so frail a being made me tremble. She stood like the sculptured Madonna in Hugh's tower, calm and immovable, however weak in appearance.

The eyes of the count kindled with an ominous fire. I tried to make the young countess understand by signs how gladly I would hear her give the least hope, and calm his rising passion, but she seemed not to see me.

"So," he cried in a smothered tone, as if he were strangling, "so you will look on and see your father perish? A word would restore him to life, and you refuse to speak that one word?"

"Life is not in the hand of man, for it is God's gift. My word can be of no avail."

"Those are nothing but pious maxims," answered the count scornfully, "to release you from your plain duty. But has not God said, 'Honour thy father and thy mother?'"

"I do honour you," she replied gently. "But it is my duty not to marry."

I could hear the grinding and gnashing of the man's teeth. He lay apparently calm, but presently turned abruptly and cried, "Leave me. The sight of you is offensive to me!"

And addressing me as I stood by agitated with conflicting feelings, he cried with a savage grin, "Doctor, have you any violent malignant poison about you to give me—something that will destroy me like a thunderbolt? It would be a mercy to poison me like a dog, rather than let me suffer as I am doing."

His features writhed convulsively, his colour became livid.

Odile rose and advanced to the door.

"Stay!" he howled furiously, "Stay till I have cursed you!"

So far I had stood by without speaking, not venturing to interfere between Father and Daughter, but now I could refrain no longer.

"Monseigneur," I cried, "for the sake of your own health, for the sake of mere justice and fairness, do calm yourself. Your life is at stake."

"What matters my life? What matters the future? Is there a knife here to put an end to me? Let me die!"

His excitement rose every minute. I seemed to dread lest in some frenzied moment he should spring from the bed and destroy his child's life. But she, calm though deadly pale, knelt at the door, which was standing open, and outside I could see Sperver, whose features betrayed the deepest anxiety. He drew near without noise, and bent towards Odile.

"Oh, mademoiselle!" he whispered, "mademoiselle, the count is such a worthy, good man. If you would but just say only, 'Perhaps, by-and-by, we will see.'"

She made no reply, and did not change her attitude.

At this moment I persuaded the Lord of Nideck to take a few drops of Laudanum. He sank back with a sigh, and soon his panting and irregular breathing became more measured under the influence of a deep and heavy slumber.

Odile arose, and her aged friend, who had not opened her lips, went out with her. Sperver and I watched their slowly retreating figures. There was a calm grandeur in the step of the young countess which seemed to express a consciousness of duty fulfilled.

When she had disappeared down the long corridor Gideon turned towards me.

"Well, Fritz," he said gravely, "what is your opinion?"

I bent my head down without answering. This girl's incredible firmness astonished and bewildered me.

CHAPTER VI

S PERVER'S INDIGNATION was mounting. "There's the happiness and felicity of the rich! What is the good of being master of Nideck, with castles, forests, lakes, and all the best parts of the Black Forest, when an innocent looking damsel comes and says to you in her sweet soft voice, 'Is that your will? Well, it is not mine. Do you say I must? Well, I say no, I won't.' Is it not awful? Would it not be better to be a woodcutter's son and live quietly upon the wages of your day's work? Come on, Fritz, let us be off. I am suffocating here. I want to get into the open air."

And the good fellow, seizing my arm, dragged me down the corridor.

It was now about nine. The sky had been fair when we got up, but now the clouds had again covered the dreary earth, the north wind was raising the snow in ghostly eddies against the windowpanes, and I could scarcely distinguish the summits of the neighbouring mountains.

We were going down the stairs which led into the hall, when, at a turn in the corridor, we found ourselves face to face with Tobias Offenloch, the worthy major-domo, in a great state of palpitation.

"Halloo!" he cried, closing our way with his stick right across the passage. "Where are you off to in such a hurry? What about our breakfast?"

"Breakfast! Which breakfast do you mean?" asked Sperver.

"What do you mean by pretending to forget what breakfast? Are not you and I to breakfast this very morning with Doctor Fritz?"

"Aha! So we are! I had forgotten all about it."

And Offenloch burst into a great laugh which divided his jolly face from ear to ear.

"Ha, ha! This is rather beyond a joke. And I was afraid of being too late! Come, let us be moving. Kasper is upstairs waiting. I ordered him to lay the breakfast in your room. I thought we should be more comfortable there. Good-bye for the present, doctor."

"Are you not coming up with us?" asked Sperver.

"No, I am going to tell the countess that the Baron de Zimmer-Bluderich begs the honour to thank her in person before he leaves the castle."

"The Baron de Zimmer?"

"Yes, that stranger who came yesterday in the middle of the

night."

"Well, you must make haste."

"Yes, I shall not be long. Before you have done uncorking the bottles I shall be with you again."

And he hobbled away as fast as he could.

The mention of breakfast had given a different turn to Sperver's thoughts.

"Exactly so," he observed, turning back. "The best way to drown all your cares is to drink a draught of good wine. I am very glad we are going to breakfast in my room. Under those great high vaults in the fencing-school, sitting round a small table, you feel just like mice nibbling a nut in a corner of a big church. Here we are, Fritz. Just listen to the wind whistling through the arrow-slits. In half-an-hour there will be a storm."

He pushed the door open and Kasper, who was only drumming with his fingers upon the windowpanes, seemed very glad to see us. That little man had flaxen hair and a snub nose. Sperver had made him his factotum. It was he who took to pieces and cleaned his guns, mended the riding horses' harness, fed the dogs in his absence, and superintended in the kitchen the preparation of his favourite dishes. On grand occasions he was outrider. He now stood with a napkin over his arm, and was gravely uncorking the long-necked bottle of Rhenish.

"Kasper," said his master, as soon as he had surveyed this satisfactory state of things, "I was very well pleased with you yesterday. Everything was excellent—the roast kid, the chicken, and the fish. I like fair-play, and when a man has done his duty I like to tell him so. Today I am quite as well satisfied. The boar's head looks excellent with its white wine sauce. So does the crayfish soup. Isn't it your opinion too, Fritz?"

I assented.

"Well," said Sperver, "since it is so, you shall have the honour of filling our glasses. I mean to raise you step by step, for you are a very deserving fellow."

Kasper looked down bashfully and blushed. He seemed to enjoy his master's praises.

We took our places, and I was wondering at this quondam poacher, who in years gone by was content to cook his own potatoes in his cottage, now assuming all the airs of a great seigneur. Had he been born Lord of Nideck he could not have put on a more noble and dignified attitude at table. A single glance brought Kasper to his side, made him bring such and such a bottle, or bring the dish he required.

We were just going to attack the boar's head when Master Tobias appeared in person, followed by no less a personage than the Baron of Zimmer-Bluderich, attended by his groom.

We rose from our seats. The young baron advanced to meet us with head uncovered. It was a noble-looking head, pale and haughty, with a surrounding of fine dark hair. He stopped before Sperver.

"Monsieur," said he in that pure Saxon accent which no other dialect can approach, "I am come to ask you for information as to this locality. Madame la Comtesse de Nideck tells me that no one knows these mountains so well as yourself."

"That is quite true, monseigneur, and I am quite at your service."

"Circumstances of great urgency oblige me to start in the midst of the storm," replied the baron, pointing to the window-panes thickly covered with flakes of snow. "I must reach Wald Horn, six leagues from this place!"

"That will be a hard matter, my lord, for all the roads are blocked up with snow."

"I am aware of that, but necessity obliges."

"You must have a guide, then. I will go, if you will allow me, to Sébalt Kraft, the head huntsman at Nideck. He knows the mountains almost as well as I do."

"I am much obliged to you for your kind offers, and I am very grateful, but still I cannot accept them. Your instructions will be quite sufficient."

Sperver bowed, then advancing to a window, he opened it wide. A furious blast of wind rushed in, driving the whirling snow as far as the corridor, and slammed the door with a crash.

I remained by my chair, leaning on its back. Kasper slunk into a corner. Sperver and the baron, with his groom, stood at the open window.

"Gentlemen," said Sperver with a loud voice to make himself heard above the howling winds, and with arm extended, "you see the country mapped out before you. If the weather was fair I would take you up into the tower, and then we could see the whole of the Black Forest at our feet, but it is no use now. Here you can see the peak of the Altenberg. Farther on behind that white ridge you may see the Wald Horn, beaten by a furious storm. You must make straight for the Wald Horn. From the summit of the rock, which seems formed like a mitre, and is called Roche Fendue, you will see three peaks, the Behrenkopp, the Geierstein, and the Trielfels. It is by this last one at the right that you must proceed. There is a torrent across the valley of the Rhéthal, but it must be frozen now. In any case, if you can get no farther, you will find on your left, on following the bank, a cavern half-way up the hill, called Roche Creuse. You can spend the night there, and tomorrow very likely, if the wind falls, you will see the Wald Horn before you. If you are lucky enough to meet with a charcoal-burner, he might, perhaps, show you where there is a ford over the stream, but I doubt whether one will be found anywhere on such a day as this. There are none from our neighbourhood. Only be careful to go right round the base of the Behrenkopp, for you could not get down the other side. It is a precipice."

During these observations I was watching Sperver, whose clear, energetic tones indicated the different points in the road with the greatest precision, and I watched, too, the young bar-on, who was listening with the closest attention. No obstacle seemed to alarm him. The old groom seemed not less bent upon the enterprise.

Just as they were leaving the window a momentary light broke through the grey snow-clouds, just one of those moments when the eddying wind lays hold of the falling clouds of snow and flings them back again like floating garments of white. Then for a moment there was a glimpse of the distance. The three peaks stood out behind the Altenberg. The description which Sperver had given of invisible objects became visible for a few moments, then the air again was veiled in ghostly clouds of flying snow.

"Thank you," said the baron. "Now I have seen the point I am to make for, and, thanks to your explanations, I hope to reach it."

Sperver bowed without answering. The young man and his servant, having saluted us, retired slowly and gravely.

Gideon shut the window, and addressing Master Tobias and me, said, "The deuce must be in the man to start off in such horrible weather as this. I could hardly turn out a wolf on such a day as this. However, it is their business, not mine. I seem to remember that young man's face, and his servant's too. Now let us drink! Maître Tobie, your health!"

I had gone to the window, and as the Baron Zimmer and his groom mounted on horseback in the middle of the courtyard, in spite of the snow which was filling the air, I saw at the left in a turret, pierced with long Gothic windows, the pale countenance of Odile directed long and anxiously towards the young man.

"Halloo, Fritz! What are you doing?"

"I am only looking at those strangers' horses."

"Oh, the Wallachians! I saw them this morning in the stable. They are splendid animals."

The horsemen galloped away at full speed, and the curtain in the turret-window dropped.

CHAPTER VII

S EVERAL UNEVENTFUL DAYS followed. My life at Nideck was becoming dull and monotonous. Every morning there was the doleful bugle-call of the huntsman, whose occupation was gone, then came a visit to the count. After that, breakfast, with Sperver's interminable speculations upon the Black Plague, the incessant gossiping and chattering of Marie Lagoutte, Maître Tobias, and all that pack of idle servants, who had nothing to do but eat and drink, smoke, and go to sleep. The only man who had any kind of individual existence was Knapwurst, who sat buried up to the tip of his red nose in old chronicles all the day long, careless of the cold so long as there was anything left to find out in his curious researches.

My weariness of all this may easily be imagined. Ten times had Sperver taken me over the stables and the kennels; the dogs were beginning to know me. I knew by heart all the coarse pleasantries of the major-domo over his bottles and Marie Lagoutte's invariable replies. Sébalt's melancholy was infecting me; I would gladly have blown a little on his horn to tell the mountains of my ennui, and my eyes were incessantly directed towards Fribourg.

Still the disorder of Yeri-Hans, lord of Nideck, was taking its usual course, and this gave my only occupation any serious interest. All the particulars which Sperver had made me acquainted with appeared clearly before me. Sometimes the count, waking up with a start, would half rise, and supported on his elbow, with neck outstretched and haggard eyes, would mutter, "She is coming, she is coming!"

Then Gideon would shake his head and ascend the signal-tower, but neither right nor left could the Black Plague be discovered.

After long reflection upon this strange malady I had come to the conclusion that the sufferer was insane. The strange influence that the old hag exercised over him, his alternate phases of madness and lucidity, all confirmed me in this view.

Medical men who have given especial attention to the subject of mental aberrations are well aware that periodical madness is of not unfrequent occurrence. In some cases the illness appears several times in the year, in others at only particular seasons of the year. I know at Fribourg an old lady who for thirty years past has regularly presented herself at the door of the asylum. At her own request they place her in confinement, then the unhappy woman every night passes through the terrible scenes of the French Revolution, of which she was a witness in her youth. She trembles in the hands of the executioner, she fancies herself drenched with the blood of the victims, she weeps and cries aloud incessantly. In the course of a few weeks the mind returns to its wonted seat, and she is restored to liberty with the full expectation that she will return again in a year.

"The Count of Nideck is suffering from a similar attack," I said. "Unknown chains unite his fate with that of the Black Plague. Who can tell?" thought I. "That woman once was young, perhaps beautiful!"

And my imagination, once launched, carried me into the interesting regions of romance, but I was careful to tell no one what I thought. If I had opened out those conjectures to Sperver he would never have forgiven me for imagining that there could have been any intimacy between his master and the Black Plague, and as for Mademoiselle Odile, I dared not suggest insanity to her.

The poor young lady was evidently most unhappy. Her refusal to marry had so embittered the count against her that he could scarcely endure to have her in his presence. He bitterly reproached her with her ingratitude and disobedience, and expatiated upon the cruelty of ungrateful children. Sometimes even violent curses followed his daughter's visits. Things at last were so bad that I thought myself obliged to interfere. I therefore waited one evening on the countess in the antechamber and entreated her to relinquish her personal attendance upon her father. But here arose, contrary to all expectations, quite an unforeseen obstacle. In spite of all my entreaties she steadily insisted on watching by her father and nursing him as she had done hitherto.

"It is my duty," she repeated, "and no arguments will shake my purpose," she said firmly.

"Madam," I replied as a last effort, "the medical profession, too, has its duties, and an honourable man must fulfil them even to harshness and cruelty. Your presence is killing your father."

I shall remember all my life the sudden change in the expression of the face of Odile.

My solemn words of warning seemed to cause the blood to flow back to the heart. Her face became white as marble, and her large blue eyes, fixed steadily upon mine, seemed to read into the most secret recesses of my soul.

"Is that possible, sir?" she stammered. "Upon your honour, do you declare this? Tell me truly!"

"Yes, madam, upon my honour."

There was a long and painful silence, only broken at last by these words in a low voice: "Let God's will be done!"

And with downcast eyes she withdrew.

The day after this scene, about eight in the morning, I was pacing up and down in Hugh Lupus's tower, thinking of the count's illness, of which I could not foretell the issue, and I was thinking too of my patients at Fribourg, whom I might lose by too prolonged an absence, when three discreet taps upon my door turned my thoughts into another channel.

"Come in!"

The door opened, and Marie Lagoutte stood within, dropping me a low curtsey.

This old dame's visit put me out, and I was going to beg her to postpone her visit, when something mysterious in her countenance caught my attention. She had thrown over her shoulders a red-and-green shawl. She was biting her lips, with her head down, and as soon as she had closed the door she opened it again, and peeped out, to make sure that no one had followed her.

"What does she want with me?" I thought. "What is the meaning of all these precautions?"

And I was quite puzzled.

"Monsieur le Docteur," said the worthy lady, advancing towards me, "I beg your pardon for disturbing you so early in the morning, but I have a very serious thing to tell you."

"Pray tell me all about it, then."

"It is the count."

"Indeed!"

"Yes, sir. You know that I sat up with him last night."

"I know. Pray sit down."

She sat before me in a great armchair, and I could not help noticing the energetic character of her head, which on the evening of my arrival at the castle had only seemed to me grotesque.

"Doctor," she resumed after a short pause and with her dark eyes upon me, "you know I am not timid or easily frightened. I have seen so many dreadful things in the course of my life that I am astonished at nothing now. When you have seen Marengo, Austerlitz, and Moscow, there is nothing left that can put you out."

"I am sure of that, ma'am."

"I don't want to boast, that is not my reason for telling you this, but it is to show you that I am not an escaped lunatic, and that you may believe me when I tell you what I say I have seen."

This was becoming interesting.

"Well," the good woman resumed, "last night, between nine and ten, just as I was going to bed, Offenloch came in and said to me, 'Marie, you will have to sit up with the count tonight.' At first I felt surprised. 'What! Is not mademoiselle going to sit up?' 'No, mademoiselle is poorly, and you will have to take her place.' Poor girl, she is ill. I knew that would be the end of it, I told her so a hundred times, but it is always so. Young people won't believe those who are older, and then, it is her Father. So I took my knitting, said goodnight to Tobias, and went into monseigneur's room. Sperver was there waiting for me, and went to bed. So there I was, all alone."

Here the good woman stopped a moment, indulged in a pinch of snuff, and tried to arrange her thoughts. I listened with eager attention for what was coming.

"About half-past ten," she went on, "I was sitting near the bed, and from time to time drew the curtain to see what the count was doing. He made no movement. He was sleeping as quietly as a child. It was all right until eleven o'clock, then I began to feel tired. An old woman, sir, cannot help herself—she must drop off to sleep in spite of everything. I did not think anything was going to happen, and I said to myself, 'He is sure to sleep till daylight.' About twelve the wind went down. The big windows had been rattling, but now they were quiet. I got up to see if anything was stirring outside. It was all as black as ink, so I came back to my armchair. I took another look at the patient. I saw that he had not stirred an inch, and I took up my knitting, but in a few minutes more I began nodding, nodding, and I dropped right off to sleep. I could not help it, the armchair was so soft and the room was so warm, who could have helped it? I had been asleep an hour, I suppose, when a sharp current of wind woke me up. I opened my eyes, and what do you think I saw? The tall middle window was wide open, the curtains were drawn, and there in the opening stood the count in his white night-dress, right on the window sill."

"The count?"

"Yes."

"Nay, it is impossible. He cannot move!"

"So I thought too, but that is just how I saw him. He was standing with a torch in his hand. The night was so dark and the air so still that the flame stood up quite straight."

I gazed upon Marie Anne with astonishment.

"First of all," she said, after a moment's silence, "to see that long, thin man standing there with his bare legs, I can assure you it had such an effect upon me! I wanted to scream, but then I thought, 'Perhaps he is walking in his sleep. If I shout he will wake up, he will jump down, and then—' So I did not say a word, but I stared and stared till I saw him lift up his torch in the air over his head, then he lowered it, then up again and down again, and he did this three times, just like a man making signals, then he threw it down upon the ramparts, shut the window, drew the curtains, passed before me without speaking, and got into bed muttering some words I could not make out."

"Are you sure you saw all that, ma'am?"

"Quite sure."

"Well, it is strange."

"I know it is, but it is true. Ah! It did astonish me at first, and then when I saw him get into bed again and cross his hands over his breast just as if nothing had happened, I said to myself, 'Marie Anne, you have had a bad dream. It cannot be true,' and so I went to the window, and there I saw the torch still burning. It had fallen into a bush near the third gate, and there it was shining just like a spark of fire. There was no denying it."

Marie Lagoutte looked at me a few moments without speaking.

"You may be sure, doctor, that after that I had no more sleep. I sat watching and ready for anything. Every moment I fancied I could hear something behind the armchair. I was not afraid, it was not that, but I was uneasy and restless. When morning came, very early I ran and woke Offenloch and sent him to the count. Passing down the corridor I noticed that there was no torch in the first ring, and I came down and found it near the narrow path to the Schwartzwald. Here it is!"

And the good woman took from under her apron the end of a torch, which she threw upon the table.

I was confounded.

How had that man, whom I had seen the night before feeble and exhausted, been able to rise, walk, lift up and close down that heavy window? What was the meaning of that signal by night? I seemed to myself to witness this strange, mysterious scene, and my thoughts went off at once to the Black Plague. When I aroused myself from this contemplation of my own thoughts, I saw Marie Lagoutte rising and preparing to go.

"You have done quite right," I said as I took her to the door, "to tell me of these things, and I am much obliged to you. Have you told any one else of this adventure?"

"No one, sir. Such things are only to be told to the priest and the doctor."

"Come, I see you are a very wise, sensible woman."

These words were exchanged at the door of my tower. At this moment Sperver appeared at the end of the gallery, followed by his friend Sébalt.

"Fritz!" he shouted, "I have got news to tell you."

"Oh, come!" thought I, "more news! This is a strange condition of things."

Marie Lagoutte had disappeared, and the huntsman and his friend entered the tower.

CHAPTER VIII

ON THE COUNTENANCE of Sperver was an expression of suppressed wrath, on that of his companion bitter irony. This worthy sportsman, whose woeful physiognomy had struck me on my first arrival at Nideck, was as thin and dry as a lath. His hunting-jacket was girded tightly about him by his belt, from which hung a hunting-knife with a horn handle. Long leathern gaiters came above his knees, the horn went over his shoulder from right to left, the wide-expanded opening under his arm, on his head a wide-brimmed hat, with a heron's plume in the buckle. His profile, coming to a point in a reddish tuft, looked not unlike a goat's.

"Yes," cried Sperver, "I have got strange things to tell you."

He threw himself in a chair, seizing his head between his clenched hands, while dismal Sébalt calmly drew his horn over his head and laid it on the table.

"Now, Sébalt," cried Gideon, "speak out."

"The witch is hanging about the castle."

This piece of intelligence would have failed to interest me before seeing Marie Lagoutte, but now it struck more forcibly. There certainly was some mysterious connection between the lord of Nideck and that old woman. I knew nothing of the nature of this connection, and I felt that, at whatever cost, I must know it.

"Just wait a moment, friends," said I to Sperver and his comrade. "I want to know, first of all, where does this Black Pest come from?"

Sperver stared at me with astonishment.

"Come from? Who can tell that?"

"Very well, you can't. But when does she come within sight of Nideck?"

"As I told you, ten days before Christmas, at the same time every year."

"And how long does she stay?"

"A fortnight or three weeks."

"Is she ever seen before? Not even on her way? Nor after?"

"No."

"Then we shall have to catch her, seize upon her," I cried. "This is contrary to nature. We must find out where she comes from, what she wants here, what she is."

"Lay hold of her!" exclaimed Sperver. "Seize her! Do you mean it?" and he shook his head. "Fritz, your advice is good enough in its way, but it is easier said than done. I could very easily send a bullet after her, almost at any time, but the count won't consent to that measure, and as for catching in any other way than by powder and shot, why, you had better go first and catch a squirrel by the tail! Listen to Sébalt's story, and you shall judge for yourself."

The master of the hounds, sitting on the table with his long legs crossed, fixed his eyes mournfully upon me, and began his tale.

"This morning, as I was coming down from the Altenberg, I followed the hollow road to Nideck. The snow filled it up entirely. I was going on my way, thinking of nothing particular, when I noticed a foot-track. It was deep down, and went across the road. The person had come down the bank and gone up on the other side. It was not a soft hare's foot, which hardly leaves an impression, it was not forked like a wild boar's track, it was not like a cloven hoof, such as the wolf's—it was a deep hole. I stopped and stooped down, and cleared away the loose snow that fell round, and came upon the very track of the Black Pest!"

"Are you sure it was that?"

"Of course I am. I know the old woman by her foot better than by her figure, for I always go, sir, with my eyes on the ground. I know everybody by their tracks, and as for this one, a child might know it."

"What, then, distinguishes this foot so particularly?"

"It is so small that you could cover it with your hand. It is finely shaped, the heel is rather long, the outline clean, the great toe lies close to the other toes, and they are all as fine as if they were in a lady's slipper. It is a lovely foot. Twenty years ago I should have fallen in love with a foot like that. Whenever I come across it, it has such an effect upon me! No one would believe that such a foot could belong to the Black Plague."

And the poor fellow, joining his hands together, contemplated the stone floor with doleful eyes.

"Well, Sébalt, what next?" asked Sperver impatiently.

"Ah, yes, to be sure! Well, I recognised that track and started off in pursuit. I was hoping to catch the creature in her lair, but I will tell you the way she took me. I climbed up the bank by the roadside, only two gunshots from Nideck. I go along the hill, keeping the track on my right. It led along the side of the wood in the Rhéthal. All at once it jumps over the ditch into the wood. I stuck to it, but, happening to look a little to my left, I saw another track which had, been following the Black Plague. I stopped short: was it Sperver's? or Kasper Trumpfs? or whose? I came to it, and you may fancy how astounded I was when I saw that it was nobody from our place! I know every foot in the Schwartzwald from Fribourg to Nideck. That foot was like none of ours. It must have come from a distance. The boot—for it was a kind of well-made, soft gentleman's boot, with spurs, which leave a little print behind them—the boot was not round at the toes, but square. The sole was thin, and bent with every step, and it had no nails in it. The walk was rapid, and the short steps were like those of a young man of twenty to five-and-twenty. I noticed the stitches in the side leather at once, and I think I never saw finer."

"Who can this be?" Sperver exclaimed.

Sébalt raised his shoulders and extended his hands, but said nothing.

"Who can have any object in following the old woman?" I asked Sperver.

"No one on earth can tell," was the reply.

And so we sat a few minutes meditating over what we had heard.

At last he went on again with his narrative:

"I kept following the track. It went up the next ridge through the pine forest. When it doubled round the Koche Fendue I said to myself, 'Ah, you accursed plague! If there was much game of your sort there would not be much sport.' So we all three arrive, the two tracks and I, at the top of the Schnéeberg. There the wind had been blowing hard, the snow was knee-deep, but no matter! I must get on! I got to the edge of the torrent of the Steinbach, and there I lost the track. I halted, and I saw that, after trying up and down in several directions, the gentleman's boots had gone down the Tiefenbach. That was a bad sign. I looked along the other side of the torrent, but there was no appearance of a track there—none at all! The old hag had paddled up and down the stream to throw any one off the scent who should try to follow her. Where was I to go to? Right, or left, or straight on? Not knowing, I came back to Nideck."

"You haven't told us about her breakfast," said Sperver.

"No, I was forgetting. At the foot of Roche Fendue I saw there had been a fire. There was a black place. I laid my hand upon it, thinking it might be warm, which would have proved that the Black Plague had not gone far, but it was as cold as ice. Close by I saw a wire trap in the bushes. It seems the creature knows how to snare game. A hare had been caught in it. The print of its body was still plain, lying flat in the snow. The witch had lighted the fire to cook it. She had had a good breakfast, I'll be bound."

At this Sperver cried indignantly, "Just fancy that old witch living on meat while so many honest folks in our villages have nothing better than potatoes to eat! That's what upsets me, Fritz! Ah! If I had but—"

But his thoughts remained untold. He turned deadly pale, and all three of us, in a moment, stood rigid and motionless, staring with horror at each other's ghastly countenances.

A yell, the howling cry of the wolf in the long, cold days of winter, the cry which none can imagine who has not heard the most fearful and harrowing of all bestial sounds, that fearful cry was echoing through the castle not far from us! It rose up the spiral staircase, it filled the massive building as if the hungry, savage beast was at our door!

Travellers speak of the deep roar of the lion troubling the silence of the night amidst the rocky deserts of Africa, but while the tropical regions, sultry and baked, resound with the vibrations of the mighty voice of the savage monarch of the desert, making the air tremble with the distant thunder of his awful cry, the vast snowy deserts of the North too have their characteristic cry—a strange, lamentable yell that seems to suit the character of the dreary winter scene. That voice of the Northern desert is the howl of the wolf!

The instant after this awful sound had broken upon the silence followed another formidable body of discordant sounds—the baying and yelling of sixty hounds—answering from the ramparts of Nideck. The whole pack gave voice at the same moment—the deep bay of the bloodhound, the sharp cry of the pointer, the plaintive yelpings of the spaniels, and the melancholy howl of the mastiffs, all mingling in confusion with the rattling of dog-chains, the shaking of the kennels under the struggles of the hounds to get loose, and, dominating over all, the long, dismal, prolonged note of the wolf's monotonous howl. His was the leading part in this horrible canine concert!

Sperver sprang from his seat and ran out upon the platform to see if a wolf had dropped into the moat. But no, the howling came from neither.

Then turning to us he cried, "Fritz! Sébalt! Come, come quickly!"

We flew down the steps four at a time and rushed into the fencing school. Here we heard the cry of the wolf alone, prolonged beneath the echoing arches the distant barking and yelling of the pack became almost inaudible in the distance. The dogs were hoarse with rage and excitement, their chains were getting entangled together. Perhaps they were strangling each other.

Sperver drew the keen blade of his hunting knife. Sébalt did the same. They preceded me down the gallery.

Then the fearful sounds became our guide to the sick man's room. Sperver spoke no more. He hurried forward. Sébalt stretched his long legs. I felt a shuddering horror creep through my whole frame, a horrible presentiment of something shocking and abominable came over us.

As we approached the apartments of the count we met the whole household afoot—the gamekeepers, the huntsmen, the kennel-keepers, the scullions were all mingled and jostling each other, asking "What is the matter? Where are those cries coming from?"

Without stopping we ran into the passage which led into the count's bedroom, where we met poor Marie Lagoutte, who alone had had the courage to penetrate thither before us. She was holding in her arms the young countess, who had fainted, her head falling back, her hair flowing down behind her. She was carrying her away as fast as she could.

We passed her so rapidly that we scarcely had time to witness this sad sight. But it has since returned to my memory, and the pale face of Odile lying on the ample shoulders of the good servant still makes a vivid impression upon my memory, resembling the poor lamb presenting its throat to the knife without a complaint, dying with fear before the stroke falls.

At last we had reached the count's chamber.

The howling came from behind his door.

We stole fearful glances at one another without attempting to account for the hideous noise, or explaining the presence of such a wild guest in the house. Indeed, we had no time. Our ideas were in dire and utter confusion.

Sperver hastily pushed the door open, and, knife in hand, was darting into the room, but he stood arrested on the threshold motionless as a stone.

Never have I seen such a picture of horror as he displayed standing rooted there, with his eyes starting from his head, and his mouth wide open and gasping for breath.

I gazed over his shoulder, and the sight that met my eyes made the blood run chill as snow in my veins.

The lord of Nideck, crouching on all fours upon his bed, with his arms bending forward, his head carried low, his eyes glaring with fierce fires, was uttering loud, protracted howlings!

He was the wolf!

That low receding forehead, that sharp-pointed face, that foxy-looking beard, bristling off both cheeks, the long meagre figure, the sinewy limbs, the face, the cry. The attitude, declared the presence of the wild beast half-hidden, half-revealed under a human mask!

At times he would stop for a second and listen attentively with head awry, and then the crimson hangings would tremble with the quivering of his limbs, like foliage shaken by the wind, then the melancholy wail would open afresh.

Sperver, Sébalt, and I stood nailed to the floor. We held our breath, petrified with fear.

Suddenly the count stopped. As a wild beast scents the wind, he lifted his head and listened again.

There, there, far away, down among the thick fir forests, whitened with dense patches of snow, a cry was heard in reply. Weak at first, then the sound rose and swelled in a long protracted howl, drowning the feebler efforts of the hounds. It was the she-wolf answering the wolf!

Sperver, turning round awe-stricken, his countenance pale as ashes, pointed to the mountain, and murmured low, "Listen, there's the witch!"

And the count still crouching motionless, but with his head now raised in the attitude of attention, his neck outstretched, his eyes burning, seemed to understand the meaning of that distant voice, lost amidst the passes and peaks of the Schwartzwald, and a kind of fearful joy gleamed in his savage features.

At this moment, Sperver, unable or unwilling to restrain himself any longer, cried in a voice broken with emotion, "Count of Nideck, what are you doing?"

The count fell back thunderstruck. We rushed into the room

to his help. It was time. The third attack had commenced, and it was terrible to witness!

CHAPTER IX

THE LORD OF NIDECK was in a dying state. What can science do in presence of the great mortal strife between Death and Life? At the supreme hour, when the invisible wrestlers are writhed together body to body and limb to limb, panting, each in turn overthrowing and overthrown, what avails the healing art? One can but watch, and tremble, and listen!

At times the struggle seems suspended—a truce has sounded. Life has retired into her hold. She is resting, she is collecting the courage of despair. But the relentless enemy beats at the gates, he bursts in, then Life springs to the rescue, and again grapples with her adversary. The strife is renewed with fresh fuel added to the fire of mortal energy as the fatal issue draws closer and nearer.

And the exhausted patient, himself the field of battle, weltering in the cold sweat of death, the eye set and the arm powerless, can do nothing for himself. His breathing, sometimes short, broken, and distressing, sometimes long, deep, laboured, and heavy, indicates the varying phases of this dreadful struggle.

The bystanders watch each other's faces, and they think, "The day will come when we in our turns shall be the field of the same strife, and victorious Death will bear us away into the grave, his den, as the spider carries away the fly." But the true life, the only life, the soul, spreading her immortal wings, will speed her flight to another world, with the exulting cry, "I have fought the good fight. I have finished my course. I have kept the faith!" And Death, disappointed of its prey, will look up at the emancipated being, unable to follow, and holding in its clutches only a cold and decaying corpse, soon to be a handful of dust. "O death, where is thy sting? O grave, where is thy victory?" O best and only consolation, the hope and belief in the final triumph of justice, the certainty of immortal life through Jesus Christ the Saviour! Cruel indeed is he who would rob man of the chief brightness and glory of life!

Towards midnight the Count of Nideck seemed almost gone. The agony of death was at hand. The broken, weakened pulse indicated the sinking of the vital powers, then, it might return to a more active state, but there seemed no hope.

My only duty left was to stay and see this unhappy man die.

I was exhausted with fatigue and anxiety. Whatever art could do I had tried.

I told Sperver to sit up, and close his master's eyes in death. The poor faithful fellow was in the utmost distress. He reproached himself with his involuntary cry, "Count of Nideck, what are you doing?" and tore his hair in bitter repentance.

I went away alone to Hugh Lupus's tower, having had scarcely any time to take food, but I did not feel the want of it.

There was a bright fire on the hearth. I threw myself dressed upon the bed, and sleep soon came to relieve my weight of apprehension, that heavy sleep broken by the consciousness that you may any minute be awoke by tears and lamentations.

I was sleeping thus, with my face turned towards the fire, and as it often happens, the flame fitfully rising, and falling threw a fluttering, flickering light like those of ruddy flapping wings against the walls, and wearied still more my dropping eyelids.

Lost in a dreamy slumber, I was half opening my eyes to see the cause of these alternate lights and shadows, but the strangest sight surprised me.

Close by the hearth, hardly revealed by the feeble light of a few dying embers, I recognised with dismay the dark profile of the Black Plague!

She sat upon a low stool, and was evidently warming herself.

At first I thought myself deceived by my senses, which would have been natural enough after the exciting scenes of the last few days. I raised myself upon my elbow, gazing with my eyes starting with fear and horror.

It was she indeed! I lay horrified, for there she sat calm and immovable, with her hands clasped over her skinny knees, just as I had seen her in the snow, with her long scraggy neck outstretched, her hooked nose, her compressed lips.

How had the Black Pest got here? How had she found her way into this high tower crowning the dangerous precipices? Everything that Sperver had told me of this mysterious being seemed to be coming true! And now the unaccountable behaviour of Lieverlé, growling so fiercely against the wall, seemed clear as the daylight. I huddled myself close up into the alcove, hardly daring to breathe, and staring upon this motionless profile just as a mouse out of its hole fixes its paralysed stare upon the cat that is watching for it.

The old woman stirred no more than the rock-hewn pillars on each side of the hearthstone, and her lips were mumbling inarticulate sounds.

My heart was palpitating, my fears increased momentarily during the long silence, made more startling by the motionless supernatural figure that sat there before me.

This had lasted a quarter of an hour when, the fire catching a splinter of fir-wood, a flash of light broke out, the shaving twisted and flamed, and a few rays of light flared to the end of the room.

That luminous jet was sufficient to show me that the creature was clothed in an old dress of rich purple silk as stiff as cardboard, with a violet pattern; there was a massive bracelet upon her left wrist, and a gold arrow stuck through her thick grey hair twisted over the back of her head. It was like an apparition out of the ages past.

Still the Plague could have had no hostile intentions towards me, or she might easily have taken advantage of my sleep to have put them in execution.

That thought was beginning to give me some confidence, when suddenly she rose from her seat and with slow steps approached my bed, holding in her hand a torch which she had just lighted. I then observed that her eyes were fixed and haggard.

I made an effort to rise and cry aloud, but not a muscle of my body would obey my wishes, not a breath came to my lips, and the old woman, bending over me between the curtains, fixed her stony stare upon me with a strange unearthly smile. I wanted to call for help, I wanted to drive her from me, but her petrifying stare seemed to fascinate and paralyse me, just as that of the serpent fixes the little bird motionless before it.

During this speechless contemplation minutes seemed like hours. What was she about to do? I was ready for any event.

Suddenly she turned her head, went round upon her heel, listened, strode across the room, and opened the door.

At last I recovered a little courage. An effort of the will brought me to my feet as if I were acted on by a spring. I darted after her footsteps. She with one hand was holding her torch on high, and with the other kept the door open.

I was about to seize her by the hair, when at the end of the long gallery, under the Gothic archway of the castle leading to the ramparts, I saw—a tall figure.

It was the Count of Nideck!

The Count of Nideck, whom I had thought a dying man, clad in a huge wolf-skin thrown with its upper jaw projecting grimly over his eyes like a visor, the formidable claws hanging over each shoulder, and the tail dragging behind him along the flags.

He wore stout heavy shoes, a silver clasp gathered the wolf-skin round his neck, and his whole aspect, but for the ice-cold deathly expression of his face, proclaimed the man born for command—the master!

In the presence of such an imposing personage my ideas became vague and confused. Flight was no longer possible, yet I had the presence of mind to throw myself into the embrasure of the window.

The count entered my room with his eyes fixed on the old woman and his features unrelaxed. They spoke to one another in hoarse whispers, so low that I could not distinguish a word. But there was no mistaking their gestures. The woman was pointing to the bed.

They approached the fireplace on tiptoe. There in the dark shadow of the recess at its side the Black Plague, with a horrible smile, unrolled a large bag.

As soon as the count saw the bag he made a bound towards the bed and kneeled upon it with one knee. There was a shaking of the curtains, his body disappeared beneath their folds, and I could only see one leg still resting on the floor, and the wolf's tail undulating irregularly from side to side.

They seemed to be acting a murder in ghastly pantomime. No real scene, however frightful, could have agitated me more than this mute representation of some horrible deed.

Then the old woman ran to his assistance, carrying the bag with her. Again the curtains shook and the shadows crossed the walls, but the most horrible of all was that I fancied I saw a pool of blood creeping across the floor and slowly reaching the hearth. But it was only the snow that had clung to the count's boots, and was melting in the heat.

I was still gazing upon this dark stream, feeling my dry tongue cleave to the roof of my mouth, when there was a great movement. The old woman and the count were stuffing the sheets of the bed into the sack, they were thrusting and stamping them in with just the same haste as a dog scratching at a hole, then the lord of Nideck flung this unshapely bundle over his shoulder and made for the door, a sheet dragging behind him, and the old woman followed him torch in hand. They went across the court.

My knees were almost giving way under me. They knocked together for fear. I prayed for strength.

In a couple of minutes I was on their footsteps, dragged forward by a sudden irresistible impulse.

I crossed the court at a run, and was just going to enter the door of the tower when I perceived a deep but narrow pit at my feet, down which went a winding staircase, and there far below I could see the torch describing a spiral course around the stone rail like a little star; at last it was lost in the distance.

Now I also descended the first steps of this newly-discovered staircase, directing my course after this distant light. Suddenly it vanished. The old woman and the count had reached the bottom of the precipice. Supported by the stone rail I continued my descent, safe to be able to mount again if I found my further progress stopped.

Soon I came to the last step. I looked around me, and discovered on my left hand a narrow streak of moonlight shining under a low door, through the nettles and brambles. I kicked a way through these obstacles, clearing the snow away with my feet, and then found that I was at the very foot of the keep, Hugh's donjon tower.

Who would have supposed that such a hole would have led up into the castle? Who had shown it to the old woman? I did not stay to satisfy myself on these points.

The vast plain lay spread before me bathed in a light almost equal to that of day. On the right lay extended wide the dark line of the Black Forest with its craggy rocks, its gullies, its passes stretching away as far as the sight could reach.

The night air was keen and sharp, but perfectly calm, and I felt myself awakened to the highest degree, almost as if my senses were volatilised by the still and ice-cold air.

My first examination of the horizon was for the figures of the count and his strange companion. I soon distinguished their tall dark forms standing out sharply against the star-spangled purple heavens. I nearly overtook them at the bottom of the ravine.

The count was moving with deliberate steps, the imaginary

winding-sheet dragging slowly after him. There was an automatic precision in the movements of both.

I kept six or eight yards behind them down the hollow road to the Altenberg, now in the shade, now in the full light, for the moon was shining with astonishing brilliancy. A few clouds floated idly across the zenith, seeming to want to clasp her in their long arms, but she ever eluded their grasp, and her rays, keen as a blade of steel, cut me to the marrow of my bones.

I could have wished to turn back, but some invisible power impelled me onwards to follow this funeral procession in pantomime. Even to this day I fancy still I can see the rough mountain path through the Black Forest, I can hear the crisp snow crackling under foot, and the dead leaves rustling in the light north wind. I can see myself following those two silent beings, but I cannot understand what mysterious power drew me in their footsteps.

At last we reach the forest, and advance amongst the tall bare-branched beeches. The dark shadows of their higher boughs intersect the lower branches, and fall broken upon the snow-encumbered road. Sometimes I fancy I can hear steps behind me. I turn sharply round, but can see no one.

We had just reached the long rocky ridge that forms the crest of the Altenberg. Behind it flows the torrent of the Schnéeberg, but in winter no current is visible. Scarcely does a mere thread of its blue waters trickle under the thick crust of ice. Here the deep solitude is broken by no murmuring brooks, no warblings of birds, no thunder of the waterfall. In the vast unbroken solitudes the awful silence is terrible.

The Count of Nideck and the old woman found a gap in the face of the rock, up which they mounted straight with marvellous celerity, whilst I had to pull myself up by the help of the bushes.

Hardly had they reached the ridge of the crags, which came almost to a point, when I was within three yards of them, and

I beheld beyond a dreadful precipice of which I could not see the bottom. At the left hung in the air like a vast sheet the fall of the Schnéeberg, a mass of ice. That resemblance to an immense wave taking the precipice at one bound, bearing trees on its breast, fringed with the bushes, and winding out the long ivy sprays, which exhibit in their delicate tracery the form of the rigid glassy billow. That mere semblance of movement amidst the stillness and immovableness of death, and the presence of those two speechless creatures pursuing their ghastly work with automatic precision, added to the terror with which I already trembled.

Nature herself seemed to shrink with horror.

The count had laid down his burden. The old woman and he took it up together, swung it for a moment over the edge of the precipice, then the long shroud floated over the abyss, and the imaginary murderers in silence bent forward to see it fall.

That long white sheet floating in the air is still present before my eyes. It descends, it falls like a wild swan shot in the clouds, spreading its wide wings, the long neck thrown back, whirling down to earth to die.

The white burden disappeared in the dark depths of the precipice.

At last the cloud which I had long seen threatening to cover the moon's bright disc veiled her in its steel-blue folds, and her rays ceased to shine.

The old woman, holding the count by the hand and dragging him forward with hurried steps, came for a moment into view.

The cloud had overshadowed the moon, and I could not move out of their way without danger of falling over the precipice.

After a few minutes, during which I lay as close as I could, there was a rift in the cloud. I looked out again. I stood alone on the point of the peak with the snow up to my knees.

Full of horror and apprehension, I descended from my perilous position, and ran to the castle in as much consternation as if I had been guilty of some great crime.

As for the lord of Nideck and his companion, I lost sight of them.

CHAPTER X

I WANDERED AROUND the castle of Nideck unable to find the exit from which I had commenced my melancholy journey.

So much anxiety and uneasiness were beginning to tell upon my mind. I staggered on, wondering if I was not mad, unable to believe in what I had seen, and yet alarmed at the clearness of my own perceptions.

My mind in confusion passed in review that strange man waving his torch overhead in the darkness, howling like a wolf, coldly and accurately going through all the details of an imaginary murder without the omission of one ghastly detail or circumstance, then escaping and committing to the furious torrent the secret of his crime. These things all harassed my mind, hurried confusedly past my eyes, and made me feel as if I were labouring under a nightmare.

Lost in the snow, I ran to and fro panting and alarmed, and unable to judge which way to direct my steps.

As day drew near the cold became sharper. I shivered, I execrated Sperver for having brought me from Fribourg to bear a part in this hideous adventure.

At last, exhausted, my beard a mass of ice, my ears nearly frostbitten, I discovered the gate and rang the bell with all my might.

It was then about four in the morning. Knapwurst made me wait a terribly long time. His little lodge, cut in the rock, remained silent. I thought the little humpbacked wretch would never have done dressing, for of course I supposed he would be in bed and asleep.

I rang again.

This time his grotesque figure appeared abruptly, and he cried to me from the door in a fury, "Who are you?"

"I? Doctor Fritz."

"Oh, that alters the case," and he went back into his lodge for a lantern, crossed the outer court where the snow came up to his middle, and staring at me through the grating, he exclaimed, "I beg your pardon, Doctor Fritz. I thought you would be asleep up there in Hugh Lupus's tower. Were you ringing? Now that explains why Sperver came to me about midnight to ask if anybody had gone out. I said no, which was quite true, for I never saw you going out."

"But pray, Monsieur Knapwurst, do for pity's sake let me in, and I will tell you all about that by-and-by."

"Come, come, sir, a little patience."

And the hunchback, with the slowest deliberation, undid the padlock and slipped the bars, whilst my teeth were chattering, and I stood shivering from head to foot.

"You are very cold, doctor," said the diminutive man, "and you cannot get into the castle. Sperver has fastened the inside door, I don't know why. He does not usually do so; the outer gate is enough. Come in here and get warm. You won't find my little hole very inviting, though. It is nothing but a sty, but when a man is as cold as you are he is not apt to be particular."

Without replying to his chatter I followed him in as quickly as I could.

We went into the hut, and in spite of my complete state of numbness, I could not help admiring the state of picturesque disorder in which I found the place. The slate roof leaning against the rock, and resting by its other side on a wall not more than six feet high, showed the smoky, blackened rafters from end to end.

The whole edifice consisted of but one apartment, furnished with a very uninviting bed, which the dwarf did not often take the trouble to make, and two small windows with hexagonal panes, weather-stained with the rainbow tints of mother-of-pearl. A large square table filled up the middle, and it would be difficult to account for that massive oak slab being got in unless by supposing it to have been there before the hut was built.

On shelves against the wall were rolls of parchment, and old books great and small. Wide open on the table lay a fine black-letter volume, with illuminations, bound in vellum, clasped and cornered with silver, apparently a collection of old chronicles. Besides there was nothing but two leathern armchairs, bearing on them the unmistakable impression of the misshapen figure of this learned gentleman.

I need not stay to do more than mention the pens, the jar of tobacco, five or six pipes lying here and there, and in a corner a small cast-iron stove, with its low, open door wide open, and throwing out now and then a volley of bright sparks, and to complete the picture, the cat arching her back, and spitting threateningly at me with her armed paw uplifted.

All this scene was tinted with that deep rich amber light in which the old Flemish painters delighted, and of which they alone possessed the secret, and never left it to the generations after them.

"So you went out last night, doctor?" inquired my host, after we had both installed ourselves, and while I had my hands in a warm place upon the stove.

"Yes, pretty early," I answered. "I had to look after a patient."

This brief explanation seemed to satisfy the little hunchback, and he lighted his blackened boxwood pipe, which was hanging over his chin.

"You don't smoke, doctor?"

"I beg your pardon, I do."

"Well, fill any one of these pipes. I was here," he said, spreading his yellow hand over the open volume. "I was reading the chronicles of Hertzog when you came."

"Ah, that accounts for the time I had to wait! Of course you stayed to finish the chapter?" I said, smiling.

He owned it, grinning, and we both laughed together.

"But if I had known it was you," he said, "I should have finished the chapter another time."

There was a short silence, during which I was observing the very peculiar physiognomy of this misshapen being—those long deep wrinkles that moated in his wide mouth, his small eyes with the crow's feet at the outer corners, that contorted nose, bulbous at its end, and especially that huge double-storied forehead of his. The whole figure reminded me not a little of the received pictures of Socrates, and while warming myself and listening to the crackling of the fire, I went off into contemplations on the very diversified fortunes of mankind.

"Here is this dwarf," I thought, "an ill-shaped, stunted caricature, banished into a corner of Nideck, and living just like the cricket that chirps beneath the hearthstone. Here is this little Knapwurst, who in the midst of excitement, grand hunts, gallant trains of horsemen coming and going, the barking of the hounds, the trampling of the horses, and the shouts of the hunters, is living quietly all alone, buried in his books, and thinking of nothing but the times long gone by, whilst joy or sorrow, songs or tears, fill the world around him, while spring and summer, autumn and winter, come and look in through his dim windows, by turns brightening, warming, and benumbing the face of nature outside. Whilst men in the outer world are subject to the gentle influences of love, or the sterner impulses of ambition or avarice, hoping, coveting, longing, and desiring, he neither hopes, nor desires, nor covets anything. As long as he is smoking his pipe, with his eyes feasting on a musty parchment, he lives in the enjoyment of dreams, and he goes into raptures over things long, long ago gone by, or which have never existed at all. It is all one to him. 'Hertzog says so and so, somebody else tells the tale a different way,' and he is perfectly happy! His leathery face gets more and more deeply wrinkled, his broken angular back bends into sharper angles and corners, his pointed elbows dig beds for themselves in the oak table, his skinny fingers bury themselves in his cheeks, his piggish grey eyes get redder over manuscripts, Latin, Greek, or mediaeval. He falls into raptures, he smacks his lips, he licks his chops like a cat over a dainty dish, and then he throws himself upon that dirty litter, with his knees up to his chin, and he thinks he has had a delightful day! Oh, Providence of God, is a man's duty best done, are his responsibilities best discharged, at the top or at the bottom of the scale of human life?"

But the snow was melting away from my legs, the balmy warmth of the stove was shedding a pleasant influence over my feelings, and I felt myself reviving in this mixed atmosphere of tobacco-smoke and burning pine-wood.

Knapwurst gravely laid his pipe on the table, and reverently spreading his hand upon the folio, said in a voice that seemed to issue from the bottom of his consciousness, or, if you like it better, from the bottom of a twenty-gallon cask, "Doctor Fritz, here is the law and the prophets!"

"How so? What do you mean?"

"Parchment, old parchment, that is what I love! These old yellow, rusty, worm-eaten leaves are all that is left to us of the past, from the days of Charlemagne until this day. The oldest families disappear, the old parchments remain. Where would be the glory of the Hohenstauffens, the Leiningens, the Nidecks, and of so many other families of renown? Where would be the fame of their titles, their deeds of arms, their magnificent armour, their expeditions to the Holy Land, their alliances, their claims to remote antiquity, their conquests once complete, now long ago annulled? Where would be all those grand claims to historic fame without these parchments? Nowhere at all. Those high and mighty barons, those great dukes and princes, would be as if they had never been—they and everything that related to them far and near. Their strong castles, their palaces, their fortresses fall and moulder away into masses of ruin, vague remembrancers! Of all that greatness one monument alone remains—the chronicles, the songs of bards and minnesingers. Parchment alone remains!"

He sat silent for a moment, and then pursued his reflections.

"And in those distant times, while knights and squires rode out to war, and fought and conquered or fought and fell over the possession of a nook in a forest, or a title, or a smaller matter still, with what scorn and contempt did they not look down upon the wretched little scribbler, the man of mere letters and jargon, half-clothed in untanned hides, his only weapon an ink-horn at his belt, his pennon the feather of a goosequill! How they laughed at him, calling him an atom or a flea, good for nothing! 'He does nothing, he cannot even collect our taxes, or look after our estates, whilst we bold riders, armed to the teeth, sword in hand and lance on thigh, we fight, and we are the finest fellows in the land!' So they said when they saw the poor devil dragging himself on foot after their horses' heels, shivering in winter and sweating in summer, rusting and decaying in old age. Well, what has happened? That flea, that vermin, has kept them in the memory of men longer than their castles stood, long after their arms and their armour had rusted in the ground. I love those old parchments. I respect and revere them. Like ivy, they clothe the ruins and keep the ancient walls from crumbling into dust and perishing in oblivion!"

Having thus delivered himself, a solemn expression stole over his features, and his own eloquence made the tears of moved affection to steal down his furrowed cheeks.

The poor hunchback evidently loved those who had borne with and protected his unwarlike but clever ancestors. And after all he spoke truly, and there was profound good sense in his words.

I was surprised, and said, "Monsieur Knapwurst, do you

know Latin?"

"Yes, sir," he answered, but without conceit, "both Latin and Greek. I taught myself. Old grammars were quite enough. There were some old books of the count's, thrown by as rubbish. They fell into my hands, and I devoured them. A little while after, the count, hearing me drop a Latin quotation, was quite astonished, and said, 'When did you learn Latin, Knapwurst?' 'I taught myself, monseigneur.' He asked me a few questions, to which I gave pretty good answers. 'Parbleu!' he cried, 'Knapwurst knows more than I do. He shall keep my records.' So he gave me the keys of the archives. That was thirty years ago. Since that time I have read every word. Sometimes, when the count sees me mounted upon my ladder, he says, 'What are you doing now, Knapwurst?' 'I am reading the family archives, monseigneur.' 'Aha! is that what you enjoy?' 'Yes, very much.' 'Come, come, I am glad to hear it, Knapwurst, but for you, who would know anything about the glory of the house of Nideck?' And off he goes laughing. I do just as I please."

"So he is a very good master, is he?"

"Oh, Doctor Fritz, he is the kindest-hearted master! He is so frank and so pleasant!" cried the dwarf, with hands clasped. "He has but one fault."

"And what may that be?"

"He has no ambition."

"How do you prove that?"

"Why, he might have been anything he pleased. Think of a Nideck, one of the very noblest families in Germany! He had but to ask to be made a minister or a field-marshal. Well, he desired nothing of the sort. When he was no longer a young man he retired from political life. Except that he was in the campaign in France at the head of a regiment he raised at his own expense, he has always lived far away from noise and battle. Plain and simple, and almost unknown, he seemed to think of nothing but his hunting."

These details were deeply interesting to me. The conversation was of its own accord taking just the turn I wished it to take, and I resolved to get my advantage out of it.

"So the count has never had any exciting deeds in hand?"

"None, Doctor Fritz, none whatever, and that is the pity. A noble excitement is the glory of great families. It is a misfortune for a noble race when a member of it is devoid of ambition. He allows his family to sink below its level. I could give you many examples. That which would be very fortunate in a trader's family is the greatest misfortune in a nobleman's."

I was astonished, for all my theories upon the count's past life were falling to the earth.

"Still, Monsieur Knapwurst, the lord of Nideck has had great sorrows, had he not?"

"Such as what?"

"The loss of his wife."

"Yes, you are right there. His wife was an angel. He married her for love. She was a Zaân, one of the oldest and best nobility of Alsace, but a family ruined by the Revolution. The Countess Odile was the delight of her husband. She died of a decline which carried her off after five years' illness. Every plan was tried to save her life. They travelled in Italy together but she returned worse than she went, and died a few weeks after their return. The count was almost broken-hearted, and for two years he shut himself up and would see no one. He neglected his hounds and his horses. Time at last calmed his grief, but there is always a remainder of grief," said the hunchback, pointing with his finger to his heart, "you understand very well, there is still a bleeding wound. Old wounds you know, make themselves felt in change of weather, and old sorrows too, in spring when the flowers bloom again, and in autumn when the dead leaves cover the soil. But the count would not marry again; all his love is given to his daughter."

"So the marriage was a happy one throughout?"

"Happy! Why it was a blessing for everybody."

I said no more. It was plain that the count had not committed, and could not have committed, a crime. I was obliged to yield to evidence. But, then, what was the meaning of that scene at night, that strange connection with the Black Pest, that fearful acting, that remorse in a dream, which impelled the guilty to betray their past atrocities?

I lost myself in vain conjectures.

Knapwurst relighted his pipe, and handed me one, which I accepted.

By that time the icy numbness which had laid hold of me had nearly passed away, and I was enjoying that pleasant sense of relief which follows great fatigue when by the chimney-corner in a comfortable easy-chair, veiled in wreaths of tobacco smoke, you yield to the luxury of repose, and listen idly to the duet between the chirping of a cricket on the hearth and the hissing of the burning log.

So we sat for a quarter of an hour.

At last I ventured to remark, "But sometimes the count gets angry with his daughter?"

Knapwurst started, and fixing a sinister, almost a fierce and hostile eye upon me, answered, "I know, I know!"

I watched him narrowly, thinking I might learn something now in support of my theory, but he simply added ironically, "The towers of Nideck are high, and slander flies too low to reach their elevation!"

"No doubt, but still it is a fact, is it not?"

"Oh yes, so it is, but after all it is only a craze, an effect of his complaint. As soon as the crisis is past all his love for mademoiselle comes back. I assure you, sir, that a lover of twenty could not be more devoted, more affectionate, than he is. That young girl is his pride and his joy. A dozen times have I seen him riding away to get a dress, or flowers, or what not, for her. He went off alone, and brought back the articles in triumph, blowing his horn. He would have entrusted so delicate a commission to no one, not even to Sperver, whom he is so fond of. Mademoiselle never dares express a wish in his hearing lest he should start off and fulfill it at once. The lord of Nideck is the worthiest master, the tenderest father, and the kindest and most upright of men. Those poachers who are forever infesting our woods, the old Count Ludwig would have strung them up without mercy. Our count winks at them. He even turns them into gamekeepers. Look at Sperver! Why, if Count Ludwig was alive, Sperver's bones would long ago have been rattling in chains, instead of which he is head huntsman at the castle."

All my theories were now in a state of disorganisation. I laid my head between my hands and thought a long while.

Knapwurst, supposing that I was asleep, had turned to his folio again.

The grey dawn was now peeping in, and the lamp turning pale. Indistinct voices were audible in the castle.

Suddenly there was a noise of hurried steps outside. I saw someone pass before the window, the door opened abruptly, and Gideon appeared at the threshold.

CHAPTER XI

SPERVER'S PALE FACE and glowing eyes announced that events were on their way. Yet he was calm, and did not seem surprised at my presence in Knapwurst's room.

"Fritz," he said briefly, "I am come to fetch you." I rose without answering and followed him. Scarcely were we out of the hut when he took me by the arm and drew me on to the castle.

"Mademoiselle Odile wants to see you," he whispered.

"What! Is she ill?"

"No, she is much better, but something or other that is strange is going on. This morning about one o'clock, thinking that the count was nearly breathing his last, I went to wake the countess. With my hand on the bell my heart failed me. 'Why should I break her heart?' I said to myself, 'She will learn her misfortune only too soon, and then to wake her up in the middle of the night, weak and frail as she is, after such shocks, might kill her at a stroke.' I took a few minutes to consider, and then I resolved I would take it all on myself. I returned to the count's room. I looked in—not a soul was there! Impossible! The man was in the last agonies of death. I ran into the corridor like a madman. No one was there! Into the long gallery—no one! Then I lost my presence of mind, and rushing again into the young countess's room, I rang again. This time she appeared, crying out, 'Is my father dead?' 'No.' 'Has he disappeared?' 'Yes, madam. I had gone out for a minute—when I came in again—' 'And Doctor Fritz, where is he?' 'In Hugh Lupus's tower.' 'In that tower?' She started. She threw a dressing-gown around her, took her lamp, and went out. I stayed behind. A quarter of an hour after she came back, her feet covered with snow, and so pale and so cold! She set her lamp upon the chimney-piece, and looking at me fixedly, said, 'Was it you who put the doctor into that tower?' 'Yes, madam.' 'Unhappy man! You will never know the extent of the harm you have done.' I was about to answer, but she interrupted me, 'No more. Go and fasten every door and lie down. I will sit up. Tomorrow morning you will find Doctor Fritz at Knapwurst's, and bring him to me. Make no noise, and mind, you have seen nothing and know nothing!'"

"Is that all, Sperver?" I asked.

He nodded gravely.

"And about the count?"

"He is in again. He is better."

We had got to the antechamber. Gideon knocked at the door gently, then he opened it, announcing, "Doctor Fritz."

I took a pace forward, and stood in the presence of Odile. Sperver had retired, closing the door.

A strange impression crossed my mind at the sight of the

young countess standing pale and still, leaning upon the back of an armchair, her eyes of feverish brightness, and robed in a long dress of rich black velvet. But she stood calm and firm.

"Doctor," she said, motioning me to a chair, "pray sit down. I have a very serious matter to speak to you about."

I obeyed in silence.

In her turn she sat down and seemed to be collecting her thoughts.

"Providence or an evil destiny, I know not which, has made you witness of a mystery in which lies involved the honour of my family."

So she knew it all!

I sat confounded and astonished.

"Madam, believe me, it was but by chance—"

"It is useless," she interrupted. "I know it all, and it is frightful!"

Then, in a heartrending appealing voice, she cried, "My father is not a guilty man!"

I shuddered, and with hands outstretched cried, "Madam, I know it. I know that the life of your father has been one of the noblest and loveliest."

Odile had half-risen from her seat, as if to protest, by anticipation, against any supposition that might be injurious to her father. Hearing me myself taking up his defence, she sank back again, and covering her face with her hands, the tears began to flow.

"God bless you, sir!" she exclaimed. "I should have died with the very thought that a breath of suspicion was harboured against him."

"Ah! Madam, who could possibly attach any reality to the action of a somnambulist?"

"That is quite true, sir. I had had that thought myself, but appearances, pardon me, yet I feared, still I knew Doctor Fritz was a man of honour."

"Pray, madam, be calm."

"No," she cried, "let me weep on. It is such a relief. For ten years I have suffered in secret. Oh, how I suffered! That secret, so long shut up in my breast, was killing me. I should soon have died, like my dear mother. God has had pity upon me, and has sent you, and made you share it with me. Let me tell you all, sir, do let me!"

She could speak no more. Sobs and tears broke her voice. So it always is with proud and lofty natures. After having conquered grief, and imprisoned it, buried, and, as it were, crushed down in the secret depths of the mind, they seem happy, or, at any rate, indifferent to the eyes of the uninformed around, and the eye of the most watchful observer might be mistaken, but let a sudden shock break the seal, an unexpected rending of a portion of the veil, then, as with the crash of a thunderstorm, the tower in which the sufferer hid his sorrow falls in ruins to the ground. The conquered foe rises more fierce than before his defeat and captivity. He shakes with fury the prison doors, the frame trembles with long shudderings, sobs and sighs heave the breast, the tears, too long contained within bounds, overflow their swollen banks, bounding and rushing as if after the heavy rain of a thunderstorm.

Such was Odile.

At length she lifted her beautiful head. She wiped her tear-stained cheeks, and with her arm on the elbow of her chair, her cheek resting on her hand, and her eyes tenderly fixed on a picture on the wall, she resumed in slow and melancholy tones.

"When I go back into the past, sir, when I return to my first impressions, my mother's is the picture before me. She was a tall, pale, and silent woman. She was still young at the period to which I am referring. She was scarcely thirty, and yet you would have thought her fifty. Her brow was silvered round with hair white as snow. Her thin, hollow cheeks, her sharp, clear profile, her lips ever closed together with an expression of pain, gave to her features a strange character in which pride and pain seemed to contend for the mastery. There was nothing left of the elasticity of youth in that aged woman of thirty—nothing but her tall, upright figure, her brilliant eyes, and her voice, which was always as gentle and as sweet as a dream of childhood. She often walked up and down for hours in this very room, with her head hanging down, and I, an unthinking child, ran happily along by her side, never aware that my mother was sad, never understanding the meaning of the deep melancholy revealed by those furrows that traversed her fair brow. I knew nothing of the past, to me the present was joy and happiness, and oh, the future, the dark, miserable future! There was none! My only future was tomorrow's play!"

Odile smiled bitterly and went on.

"Sometimes I would happen, in my noisy play, to disturb my mother in her silent walk, then she would stop, look down, and, seeing me at her feet, would slowly bend, kiss me with an absent smile, and then again resume her interrupted walk and her sad gait. Since then, sir, whenever I have desired to search back in my memory for remembrances of my early days that tall, pale woman has risen before me, the image of melancholy. There she is," pointing to a picture on the wall, "there she is! Not such as illness made her as my father supposes, but that fatal and terrible secret. See!"

I turned round, and as my eye dwelt upon the portrait the lady pointed to, I shuddered.

It was a long, pale, thin face, cold and rigid as death, and only luridly lighted up by two dark, deep-set eyes, fixed, burning, and of a terrible intensity.

There was a moment's silence.

"How much that woman must have suffered!" I said to myself with a pain striking at my heart.

"I know not how my mother made that terrible discovery," added Odile, "but she became aware of the mysterious attraction of the Black Pest and their meetings in Hugh Lupus's tower. She knew it all—all! She never suspected my father—ah no!—but she perished away by slow degrees under this consuming influence! And I myself am dying."

I bowed my head into my hands and wept in silence.

"One night," she went on, "one night, I was only ten, and my mother, with the remains of her superhuman energy, for she was near her end that night, came to me when I lay asleep. It was in winter, a stony cold hand caught me by the wrist. I looked up. Before me stood a tall woman. In one hand she held a flaming torch, with the other she held me by the arm. Her robe was sprinkled with snow. There was a convulsive movement in all her limbs and her eyes were fired with a gloomy light through the long locks of white hair which hung in disorder round her face. It was my mother, and she said, 'Odile, my child, get up and dress! You must know it all!' Then taking me to Hugh Lupus's tower she showed me the open subterranean passage. 'Your father will come out that way,' she said, pointing to the tower. 'He will come out with the she-wolf. Don't be frightened, he won't see you.' And presently my father, bearing his funereal burden, came out with the old woman. My mother took me in her arms and followed. She showed me the dismal scene on the Altenberg of which you know. 'Look, my child,' she said, 'you must for I... am going to die soon. You will have to keep that secret. You alone are to sit up with your father,' she said impressively, 'you alone. The honour of your family depends upon you!' And so we returned. A fortnight after my mother died, leaving me her will to accomplish and her example to follow. I have scrupulously obeyed her injunctions as a sacred command, but oh, at what a sacrifice! You have seen it all. I have been obliged to disobey my father and to rend his heart. If I had married I should have brought a stranger into the house and betrayed the secret of our race. I resisted. No one in this castle knows of the somnambulism of my father, and but for yesterday's crisis, which broke down my strength completely and prevented me from sitting up with my father, I should still have been its sole depositary. God has decreed otherwise, and has placed the honour and reputation of my family in your keeping. I might demand of you, sir, a solemn promise never to reveal what you have seen tonight. I should have a right to do so."

"Madam," I said, rising, "I am ready."

"No, sir," she replied with much dignity, "I will not put such an affront upon you. Oaths fail to bind base men, and honour alone is a sufficient guarantee for the upright. You will keep that secret, sir, I know you will keep it, because it is your duty to do so. But I expect more than this of you, much more, and this is why I consider myself obliged to tell you all!"

She rose slowly from her seat.

"Doctor Fritz," she resumed in a voice which made every nerve within me quiver with deep emotion, "my strength is unequal to my burden. I bend beneath it. I need a helper, a friend. Will you be that friend?"

"Madam," I replied, rising from my seat, "I gratefully accept your offer of friendship. I cannot tell you how proud I am of your confidence, but still, allow me to unite with it one condition."

"Pray speak, sir."

"I mean that I will accept that title of friend with all the duties and obligations which it shall impose upon me."

"What duties do you mean?"

"There is a mystery overhanging your family. That mystery must be discovered and solved at any cost. That Black Pest must be apprehended. We must find out where she comes from, what she is, and what she wants!"

"Oh, but that is impossible!" she said with a movement of despair.

"Who can tell that, madam? Perhaps Divine Providence may have had a design connected with me in sending Sperver to fetch me here.”

“You are right, sir. God never acts without consummate wisdom. Do whatever you think right. I give my approval in advance.”

I raised to my lips the hand which she tremblingly placed in mine, and went out full of admiration for this frail and feeble woman, who was, nevertheless, so strong in the time of trial. Is anything grander than duty nobly accomplished?

CHAPTER XII

AN HOUR after the conversation with Odile, Sperver and I were riding hard, and leaving Nideck rapidly behind us.

The huntsman, bending forward over his horse’s neck, encouraged him with voice and action.

He rode so fast that his tall Mecklemburger, her mane flying, tail outstretched, and legs extended wide, seemed almost motionless, so swiftly did she cleave the air. As for my little Ardenne pony, I think he was running right away with his rider. Lieverlé accompanied us, flying alongside of us like an arrow from the bow. A whirlwind seemed to sweep us in our headlong way.

The towers of Nideck were far away, and Sperver was keeping ahead as usual when I shouted—

“Halloo, comrade, pull up! Halt! Before we go any farther let us know what we are about.”

He faced round.

“Only just tell me, Fritz, is it right or is it left?”

“No, that won’t do. It is of the first importance that you should know the object of our journey. In short, we are going to catch the hag.”

A flush of pleasure brightened up the long sallow face of the old poacher, and his eyes sparkled.

“Ha, ha!” he cried, “I knew we should come to that at last!”

And he slipped his rifle round from his shoulder into his

hand.

This significant action roused me.

"Wait, Sperver, we are not going to kill the Black Pest, but to take her alive!"

"Alive?"

"No doubt, and it will spare you a good deal of remorse perhaps if I declare to you that the life of this old woman is bound up with that of your master. The ball that hits her hits your lord."

Sperver gazed at me in astonishment.

"Is this really true, Fritz?"

"Positively true."

There was a long silence. Our mounts, Fox and Rappel, tossed their heads at each other as if in the act of saluting one another, scraping up the snow with their hoofs in congratulation upon so pleasant an expedition. Lieverlé opened wide his red mouth, gaping with impatience, extending and bending his long meagre body like a snake, and Sperver sat motionless, his hand still upon his gun.

"Well, let us try and catch her alive. We will put on gloves if we have to touch her, but it is not so easy as you think, Fritz."

And pointing out with extended hand the panorama of mountains which lay unrolled about us like a vast amphitheatre, he added, "Look! There's the Altenberg, the Schnéeberg, the Oxenhorn, the Rhéthal, the Behrenkopf, and if we only got up a little higher we should see fifty more mountain tops far away, right into the Palatinate. There are rocks and ravines, passes and valleys, torrents and waterfalls, forests, and more mountains, here beeches, there firs, then oaks, and the old woman has got all that for her camping ground. She tramps everywhere, and lives in a hole wherever she pleases. She has a sure foot, a keen eye, and can scent you a couple of miles off. How are you going to catch her, then?"

"If it was an easy matter where would be the merit? I should not then have chosen you to take a part in it."

"That is all very fine, Fritz. If we only had one end of her trail, who knows but with courage and perseverance—"

"As for her trail, don't trouble about that. That's my business."

"Yours?"

"Yes, mine."

"What do you know about following up a trail?"

"Why should not I?"

"Oh, if you are so sure of it, and you know more about it than I do, of course march on, and I'll follow!"

It was easy to see that the old hunter was vexed that I should presume to trespass upon his special province. Therefore, only laughing inwardly, I required no repetition of the request to lead on, and I turned sharply to the left, sure of coming across the old woman's trail, who, after having left the count at the postern gate, must have crossed the plain to reach the mountain. Sperver rode behind me now, whistling rather contemptuously, and I could hear him now and then grumbling.

"What is the use of looking for the track of the she-wolf in the plain? Of course she went along the forest side just as usual. But it seems she has altered her habits, and now walks about with her hands in her pockets, like a respectable Fribourg tradesman out for a walk."

I turned a deaf ear to his hints, but in a moment I heard him utter an exclamation of surprise, then, fixing a keen eye upon me, he said, "Fritz, you know more than you choose to tell."

"How so, Gideon?"

"The track that I should have been a week finding, you have got it at once. Come, that's not all right!"

"Where do you see it, then?"

"Oh, don't pretend to be looking at your feet."

And pointing out to me at some distance a scarcely perceptible white streak in the snow, "There she is!"

Immediately he galloped up to it. I followed in a couple of minutes. We had dismounted, and were examining the track of the Black Pest.

"I should like to know," cried Sperver, "how that track came here?"

"Don't let that trouble you," I replied.

"You are right, Fritz. Don't mind what I say. Sometimes I do speak rather at random. What we want now is to know where that track will lead us to."

And now the huntsman knelt on the ground.

I was all ears. He was closely examining.

"It is a fresh track," he pronounced. "Last night's. It is a strange thing, Fritz, during the count's last attack that old witch was hanging about the castle."

Then examining with greater care, "She passed here between three and four o'clock this morning."

"How can you tell that?"

"It is quite a fresh track. There is sleet all round it. Last night, about twelve, I came out to shut the doors. There was sleet falling then, there is none upon the footsteps, therefore she has passed since."

"That is true enough, Sperver, but it may have been made much later, for instance, at eight or nine."

"No, look, there is frost upon it! The fog that freezes on the snow only comes at daybreak. The creature passed here after the sleet and before the fog, that is, about three or four this morning."

I was astonished at Sperver's exactitude.

He rose from his knee, clapping his hands together to get rid of the snow, and looking at me thoughtfully, as if speaking to himself, said, "It is twelve, is it not, Fritz?"

"A quarter to twelve."

"Very well, then the old woman has got seven hours' start of us. We must follow upon her trail step by step. On horseback we can do it in half the time, and, if she is still going, about seven or eight tonight we have got her, Fritz. Now then, we're off."

And we started afresh upon the track. It led us straight to the mountains.

Galloping away, Sperver said, "If good luck only would have it that she had rested an hour or two in a hole in a rock, we might be up with her before the daylight is gone."

"Let us hope so, Gideon."

"Oh, don't think of it. The old she-wolf is always moving. She never tires. She tramps along all the hollows in the Black Forest. We must not flatter ourselves with vain hopes. If, perhaps, she has stopped on her journey, so much the better for us, and if she still keeps going, we won't let that discourage us. Come on at a gallop."

It is a very strange feeling to be hunting down a fellow creature, for, after all, that unhappy woman was of our own kind and nature. Endowed like ourselves with an immortal soul to be saved, she felt, and thought, and reflected like ourselves. It is true that a strange perversion of human nature had brought her near to the nature of the wolf, and that some great mystery overshadowed her being. No doubt a wandering life had obliterated the moral sense in her, and even almost effaced the human character, but still nothing in the world can give one man a right to exercise over another the dominion of the man over the brute.

And yet a burning ardour hurried us on in pursuit. My blood was at fever heat. I was determined to stand at no obstacle in laying hold of this extraordinary being. A wolf-hunt or a boar-hunt would not have excited me near so much.

The snow was flying in our rear. Sometimes splinters of ice, bitten off by the horse-shoes, like shavings of iron from machinery, whizzed past our ears.

Sperver, sometimes with his nose in the air and his red moustache floating in the wind, sometimes with his grey eyes intently following the track, reminded me of those famous Cossacks that

I had seen pass through Germany when I was a boy, and his tall, lanky horse, muscular and full-maned, its body as slender as a greyhound's, completed the illusion.

Lieverlé, in a high state of enthusiasm and excitement, took bounds sometimes as high as our horses' backs, and I could not but tremble at the thought that when we came up at last with the Pest he might tear her in pieces before we could prevent him.

But the old woman gave us all the trouble she could. On every hill she doubled, at every hillock there was a false track.

"After all, it is easy here," cried Sperver, "to what it will be in the wood. We shall have to keep our eyes open there! Do you see the accursed beast? Here she has confused the track! There she has been amusing herself sweeping the trail, and then from that height which is exposed to the wind she has slipped down to the stream, and has crept along through the cresses to get to the underwood. But for those two footsteps she would have sold us completely."

We had just reached the edge of a pine-forest. In woods of this description the snow never reaches the ground except in the open spaces between the trees, the dense foliage intercepting it in its fall. This was a difficult part of our enterprise. Sperver dismounted to see our way better, and placed me on his left so as not to be hindered by my shadow.

Here were large spaces covered with dead leaves and the needles and cones of the fir trees, which retain no footprint. It was, therefore, only in the open patches where the snow had fallen on the ground that Sperver found the track again.

It took us an hour to get through this thicket. The old poacher bit his moustache with excitement and vexation, and his long nose visibly bent into a hook. When I was only opening my mouth to speak, he would impatiently say—

"Don't speak—it bothers me!"

At last we descended a valley to the left and Gideon pointing to the track of the she-wolf outside the edge of the brushwood, triumphantly remarked, "There is no feint in this sortie, for once. We may follow this track confidently."

"Why so?"

"Because the Pest has a habit every time she doubles of going three paces to the right, then she retraces her steps four, five, or six in the other direction, and jumps away into a clear place. But when she thinks she has sufficiently disguised her trail she breaks out without troubling herself to make any feints. There now! What did I say? Now she is burrowing beneath the brushwood like a wild boar, and it won't be so difficult to follow her up."

"Well, let us put the track between us and smoke a pipe."

We halted, and the honest fellow, whose countenance was beginning to brighten up, looking up at me with enthusiasm, cried, "Fritz, if we have luck this will be one of the finest days in my life. If we catch the old hag I will strap her across my horse behind me like a bundle of old rags. There is only one thing troubles me."

"And what is that?"

"That I forgot my bugle. I should have liked to have sounded the return on getting near the castle! Ha, ha, ha!"

He lighted his stump of a pipe and we galloped off again.

The track of the she-wolf now passed on to the heights of the forest by so steep an ascent that several times we had to dismount and lead our horses by the bridle.

"There she is, turning to the right," said Sperver. "In this direction the mountains are craggy. Perhaps one of us will have to lead both horses while the other climbs to look after the trail. But don't you think the light is going?"

The landscape now was assuming an aspect of grandeur and magnificence. Vast grey rocks, sparkling with long icicles, raised here and there their sharp peaks like breakers amidst a snowy sea.

There is nothing more sadly impressive than the aspect of winter in a mountainous region. The jagged crests of the precipices, the deep, dark ravines, the woods sparkling with hoar-frost like diamonds, all form a picture of desertion, desolation, and unspeakable melancholy. The silence is so profound that you hear a dead leaf rustling on the snow, or the needle of the fir dropping to the ground. Such a silence is oppressive as the tomb. It urges on the mind the idea of man's nothingness in the vastness of creation.

How frail a being is man! Two winters together, without a summer between, would sweep him off the earth!

At times we felt it a necessity to be saying something if only to show that we were keeping up our spirits.

"Ah, we are getting on! How fearfully cold! Lieverlé, what is the matter? What have you found now?"

Unfortunately Fox and Rappel were beginning to tire. They sank deeper in the snow and no longer neighed joyfully.

And added to this the endless mazes of the Black Forest wearied us too. The old woman affected this solitary region greatly. Here she had trotted round a deserted charcoal-burner's hut, farther on she had torn out the roots that projected from a moss-grown rock, there she had sat at the foot of a tree, and that very recently—not more than two hours since, for the track was quite fresh—and our hope and our ardour rose together. But the daylight was slowly fading away!

Very strangely, ever since our departure from Nideck we had met neither wood-cutters, nor charcoal-burners, nor timber-carriers. At this season the silence and solitude of the Black Forest is as deep as that of the North American steppes.

At five o'clock it was almost dark. Sperver halted and said, "Fritz, my lad, we have started a couple of hours too late. The she-wolf has had too long a start. In ten minutes it will be as dark as a dungeon. The best way would be to reach Roche Creuse, which is twenty minutes' ride from here, light a good fire, and eat our provisions and empty our flasks. When the moon is up we will follow the trail again, and unless the old hag is the foul fiend himself, ten to one we shall find her dead and stiff with cold against the foot of a tree, for nothing can live after such a tremendous tramp in weather like this. Sébalt is the best walker in the Black Forest, and he would not have stood it. Come, Fritz, what is your opinion?"

"I am not so mad as to think differently. Besides, I am perishing with hunger!"

"Well, let us start again."

He took the lead and passed into a close and narrow glen between two precipitous faces of rock. The fir trees met over our heads. Under our feet ran a mere thread of the stream, and from time to time some ray from above was dimly reflected in the depths below and glinted with a dull leaden light.

The darkness was now such that I thought it prudent to drop my bridle on Rappel's neck. The steps of our horses on the slippery gravel awoke strange discordant sounds like the screaming of monkeys at play. The echoes from rock to rock caught up and repeated every sound, and in the distance a tiny space of deep blue widened as we advanced; it was the issue from the glen.

"Fritz," said Sperver, "we are in the bed of the Tunkelbach. This is the wildest spot in the Black Forest. The end is a pit called La Marmite du Grand Gueulard, the muckle-mouthed giant's kettle. In the spring, when the snow is melting, the Tunkelbach hurls all its waters into it, a depth of two hundred feet. There is an awful uproar, the waters dash down and then splash up again and fall in spray on all the hills around. Sometimes it even fills the Roche Creuse, but just now it must be as dry as a powder flask."

Whilst I was listening to Gideon's explanations I was at the same time meditating upon this dark and fearful glen, and I reflected that the instinct which attracts the brutes into such retreats as these, far from the light of heaven, away from everything bright and cheerful, must partake of the nature of remorse. Those animals which love the open sunshine—the goat aloft upon a high conspicuous peak, the horse flying across the wide plain, the dog capering round his master, the bird bathed in sunlight—all breathe joy and happiness. They bask, and sing, and rejoice in dancing and delight. The kid nibbling the tender grass under the shade of the great trees is as poetic an object as the shelter that it loves. The fierce boar is as rough as the tangled brakes through which he loves to run his huge bristly back. The eagle is as proud and lofty as the sky-piercing crags on which he perches as his home. The lion is as majestic as the arching vaults of the caves where he makes his den, but the wolf, the fox, and the ferret seek the darkness that conforms to their ugly deeds. Fear and remorse dog their steps.

I was still dreamily pursuing these thoughts, and I was beginning to feel the keen air moving upon my face, for we were approaching the outlet of the gorge, when all at once a red light struck the rock a hundred feet above us, purpling the dark green of the fir trees and lighting up the wreaths of snow.

"Ha!" cried Sperver, "we have got her at last!"

My heart leaped. We stood, closely pressed, the one against the other.

The dog growled low and deep.

"Cannot she escape?" I asked in a whisper.

"No, she is caught like a rat in a trap. There is no way out of La Marmite du Grand Gueulard but this, and everywhere all round the rocks are two hundred feet high. Now, vile hag, I hold you!"

He alighted in the ice-cold stream, handing me his bridle. I caught in the silence the click of the lock of his gun, and that slight noise threw me into a tremor of apprehension.

"Sperver, what are you about?"

"Don't be alarmed. It is only to frighten her."

"Very well, then, but no blood. Remember what I told you— the ball which strikes the Pest slays the count!"

"Don't trouble yourself," was the answer.

He went away without further parley. I could hear the splash of his feet in the water, then I saw his tall figure emerge at the opening of the dark glen, black against a purple background. He stood five minutes motionless. Attentive, bending forward, I looked and listened, still moving onward. As he returned I was but a few yards from him.

"Hark!" he whispered mysteriously. "Look there!"

At the end of the hollow, scooped out perpendicularly like a quarry in the mountain side, I saw a bright fire unrolling its golden spires beneath the vault of a cave, and before the fire sat a man with his hands clasped about his knees, whom I recognised by his dress as the Baron de Zimmer-Bluderich.

He sat motionless, his forehead resting between his hands. Behind him lay a dark gaunt form extended on the ground. Farther on, his horse, half lost in the shade, reared his neck, gazed on us with eyes fixed, ears erect, and nostrils distended.

I stood rooted to the ground.

How did the Baron de Zimmer happen to be in that lonely wilderness at such a time? What did he want here? Had he lost his way?

The most contradictory conjectures were passing in confusion through my excited brain, and I could not tell what conclusion to arrive at, when the baron's horse began to neigh, and the master raised his head.

"Well, Donner, what is the matter now?" said he.

Then he, too, directed his gaze our way, straining his eyes through the darkness.

That pale face, with its strongly-marked features, thin lips, and thick black eyebrows meeting together, and forming a deep hollow on the brow in the form of a long vertical wrinkle, would have struck me with admiration at any other time, while now an inexplicable anxiety laid hold of me, and I was filled with vague apprehensions.

Suddenly the young man exclaimed, "Who goes there?"

"I, monseigneur," answered Sperver, coming forward, "Sperver, chief huntsman to the lord of Nideck."

A flash shot from the baron's quick eye, not a muscle of his countenance quailed. He rose to his feet, gathering his pelisse over his shoulders. I drew towards me the horses and the dog, and this animal suddenly began howling fearfully.

Is not every one, more or less, subject to superstitious fears? At these dismal sounds I trembled, and a cold shudder crept through my whole body.

Sperver and the baron stood at a distance of fifty yards from each other, the first immovable in the midst of the deep glen, his gun unslung from his shoulder, the other erect upon the level platform outside of the cave, carrying his head high, fixing on us a haughty eye and a proud look of superiority.

"What do you want here?" he asked aggressively.

"We are looking for a woman," replied the old poacher. "A woman who comes every year prowling about Nideck, and our orders are to take her."

"Has she stolen anything?"

"No."

"Has she committed murder?"

"No, monseigneur."

"Then what do you want with her? What right have you to pursue her?"

"And you, what right have you over her?" answered Sperver with an ironical smile. "See, there she is. I can see her at the bottom of the cave. What right have you to meddle with our affairs? Don't you know that we are here in the domains of Nideck, and that we administer justice and execute our own decrees?"

The young man changed colour, and said coldly, "I have no account to render to you."

"Beware," replied Sperver. "I am come with proposals of peace and conciliation. I am here on behalf of the lord Yeri-Hans. I am in the execution of my duty, and you are putting yourself in the wrong."

"Your duty!" cried the young man bitterly. "If you talk about your duty you will oblige me to do mine!"

"Well, do it!" cried the huntsman, whose features were becoming disturbed with anger.

"No," replied the baron, "I am not responsible to you, and you shall not come here!"

"That's what we shall soon see!" said Sperver, drawing nearer to the cave.

The young man drew his hunting knife. Perceiving this menacing action, I was about to dart between them, but happily the hound which I was holding by his collar slipped from me with a violent shock and threw me on the ground. I thought the baron would be lost, but at that instant a wild shriek rose from the dark bottom of the cavern, and as I rose to my feet I saw the old woman standing erect before the fire, her tattered garments hanging loosely about her, her grey and tangled locks floating wildly in the wind. She flung her bony arms in the air and uttered prolonged piercing howls like the cry of agony of the hungry wolf in the long cold nights of winter when famine is gnawing his entrails.

Never in my life have I seen a more fearful apparition. Sperver, motionless, his eyes riveted on the fearful object before him, and his mouth open with astonishment, stood as if rooted to the earth. But the powerful dog, surprised himself at this unexpected sight, stood still for a moment, then with a bend of his bristling back in preparation for a mighty leap, he made a rush with a deep, impatient growl which made me tremble. The platform before the cave was about eight or nine feet from the level where we stood, or he would have reached it at a single bound. I can yet hear him clearing a way through the snowy brambles, the baron flinging himself before the woman with a piercing cry, "My mother!" then the dog taking another spring, and Sperver, quick as lightning, raising his gun, and bringing down the poor animal dead at the young man's feet.

This was but the work of a second. The gulf had been illuminated with a momentary flash, and the wild echoes were vibrating with the explosion from rock to rock, till it died in the far distance. Then silence again settled on the gloomy scene, as darkness after the lightning.

When the smoke of the explosion had cleared away I saw Lieverlé lying outstretched at the foot of the rock, and the woman fainting in the arms of the young man. Sperver, pale with concentrated rage and excitement, and eyeing the young baron darkly, dropped the butt of his gun to the ground, his features discomposed, and his eyes half-hid in his gloomy frown.

"Seigneur de Bluderich," he cried, with his hand extended, "I have killed my best friend to save the life of that unhappy woman, your mother! Thank God that her life is bound up with that of the Count of Nideck! Take her away! Take her hence, and never let her return here again. If you do I cannot answer for what old Sperver may be driven to do!"

Then, with a glance at the poor dog—

"Oh! Lieverlé, Lieverlé!" he cried, "was it to end thus? Come, Fritz, let us go. I cannot stay here. I might do something that I should have to repent of!"

And, laying hold of Fox by the mane, he was going to throw himself into the saddle, but suddenly his feelings of distress overcame all restraint, and bowing his head upon his horse's neck, he burst into sobs and tears, and wept like a child.

CHAPTER XIII

S PERVER HAD GONE, bearing the body of poor Lieverlé in his cloak. I had declined to follow. My sense of duty kept me by this unhappy woman, and I could not leave her without violence to my own feelings.

Besides, I must confess I was curious to see a little more closely this strange mysterious being, and therefore as soon as Sperver had disappeared in the darkness of the glen I began to climb up to reach the cavern.

There I beheld a strange sight.

Extended upon a large cloak of white fur lay the aged woman in a long and ragged robe of purple, her fingers clutching her breast, a golden arrow through her grey hair.

Never shall I forget the figure of this strange woman. Her vulture-like features distorted with the last agonies of death, her eyes set, her gasping mouth, were fearful to look upon. Such might have been the terrible Queen Frédégonde.

The baron, on his knees at her side, was trying to restore her to animation, but I saw at a glance that the wretched creature was dying, and it was not without a profound sense of pity that I took her by the arm.

"Leave madame alone—don't touch her," cried the young man with irritation.

"I am a surgeon, monseigneur."

He looked in silence at me for a moment, then rising, said, "Pardon me, sir. Pray forgive my hasty language."

He trembled with excitement, scarcely yet subdued, and presently he went on.

"What is your opinion, sir?"

"It is over. She is dead!"

Then, without speaking another word, he sat upon a large stone, with his forehead resting upon his hand and his elbow on his knee, his eyes motionless, as still as a statue.

I sat near the fire, watching the flames rising to the vaulted roof of the cave, and casting lurid reflections upon the rigid features of the corpse.

We had sat there an hour as motionless as statues, each deep in thought, when, suddenly lifting his head, the baron said, "Sir, all this utterly confounds me. Here is my mother, for twenty-six years I thought I knew her, and now an abyss of horrible mysteries opens before me. You are a doctor. Tell me, did you ever know anything so dreadful?"

"Monseigneur," I replied, "the Count of Nideck is afflicted with a complaint strikingly similar to that from which your mother appears to have suffered. If you feel enough confidence in me to communicate to me the facts which you have yourself observed, I will gladly tell you what I know myself, for perhaps this exchange of our experiences might supply me with the means to save my patient."

"Willingly, sir," he replied, and without any further prelude he informed me that the Baroness de Bluderich, a member of one of the noblest families in Saxony, took, every year towards autumn, a journey into Italy, with no attendant besides an old man-servant, who possessed her entire confidence. That that man, being at the point of death, had desired a private interview with the son of his old master, and that at that last hour, prompted, no doubt, by the pangs of remorse, he had told the young man that his mother's visit to Italy was only a pretence to enable her to make, you observed, a certain excursion into the Black Forest, the object of which was unknown to himself, but which must have had something fearful in its character, since the baroness returned always in a state of physical prostration, ragged, half dead, and that weeks of rest alone could restore her after the hideous labours of those few days.

This was the purport of the old servant's disclosures to the young baron, who believed that in so doing he was only fulfilling his duty.

The son, anxious at any sacrifice to know the truth of this account, had, that very year, ascertained it, first by following his mother to Baden, and then by penetrating on her track into the gorges of the Black Forest. The footsteps which Sébalt had tracked in the woods were his.

When the baron had thus imparted his knowledge to me, I thought I ought not to conceal from him the mysterious influence which the appearance of the old woman in the neighborhood of the castle exercised over the count, nor the other circumstances of this unaccountable series of events.

We were both amazed at the extraordinary coincidence between the facts narrated, the mysterious attraction which these beings unconsciously exercised the one over the other, the tragic drama which they performed in union, the familiarity which the old woman had shown with the castle, and its most secret passages, without any previous examination of them, the costume which she had discovered in which to carry out this secret act, and which could only have been rummaged out of some mysterious retreat revealed to her by the strange instinct of insanity. Finally, we were agreed that there are unknown, unfathomed depths in our being, and that the mystery of death is not the only secret which God has veiled from our eyes, although it may seem to us the most important.

But the darkness of night was beginning to yield to the pale tints of early dawn. A bat was sounding the departure of the hours of darkness with a singular note resembling the gurgling of liquid from a narrow bottle-neck. A neighing of horses was heard far up the defile, then, with the first rays of dawn, we distinguished a sledge driven by the baron's servant. Its bottom was littered with straw. On this the body was laid.

I mounted my horse, who seemed not sorry to use his limbs again, which had been numbed by standing upon ice and snow the whole night through. I rode after the sledge to the exit from the defile, when, after a grave salutation, the usual token of courtesy between the nobility and the people, they drove off in the direction of Hirschland and I rode towards the towers of Nideck.

At nine I was in the presence of Mademoiselle Odile, to whom I gave a faithful narrative of all that had taken place.

Then repairing to the count's apartments, I found him in a very satisfactory state of improvement. He felt very weak, as was to be expected after the terrible shocks of such crises as he had gone through, but had returned to the full possession of his clear faculties, and the fever had left him the evening before. There was, therefore, every prospect of a speedy cure.

A few days later, seeing the old lord in a state of convalescence, I expressed a desire to return to Fribourg, but he entreated me so earnestly to stay altogether at Nideck, and offered me terms so honourable and advantageous, that I felt myself unable to refuse compliance with his wishes.

I shall long remember the first boar-hunt in which I had the honour to join with the count, and especially the magnificent return home in a torchlight procession after having sat in the saddle for twelve hours together.

I had just had supper, and was going up into Hugh Lupus's tower completely knocked up, when, passing Sperver's room, whose door was half open, shouts and cries of joy reached my ears. I stopped, when the most jovial spectacle burst upon me. Around the massive oaken table beamed twenty square rosy faces, bright and ruddy with health and fun.

The hob and nobbing of the glasses gave out an incessant tinkling and clattering. There was sitting Sperver with his bossy forehead, his moustaches bedewed with Rhenish wine, his eyes sparkling, and his grey hair rather disordered. At his right was Marie Lagoutte, on his left Knapwurst. He was raising aloft the ancient silver-gilt and chased goblet dimmed with age, and on his manly chest glittered the silver plate of his shoulder-belt, for, according to his custom on a hunting day, he was still wearing the uniform of his office.

The colour of Marie Lagoutte's cheeks, rather redder even than usual, told of an evening of jollity, and her broad cap-frills seemed as if they were wanting to fly all abroad. She sat laughing, now with one, then with another.

Knapwurst, squatting in his armchair, with his head on a level with Sperver's elbow, looked like a big pumpkin. Then came Tobias Offenloch, so red that you would have thought he had bathed his face in the red wine, leaning back with his wig upon the chair-back and his wooden leg extended under the table. Farther on loomed the melancholy long face of Sébalt, who was peeping with a sickly smile into the bottom of his wine-glass.

Besides these worthies there were present the waiting-people, men and women servants, comprising all that little community which springs up around the board of the great people of the land and belongs to them as the ivy, and the moss, and the wild convolvulus belong to the monarch of the forests.

Upon the groaning board lay a vast ham, displaying its concentric circles of pink and white. Then among the gaily-patterned plates and dishes came the long-necked bottles containing the produce of the vineyards that border the broad and flowing Rhine, long German pipes with little silver chains, and long shining blades of steel.

The light of the lamp shed over the whole scene its amber-colored hue and left in the shade the old grey and time-stained walls, where hung in ample numbers the brazen convolutions of the hunting-horns and bugles.

What an original picture! The vaulted roof was ringing with the joyous shouts of laughter.

Sperver, as I have already told, was lifting high the full bumper and singing the song of Black Hatto, the Burgrave, "I am king on these mountains of mine," while the rosy dew of Affénthal hung trembling from his long moustaches. As soon as he caught sight of me he stopped, and holding out his hand, "Fritz," said he, "we only wanted you. It is a long time since I felt so comfortable as I do tonight. You are welcome, old boy!"

As I gazed upon him with surprise, for since the death of Lieverlé I had never seen him smile, he added more seriously, "We are celebrating the return of monseigneur to his health, and Knapwurst is telling us stories."

All the guests turned my way, and I was saluted with kindly welcomes on all sides.

I was dragged in by Sébalt, seated near Marie Lagoutte, and found a large glass of Bohemian wine in my hand before I could quite understand the meaning of it all.

The old hall was echoing with merry peals of laughter, and Sperver, throwing his arm round my neck, holding his cup high, and with an attempt at gravity which showed plainly that the wine was up in his head, he shouted.

"Here is my son! He and I, I and he, until death! Here's the health of Doctor Fritz!"

Knapwurst, standing as high as he was able upon the seat of his armchair, not unlike a turnip half divided in two, leaned towards me and held me out his glass. Marie Lagoutte shook out the long streamers of her cap, and Sébalt, upright before his chair, as gaunt and lean as the shade of the wild jäger amongst the heather, repeated, "Your health, Doctor Fritz!" whilst the flakes of silvery foam ran down his cup and floated gently down upon the stone-flagged floor.

Then there was a moment's silence. Every guest drank. Then, with a single clash, every glass was set vigorously down upon the table.

"Bravo!" cried Sperver. Then turning to me, "Fritz, we have already drunk to the health of the count and of Mademoiselle Odile. You will do the same."

Twice had I to drain the cup before the vigilant eyes of the whole table. Then I too began to look grave. Could it have been drunken gravity? A luminous radiance seemed shed on every object. Faces stood out brightly from the darkness, and looked more nearly upon me. In truth, there were youthful faces and aged, pretty and ugly, but all alike beamed upon me kindly, and lovingly, and tenderly, but it was the youngest, at the other end of the table, whose bright eyes attracted me, and we exchanged long and wistful glances, full of affection and sympathy!

Sperver kept on humming and laughing. Suddenly putting his hand upon the dwarf's misshapen back, he cried, "Silence!

Here is Knapwurst, our historian and chronicler! He is preparing to speak. This hump holds all the history of the house of Nideck from the beginning of time!"

The little hunchback, not at all indignant at so ambiguous a compliment, directed his benevolent eyes upon the face of the huntsman, and replied, "You, Sperver, you are one of the reiters whose story I have been telling you. You have the arm, and the courage, and the whiskers of a reiter of old! If that window opened wide, and a reiter was to hold out his hand at the end of his long arm to you, what would you say to him?"

"I would say, 'You are welcome, comrade. Sit down and drink. You will find the wine just as good and the girls just as pretty as they were in the days of old Hugh Lupus.' Look!"

And he pointed with his glass at the jolly young faces that brightened the farther end of the table.

Certainly the damsels of Nideck were lovely. Some were blushing with pleasure to hear their own praises, others half-veiled their rosy cheeks with their long drooping eyelashes, while one or two seemed rather to prefer to display their sweet blue eyes by raising them to the smoky ceiling. I wondered at my own insensibility that I had never before noticed these fair roses blooming in the towers of the ancient manor.

"Silence!" cried Sperver for the second time. "Our friend Knapwurst is going to tell us again the legend he related to us just now."

"Won't you have another instead?" asked the hunchback.

"No. I like this best."

"I know better ones than that."

"Knapwurst," insisted the huntsman, raising his finger impressively, "I have reasons for wishing to hear the same again and no other. Cut it shorter if you like. There is a great deal in it. Now, Fritz, listen!"

The dwarf, rather under the influence of the sparkling wine he had taken, rested his elbows on the table, and with his cheeks clutched in his bony fingers, and his eyes starting from his head with his concentrated efforts to speak with becoming seriousness, he cried as if he were publishing a proclamation.

"Bernard Hertzog relates that the burgrave Hugh, surnamed Lupus, or the Wolf, when he was old, used to wear a cowl, which was a kind of knitted cap that covered in the crest of the knight's helmet when engaged in fighting. When the helmet tired him he would take it off and put on the knitted cowl, and its long cape fell around his shoulders.

"Up to his eighty-second year Hugh still wore his armour, though he could hardly breathe in it.

"Then he sent for Otto of Burlach, his chaplain, his eldest son Hugh, his second son Berthold, and his daughter the red-haired Bertha, wife of a Saxon chief named Bluderich, and said to them, "'Your mother the she-wolf has bequeathed you her claws. Her blood flows, mingled with mine, in your veins. In you the wolf's blood will flow from generation to generation. It shall weep and howl among the snows of the Black Forest. Some will say, "Hark! The wind howls!" others, "No, it is the owl hooting!" But not so. It is your blood, mine and the blood of the she-wolf who drove me to murder Hedwige, my wife before God and the Church. She died under my bloody hands! Cursed be the she-wolf! For it is written, "I will visit the sins of the fathers upon the children." The crime of the father shall be visited upon the children until justice shall have been satisfied!'

"Then old Hugh the Wolf died.

"From that dreary day the north wind has howled across the wilds, and the owl has hooted in the dark, and travellers by night know not that it is the blood of the she-wolf weeping for the day of vengeance that will come, whose blood will be renewed from generation to generation—so says Hertzog—until the day when the first wife of Hugh, Hedwige the Fair, shall reappear at Nideck under the form of an angel to comfort and to forgive!"

Then Sperver, rising from his seat, took a lamp and demanded of Knapwurst the keys of the library, and beckoned to me to follow him.

We rapidly traversed the long dark gallery, then the armoury, and soon the archive chamber appeared at the end of the great corridor.

All noises had died away in the distance. The place seemed quite deserted.

Once or twice I turned round, and could then see with a creeping feeling of dread our two long fantastic shadows in ghostly fashion writhing in strange distortions upon the high tapestry.

Sperver quickly opened the old oak door, and with torch uplifted, his hair all bristling in disorder, and excited features, walked in the first. Standing before the portrait of Hedwige, whose likeness to the young countess had struck me at our first visit to the library, he addressed me in these solemn words.

"Here is she who was to return to comfort and pity me! She has returned! At this moment she is downstairs with the old count. Look well, Fritz. Do you recognise her? Is it not Odile?"

Then turning to the picture of Hugh's second wife, "There," he said, "is Huldine, the she-wolf. For a thousand years she has wept in the deep gorges amongst the pine forests of the Schwartz-wald. She was the cause of the death of poor Lieverlé, but henceforward the lords of Nideck may rest securely, for justice is done, and the good angel of this lordly house has returned!"

THE WEREWOLF

by Clemence Housman

THE GREAT FARM HALL was ablaze with the fire-light, and noisy with laughter and talk and many-sounding work. None could be idle but the very young and the very old: little Rol, who was hugging a puppy, and old Trella, whose palsied hand fumbled over her knitting. The early evening had closed in, and the farm servants, come from their outdoor work, had assembled in the ample hall, which gave space for a score or more of workers. Several of the men were engaged in carving, and to these were yielded the best place and light. Others made or repaired fishing tackle and harness, and a great seine net occupied three pairs of hands. Of the women most were sorting and mixing eider feather and chopping straw to add to it. Looms were there, though not in present use, but three wheels whirred emulously, and the finest and swiftest thread of the three ran between the fingers of the house-mistress. Near her were some children, busy too, plaiting wicks for candles and lamps. Each group of workers had a lamp in its centre, and those farthest from the fire had live heat from two braziers filled with glowing wood embers, replenished now and again from the generous hearth. But the flicker of the great fire was manifest to remotest corners, and prevailed beyond the limits of the weaker lights.

Little Rol grew tired of his puppy, dropped it incontinently, and made an onslaught on Tyr, the old wolf-hound, who basked dozing, whimpering and twitching in his hunting dreams. Prone went Rol beside Tyr, his young arms round the shaggy neck, his curls against the black jowl. Tyr gave a perfunctory lick, and stretched with a sleepy sigh. Rol growled and rolled and shoved invitingly, but could only gain from the old dog placid toleration and a half-observant blink. "Take that then!" said Rol, indignant at this ignoring of his advances, and sent the puppy sprawling against the dignity that disdained him as playmate. The dog took no notice, and the child wandered off to find amusement elsewhere.

The baskets of white eider feathers caught his eye far off in a distant corner. He slipped under the table, and crept along on all-fours, the ordinary commonplace custom of walking down a room upright not being to his fancy. When close to the women he lay still for a moment watching, with his elbows on the floor and his chin in his palms. One of the women seeing him nodded and smiled, and presently he crept out behind her skirts and passed, hardly noticed, from one to another, till he found opportunity to possess himself of a large handful of feathers. With these he traversed the length of the room, under the table again, and emerged near the spinners. At the feet of the youngest he curled himself round, sheltered by her knees from the observation of the others, and disarmed her of interference by secretly displaying his handful with a confiding smile. A dubious nod satisfied him, and presently he started on the play he had devised. He took a tuft of the white down, and gently shook it free of his fingers close to the whirl of the wheel. The wind of the swift motion took it, spun it round and round in widening circles, till it floated above like a slow white moth. Little Rol's eyes danced, and the row of his small teeth shone in a silent laugh of delight. Another and another of the white tufts was sent whirling round like a winged thing in a spider's web, and floating clear at last. Presently the handful failed.

Rol sprawled forward to survey the room, and contemplate another journey under the table. His shoulder, thrusting forward, checked the wheel for an instant. He shifted hastily. The wheel flew on with a jerk, and the thread snapped. "Naughty

Rol!" said the girl. The swiftest wheel stopped also, and the house-mistress, Rol's aunt, leaned forward, and sighting the low curly head, gave a warning against mischief, and sent him off to old Trella's corner.

Rol obeyed, and after a discreet period of obedience, sidled out again down the length of the room farthest from his aunt's eye. As he slipped in among the men, they looked up to see that their tools might be, as far as possible, out of reach of Rol's hands, and close to their own. Nevertheless, before long he managed to secure a fine chisel and take off its point on the leg of the table. The carver's strong objections to this disconcerted Rol, who for five minutes thereafter effaced himself under the table.

During this seclusion he contemplated the many pairs of legs that surrounded him, and almost shut out the light of the fire. How very odd some of the legs were. Some were curved where they should be straight, some were straight where they should be curved, and, as Rol said to himself, "they all seemed screwed on differently." Some were tucked away modestly under the benches, others were thrust far out under the table, encroaching on Rol's own particular domain. He stretched out his own short legs and regarded them critically, and, after comparison, favourably. Why were not all legs made like his, or like his?

These legs approved by Rol were a little apart from the rest. He crawled opposite and again made comparison. His face grew quite solemn as he thought of the innumerable days to come before his legs could be as long and strong. He hoped they would be just like those, his models, as straight as to bone, as curved as to muscle.

A few moments later Sweyn of the long legs felt a small hand caressing his foot, and looking down, met the upturned eyes of his little cousin Rol. Lying on his back, still softly patting and stroking the young man's foot, the child was quiet and happy for a good while. He watched the movement of the strong deft hands, and the shifting of the bright tools. Now and then, minute chips of wood, puffed off by Sweyn, fell down upon his face. At last he raised himself, very gently, lest a jog should wake impatience in the carver, and crossing his own legs round Sweyn's ankle, clasping with his arms too, laid his head against the knee. Such act is evidence of a child's most wonderful hero-worship. Quite content was Rol, and more than content when Sweyn paused a minute to joke, and pat his head and pull his curls. Quiet he remained, as long as quiescence is possible to limbs young as his. Sweyn forgot he was near, hardly noticed when his leg was gently released, and never saw the stealthy abstraction of one of his tools.

Ten minutes thereafter was a lamentable wail from low on the floor, rising to the full pitch of Rol's healthy lungs, for his hand was gashed across, and the copious bleeding terrified him. Then was there soothing and comforting, washing and binding, and a modicum of scolding, till the loud outcry sank into occasional sobs, and the child, tear-stained and subdued, was returned to the chimney-corner settle, where Trella nodded.

In the reaction after pain and fright, Rol found that the quiet of that fire-lit corner was to his mind. Tyr, too, disdained him no longer, but, roused by his sobs, showed all the concern and sympathy that a dog can by licking and wistful watching. A little shame weighed also upon his spirits. He wished he had not cried quite so much. He remembered how once Sweyn had come home with his arm torn down from the shoulder, and a dead bear, and how he had never winced nor said a word, though his lips turned white with pain. Poor little Rol gave another sighing sob over his own faint-hearted shortcomings.

The light and motion of the great fire began to tell strange stories to the child, and the wind in the chimney roared a corroborative note now and then. The great black mouth of the chimney, impending high over the hearth, received as into a mysterious gulf murky coils of smoke and brightness of aspiring sparks, and beyond, in the high darkness, were muttering and wailing and strange doings, so that sometimes the smoke rushed back in panic, and curled out and up to the roof, and condensed itself to invisibility among the rafters. And then the wind would rage after its lost prey, and rush round the house, rattling and shrieking at window and door.

In a lull, after one such loud gust, Rol lifted his head in surprise and listened. A lull had also come on the babel of talk, and thus could be heard with strange distinctness a sound outside the door—the sound of a child's voice, a child's hands. "Open, open, let me in!" piped the little voice from low down, lower than the handle, and the latch rattled as though a tiptoe child reached up to it, and soft small knocks were struck. One near the door sprang up and opened it. "No one is here," he said. Tyr lifted his head and gave utterance to a howl, loud, prolonged, most dismal.

Sweyn, not able to believe that his ears had deceived him, got up and went to the door. It was a dark night. The clouds were heavy with snow, that had fallen fitfully when the wind lulled. Untrodden snow lay up to the porch. There was no sight nor sound of any human being. Sweyn strained his eyes far and near, only to see dark sky, pure snow, and a line of black fir trees on a hill brow, bowing down before the wind. "It must have been the wind," he said, and closed the door.

Many faces looked scared. The sound of a child's voice had been so distinct, and the words "Open, open, let me in!" The wind might creak the wood, or rattle the latch, but could not speak with a child's voice, nor knock with the soft plain blows that a plump fist gives. And the strange unusual howl of the wolf-hound was an omen to be feared, be the rest what it might. Strange things were said by one and another, till the rebuke of the house-mistress quelled them into far-off whispers. For a time after there was uneasiness, constraint, and silence, then the chill fear thawed by degrees, and the babble of talk flowed on again.

Yet half-an-hour later a very slight noise outside the door sufficed to arrest every hand, every tongue. Every head was raised, every eye fixed in one direction. "It is Christian, he is late," said Sweyn.

No, no, this is a feeble shuffle, not a young man's tread. With the sound of uncertain feet came the hard tap-tap of a stick against the door, and the high-pitched voice of eld, "Open, open, let me in!" Again Tyr flung up his head in a long doleful howl.

Before the echo of the tapping stick and the high voice had fairly died away, Sweyn had sprung across to the door and flung it wide. "No one again," he said in a steady voice, though his eyes looked startled as he stared out. He saw the lonely expanse of snow, the clouds swagging low, and between the two the line of dark fir-trees bowing in the wind. He closed the door without a word of comment, and re-crossed the room.

A score of blanched faces were turned to him as though he must be solver of the enigma. He could not be unconscious of this mute eye-questioning, and it disturbed his resolute air of composure. He hesitated, glanced towards his mother, the house-mistress, then back at the frightened folk, and gravely, before them all, made the sign of the cross. There was a flutter of hands as the sign was repeated by all, and the dead silence was stirred as by a huge sigh, for the held breath of many was freed as though the sign gave magic relief.

Even the house-mistress was perturbed. She left her wheel and crossed the room to her son, and spoke with him for a moment in a low tone that none could overhear. But a moment later her voice was high-pitched and loud, so that all might benefit by her rebuke of the "heathen chatter" of one of the girls. Perhaps she essayed to silence thus her own misgivings and forebodings.

No other voice dared speak now with its natural fullness. Low tones made intermittent murmurs, and now and then silence drifted over the whole room. The handling of tools was as noiseless as might be, and suspended on the instant if the door rattled in a gust of wind. After a time Sweyn left his work, joined the group nearest the door, and loitered there on the pretence of giving advice and help to the unskilful.

A man's tread was heard outside in the porch. "Christian!" said Sweyn and his mother simultaneously, he confidently, she authoritatively, to set the checked wheels going again. But Tyr flung up his head with an appalling howl.

"Open, open, let me in!"

It was a man's voice, and the door shook and rattled as a man's strength beat against it. Sweyn could feel the planks quivering, as on the instant his hand was upon the door, flinging it open, to face the blank porch, and beyond only snow and sky, and firs aslant in the wind.

He stood for a long minute with the open door in his hand. The bitter wind swept in with its icy chill, but a deadlier chill of fear came swifter, and seemed to freeze the beating of hearts. Sweyn stepped back to snatch up a great bearskin cloak.

"Sweyn, where are you going?"

"No farther than the porch, mother," and he stepped out and closed the door.

He wrapped himself in the heavy fur, and leaning against the most sheltered wall of the porch, steeled his nerves to face the devil and all his works. No sound of voices came from within; the most distinct sound was the crackle and roar of the fire.

It was bitterly cold. His feet grew numb, but he forbore stamping them into warmth lest the sound should strike panic within. Nor would he leave the porch, nor print a foot-mark on the untrodden white that declared so absolutely how no human voices and hands could have approached the door since snow fell two hours or more ago. "When the wind drops there will be more snow," thought Sweyn.

For the best part of an hour he kept his watch, and saw no living thing, heard no unwonted sound. "I will freeze here no longer," he muttered, and re-entered.

One woman gave a half-suppressed scream as his hand was laid on the latch, and then a gasp of relief as he came in. No one questioned him, only his mother said, in a tone of forced unconcern, "Could you not see Christian coming?" as though she were made anxious only by the absence of her younger son. Hardly had Sweyn stamped near to the fire than clear knocking was heard at the door. Tyr leapt from the hearth, his eyes red as the fire, his fangs showing white in the black jowl, his neck ridged and bristling, and overleaping Rol, ramped at the door, barking furiously.

Outside the door a clear mellow voice was calling. Tyr's bark made the words undistinguishable. No one offered to stir towards the door before Sweyn.

He stalked down the room resolutely, lifted the latch, and swung back the door.

A white-robed woman glided in.

No wraith! Living, beautiful, young.

Tyr leapt upon her.

Lithely she baulked the sharp fangs with folds of her long fur robe, and snatching from her girdle a small two-edged axe, whirled it up for a blow of defence.

Sweyn caught the dog by the collar, and dragged him off yelling and struggling.

The stranger stood in the doorway motionless, one foot set forward, one arm flung up, till the house-mistress hurried down the room, and Sweyn, relinquishing to others the furious Tyr, turned again to close the door, and offer excuse for so fierce a greeting. Then she lowered her arm, slung the axe in its place at her waist, loosened the furs about her face, and shook over her shoulders the long white robe, all as it were with the sway of one movement.

She was a maiden, tall and very fair. The fashion of her dress was strange, half masculine, yet not unwomanly. A fine fur tunic, reaching but little below the knee, was all the skirt she wore.

Below were the cross-bound shoes and leggings that a hunter wears. A white fur cap was set low upon the brows, and from its edge strips of fur fell lappet-wise about her shoulders; two of these at her entrance had been drawn forward and crossed about her throat, but now, loosened and thrust back, left unhidden long plaits of fair hair that lay forward on shoulder and breast, down to the ivory-studded girdle where the axe gleamed.

Sweyn and his mother led the stranger to the hearth without question or sign of curiosity, till she voluntarily told her tale of a long journey to distant kindred, a promised guide unmet, and signals and landmarks mistaken.

"Alone!" exclaimed Sweyn in astonishment. "Have you journeyed thus far, a hundred leagues, alone?"

She answered "Yes" with a little smile.

"Over the hills and the wastes! Why, the folk there are savage and wild as beasts."

She dropped her hand upon her axe with a laugh of some scorn.

"I fear neither man nor beast. Some few fear me." And then she told strange tales of fierce attack and defence, and of the bold free huntress life she had led.

Her words came a little slowly and deliberately, as though she spoke in a scarce familiar tongue. Now and then she hesitated, and stopped in a phrase, as though for lack of some word.

She became the centre of a group of listeners. The interest she excited dissipated, in some degree, the dread inspired by the mysterious voices. There was nothing ominous about this young, bright, fair reality, though her aspect was strange.

Little Rol crept near, staring at the stranger with all his might. Unnoticed, he softly stroked and patted a corner of her soft white robe that reached to the floor in ample folds. He laid his cheek against it caressingly, and then edged up close to her knees.

"What is your name?" he asked.

The stranger's smile and ready answer, as she looked down,

saved Rol from the rebuke merited by his unmannerly question.

"My real name," she said, "would be uncouth to your ears and tongue. The folk of this country have given me another name, and from this" (she laid her hand on the fur robe) "they call me 'White Fell.'"

Little Rol repeated it to himself, stroking and patting as before. "White Fell, White Fell."

The fair face, and soft, beautiful dress pleased Rol. He knelt up, with his eyes on her face and an air of uncertain determination, like a robin's on a doorstep, and plumped his elbows into her lap with a little gasp at his own audacity.

"Rol!" exclaimed his aunt, but, "Oh, let him!" said White Fell, smiling and stroking his head, and Rol stayed.

He advanced farther, and panting at his own adventurousness in the face of his aunt's authority, climbed up on to her knees. Her welcoming arms hindered any protest. He nestled happily, fingering the axe head, the ivory studs in her girdle, the ivory clasp at her throat, the plaits of fair hair, rubbing his head against the softness of her fur-clad shoulder, with a child's full confidence in the kindness of beauty.

White Fell had not uncovered her head, only knotted the pendant fur loosely behind her neck. Rol reached up his hand towards it, whispering her name to himself, "White Fell, White Fell," then slid his arms round her neck, and kissed her, once, twice. She laughed delightedly, and kissed him again.

"The child plagues you?" said Sweyn.

"No, indeed," she answered, with an earnestness so intense as to seem disproportionate to the occasion.

Rol settled himself again on her lap, and began to unwind the bandage bound round his hand. He paused a little when he saw where the blood had soaked through, then went on till his hand was bare and the cut displayed, gaping and long, though only skin deep. He held it up towards White Fell, desirous of her pity and sympathy.

At sight of it, and the blood-stained linen, she drew in her breath suddenly, clasped Rol to her—hard, hard—till he began to struggle. Her face was hidden behind the boy, so that none could see its expression. It had lighted up with a most awful glee.

Afar, beyond the fir-grove, beyond the low hill behind, the absent Christian was hastening his return. From daybreak he had been afoot, carrying notice of a bear hunt to all the best hunters of the farms and hamlets that lay within a radius of twelve miles. Nevertheless, having been detained till a late hour, he now broke into a run, going with a long smooth stride of apparent ease that fast made the miles diminish.

He entered the midnight blackness of the fir-grove with scarcely slackened pace, though the path was invisible, and passing through into the open again, sighted the farm lying a furlong off down the slope. Then he sprang out freely, and almost on the instant gave one great sideways leap, and stood still. There in the snow was the track of a great wolf.

His hand went to his knife, his only weapon. He stooped, knelt down, to bring his eyes to the level of a beast, and peered about. His teeth set, his heart beat a little harder than the pace of his running insisted on. A solitary wolf, nearly always savage and of large size, is a formidable beast that will not hesitate to attack a single man. This wolf-track was the largest Christian had ever seen, and, so far as he could judge, recently made. It led from under the fir-trees down the slope. Well for him, he thought, was the delay that had so vexed him before. Well for him that he had not passed through the dark fir-grove when that danger of jaws lurked there. Going warily, he followed the track.

It led down the slope, across a broad ice-bound stream, along the level beyond, making towards the farm. A less precise knowledge had doubted, and guessed that here might have come straying big Tyr or his like, but Christian was sure, knowing better than to mistake between footmark of dog and wolf.

Straight on—straight on towards the farm.

Surprised and anxious grew Christian, that a prowling wolf should dare so near. He drew his knife and pressed on, more hastily, more keen-eyed. Oh that Tyr were with him!

Straight on, straight on, even to the very door, where the snow failed. His heart seemed to give a great leap and then stop. There the track ended.

Nothing lurked in the porch, and there was no sign of return. The firs stood straight against the sky, the clouds lay low, for the wind had fallen and a few snowflakes came drifting down. In a horror of surprise, Christian stood dazed a moment, then he lifted the latch and went in. His glance took in all the old familiar forms and faces, and with them that of the stranger, fur-clad and beautiful. The awful truth flashed upon him. He knew what she was.

Only a few were startled by the rattle of the latch as he entered. The room was filled with bustle and movement, for it was the supper hour, when all tools were laid aside, and trestles and tables shifted. Christian had no knowledge of what he said and did. He moved and spoke mechanically, half thinking that soon he must wake from this horrible dream. Sweyn and his mother supposed him to be cold and dead-tired, and spared all unnecessary questions. And he found himself seated beside the hearth, opposite that dreadful Thing that looked like a beautiful girl, watching her every movement, curdling with horror to see her fondle the child Rol.

Sweyn stood near them both, intent upon White Fell also, but how differently! She seemed unconscious of the gaze of both, neither aware of the chill dread in the eyes of Christian, nor of Sweyn's warm admiration.

These two brothers, who were twins, contrasted greatly, despite their striking likeness. They were alike in regular profile, fair brown hair, and deep blue eyes, but Sweyn's features were perfect as a young god's, while Christian's showed faulty details. Thus, the line of his mouth was set too straight, the eyes shelved too deeply back, and the contour of the face flowed in less generous curves than Sweyn's. Their height was the same, but Christian was too slender for perfect proportion, while Sweyn's well-knit frame, broad shoulders, and muscular arms, made him pre-eminent for manly beauty as well as for strength. As a hunter Sweyn was without rival, as a fisher without rival. All the countryside acknowledged him to be the best wrestler, rider, dancer, singer. Only in speed could he be surpassed, and in that only by his younger brother. All others Sweyn could distance fairly, but Christian could outrun him easily. Ay, he could keep pace with Sweyn's most breathless burst, and laugh and talk the while. Christian took little pride in his fleetness of foot, counting a man's legs to be the least worthy of his members. He had no envy of his brother's athletic superiority, though to several feats he had made a moderate second. He loved as only a twin can love—proud of all that Sweyn did, content with all that Sweyn was, humbly content also that his own great love should not be so exceedingly returned, since he knew himself to be so far less love-worthy.

Christian dared not, in the midst of women and children, launch the horror that he knew into words. He waited to consult his brother, but Sweyn did not, or would not, notice the signal he made, and kept his face always turned towards White Fell. Christian drew away from the hearth, unable to remain passive with that dread upon him.

"Where is Tyr?" he said suddenly. Then, catching sight of the dog in a distant corner, "Why is he chained there?"

"He flew at the stranger," one answered.

Christian's eyes glowed. "Yes?" he said, interrogatively.

"He was within an ace of having his brain knocked out."

"Tyr?"

"Yes, she was nimbly up with that little axe she has at her waist. It was well for old Tyr that his master throttled him off."

Christian went without a word to the corner where Tyr was

chained. The dog rose up to meet him, as piteous and indignant as a dumb beast can be. He stroked the black head. "Good Tyr! brave dog!"

They knew, they only, and the man and the dumb dog had comfort of each other.

Christian's eyes turned again towards White Fell. Tyr's also, and he strained against the length of the chain. Christian's hand lay on the dog's neck, and he felt it ridge and bristle with the quivering of impotent fury. Then he began to quiver in like manner, with a fury born of reason, not instinct, as impotent morally as was Tyr physically. Oh, the woman's form that he dare not touch! Anything but that, and he with Tyr would be free to kill or be killed.

Then he returned to ask fresh questions.

"How long has the stranger been here?"

"She came about half-an-hour before you."

"Who opened the door to her?"

"Sweyn. No one else dared."

The tone of the answer was mysterious.

"Why?" queried Christian. "Has anything strange happened? Tell me."

For answer he was told in a low undertone of the summons at the door thrice repeated without human agency, and of Tyr's ominous howls, and of Sweyn's fruitless watch outside.

Christian turned towards his brother in a torment of impatience for a word apart. The board was spread, and Sweyn was leading White Fell to the guest's place. This was more awful. She would break bread with them under the roof-tree!

He started forward, and touching Sweyn's arm, whispered an urgent entreaty. Sweyn stared, and shook his head in angry impatience.

Thereupon Christian would take no morsel of food.

His opportunity came at last. White Fell questioned of the landmarks of the country, and of one Cairn Hill, which was an appointed meeting-place at which she was due that night. The house-mistress and Sweyn both exclaimed.

"It is three long miles away," said Sweyn, "with no place for shelter but a wretched hut. Stay with us this night, and I will show you the way tomorrow."

White Fell seemed to hesitate. "Three miles," she said, "then I should be able to see or hear a signal."

"I will look out," said Sweyn, "then, if there be no signal, you must not leave us."

He went to the door. Christian rose silently, and followed him out.

"Sweyn, do you know what she is?"

Sweyn, surprised at the vehement grasp, and low hoarse voice, made answer: "She? Who? White Fell?"

"Yes."

"She is the most beautiful girl I have ever seen."

"She is a Were-Wolf."

Sweyn burst out laughing. "Are you mad?" he asked.

"No, here, see for yourself."

Christian drew him out of the porch, pointing to the snow where the footmarks had been. Had been, for now they were not. Snow was falling fast, and every dint was blotted out.

"Well?" asked Sweyn.

"Had you come when I signed to you, you would have seen for yourself."

"Seen what?"

"The footprints of a wolf leading up to the door, none leading away."

It was impossible not to be startled by the tone alone, though it was hardly above a whisper. Sweyn eyed his brother anxiously, but in the darkness could make nothing of his face. Then he laid his hands kindly and reassuringly on Christian's shoulders and felt how he was quivering with excitement and horror.

"One sees strange things," he said, "when the cold has got

into the brain behind the eyes. You came in cold and worn out."

"No," interrupted Christian. "I saw the track first on the brow of the slope, and followed it down right here to the door. This is no delusion."

Sweyn in his heart felt positive that it was. Christian was given to daydreams and strange fancies, though never had he been possessed with so mad a notion before.

"Don't you believe me?" said Christian desperately. "You must. I swear it is sane truth. Are you blind? Why, even Tyr knows."

"You will be clearer headed tomorrow after a night's rest. Then come too, if you will, with White Fell, to the Hill Cairn, and if you have doubts still, watch and follow, and see what footprints she leaves."

Galled by Sweyn's evident contempt, Christian turned abruptly to the door. Sweyn caught him back.

"What now, Christian? What are you going to do?"

"You do not believe me. My mother shall."

Sweyn's grasp tightened. "You shall not tell her," he said authoritatively.

Customarily Christian was so docile to his brother's mastery that it was now a surprising thing when he wrenched himself free vigorously, and said as determinedly as Sweyn, "She shall know!" but Sweyn was nearer the door and would not let him pass.

"There has been scare enough for one night already. If this notion of yours will keep, broach it tomorrow." Christian would not yield.

"Women are so easily scared," pursued Sweyn, "and are ready to believe any folly without shadow of proof. Be a man, Christian, and fight this notion of a Were-Wolf by yourself."

"If you would believe me," began Christian.

"I believe you to be a fool," said Sweyn, losing patience. "Another, who was not your brother, might believe you to be a knave, and guess that you had transformed White Fell into a Were-Wolf because she smiled more readily on me than on you."

The jest was not without foundation, for the grace of White Fell's bright looks had been bestowed on him, on Christian never a whit. Sweyn's coxcombery was always frank, and most forgiveable, and not without fair colour.

"If you want an ally," continued Sweyn, "confide in old Trella. Out of her stores of wisdom, if her memory holds good, she can instruct you in the orthodox manner of tackling a Were-Wolf. If I remember aright, you should watch the suspected person till midnight, when the beast's form must be resumed, and retained ever after if a human eye sees the change, or, better still, sprinkle hands and feet with holy water, which is certain death. Oh, never fear, but old Trella will be equal to the occasion."

Sweyn's contempt was no longer good-humoured. Some touch of irritation or resentment rose at this monstrous doubt of White Fell. But Christian was too deeply distressed to take offence.

"You speak of them as old wives' tales, but if you had seen the proof I have seen, you would be ready at least to wish them true, if not also to put them to the test."

"Well," said Sweyn, with a laugh that had a little sneer in it, "put them to the test! I will not object to that, if you will only keep your notions to yourself. Now, Christian, give me your word for silence, and we will freeze here no longer."

Christian remained silent.

Sweyn put his hands on his shoulders again and vainly tried to see his face in the darkness.

"We have never quarrelled yet, Christian?"

"I have never quarrelled," returned the other, aware for the first time that his dictatorial brother had sometimes offered occasion for quarrel, had he been ready to take it.

"Well," said Sweyn emphatically, "if you speak against White Fell to any other, as tonight you have spoken to me, we shall."

He delivered the words like an ultimatum, turned sharp round, and re-entered the house. Christian, more fearful and wretched than before, followed.

"Snow is falling fast. Not a single light is to be seen."

White Fell's eyes passed over Christian without apparent notice, and turned bright and shining upon Sweyn.

"Nor any signal to be heard?" she queried. "Did you not hear the sound of a sea-horn?"

"I saw nothing, and heard nothing, and signal or no signal, the heavy snow would keep you here perforce."

She smiled her thanks beautifully. And Christian's heart sank like lead with a deadly foreboding, as he noted what a light was kindled in Sweyn's eyes by her smile.

That night, when all others slept, Christian, the weariest of all, watched outside the guest chamber till midnight was past. No sound, not the faintest, could be heard. Could the old tale be true of the midnight change? What was on the other side of the door, a woman or a beast? He would have given his right hand to know. Instinctively he laid his hand on the latch, and drew it softly, though believing that bolts fastened the inner side. The door yielded to his hand. He stood on the threshold, a keen gust of air cut at him. The window stood open, the room was empty.

So Christian could sleep with a somewhat lightened heart.

In the morning there was surprise and conjecture when White Fell's absence was discovered. Christian held his peace. Not even to his brother did he say how he knew that she had fled before midnight, and Sweyn, though evidently greatly chagrined, seemed to disdain reference to the subject of Christian's fears.

The elder brother alone joined the bear hunt. Christian found pretext to stay behind. Sweyn, being out of humour, manifested his contempt by uttering not a single expostulation.

All that day, and for many a day after, Christian would never go out of sight of his home. Sweyn alone noticed how he manœuvred for this, and was clearly annoyed by it. White Fell's name was never mentioned between them, though not seldom was it heard in general talk. Hardly a day passed but little Rol asked when White Fell would come again, pretty White Fell, who kissed like a snowflake. And if Sweyn answered, Christian would be quite sure that the light in his eyes, kindled by White Fell's smile, had not yet died out.

Little Rol! Naughty, merry, fairhaired little Rol. A day came when his feet raced over the threshold never to return, when his chatter and laugh were heard no more, when tears of anguish were wept by eyes that never would see his bright head again: never again, living or dead.

He was seen at dusk for the last time, escaping from the house with his puppy, in freakish rebellion against old Trella. Later, when his absence had begun to cause anxiety, his puppy crept back to the farm, cowed, whimpering and yelping, a pitiful, dumb lump of terror, without intelligence or courage to guide the frightened search.

Rol was never found, nor any trace of him. Where he had perished was never known. How he had perished was known only by an awful guess—a wild beast had devoured him.

Christian heard the conjecture "a wolf", and a horrible certainty flashed upon him that he knew what wolf it was. He tried to declare what he knew, but Sweyn saw him start at the words with white face and struggling lips, and, guessing his purpose, pulled him back, and kept him silent, hardly, by his imperious grip and wrathful eyes, and one low whisper.

That Christian should retain his most irrational suspicion against beautiful White Fell was, to Sweyn, evidence of a weak obstinacy of mind that would but thrive upon expostulation and argument. But this evident intention to direct the passions of grief and anguish to a hatred and fear of the fair stranger, such as his own, was intolerable, and Sweyn set his will against it. Again Christian yielded to his brother's stronger words and will, and against his own judgment consented to silence.

Repentance came before the new moon, the first of the year, was old. White Fell came again, smiling as she entered, as though assured of a glad and kindly welcome, and, in truth, there was only one who saw again her fair face and strange white garb without pleasure. Sweyn's face glowed with delight, while Christian's grew pale and rigid as death. He had given his word to keep silence, but he had not thought that she would dare to come again. Silence was impossible, face to face with that Thing, impossible. Irrepressibly he cried out:

"Where is Rol?"

Not a quiver disturbed White Fell's face. She heard, yet remained bright and tranquil. Sweyn's eyes flashed round at his brother dangerously. Among the women some tears fell at the poor child's name, but none caught alarm from its sudden utterance, for the thought of Rol rose naturally. Where was little Rol, who had nestled in the stranger's arms, kissing her, and watched for her since, and prattled of her daily?

Christian went out silently. One only thing there was that he could do, and he must not delay. His horror overmastered any curiosity to hear White Fell's smooth excuses and smiling apologies for her strange and uncourteous departure, or her easy tale of the circumstances of her return, or to watch her bearing as she heard the sad tale of little Rol.

The swiftest runner of the countryside had started on his hardest race: little less than three leagues and back, which he reckoned to accomplish in two hours, though the night was moonless and the way rugged. He rushed against the still cold air till it felt like a wind upon his face. The dim homestead sank below the ridges at his back, and fresh ridges of snowlands rose out of the obscure horizon level to drive past him as the stirless air drove, and sink away behind into obscure level again. He took no conscious heed of landmarks, not even when all sign of a path was gone under depths of snow. His will was set to reach his goal with unexampled speed, and thither by instinct his physical forces bore him, without one definite thought to guide.

And the idle brain lay passive, inert, receiving into its vacancy restless siftings of past sights and sounds: Rol, weeping, laughing, playing, coiled in the arms of that dreadful Thing, Tyr—O Tyr!—white fangs in the black jowl, the women who wept on, the foolish puppy, precious for the child's last touch, footprints from pine wood to door, the smiling face among furs, of such womanly beauty, smiling, smiling. And Sweyn's face.

"Sweyn, Sweyn, O Sweyn, my brother!"

Sweyn's angry laugh possessed his ear within the sound of the wind of his speed. Sweyn's scorn assailed more quick and keen than the biting cold at his throat. And yet he was unimpressed by any thought of how Sweyn's anger and scorn would rise, if this errand were known.

Sweyn was a sceptic. His utter disbelief in Christian's testimony regarding the footprints was based upon positive scepticism. His reason refused to bend in accepting the possibility of the supernatural materialised. That a living beast could ever be other than palpably bestial, pawed, toothed, shagged, and eared as such, was to him incredible, far more that a human presence could be transformed from its god-like aspect, upright, free-handed, with brows, and speech, and laughter. The wild and fearful legends that he had known from childhood and then believed, he regarded now as built upon facts distorted, overlaid by imagination, and quickened by superstition. Even the strange summons at the threshold, that he himself had vainly answered, was, after the first shock of surprise, rationally explained by him as malicious foolery on the part of some clever trickster, who withheld the key to the enigma.

To the younger brother all life was a spiritual mystery, veiled from his clear knowledge by the density of flesh. Since he knew his own body to be linked to the complex and antagonistic forces that constitute one soul, it seemed to him not impossibly strange that one spiritual force should possess diverse forms for widely various manifestation. Nor, to him, was it great effort to believe that as pure water washes away all natural foulness, so water, holy by consecration, must needs cleanse God's world from that supernatural evil Thing. Therefore, faster than ever man's foot had covered those leagues, he sped under the dark, still night, over the waste, trackless snow-ridges to the far-away church, where salvation lay in the holy-water stoup at the door. His faith was as firm as any that wrought miracles in days past, simple as a child's wish, strong as a man's will.

He was hardly missed during these hours, every second of which was by him fulfilled to its utmost extent by extremest effort that sinews and nerves could attain. Within the homestead the while, the easy moments went bright with words and looks of unwonted animation, for the kindly, hospitable instincts of the inmates were roused into cordial expression of welcome and interest by the grace and beauty of the returned stranger.

But Sweyn was eager and earnest, with more than a host's courteous warmth. The impression that at her first coming had charmed him, that had lived since through memory, deepened now in her actual presence. Sweyn, the matchless among men, acknowledged in this fair White Fell a spirit high and bold as his own, and a frame so firm and capable that only bulk was lacking for equal strength. Yet the white skin was moulded most smoothly, without such muscular swelling as made his might evident. Such love as his frank self-love could concede was called forth by an ardent admiration for this supreme stranger. More admiration than love was in his passion, and therefore he was free from a lover's hesitancy and delicate reserve and doubts. Frankly and boldly he courted her favour by looks and tones, and an address that came of natural ease, needless of skill by practice.

Nor was she a woman to be wooed otherwise. Tender whispers and sighs would never gain her ear, but her eyes would brighten and shine if she heard of a brave feat, and her prompt hand in sympathy fall swiftly on the axe-haft and clasp it hard. That movement ever fired Sweyn's admiration anew. He watched for it, strove to elicit it, and glowed when it came. Wonderful and beautiful was that wrist, slender and steel-strong, also the smooth shapely hand, that curved so fast and firm, ready to deal instant death.

Desiring to feel the pressure of these hands, this bold lover schemed with palpable directness, proposing that she should hear how their hunting songs were sung, with a chorus that signalled hands to be clasped. So his splendid voice gave the verses, and, as the chorus was taken up, he claimed her hands, and, even through the easy grip, felt, as he desired, the strength that was latent, and the vigour that quickened the very fingertips, as the song fired her, and her voice was caught out of her by the rhythmic swell, and rang clear on the top of the closing surge.

Afterwards she sang alone. For contrast, or in the pride of swaying moods by her voice, she chose a mournful song that drifted along in a minor chant, sad as a wind that dirges:

> "Oh, let me go!
> Around spin wreaths of snow;
> The dark earth sleeps below.
> Far up the plain
> Moans on a voice of pain:
> 'Where shall my babe be lain?'
> In my white breast
> Lay the sweet life to rest!
> Lay, where it can lie best!
> 'Hush! Hush its cries!
> Dense night is on the skies:
> Two stars are in thine eyes.'
> Come, babe, away!
> But lie thou till dawn be grey,

Who must be dead by day.
This cannot last;
But, ere the sickening blast,
All sorrow shall be past;
And kings shall be
Low bending at thy knee,
Worshipping life from thee.
For men long sore
To hope of what's before,
To leave the things of yore.
Mine, and not thine,
How deep their jewels shine!
Peace laps thy head, not mine."

Old Trella came tottering from her corner, shaken to additional palsy by an aroused memory. She strained her dim eyes towards the singer, and then bent her head, that the one ear yet sensible to sound might avail of every note. At the close, groping forward, she murmured with the high-pitched quaver of old age: "So she sang, my Thora, my last and brightest. What is she like, she whose voice is like my dead Thora's? Are her eyes blue?"

"Blue as the sky."

"So were my Thora's! Is her hair fair, and in plaits to the waist?"

"Even so," answered White Fell herself, and met the advancing hands with her own, and guided them to corroborate her words by touch.

"Like my dead Thora's," repeated the old woman, and then her trembling hands rested on the fur-clad shoulders, and she bent forward and kissed the smooth fair face that White Fell upturned, nothing loth, to receive and return the caress.

So Christian saw them as he entered.

He stood a moment. After the starless darkness and the icy night air, and the fierce silent two hours' race, his senses reeled on sudden entrance into warmth, and light, and the cheery hum of voices. A sudden unforeseen anguish assailed him, as now first he entertained the possibility of being overmatched by her wiles and her daring, if at the approach of pure death she should start up at bay transformed to a terrible beast, and achieve a savage glut at the last. He looked with horror and pity on the harmless, helpless folk, so unwitting of outrage to their comfort and security. The dreadful Thing in their midst, that was veiled from their knowledge by womanly beauty, was a centre of pleasant interest. There, before him, signally impressive, was poor old Trella, weakest and feeblest of all, in fond nearness. And a moment might bring about the revelation of a monstrous horror, a ghastly, deadly danger, set loose and at bay, in a circle of girls and women and careless defenceless men: so hideous and terrible a thing as might crack the brain, or curdle the heart stone dead.

And he alone of the throng prepared!

For one breathing space he faltered, no longer than that, while over him swept the agony of compunction that yet could not make him surrender his purpose.

He alone? Nay, but Tyr also, and he crossed to the dumb sole sharer of his knowledge.

So timeless is thought that a few seconds only lay between his lifting of the latch and his loosening of Tyr's collar, but in those few seconds succeeding his first glance, as lightning-swift had been the impulses of others, their motion as quick and sure. Sweyn's vigilant eye had darted upon him, and instantly his every fibre was alert with hostile instinct, and, half divining, half incredulous, of Christian's object in stooping to Tyr, he came hastily, wary, wrathful, resolute to oppose the malice of his wild-eyed brother.

But beyond Sweyn rose White Fell, blanching white as her furs, and with eyes grown fierce and wild. She leapt down the room to the door, whirling her long robe closely to her. "Hark!" she panted. "The signal horn! Hark, I must go!" as she snatched at the latch to be out and away.

For one precious moment Christian had hesitated on the half-loosened collar, for, except the womanly form were exchanged for the bestial, Tyr's jaws would gnash to rags his honour of manhood. Then he heard her voice, and turned, too late.

As she tugged at the door, he sprang across grasping his flask, but Sweyn dashed between, and caught him back irresistibly, so that a most frantic effort only availed to wrench one arm free. With that, on the impulse of sheer despair, he cast at her with all his force. The door swung behind her, and the flask flew into fragments against it. Then, as Sweyn's grasp slackened, and he met the questioning astonishment of surrounding faces, with a hoarse inarticulate cry: "God help us all!" he said. "She is a Were-Wolf."

Sweyn turned upon him, "Liar, coward!" and his hands gripped his brother's throat with deadly force, as though the spoken word could be killed so, and as Christian struggled, lifted him clear off his feet and flung him crashing backward. So furious was he, that, as his brother lay motionless, he stirred him roughly with his foot, till their mother came between, crying shame, and yet then he stood by, his teeth set, his brows knit, his hands clenched, ready to enforce silence again violently, as Christian rose staggering and bewildered.

But utter silence and submission were more than he expected, and turned his anger into contempt for one so easily cowed and held in subjection by mere force. "He is mad!" he said, turning on his heel as he spoke, so that he lost his mother's look of pained reproach at this sudden free utterance of what was a lurking dread within her.

Christian was too spent for the effort of speech. His hard-drawn breath laboured in great sobs. His limbs were powerless and unstrung in utter relax after hard service. Failure in his endeavour induced a stupor of misery and despair. In addition was the wretched humiliation of open violence and strife with his brother, and the distress of hearing misjudging contempt expressed without reserve, for he was aware that Sweyn had turned to allay the scared excitement half by imperious mastery, half by explanation and argument, that showed painful disregard of brotherly consideration. All this unkindness of his twin he charged upon the fell Thing who had wrought this their first dissension, and, ah, most terrible thought, interposed between them so effectually, that Sweyn was wilfully blind and deaf on her account, resentful of interference, arbitrary beyond reason.

Dread and perplexity unfathomable darkened upon him, unshared, the burden was overwhelming, a foreboding of unspeakable calamity, based upon his ghastly discovery, bore down upon him, crushing out hope of power to withstand impending fate.

Sweyn the while was observant of his brother, despite the continual check of finding, turn and glance when he would, Christian's eyes always upon him, with a strange look of helpless distress, discomposing enough to the angry aggressor. "Like a beaten dog!" he said to himself, rallying contempt to withstand compunction. Observation set him wondering on Christian's exhausted condition. The heavy labouring breath and the slack inert fall of the limbs told surely of unusual and prolonged exertion. And then why had close upon two hours' absence been followed by open hostility against White Fell?

Suddenly, the fragments of the flask giving a clue, he guessed all, and faced about to stare at his brother in amaze. He forgot that the motive scheme was against White Fell, demanding derision and resentment from him, that was swept out of remembrance by astonishment and admiration for the feat of speed and endurance. In eagerness to question he inclined to attempt a generous part and frankly offer to heal the breach, but Christian's depression and sad following gaze provoked him to self-justification by recalling the offence of that outrageous utterance against White Fell, and the impulse passed. Then other considerations counselled silence, and afterwards a humour possessed him to wait and see how Christian would find opportunity to proclaim his performance and establish the fact, without exciting ridicule on account of the absurdity of the errand.

This expectation remained unfulfilled. Christian never attempted the proud avowal that would have placed his feat on record to be told to the next generation.

That night Sweyn and his mother talked long and late together, shaping into certainty the suspicion that Christian's mind had lost its balance, and discussing the evident cause. For Sweyn, declaring his own love for White Fell, suggested that his unfortunate brother, with a like passion, they being twins in loves as in birth, had through jealousy and despair turned from love to hate, until reason failed at the strain, and a craze developed, which the malice and treachery of madness made a serious and dangerous force.

So Sweyn theorised, convincing himself as he spoke, convincing afterwards others who advanced doubts against White Fell, fettering his judgment by his advocacy, and by his staunch defence of her hurried flight silencing his own inner consciousness of the unaccountability of her action.

But a little time and Sweyn lost his vantage in the shock of a fresh horror at the homestead. Trella was no more, and her end a mystery. The poor old woman crawled out in a bright gleam to visit a bed-ridden gossip living beyond the fir-grove. Under the trees she was last seen, halting for her companion, sent back for a forgotten present. Quick alarm sprang, calling every man to the search. Her stick was found among the brushwood only a few paces from the path, but no track or stain, for a gusty wind was sifting the snow from the branches, and hid all sign of how she came by her death.

So panic-stricken were the farm folk that none dared go singly on the search. Known danger could be braced, but not this stealthy Death that walked by day invisible, that cut off alike the child in his play and the aged woman so near to her quiet grave.

"Rol she kissed. Trella she kissed!" So rang Christian's frantic cry again and again, till Sweyn dragged him away and strove to keep him apart, albeit in his agony of grief and remorse he accused himself wildly as answerable for the tragedy, and gave clear proof that the charge of madness was well founded, if strange looks and desperate, incoherent words were evidence enough.

But thenceforward all Sweyn's reasoning and mastery could not uphold White Fell above suspicion. He was not called upon to defend her from accusation when Christian had been brought to silence again, but he well knew the significance of this fact, that her name, formerly uttered freely and often, he never heard now. It was huddled away into whispers that he could not catch.

The passing of time did not sweep away the superstitious fears that Sweyn despised. He was angry and anxious, eager that White Fell should return, and, merely by her bright gracious presence, reinstate herself in favour, but doubtful if all his authority and example could keep from her notice an altered aspect of welcome, and he foresaw clearly that Christian would prove unmanageable, and might be capable of some dangerous outbreak.

For a time the twins' variance was marked, on Sweyn's part by an air of rigid indifference, on Christian's by heavy downcast silence, and a nervous apprehensive observation of his brother. Superadded to his remorse and foreboding, Sweyn's displeasure weighed upon him intolerably, and the remembrance of their violent rupture was a ceaseless misery. The elder brother, self-sufficient and insensitive, could little know how deeply his unkindness stabbed. A depth and force of affection such as Christian's was unknown to him. The loyal subservience that he could not appreciate had encouraged him to domineer. This strenuous opposition to his reason and will was accounted as furious malice, if not sheer insanity.

Christian's surveillance galled him incessantly, and embarrassment and danger he foresaw as the outcome. Therefore, that suspicion might be lulled, he judged it wise to make overtures for peace. Most easily done. A little kindliness, a few evidences of consideration, a slight return of the old brotherly imperiousness, and Christian replied by a gratefulness and relief that might have touched him had he understood all, but instead, increased his secret contempt.

So successful was this finesse, that when, late on a day, a message summoning Christian to a distance was transmitted by Sweyn, no doubt of its genuineness occurred. When, his errand proved useless, he set out to return, mistake or misapprehension was all that he surmised. Not till he sighted the homestead, lying low between the night-grey snow ridges, did vivid recollection of the time when he had tracked that horror to the door rouse an intense dread, and with it a hardly-defined suspicion.

His grasp tightened on the bear-spear that he carried as a staff. Every sense was alert, every muscle strung. Excitement urged him on, caution checked him, and the two governed his long stride, swiftly, noiselessly, to the climax he felt was at hand.

As he drew near to the outer gates, a light shadow stirred and went, as though the grey of the snow had taken detached motion. A darker shadow stayed and faced Christian, striking his life-blood chill with utmost despair.

Sweyn stood before him, and surely, the shadow that went was White Fell.

They had been together, close. Had she not been in his arms, near enough for lips to meet?

There was no moon, but the stars gave light enough to show that Sweyn's face was flushed and elate. The flush remained, though the expression changed quickly at sight of his brother. How, if Christian had seen all, should one of his frenzied outbursts be met and managed. By resolution? By indifference? He halted between the two, and as a result, he swaggered.

"White Fell?" questioned Christian, hoarse and breathless.

"Yes?"

Sweyn's answer was a query, with an intonation that implied he was clearing the ground for action.

From Christian came: "Have you kissed her?" like a bolt direct, staggering Sweyn by its sheer prompt temerity.

He flushed yet darker, and yet half-smiled over this earnest of success he had won. Had there been really between himself and Christian the rivalry that he imagined, his face had enough of the insolence of triumph to exasperate jealous rage.

"You dare ask this!"

"Sweyn, O Sweyn, I must know! You have!"

The ring of despair and anguish in his tone angered Sweyn, misconstruing it. Jealousy urging to such presumption was intolerable.

"Mad fool!" he said, constraining himself no longer. "Win for yourself a woman to kiss. Leave mine without question. Such an one as I should desire to kiss is such an one as shall never allow a kiss to you."

Then Christian fully understood his supposition.

"I—I!" he cried. "White Fell—that deadly Thing! Sweyn, are you blind, mad? I would save you from her, a Were-Wolf!"

Sweyn maddened again at the accusation, a dastardly way of revenge, as he conceived, and instantly, for the second time, the brothers were at strife violently.

But Christian was now too desperate to be scrupulous, for a dim glimpse had shot a possibility into his mind, and to be free to follow it the striking of his brother was a necessity. Thank God he was armed, and so Sweyn's equal.

Facing his assailant with the bear-spear, he struck up his arms, and with the butt end hit hard so that he fell. The matchless runner leapt away on the instant, to follow a forlorn hope. Sweyn, on regaining his feet, was as amazed as angry at this unaccountable flight. He knew in his heart that his brother was no coward, and that it was unlike him to shrink from an encounter because defeat was certain, and cruel humiliation from a vindictive victor probable. Of the uselessness of pursuit he was well aware. He must abide his chagrin, content to know that his time for advantage would come. Since White Fell had parted to the right, Christian to the left, the event of a sequent encounter did not occur to him. And now Christian, acting on the dim glimpse he had had, just as Sweyn turned upon him, of something that moved against the sky along the ridge behind the homestead, was staking his only hope on a chance, and his own superlative speed. If what he saw was really White Fell, he guessed she was bending her steps towards the open wastes, and there was just a possibility that, by a straight dash, and a desperate perilous leap over a sheer bluff, he might yet meet her or head her. And then, he had no further thought.

It was past, the quick, fierce race, and the chance of death at the leap, and he halted in a hollow to fetch his breath and to look. Did she come? Had she gone?

She came.

She came with a smooth, gliding, noiseless speed, that was neither walking nor running. Her arms were folded in her furs that were drawn tight about her body. The white lappets from her head were wrapped and knotted closely beneath her face. Her eyes were set on a far distance. So she went till the even sway of her going was startled to a pause by Christian.

"Fell!"

She drew a quick, sharp breath at the sound of her name thus mutilated, and faced Sweyn's brother. Her eyes glittered, her upper lip was lifted, and shewed the teeth. The half of her name, impressed with an ominous sense as uttered by him, warned her of the aspect of a deadly foe. Yet she cast loose her robes till they trailed ample, and spoke as a mild woman.

"What would you?"

Then Christian answered with his solemn dreadful accusation: "You kissed Rol, and Rol is dead! You kissed Trella, she is dead! You have kissed Sweyn, my brother, but he shall not die!"

He added, "You may live till midnight."

The edge of the teeth and the glitter of the eyes stayed a moment, and her right hand also slid down to the axe haft. Then, without a word, she swerved from him, and sprang out and away swiftly over the snow.

And Christian sprang out and away, and followed her swiftly over the snow, keeping behind, but half-a-stride's length from her side.

So they went running together, silent, towards the vast wastes of snow, where no living thing but they two moved under the stars of night.

Never before had Christian so rejoiced in his powers. The gift of speed, and the training of use and endurance were priceless to him now. Though midnight was hours away, he was confident that, go where that Fell Thing would, hasten as she would, she could not outstrip him nor escape from him. Then, when came the time for transformation, when the woman's form made no longer a shield against a man's hand, he could slay or be slain to save Sweyn. He had struck his dear brother in dire extremity, but he could not, though reason urged, strike a woman.

For one mile, for two miles they ran, White Fell ever foremost, Christian ever at equal distance from her side, so near that, now and again, her out-flying furs touched him. She spoke no word, nor he. She never turned her head to look at him, nor swerved to evade him, but, with set face looking forward, sped straight on, over rough, over smooth, aware of his nearness by the regular beat of his feet, and the sound of his breath behind.

In a while she quickened her pace. From the first, Christian had judged of her speed as admirable, yet with exulting security in his own excelling and enduring whatever her efforts. But, when the pace increased, he found himself put to the test as never had he been before in any race. Her feet, indeed, flew faster than his. It was only by his length of stride that he kept his place at her side. But his heart was high and resolute, and he did not fear failure yet.

So the desperate race flew on. Their feet struck up the powdery snow, their breath smoked into the sharp clear air, and they were gone before the air was cleared of snow and vapour. Now and then Christian glanced up to judge, by the rising of the stars, of the coming of midnight. So long, so long!

White Fell held on without slack. She, it was evident, with confidence in her speed proving matchless, as resolute to outrun her pursuer as he to endure till midnight and fulfil his purpose. And Christian held on, still self-assured. He could not fail. He would not fail. To avenge Rol and Trella was motive enough for him to do what man could do, but for Sweyn more. She had kissed Sweyn, but he should not die too. With Sweyn to save he could not fail.

Never before was such a race as this. No, not when in old Greece man and maid raced together with two fates at stake, for the hard running was sustained unabated, while star after star rose and went wheeling up towards midnight, for one hour, for two hours.

Then Christian saw and heard what shot him through with fear. Where a fringe of trees hung round a slope he saw something dark moving, and heard a yelp, followed by a full horrid cry, and the dark spread out upon the snow, a pack of wolves in pursuit.

Of the beasts alone he had little cause for fear. At the pace he held he could distance them, four-footed though they were. But of White Fell's wiles he had infinite apprehension, for how might she not avail herself of the savage jaws of these wolves, akin as they were to half her nature. She vouchsafed to them nor look nor sign, but Christian, on an impulse to assure himself that she should not escape him, caught and held the back-flung edge of her furs, running still.

She turned like a flash with a beastly snarl, teeth and eyes gleaming again. Her axe shone, on the upstroke, on the downstroke, as she hacked at his hand. She had lopped it off at the wrist, but that he parried with the bear-spear. Even then, she shore through the shaft and shattered the bones of the hand at the same blow, so that he loosed perforce.

Then again they raced on as before, Christian not losing a pace, though his left hand swung useless, bleeding and broken.

The snarl, indubitable, though modified from a woman's organs, the vicious fury revealed in teeth and eyes, the sharp arrogant pain of her maiming blow, caught away Christian's heed of the beasts behind, by striking into him close vivid realisation of the infinitely greater danger that ran before him in that deadly Thing.

When he bethought him to look behind, lo! The pack had but reached their tracks, and instantly slunk aside, cowed, the yell of pursuit changing to yelps and whines. So abhorrent was that fell creature to beast as to man.

She had drawn her furs more closely to her, disposing them so that, instead of flying loose to her heels, no drapery hung lower than her knees, and this without a check to her wonderful speed, nor embarrassment by the cumbering of the folds. She held her head as before. Her lips were firmly set, only the tense nostrils gave her breath, not a sign of distress witnessed to the long sustaining of that terrible speed.

But on Christian by now the strain was telling palpably. His head weighed heavy, and his breath came labouring in great sobs. The bear spear would have been a burden now. His heart was beating like a hammer, but such a dullness oppressed his brain, that it was only by degrees he could realize his helpless state, wounded and weaponless, chasing that terrible Thing, that was a fierce, desperate, axe-armed woman, except she should assume the beast with fangs yet more formidable.

And still the far slow stars went lingering nearly an hour from midnight.

So far was his brain astray that an impression took him that she was fleeing from the midnight stars, whose gain was by such slow degrees that a time equalling days and days had gone in the race round the northern circle of the world, and days and days as long might last before the end, except she slackened, or except he failed.

But he would not fail yet.

How long had he been praying so? He had started with a self-confidence and reliance that had felt no need for that aid, and now it seemed the only means by which to restrain his heart from swelling beyond the compass of his body, by which to cherish his brain from dwindling and shrivelling quite away. Some sharp-toothed creature kept tearing and dragging on his maimed left hand. He never could see it, he could not shake it off, but he prayed it off at times.

The clear stars before him took to shuddering, and he knew why: they shuddered at sight of what was behind him. He had never divined before that strange things hid themselves from men under pretence of being snow-clad mounds or swaying trees, but now they came slipping out from their harmless covers to follow him, and mock at his impotence to make a kindred Thing resolve to truer form. He knew the air behind him was thronged. He heard the hum of innumerable murmurings together, but his eyes could never catch them, they were too swift and nimble. Yet he knew they were there, because, on a backward glance, he saw the snow mounds surge as they grovelled flatlings out of sight. He saw the trees reel as they screwed themselves rigid past recognition among the boughs.

And after such glance the stars for awhile returned to steadfastness, and an infinite stretch of silence froze upon the chill grey world, only deranged by the swift even beat of the flying feet, and his own, slower from the longer stride, and the sound of his breath. And for some clear moments he knew that his only concern was to sustain his speed regardless of pain and distress, to deny with every nerve he had her power to outstrip him or to widen the space between them, till the stars crept up to midnight. Then out again would come that crowd invisible, humming and hustling behind, dense and dark enough, he knew, to blot out the stars at his back, yet ever skipping and jerking from his sight.

A hideous check came to the race. White Fell swirled about and leapt to the right, and Christian, unprepared for so prompt a lurch, found close at his feet a deep pit yawning, and his own impetus past control. But he snatched at her as he bore past, clasping her right arm with his one whole hand, and the two swung together upon the brink.

And her straining away in self preservation was vigorous enough to counter-balance his headlong impulse, and brought them reeling together to safety.

Then, before he was verily sure that they were not to perish so, crashing down, he saw her gnashing in wild pale fury as she wrenched to be free, and since her right hand was in his grasp, used her axe left-handed, striking back at him.

The blow was effectual enough even so. His right arm dropped powerless, gashed, and with the lesser bone broken, that jarred with horrid pain when he let it swing as he leaped out again, and ran to recover the few feet she had gained from his pause at the shock.

The near escape and this new quick pain made again every faculty alive and intense. He knew that what he followed was most surely Death animate. Wounded and helpless, he was utterly at her mercy if so she should realize and take action. Hopeless to avenge, hopeless to save, his very despair for Sweyn swept him on to follow, and follow, and precede the kiss-doomed to death. Could he yet fail to hunt that Thing past midnight, out of the womanly form alluring and treacherous, into lasting restraint of the bestial, which was the last shred of hope left from the confident purpose of the outset?

"Sweyn, Sweyn, O Sweyn!" He thought he was praying, though his heart wrung out nothing but this: "Sweyn, Sweyn,

O Sweyn!"

The last hour from midnight had lost half its quarters, and the stars went lifting up the great minutes, and again his greatening heart, and his shrinking brain, and the sickening agony that swung at either side, conspired to appal the will that had only seeming empire over his feet.

Now White Fell's body was so closely enveloped that not a lap nor an edge flew free. She stretched forward strangely aslant, leaning from the upright poise of a runner. She cleared the ground at times by long bounds, gaining an increase of speed that Christian agonised to equal.

Because the stars pointed that the end was nearing, the black brood came behind again, and followed, noising. Ah! If they could but be kept quiet and still, nor slip their usual harmless masks to encourage with their interest the last speed of their most deadly congener. What shape had they? Should he ever know? If it were not that he was bound to compel the fell Thing that ran before him into her truer form, he might face about and follow them. No, no, not so. If he might do anything but what he did, race, race, and racing bear this agony, he would just stand still and die, to be quit of the pain of breathing.

He grew bewildered, uncertain of his own identity, doubting of his own true form. He could not be really a man, no more than that running Thing was really a woman. His real form was only hidden under embodiment of a man, but what it was he did not know. And Sweyn's real form he did not know. Sweyn lay fallen at his feet, where he had struck him down, his own brother. He stumbled over him, and had to overleap him and race harder because she who had kissed Sweyn leapt so fast. "Sweyn, Sweyn, O Sweyn!"

Why did the stars stop to shudder? Midnight else had surely come!

The leaning, leaping Thing looked back at him with a wild, fierce look, and laughed in savage scorn and triumph. He saw in a flash why, for within a time measurable by seconds she would have escaped him utterly. As the land lay, a slope of ice sunk on the one hand, on the other hand a steep rose, shouldering forwards. Between the two was space for a foot to be planted, but none for a body to stand, yet a juniper bough, thrusting out, gave a handhold secure enough for one with a resolute grasp to swing past the perilous place, and pass on safe.

Though the first seconds of the last moment were going, she dared to flash back a wicked look, and laugh at the pursuer who was impotent to grasp.

The crisis struck convulsive life into his last supreme effort. His will surged up indomitable, his speed proved matchless yet. He leapt with a rush, passed her before her laugh had time to go out, and turned short, barring the way, and braced to withstand her.

She came hurling desperate, with a feint to the right hand, and then launched herself upon him with a spring like a wild beast when it leaps to kill. And he, with one strong arm and a hand that could not hold, with one strong hand and an arm that could not guide and sustain, he caught and held her even so. And they fell together. And because he felt his whole arm slipping, and his whole hand loosing, to slack the dreadful agony of the wrenched bone above, he caught and held with his teeth the tunic at her knee, as she struggled up and wrung off his hands to overleap him victorious.

Like lightning she snatched her axe, and struck him on the neck, deep—once, twice—his life-blood gushed out, staining her feet.

The stars touched midnight.

The death scream he heard was not his, for his set teeth had hardly yet relaxed when it rang out, and the dreadful cry began with a woman's shriek, and changed and ended as the yell of a beast. And before the final blank overtook his dying eyes, he saw that She gave place to It. He saw more, that Life gave place to

Death—causelessly, incomprehensibly.

For he did not presume that no holy water could be more holy, more potent to destroy an evil thing than the life-blood of a pure heart poured out for another in free willing devotion.

His own true hidden reality that he had desired to know grew palpable, recognisable. It seemed to him just this: a great glad abounding hope that he had saved his brother. Too expansive to be contained by the limited form of a sole man, it yearned for a new embodiment infinite as the stars.

What did it matter to that true reality that the man's brain shrank, shrank, till it was nothing. That the man's body could not retain the huge pain of his heart, and heaved it out through the red exit riven at the neck. That the black noise came again hurtling from behind, reinforced by that dissolved shape, and blotted out for ever the man's sight, hearing, sense.

In the early grey of day Sweyn chanced upon the footprints of a man, of a runner, as he saw by the shifted snow, and the direction they had taken aroused curiosity, since a little farther their line must be crossed by the edge of a sheer height. He turned to trace them. And so doing, the length of the stride struck his attention—a stride long as his own if he ran. He knew he was following Christian.

In his anger he had hardened himself to be indifferent to the night-long absence of his brother, but now, seeing where the footsteps went, he was seized with compunction and dread. He had failed to give thought and care to his poor frantic twin, who might—was it possible?—have rushed to a frantic death.

His heart stood still when he came to the place where the leap had been taken. A piled edge of snow had fallen too, and nothing but snow lay below when he peered. Along the upper edge he ran for a furlong, till he came to a dip where he could slip and climb down, and then back again on the lower level to the pile of fallen snow. There he saw that the vigorous running had started afresh.

He stood pondering, vexed that any man should have taken that leap where he had not ventured to follow, vexed that he had been beguiled to such painful emotions, guessing vainly at Christian's object in this mad freak. He began sauntering along, half unconsciously following his brother's track, and so in a while he came to the place where the footprints were doubled.

Small prints were these others, small as a woman's, though the pace from one to another was longer than that which the skirts of women allow.

Did not White Fell tread so?

A dreadful guess appalled him, so dreadful that he recoiled from belief. Yet his face grew ashy white, and he gasped to fetch back motion to his checked heart. Unbelievable? Closer attention showed how the smaller footfall had altered for greater speed, striking into the snow with a deeper onset and a lighter pressure on the heels. Unbelievable? Could any woman but White Fell run so? Could any man but Christian run so? The guess became a certainty. He was following where alone in the dark night White Fell had fled from Christian pursuing.

Such villainy set heart and brain on fire with rage and indignation: such villainy in his own brother, till lately love-worthy, praiseworthy, though a fool for meekness. He would kill Christian; had he lives many as the footprints he had trodden, vengeance should demand them all. In a tempest of murderous hate he followed on in haste, for the track was plain enough, starting with such a burst of speed as could not be maintained, but brought him back soon to a plod for the spent, sobbing breath to be regulated. He cursed Christian aloud and called White Fell's name on high in a frenzied expense of passion. His grief itself was a rage, being such an intolerable anguish of pity and shame at the thought of his love, White Fell, who had parted from his kiss free and radiant, to be hounded straightway by his brother mad with jealousy, fleeing for more than life while her lover was housed at his ease. If he had but known, he raved, in impotent rebellion at the cruelty of events, if he had but known that his strength and love might have availed in her defence. Now the only service to her that he could render was to kill Christian.

As a woman he knew she was matchless in speed, matchless in strength, but Christian was matchless in speed among men, nor easily to be matched in strength. Brave and swift and strong though she were, what chance had she against a man of his strength and inches, frantic, too, and intent on horrid revenge against his brother, his successful rival?

Mile after mile he followed with a bursting heart. More piteous, more tragic, seemed the case at this evidence of White Fell's splendid supremacy, holding her own so long against Christian's famous speed. So long, so long that his love and admiration grew more and more boundless, and his grief and indignation therewith also. Whenever the track lay clear he ran, with such reckless prodigality of strength, that it soon was spent, and he dragged on heavily, till, sometimes on the ice of a mere, sometimes on a wind-swept place, all signs were lost, but, so undeviating had been their line that a course straight on, and then short questing to either hand, recovered them again.

Hour after hour had gone by through more than half that winter day, before ever he came to the place where the trampled snow showed that a scurry of feet had come—and gone! Wolves' feet—and gone most amazingly! Only a little beyond he came to the lopped point of Christian's bear-spear. Farther on he would see where the remnant of the useless shaft had been dropped. The snow here was dashed with blood, and the footsteps of the two had fallen closer together. Some hoarse sound of exultation came from him that might have been a laugh had breath sufficed. "O White Fell, my poor, brave love! Well struck!" he groaned, torn by his pity and great admiration, as he guessed surely how she had turned and dealt a blow.

The sight of the blood inflamed him as it might a beast that ravens. He grew mad with a desire to have Christian by the throat once again, not to loose this time till he had crushed out his life, or beat out his life, or stabbed out his life, or all these, and torn him piecemeal likewise, and ah, then, not till then, bleed his heart with weeping, like a child, like a girl, over the piteous fate of his poor lost love.

On, on, on through the aching time, toiling and straining in the track of those two superb runners, aware of the marvel of their endurance, but unaware of the marvel of their speed, that, in the three hours before midnight had overpassed all that vast distance that he could only traverse from twilight to twilight. For clear daylight was passing when he came to the edge of an old marl-pit, and saw how the two who had gone before had stamped and trampled together in desperate peril on the verge. And here fresh blood stains spoke to him of a valiant defence against his infamous brother, and he followed where the blood had dripped till the cold had staunched its flow, taking a savage gratification from this evidence that Christian had been gashed deeply, maddening afresh with desire to do likewise more excellently, and so slake his murderous hate. And he began to know that through all his despair he had entertained a germ of hope, that grew apace, rained upon by his brother's blood.

He strove on as best he might, wrung now by an access of hope, now of despair, in agony to reach the end, however terrible, sick with the aching of the toiled miles that deferred it.

And the light went lingering out of the sky, giving place to uncertain stars.

He came to the finish.

Two bodies lay in a narrow place. Christian's was one, but the other beyond not White Fell's. There where the footsteps ended lay a great white wolf.

At the sight Sweyn's strength was blasted. Body and soul he was struck down grovelling.

The stars had grown sure and intense before he stirred from

where he had dropped prone. Very feebly he crawled to his dead brother, and laid his hands upon him, and crouched so, afraid to look or stir farther.

Cold, stiff, hours dead. Yet the dead body was his only shelter and stay in that most dreadful hour. His soul, stripped bare of all skeptic comfort, cowered, shivering, naked, abject, and the living clung to the dead out of piteous need for grace from the soul that had passed away.

He rose to his knees, lifting the body. Christian had fallen face forward in the snow, with his arms flung up and wide, and so had the frost made him rigid, strange, ghastly, unyielding to Sweyn's lifting, so that he laid him down again and crouched above, with his arms fast round him, and a low heart-wrung groan.

When at last he found force to raise his brother's body and gather it in his arms, tight clasped to his breast, he tried to face the Thing that lay beyond. The sight set his limbs in a palsy with horror and dread. His senses had failed and fainted in utter cowardice, but for the strength that came from holding dead Christian in his arms, enabling him to compel his eyes to endure the sight, and take into the brain the complete aspect of the Thing. No wound, only blood stains on the feet. The great grim jaws had a savage grin, though dead-stiff. And his kiss: he could bear it no longer, and turned away, nor ever looked again.

And the dead man in his arms, knowing the full horror, had followed and faced it for his sake, had suffered agony and death for his sake. In the neck was the deep death gash, one arm and both hands were dark with frozen blood, for his sake! Dead he knew him, as in life he had not known him, to give the right meed of love and worship. Because the outward man lacked perfection and strength equal to his, he had taken the love and worship of that great pure heart as his due; he, so unworthy in the inner reality, so mean, so despicable, callous, and contemptuous towards the brother who had laid down his life to save him. He longed for utter annihilation, that so he might lose the agony of knowing himself so unworthy of such perfect love. The frozen calm of death on the face appalled him. He dared not touch it with lips that had cursed so lately, with lips fouled by kiss of the horror that had been death.

He struggled to his feet, still clasping Christian. The dead man stood upright within his arm, frozen rigid. The eyes were not quite closed. The head had stiffened, bowed slightly to one side. The arms stayed straight and wide. It was the figure of one crucified, the blood-stained hands also conforming.

So living and dead went back along the track that one had passed in the deepest passion of love, and one in the deepest passion of hate. All that night Sweyn toiled through the snow, bearing the weight of dead Christian, treading back along the steps he before had trodden, when he was wronging with vilest thoughts, and cursing with murderous hatred, the brother who all the while lay dead for his sake.

Cold, silence, darkness encompassed the strong man bowed with the dolorous burden, and yet he knew surely that that night he entered hell, and trod hell-fire along the homeward road, and endured through it only because Christian was with him. And he knew surely that to him Christian had been as Christ, and had suffered and died to save him from his sins.

The Camp of the Dog

by Algernon Blackwood

I

Islands of all shapes and sizes troop northward from Stockholm by the hundred, and the little steamer that threads their intricate mazes in summer leaves the traveller in a somewhat bewildered state as regards the points of the compass when it reaches the end of its journey at Waxholm. But it is only after Waxholm that the true islands begin, so to speak, to run wild, and start up the coast on their tangled course of a hundred miles of deserted loveliness, and it was in the very heart of this delightful confusion that we pitched our tents for a summer holiday. A veritable wilderness of islands lay about us: from the mere round button of a rock that bore a single fir, to the mountainous stretch of a square mile, densely wooded, and bounded by precipitous cliffs, so close together often that a strip of water ran between no wider than a country lane, or, again, so far that an expanse stretched like the open sea for miles.

Although the larger islands boasted farms and fishing stations, the majority were uninhabited. Carpeted with moss and heather, their coast-lines showed a series of ravines and clefts and little sandy bays, with a growth of splendid pine-woods that came down to the water's edge and led the eye through unknown depths of shadow and mystery into the very heart of primitive forest.

The particular islands to which we had camping rights by virtue of paying a nominal sum to a Stockholm merchant lay together in a picturesque group far beyond the reach of the steamer, one being a mere reef with a fringe of fairy-like birches, and two others, cliff-bound monsters rising with wooded heads out of the sea. The fourth, which we selected because it enclosed a little lagoon suitable for anchorage, bathing, night-lines, and what-not, shall have what description is necessary as the story proceeds, but, so far as paying rent was concerned, we might equally well have pitched our tents on any one of a hundred others that clustered about us as thickly as a swarm of bees.

It was in the blaze of an evening in July, the air clear as crystal, the sea a cobalt blue, when we left the steamer on the borders of civilisation and sailed away with maps, compasses, and provisions for the little group of dots in the Skägård that were to be our home for the next two months. The dinghy and my Canadian canoe trailed behind us, with tents and dunnage carefully piled aboard, and when the point of cliff intervened to hide the steamer and the Waxholm hotel we realized for the first time that the horror of trains and houses was far behind us, the fever of men and cities, the weariness of streets and confined spaces. The wilderness opened up on all sides into endless blue reaches, and the map and compasses were so frequently called into requisition that we went astray more often than not and progress was enchantingly slow. It took us, for instance, two whole days to find our crescent-shaped home, and the camps we made on the way were so fascinating that we left them with difficulty and regret, for each island seemed more desirable than the one before it, and over all lay the spell of haunting peace, remoteness from the turmoil of the world, and the freedom of open and desolate spaces.

And so many of these spots of world-beauty have I sought out and dwelt in, that in my mind remains only a composite memory of their faces, a true map of heaven, as it were, from which this particular one stands forth with unusual sharpness because of the strange things that happened there, and also, I think, because anything in which John Silence played a part has a habit of fixing itself in the mind with a living and lasting quality of vividness.

For the moment, however, Dr. Silence was not of the party. Some private case in the interior of Hungary claimed his attention, and it was not till later—the 15th of August, to be exact—that I had arranged to meet him in Berlin and then return to London together for our harvest of winter work. All the members of our party, however, were known to him more or less well, and on this third day as we sailed through the narrow opening into the lagoon and saw the circular ridge of trees in a gold and crimson sunset before us, his last words to me when we parted in London for some unaccountable reason came back very sharply to my memory, and recalled the curious impression of prophecy with which I had first heard them:

"Enjoy your holiday and store up all the force you can," he had said as the train slipped out of Victoria, "and we will meet in Berlin on the 15th, unless you should send for me sooner."

And now suddenly the words returned to me so clearly that it seemed I almost heard his voice in my ear, "Unless you should send for me sooner," and returned, moreover, with a significance I was wholly at a loss to understand that touched somewhere in the depths of my mind a vague sense of apprehension that they had all along been intended in the nature of a prophecy.

In the lagoon, then, the wind failed us this July evening, as was only natural behind the shelter of the belt of woods, and we took to the oars, all breathless with the beauty of this first sight of our island home, yet all talking in somewhat hushed voices of the best place to land, the depth of water, the safest place to anchor, to put up the tents in, the most sheltered spot for the campfires, and a dozen things of importance that crop up when a home in the wilderness has actually to be made.

And during this busy sunset hour of unloading before the dark, the souls of my companions adopted the trick of presenting themselves very vividly anew before my mind, and introducing themselves afresh.

In reality, I suppose, our party was in no sense singular. In the conventional life at home they certainly seemed ordinary enough, but suddenly, as we passed through these gates of the wilderness, I saw them more sharply than before, with characters stripped of the atmosphere of men and cities. A complete change of setting often furnishes a startlingly new view of people hitherto held for well-known. They present another facet of their personalities. I seemed to see my own party almost as new people—people I had not known properly hitherto, people who would drop all disguises and henceforth reveal themselves as they really were. And each one seemed to say, "Now you will see me as I am. You will see me here in this primitive life of the wilderness without clothes. All my masks and veils I have left behind in the abodes of men. So, look out for surprises!"

The Reverend Timothy Maloney helped me to put up the tents, long practice making the process easy, and while he drove in pegs and tightened ropes, his coat off, his flannel collar flying open without a tie, it was impossible to avoid the conclusion that he was cut out for the life of a pioneer rather than the church. He was fifty years of age, muscular, blue-eyed and hearty, and he took his share of the work, and more, without shirking. The way he handled the axe in cutting down saplings for the tent-poles was a delight to see, and his eye in judging the level was unfailing.

Bullied as a young man into a lucrative family living, he had in turn bullied his mind into some semblance of orthodox beliefs, doing the honours of the little country church with an energy that made one think of a coal-heaver tending china, and it was only in the past few years that he had resigned the living and taken instead to cramming young men for their examinations. This suited him better. It enabled him, too, to indulge his passion for spells of "wild life," and to spend the summer months of most years under canvas in one part of the world or another where he could take his young men with him and combine "reading" with open air.

His wife usually accompanied him, and there was no doubt she enjoyed the trips, for she possessed, though in less degree, the same joy of the wilderness that was his own distinguishing characteristic. The only difference was that while he regarded it as the real life, she regarded it as an interlude. While he camped out with his heart and mind, she played at camping out with her clothes and body. None the less, she made a splendid companion, and to watch her busy cooking dinner over the fire we had built among the stones was to understand that her heart was in the business for the moment and that she was happy even with the detail.

Mrs. Maloney at home, knitting in the sun and believing that the world was made in six days, was one woman, but Mrs. Maloney, standing with bare arms over the smoke of a wood fire under the pine trees, was another, and Peter Sangree, the Canadian pupil, with his pale skin, and his loose, though not ungainly figure, stood beside her in very unfavourable contrast as he scraped potatoes and sliced bacon with slender white fingers that seemed better suited to hold a pen than a knife. She ordered him about like a slave, and he obeyed, too, with willing pleasure, for in spite of his general appearance of debility he was as happy to be in camp as any of them.

But more than any other member of the party, Joan Maloney, the daughter, was the one who seemed a natural and genuine part of the landscape, who belonged to it all just in the same way that the trees and the moss and the grey rocks running out into the water belonged to it. For she was obviously in her right and natural setting, a creature of the wilds, a gipsy in her own home.

To any one with a discerning eye this would have been more or less apparent, but to me, who had known her during all the twenty-two years of her life and was familiar with the ins and outs of her primitive, utterly un-modern type, it was strikingly clear. To see her there made it impossible to imagine her again in civilisation. I lost all recollection of how she looked in a town. The memory somehow evaporated. This slim creature before me, flitting to and fro with the grace of the woodland life, swift, supple, adroit, on her knees blowing the fire, or stirring the frying-pan through a veil of smoke, suddenly seemed the only way I had ever really seen her. Here she was at home, in London she became some one concealed by clothes, an artificial doll overdressed and moving by clockwork, only a portion of her alive. Here she was alive all over.

I forget altogether how she was dressed, just as I forget how any particular tree was dressed, or how the markings ran on any one of the boulders that lay about the camp. She looked just as wild and natural and untamed as everything else that went to make up the scene, and more than that I cannot say.

Pretty, she was decidedly not. She was thin, skinny, dark-haired, and possessed of great physical strength in the form of endurance. She had, too, something of the force and vigorous purpose of a man, tempestuous sometimes and wild to passionate, frightening her mother, and puzzling her easy-going father with her storms of waywardness, while at the same time she stirred his admiration by her violence. A pagan of the pagans she was besides, and with some haunting suggestion of old-world pagan beauty about her dark face and eyes. Altogether an odd and difficult character, but with a generosity and high courage that made her very lovable.

In town life she always seemed to me to feel cramped, bored, a devil in a cage, in her eyes a hunted expression as though any moment she dreaded to be caught. But up in these spacious solitudes all this disappeared. Away from the limitations that plagued and stung her, she would show at her best, and as I watched her moving about the camp I repeatedly found myself thinking of a wild creature that had just obtained its freedom and was trying its muscles.

Peter Sangree, of course, at once went down before her. But

she was so obviously beyond his reach, and besides so well able to take care of herself, that I think her parents gave the matter but little thought, and he himself worshipped at a respectful distance, keeping admirable control of his passion in all respects save one, for at his age the eyes are difficult to master, and the yearning, almost the devouring, expression often visible in them was probably there unknown even to himself. He, better than any one else, understood that he had fallen in love with something most hard of attainment, something that drew him to the very edge of life, and almost beyond it. It, no doubt, was a secret and terrible joy to him, this passionate worship from afar, only I think he suffered more than any one guessed, and that his want of vitality was due in large measure to the constant stream of unsatisfied yearning that poured forever from his soul and body. Moreover, it seemed to me, who now saw them for the first time together, that there was an unnamable something, an elusive quality of some kind, that marked them as belonging to the same world, and that although the girl ignored him she was secretly, and perhaps unknown to herself, drawn by some attribute very deep in her own nature to some quality equally deep in his.

This, then, was the party when we first settled down into our two months' camp on the island in the Baltic Sea. Other figures flitted from time to time across the scene, and sometimes one reading man, sometimes another, came to join us and spend his four hours a day in the clergyman's tent, but they came for short periods only, and they went without leaving much trace in my memory, and certainly they played no important part in what subsequently happened.

The weather favoured us that night, so that by sunset the tents were up, the boats unloaded, a store of wood collected and chopped into lengths, and the candle lanterns hung round ready for lighting on the trees. Sangree, too, had picked deep mattresses of balsam boughs for the women's beds, and had cleared little paths of brushwood from their tents to the central fireplace. All was prepared for bad weather. It was a cosy supper and a well-cooked one that we sat down to and ate under the stars, and, according to the clergyman, the only meal fit to eat we had seen since we left London a week before.

The deep stillness, after that roar of steamers, trains, and tourists, held something that thrilled, for as we lay round the fire there was no sound but the faint sighing of the pines and the soft lapping of the waves along the shore and against the sides of the boat in the lagoon. The ghostly outline of her white sails was just visible through the trees, idly rocking to and fro in her calm anchorage, her sheets flapping gently against the mast. Beyond lay the dim blue shapes of other islands floating in the night, and from all the great spaces about us came the murmur of the sea and the soft breathing of great woods. The odours of the wilderness, smells of wind and earth, of trees and water, clean, vigorous, and mighty, were the true odours of a virgin world un-spoilt by men, more penetrating and more subtly intoxicating than any other perfume in the whole world. Oh, and dangerous-ly strong, too, no doubt, for some natures!

"Ahhh!" breathed out the clergyman after supper, with an indescribable gesture of satisfaction and relief. "Here there is freedom, and room for body and mind to turn in. Here one can work and rest and play. Here one can be alive and absorb some-thing of the earth-forces that never get within touching distance in the cities. By George, I shall make a permanent camp here and come when it is time to die!"

The good man was merely giving vent to his delight at being under canvas. He said the same thing every year, and he said it often. But it more or less expressed the superficial feelings of us all. And when, a little later, he turned to compliment his wife on the fried potatoes, and discovered that she was snoring, with her back against a tree, he grunted with content at the sight and put a ground-sheet over her feet, as if it were the most natural thing in the world for her to fall asleep after dinner, and then moved back to his own corner, smoking his pipe with great satisfaction.

And I, smoking mine too, lay and fought against the most delicious sleep imaginable, while my eyes wandered from the fire to the stars peeping through the branches, and then back again to the group about me. The Rev. Timothy soon let his pipe go out, and succumbed as his wife had done, for he had worked hard and eaten well. Sangree, also smoking, leaned against a tree with his gaze fixed on the girl, a depth of yearning in his face that he could not hide, and that really distressed me for him. And Joan herself, with wide staring eyes, alert, full of the new forces of the place, evidently keyed up by the magic of finding herself among all the things her soul recognised as "home," sat rigid by the fire, her thoughts roaming through the spaces, the blood stirring about her heart. She was as unconscious of the Canadian's gaze as she was that her parents both slept. She looked to me more like a tree, or something that had grown out of the island, than a living girl of the century, and when I spoke across to her in a whisper and suggested a tour of investigation, she started and looked up at me as though she heard a voice in her dreams.

Sangree leaped up and joined us, and without waking the others we three went over the ridge of the island and made our way down to the shore behind. The water lay like a lake before us still coloured by the sunset. The air was keen and scented, wafting the smell of the wooded islands that hung about us in the darkening air. Very small waves tumbled softly on the sand. The sea was sown with stars, and everywhere breathed and pulsed the beauty of the northern summer night. I confess I speedily lost consciousness of the human presences beside me, and I have little doubt Joan did too. Only Sangree felt otherwise, I suppose, for presently we heard him sighing, and I can well imagine that he absorbed the whole wonder and passion of the scene into his aching heart, to swell the pain there that was more searching even than the pain at the sight of such matchless and incomprehensible beauty.

The splash of a fish jumping broke the spell.

"I wish we had the canoe now," remarked Joan. "We could paddle out to the other islands."

"Of course," I said, "wait here and I'll go across for it," and was turning to feel my way back through the darkness when she stopped me in a voice that meant what it said.

"No. Mr. Sangree will get it. We will wait here and 'cooee!' to guide him."

The Canadian was off in a moment, for she had only to hint of her wishes and he obeyed.

"Keep out from shore in case of rocks," I cried out as he went, "and turn to the right out of the lagoon. That's the shortest way round by the map."

My voice travelled across the still waters and woke echoes in the distant islands that came back to us like people calling out of space. It was only thirty or forty yards over the ridge and down the other side to the lagoon where the boats lay, but it was a good mile to coast round the shore in the dark to where we stood and waited. We heard him stumbling away among the boulders, and then the sounds suddenly ceased as he topped the ridge and went down past the fire on the other side.

"I didn't want to be left alone with him," the girl said presently in a low voice. "I'm always afraid he's going to say or do something..." She hesitated a moment, looking quickly over her shoulder towards the ridge where he had just disappeared. "...something that might lead to unpleasantness."

She stopped abruptly.

"You, frightened, Joan!?" I exclaimed, with genuine surprise. "This is a new light on your wicked character. I thought the human being who could frighten you did not exist." Then I suddenly realized she was talking seriously, looking to me for help of some kind, and at once I dropped the teasing attitude.

"He's very far gone, I think, Joan," I added gravely. "You

must be kind to him, whatever else you may feel. He's exceedingly fond of you."

"I know, but I can't help it," she whispered, lest her voice should carry in the stillness. "There's something about him that, that makes me feel creepy and half afraid."

"But, poor man, it's not his fault if he is delicate and sometimes looks like death," I laughed gently, by way of defending what I felt to be a very innocent member of my sex.

"Oh, but it's not that I mean," she answered quickly, "it's something I feel about him, something in his soul, something he hardly knows himself, but that may come out if we are much together. It draws me, I feel, tremendously. It stirs what is wild in me, deep down, oh, very deep down, yet at the same time makes me feel afraid."

"I suppose his thoughts are always playing about you," I said, "but he's nice-minded and—"

"Yes, yes," she interrupted impatiently, "I can trust myself absolutely with him. He's gentle and singularly pure-minded. But there's something else that—" She stopped again sharply to listen. Then she came up close beside me in the darkness, whispering, "You know, Mr. Hubbard, sometimes my intuitions warn me a little too strongly to be ignored. Oh, yes, you needn't tell me again that it's difficult to distinguish between fancy and intuition. I know all that. But I also know that there's something deep down in that man's soul that calls to something deep down in mine. And at present it frightens me. Because I cannot make out what it is, and I know, I know, he'll do something some day that, that will shake my life to the very bottom." She laughed a little at the strangeness of her own description.

I turned to look at her more closely, but the darkness was too great to show her face. There was an intensity, almost of suppressed passion, in her voice that took me completely by surprise.

"Nonsense, Joan," I said, a little severely, "you know him

well. He's been with your father for months now."

"But that was in London, and up here it's different—I mean, I feel that it may be different. Life in a place like this blows away the restraints of the artificial life at home. I know, oh, I know what I'm saying. I feel all untied in a place like this. The rigidity of one's nature begins to melt and flow. Surely you must understand what I mean!"

"Of course I understand," I replied, yet not wishing to encourage her in her present line of thought, "and it's a grand experience, for a short time. But you're overtired tonight, Joan, like the rest of us. A few days in this air will set you above all fears of the kind you mention."

Then, after a moment's silence, I added, feeling I should estrange her confidence altogether if I blundered any more and treated her like a child, "I think, perhaps, the true explanation is that you pity him for loving you, and at the same time you feel the repulsion of the healthy, vigorous animal for what is weak and timid. If he came up boldly and took you by the throat and shouted that he would force you to love him, well, then you would feel no fear at all. You would know exactly how to deal with him. Isn't it, perhaps, something of that kind?"

The girl made no reply, and when I took her hand I felt that it trembled a little and was cold.

"It's not his love that I'm afraid of," she said hurriedly, for at this moment we heard the dip of a paddle in the water, "it's something in his very soul that terrifies me in a way I have never been terrified before, yet fascinates me. In town I was hardly conscious of his presence. But the moment we got away from civilisation, it began to come. He seems so, so real up here. I dread being alone with him. It makes me feel that something must burst and tear its way out, that he would do something, or I should do something, I don't know exactly what I mean, probably, but that I should let myself go and scream—"

"Joan!"

"Don't be alarmed," she laughed shortly. "I shan't do any-thing silly, but I wanted to tell you my feelings in case I needed your help. When I have intuitions as strong as this they are never wrong, only I don't know yet what it means exactly."

"You must hold out for the month, at any rate," I said in as matter-of-fact a voice as I could manage, for her manner had somehow changed my surprise to a subtle sense of alarm. "Sangree only stays the month, you know. And, anyhow, you are such an odd creature yourself that you should feel generously towards other odd creatures," I ended lamely, with a forced laugh.

She gave my hand a sudden pressure. "I'm glad I've told you at any rate," she said quickly under her breath, for the canoe was now gliding up silently like a ghost to our feet, "and I'm glad you're here, too," she added as we moved down towards the water to meet it.

I made Sangree change into the bows and got into the steer-ing seat myself, putting the girl between us so that I could watch them both by keeping their outlines against the sea and stars. For the intuitions of certain folk, women and children usually, I confess, I have always felt a great respect that has more often than not been justified by experience, and now the curious emotion stirred in me by the girl's words remained somewhat vividly in my consciousness. I explained it in some measure by the fact that the girl, tired out by the fatigue of many days' travel, had suffered a vigorous reaction of some kind from the strong, desolate scenery, and further, perhaps, that she had been treated to my own experience of seeing the members of the party in a new light, the Canadian, being partly a stranger, more vividly than the rest of us. But, at the same time, I felt it was quite possi-ble that she had sensed some subtle link between his personality and her own, some quality that she had hitherto ignored and that the routine of town life had kept buried out of sight. The only thing that seemed difficult to explain was the fear she had spoken of, and this I hoped the wholesome effects of camp life and exercise would sweep away naturally in the course of time.

We made the tour of the island without speaking. It was all too beautiful for speech. The trees crowded down to the shore to hear us pass. We saw their fine dark heads, bowed low with splendid dignity to watch us, forgetting for a moment that the stars were caught in the needled network of their hair. Against the sky in the west, where still lingered the sunset gold, we saw the wild toss of the horizon, shaggy with forest and cliff, gripping the heart like the motive in a symphony, and sending the sense of beauty all a-shiver through the mind, all these surrounding islands standing above the water like low clouds, and like them seeming to post along silently into the engulfing night. We heard the musical drip-drip of the paddle, and the little wash of our waves on the shore, and then suddenly we found ourselves at the opening of the lagoon again, having made the complete circuit of our home.

The Reverend Timothy had awakened from sleep and was singing to himself, and the sound of his voice as we glided down the fifty yards of enclosed water was pleasant to hear and undeniably wholesome. We saw the glow of the fire up among the trees on the ridge, and his shadow moving about as he threw on more wood.

"There you are!" he called aloud. "Good again! Been setting the night-lines, eh? Capital! And your mother's still fast asleep, Joan."

His cheery laugh floated across the water. He had not been in the least disturbed by our absence, for old campers are not easily alarmed.

"Now, remember," he went on, after we had told our little tale of travel by the fire, and Mrs. Maloney had asked for the fourth time exactly where her tent was and whether the door faced east or south, "every one takes their turn at cooking break-fast, and one of the men is always out at sunrise to catch it first. Hubbard, I'll toss you which you do in the morning and which

I do!" He lost the toss. "Then I'll catch it," I said, laughing at his discomfiture, for I knew he loathed stirring porridge. "And mind you don't burn it as you did every blessed time last year on the Volga," I added by way of reminder.

Mrs. Maloney's fifth interruption about the door of her tent, and her further pointed observation that it was past nine o'clock, set us lighting lanterns and putting the fire out for safety.

But before we separated for the night the clergyman had a time-honoured little ritual of his own to go through that no one had the heart to deny him. He always did this. It was a relic of his pulpit habits. He glanced briefly from one to the other of us, his face grave and earnest, his hands lifted to the stars and his eyes all closed and puckered up beneath a momentary frown. Then he offered up a short, almost inaudible prayer, thanking Heaven for our safe arrival, begging for good weather, no illness or accidents, plenty of fish, and strong sailing winds.

And then, unexpectedly, no one knew why exactly, he ended up with an abrupt request that nothing from the kingdom of darkness should be allowed to afflict our peace, and no evil thing come near to disturb us in the night-time.

And while he uttered these last surprising words, so strangely unlike his usual ending, it chanced that I looked up and let my eyes wander round the group assembled about the dying fire. And it certainly seemed to me that Sangree's face underwent a sudden and visible alteration. He was staring at Joan, and as he stared the change ran over it like a shadow and was gone. I started in spite of myself, for something oddly concentrated, potent, collected, had come into the expression usually so scattered and feeble. But it was all swift as a passing meteor, and when I looked a second time his face was normal and he was looking among the trees.

And Joan, luckily, had not observed him, her head being bowed and her eyes tightly closed while her father prayed.

"The girl has a vivid imagination indeed," I thought, half

laughing, as I lit the lanterns, "if her thoughts can put a glamour upon mine in this way", and yet somehow, when we said goodnight, I took occasion to give her a few vigorous words of encouragement, and went to her tent to make sure I could find it quickly in the night in case anything happened. In her quick way the girl understood and thanked me, and the last thing I heard as I moved off to the men's quarters was Mrs. Maloney crying that there were beetles in her tent, and Joan's laughter as she went to help her turn them out.

Half an hour later the island was silent as the grave, but for the mournful voices of the wind as it sighed up from the sea. Like white sentries stood the three tents of the men on one side of the ridge, and on the other side, half hidden by some birches, whose leaves just shivered as the breeze caught them, the women's tents, patches of ghostly grey, gathered more closely together for mutual shelter and protection. Something like fifty yards of broken ground, grey rock, moss and lichen, lay between, and over all lay the curtain of the night and the great whispering winds from the forests of Scandinavia.

And the very last thing, just before floating away on that mighty wave that carries one so softly off into the deeps of forgetfulness, I again heard the voice of John Silence as the train moved out of Victoria Station, and by some subtle connection that met me on the very threshold of consciousness there rose in my mind simultaneously the memory of the girl's half-given confidence, and of her distress. As by some wizardry of approaching dreams they seemed in that instant to be related, but before I could analyse the why and the wherefore, both sank away out of sight again, and I was off beyond recall.

"Unless you should send for me sooner."

II

Whether Mrs. Maloney's tent door opened south or east I

think she never discovered, for it is quite certain she always slept with the flap tightly fastened. I only know that my own little "five by seven, all silk" faced due east, because next morning the sun, pouring in as only the wilderness sun knows how to pour, woke me early, and a moment later, with a short run over soft moss and a flying dive from the granite ledge, I was swimming in the most sparkling water imaginable.

It was barely four o'clock, and the sun came down a long vista of blue islands that led out to the open sea and Finland. Nearer by rose the wooded domes of our own property, still capped and wreathed with smoky trails of fast-melting mist, and looking as fresh as though it was the morning of Mrs. Maloney's Sixth Day and they had just issued, clean and brilliant, from the hands of the great Architect.

In the open spaces the ground was drenched with dew, and from the sea a cool salt wind stole in among the trees and set the branches trembling in an atmosphere of shimmering silver. The tents shone white where the sun caught them in patches. Below lay the lagoon, still dreaming of the summer night. In the open the fish were jumping busily, sending musical ripples towards the shore, and in the air hung the magic of dawn—silent, in-communicable.

I lit the fire, so that an hour later the clergyman should find good ashes to stir his porridge over, and then set forth upon an examination of the island, but hardly had I gone a dozen yards when I saw a figure standing a little in front of me where the sunlight fell in a pool among the trees.

It was Joan. She had already been up an hour, she told me, and had bathed before the last stars had left the sky. I saw at once that the new spirit of this solitary region had entered into her, banishing the fears of the night, for her face was like the face of a happy denizen of the wilderness, and her eyes stainless and shining. Her feet were bare, and drops of dew she had shaken from the branches hung in her loose-flying hair. Obviously she had come into her own.

"I've been all over the island," she announced laughingly, "and there are two things wanting."

"You're a good judge, Joan. What are they?"

"There's no animal life, and there's no... water."

"They go together," I said. "Animals don't bother with a rock like this unless there's a spring on it."

And as she led me from place to place, happy and excited, leaping adroitly from rock to rock, I was glad to note that my first impressions were correct. She made no reference to our conversation of the night before. The new spirit had driven out the old. There was no room in her heart for fear or anxiety, and Nature had everything her own way.

The island, we found, was some three-quarters of a mile from point to point, built in a circle, or wide horseshoe, with an opening of twenty feet at the mouth of the lagoon. Pine trees grew thickly all over, but here and there were patches of silver birch, scrub oak, and considerable colonies of wild raspberry and gooseberry bushes. The two ends of the horseshoe formed bare slabs of smooth granite running into the sea and forming dangerous reefs just below the surface, but the rest of the island rose in a forty-foot ridge and sloped down steeply to the sea on either side, being nowhere more than a hundred yards wide.

The outer shoreline was much indented with numberless coves and bays and sandy beaches, with here and there caves and precipitous little cliffs against which the sea broke in spray and thunder. But the inner shore, the shore of the lagoon, was low and regular, and so well protected by the wall of trees along the ridge that no storm could ever send more than a passing ripple along its sandy marges. Eternal shelter reigned there.

On one of the other islands, a few hundred yards away—for the rest of the party slept late this first morning, and we took to the canoe—we discovered a spring of fresh water untainted by the brackish flavour of the Baltic, and having thus solved the most important problem of the camp, we next proceeded to deal with the second—fish. And in half an hour we reeled in and turned homewards, for we had no means of storage, and to clean more fish than may be stored or eaten in a day is no wise occupation for experienced campers.

And as we landed towards six o'clock we heard the clergyman singing as usual and saw his wife and Sangree shaking out their blankets in the sun, and dressed in a fashion that finally dispelled all memories of streets and civilisation.

"The Little People lit the fire for me," cried Maloney, looking natural and at home in his ancient flannel suit and breaking off in the middle of his singing, "so I've got the porridge going, and this time it's not burnt."

We reported the discovery of water and held up the fish.

"Good! Good again!" he cried. "We'll have the first decent breakfast we've had this year. Sangree'll clean 'em in no time, and the Bo'sun's Mate—"

"Will fry them to a turn," laughed the voice of Mrs. Maloney, appearing on the scene in a tight blue jersey and sandals, and catching up the frying pan. Her husband always called her the Bo'sun's Mate in camp, because it was her duty, among others, to pipe all hands to meals.

"And as for you, Joan," went on the happy man, "you look like the spirit of the island, with moss in your hair and wind in your eyes, and sun and stars mixed in your face." He looked at her with delighted admiration. "Here, Sangree, take these twelve, there's a good fellow, they're the biggest, and we'll have 'em in butter in less time than you can say Baltic island!"

I watched the Canadian as he slowly moved off to the cleaning pail. His eyes were drinking in the girl's beauty, and a wave of passionate, almost feverish, joy passed over his face, expressive of the ecstasy of true worship more than anything else. Perhaps he was thinking that he still had three weeks to come with that vision always before his eyes. Perhaps he was thinking of his dreams in the night. I cannot say. But I noticed the curious mingling of yearning and happiness in his eyes, and the strength of the impression touched my curiosity. Something in his face held my gaze for a second, something to do with its intensity. That so timid, so gentle a personality should conceal so virile a passion almost seemed to require explanation.

But the impression was momentary, for that first breakfast in camp permitted no divided attentions, and I dare swear that the porridge, the tea, the Swedish "flatbread," and the fried fish flavoured with points of frizzled bacon, were better than any meal eaten elsewhere that day in the whole world.

The first clear day in a new camp is always a furiously busy one, and we soon dropped into the routine upon which in large measure the real comfort of every one depends. About the cooking-fire, greatly improved with stones from the shore, we built a high stockade consisting of upright poles thickly twined with branches, the roof lined with moss and lichen and weighted with rocks, and round the interior we made low wooden seats so that we could lie round the fire even in rain and eat our meals in peace. Paths, too, outlined themselves from tent to tent, from the bathing places and the landing stage, and a fair division of the island was decided upon between the quarters of the men and the women. Wood was stacked, awkward trees and boulders removed, hammocks slung, and tents strengthened. In a word, camp was established, and duties were assigned and accepted as though we expected to live on this Baltic island for years to come and the smallest detail of the Community life was important.

Moreover, as the camp came into being, this sense of a community developed, proving that we were a definite whole, and not merely separate human beings living for a while in tents upon a desert island. Each fell willingly into the routine. Sangree, as by natural selection, took upon himself the cleaning of the fish and the cutting of the wood into lengths sufficient for a day's use. And he did it well. The pan of water was never without a fish, cleaned and scaled, ready to fry for whoever was hungry. The nightly fire never died down for lack of material to throw on without going farther afield to search.

And Timothy, once reverend, caught the fish and chopped down the trees. He also assumed responsibility for the condition of the boat, and did it so thoroughly that nothing in the little cutter was ever found wanting. And when, for any reason, his presence was in demand, the first place to look for him was—in the boat, and there, too, he was usually found, tinkering away with sheets, sails, or rudder and singing as he tinkered.

Nor was the "reading" neglected, for most mornings there came a sound of droning voices from the white tent by the raspberry bushes, which signified that Sangree, the tutor, and whatever other man chanced to be in the party at the time, were hard at it with history or the classics.

And while Mrs. Maloney, also by natural selection, took charge of the larder and the kitchen, the mending and general supervision of the rough comforts, she also made herself peculiarly mistress of the megaphone which summoned to meals and carried her voice easily from one end of the island to the other, and in her hours of leisure she daubed the surrounding scenery on to a sketching block with all the honesty and devotion of her determined but unreceptive soul.

Joan, meanwhile, Joan, elusive creature of the wilds, became I know not exactly what. She did plenty of work in the camp, yet seemed to have no very precise duties. She was everywhere and anywhere. Sometimes she slept in her tent, sometimes under the stars with a blanket. She knew every inch of the island and kept turning up in places where she was least expected, forever wandering about, reading her books in sheltered corners, making little fires on sunless days to "worship by to the gods," as she put it, ever finding new pools to dive and bathe in, and swimming day and night in the warm and waveless lagoon like a fish in a huge tank. She went bare-legged and bare-footed, with her hair down and her skirts caught up to the knees, and if ever a human being turned into a jolly savage within the compass of a single week, Joan Maloney was certainly that human being. She ran wild.

So completely, too, was she possessed by the strong spirit of the place that the little human fear she had yielded to so strangely on our arrival seemed to have been utterly dispossessed. As I hoped and expected, she made no reference to our conversation of the first evening. Sangree bothered her with no special attentions, and after all they were very little together. His behaviour was perfect in that respect, and I, for my part, hardly gave the matter another thought. Joan was ever a prey to vivid fancies of one kind or another, and this was one of them. Mercifully for the happiness of all concerned, it had melted away before the spirit of busy, active life and deep content that reigned over the island. Every one was intensely alive, and peace was upon all.

Meanwhile the effect of the camp life began to tell. Always a searching test of character, its results, sooner or later, are infallible, for it acts upon the soul as swiftly and surely as the hypo bath upon the negative of a photograph. A readjustment of the personal forces takes place quickly. Some parts of the personality go to sleep, others wake up, but the first sweeping change that the primitive life brings about is that the artificial portions of the character shed themselves one after another like dead skins. Attitudes and poses that seemed genuine in the city drop away. The mind, like the body, grows quickly hard, simple, uncomplex. And in a camp as primitive and close to nature as ours was, these effects became speedily visible.

Some folk, of course, who talk glibly about the simple life when it is safely out of reach, betray themselves in camp by forever peering about for the artificial excitements of civilisation which they miss. Some get bored at once, some grow slovenly, some reveal the animal in most unexpected fashion, and some, the select few, find themselves in very short order and are happy.

And, in our little party, we could flatter ourselves that we all belonged to the last category, so far as the general effect was concerned. Only there were certain other changes as well, varying with each individual, and all interesting to note.

It was only after the first week or two that these changes became marked, although this is the proper place, I think, to speak of them. For, having myself no other duty than to enjoy a well-earned holiday, I used to load my canoe with blankets and provisions and journey forth on exploration trips among the islands of several days together, and it was on my return from the first of these, when I rediscovered the party, so to speak, that these changes first presented themselves vividly to me, and in one particular instance produced a rather curious impression.

In a word, then, while every one had grown wilder, naturally wilder, Sangree, it seemed to me, had grown much wilder, and what I can only call unnaturally wilder. He made me think of a savage.

To begin with, he had changed immensely in mere physical appearance, and the full brown cheeks, the brighter eyes of absolute health, and the general air of vigour and robustness that had come to replace his customary lassitude and timidity, had worked such an improvement that I hardly knew him for the same man. His voice, too, was deeper and his manner bespoke for the first time a greater measure of confidence in himself. He now had some claims to be called nice-looking, or at least to a certain air of virility that would not lessen his value in the eyes of the opposite sex.

All this, of course, was natural enough, and most welcome. But, altogether apart from this physical change, which no doubt had also been going forward in the rest of us, there was a subtle note in his personality that came to me with a degree of surprise that almost amounted to shock.

And two things, as he came down to welcome me and pull up

the canoe, leaped up in my mind unbidden, as though connected in some way I could not at the moment divine: first, the curious judgment formed of him by Joan, and secondly, that fugitive expression I had caught in his face while Maloney was offering up his strange prayer for special protection from Heaven.

The delicacy of manner and feature, to call it by no milder term, which had always been a distinguishing characteristic of the man, had been replaced by something far more vigorous and decided, that yet utterly eluded analysis. The change which impressed me so oddly was not easy to name. The others, singing Maloney, the bustling Bo'sun's Mate, and Joan, that fascinating half-breed of undine and salamander, all showed the effects of a life so close to nature, but in their case the change was perfectly natural and what was to be expected, whereas with Peter Sangree, the Canadian, it was something unusual and unexpected.

It is impossible to explain how he managed gradually to convey to my mind the impression that something in him had turned savage, yet this, more or less, is the impression that he did convey. It was not that he seemed really less civilised, or that his character had undergone any definite alteration, but rather that something in him, hitherto dormant, had awakened to life. Some quality, latent till now, so far, at least, as we were concerned, who, after all, knew him but slightly, had stirred into activity and risen to the surface of his being.

And while, for the moment this seemed as far as I could get, it was but natural that my mind should continue the intuitive process and acknowledge that John Silence, owing to his peculiar faculties, and the girl, owing to her singularly receptive temperament, might each in a different way have divined this latent quality in his soul, and feared its manifestation later.

On looking back to this painful adventure, too, it now seems equally natural that the same process, carried to its logical conclusion, should have wakened some deep instinct in me that, wholly without direction from my will, set itself sharply and persistently upon the watch from that very moment. Thenceforward the personality of Sangree was never far from my thoughts, and I was for ever analysing and searching for the explanation that took so long in coming.

"I declare, Hubbard, you're tanned like an aboriginal, and you look like one, too," laughed Maloney.

"And I can return the compliment," was my reply, as we all gathered round a brew of tea to exchange news and compare notes.

And later, at supper, it amused me to observe that the distinguished tutor, once clergyman, did not eat his food quite as "nicely" as he did at home—he devoured it; that Mrs. Maloney ate more, and, to say the least, with less delay, than was her custom in the select atmosphere of her English dining room, and that while Joan attacked her tin plateful with genuine avidity, Sangree, the Canadian, bit and gnawed at his, laughing and talking and complimenting the cook all the while, and making me think with secret amusement of a starved animal at its first meal. While, from their remarks about myself, I judged that I had changed and grown wild as much as the rest of them.

In this and in a hundred other little ways the change showed, ways difficult to define in detail, but all proving, not the coarsening effect of leading the primitive life, but, let us say, the more direct and unvarnished methods that became prevalent. For all day long we were in the bath of the elements, wind, water, sun, and just as the body became insensible to cold and shed unnecessary clothing, the mind grew straightforward and shed many of the disguises required by the conventions of civilisation.

And in each, according to temperament and character, there stirred the life-instincts that were natural, untamed, and, in a sense, savage.

III

So it came about that I stayed with our island party, putting off my second exploring trip from day to day, and I think that this far-fetched instinct to watch Sangree was really the cause of my postponement.

For another ten days the life of the camp pursued its even and delightful way, blessed by perfect summer weather, a good harvest of fish, fine winds for sailing, and calm, starry nights. Maloney's selfish prayer had been favourably received. Nothing came to disturb or perplex. There was not even the prowling of night animals to vex the rest of Mrs. Maloney, for in previous camps it had often been her peculiar affliction that she heard the porcupines scratching against the canvas, or the squirrels dropping fir-cones in the early morning with a sound of miniature thunder upon the roof of her tent. But on this island there was not even a squirrel or a mouse. I think two toads and a small and harmless snake were the only living creatures that had been discovered during the whole of the first fortnight. And these two toads in all probability were not two toads, but one toad.

Then, suddenly, came the terror that changed the whole aspect of the place—the devastating terror.

It came, at first, gently, but from the very start it made me realize the unpleasant loneliness of our situation, our remote isolation in this wilderness of sea and rock, and how the islands in this tideless Baltic ocean lay about us like the advance guard of a vast besieging army. Its entry, as I say, was gentle, hardly noticeable, in fact, to most of us: singularly undramatic it certainly was. But, then, in actual life this is often the way the dreadful climaxes move upon us, leaving the heart undisturbed almost to the last minute, and then overwhelming it with a sudden rush of horror. For it was the custom at breakfast to listen patiently while each in turn related the trivial adventures of the night— how they slept, whether the wind shook their tent, whether the spider on the ridge pole had moved, whether they had heard the toad, and so forth—and on this particular morning Joan, in the middle of a little pause, made a truly novel announcement.

"In the night I heard the howling of a dog," she said, and then flushed up to the roots of her hair when we burst out laughing. For the idea of there being a dog on this forsaken island that was only able to support a snake and two toads was distinctly ludicrous, and I remember Maloney, half-way through his burnt porridge, capping the announcement by declaring that he had heard a "Baltic turtle" in the lagoon, and his wife's expression of frantic alarm before the laughter undeceived her.

But the next morning Joan repeated the story with additional and convincing detail.

"Sounds of whining and growling woke me," she said, "and I distinctly heard sniffing under my tent, and the scratching of paws."

"Oh, Timothy! Can it be a porcupine?" exclaimed the Bo'sun's Mate with distress, forgetting that Sweden was not Canada.

But the girl's voice had sounded to me in quite another key, and looking up I saw that her father and Sangree were staring at her hard. They, too, understood that she was in earnest, and had been struck by the serious note in her voice.

"Rubbish, Joan! You are always dreaming something or other wild," her father said a little impatiently.

"There's not an animal of any size on the whole island," added Sangree with a puzzled expression. He never took his eyes from her face.

"But there's nothing to prevent one swimming over," I put in briskly, for somehow a sense of uneasiness that was not pleasant had woven itself into the talk and pauses. "A deer, for instance, might easily land in the night and take a look round—"

"Or a bear!" gasped the Bo'sun's Mate, with a look so portentous that we all welcomed the laugh.

But Joan did not laugh. Instead, she sprang up and called to us to follow.

"There," she said, pointing to the ground by her tent on the side farthest from her mother's, "there are the marks close to my head. You can see for yourselves."

We saw plainly. The moss and lichen, for earth there was hardly any, had been scratched up by paws. An animal about the size of a large dog it must have been, to judge by the marks. We stood and stared in a row.

"Close to my head," repeated the girl, looking round at us. Her face, I noticed, was very pale, and her lip seemed to quiver for an instant. Then she gave a sudden gulp, and burst into a flood of tears.

The whole thing had come about in the brief space of a few minutes, and with a curious sense of inevitableness, moreover, as though it had all been carefully planned from all time and nothing could have stopped it. It had all been rehearsed before, had actually happened before, as the strange feeling sometimes has it. It seemed like the opening movement in some ominous drama, and that I knew exactly what would happen next. Something of great moment was impending.

For this sinister sensation of coming disaster made itself felt from the very beginning, and an atmosphere of gloom and dismay pervaded the entire camp from that moment forward.

I drew Sangree to one side and moved away, while Maloney took the distressed girl into her tent, and his wife followed them, energetic and greatly flustered.

For thus, in undramatic fashion, it was that the terror I have spoken of first attempted the invasion of our camp, and, trivial and unimportant though it seemed, every little detail of this opening scene is photographed upon my mind with merciless accuracy and precision. It happened exactly as described. This was exactly the language used. I see it written before me in black and white. I see, too, the faces of all concerned with the sudden ugly signature of alarm where before had been peace. The terror had stretched out, so to speak, a first tentative feeler toward us and had touched the hearts of each with a horrid directness. And from this moment the camp changed.

Sangree in particular was visibly upset. He could not bear to see the girl distressed, and to hear her actually cry was almost more than he could stand. The feeling that he had no right to protect her hurt him keenly, and I could see that he was itching to do something to help, and liked him for it. His expression said plainly that he would tear in a thousand pieces anything that dared to injure a hair of her head.

We lit our pipes and strolled over in silence to the men's quarters, and it was his odd Canadian expression "Gee whiz!" that drew my attention to a further discovery.

"The brute's been scratching round my tent too," he cried, as he pointed to similar marks by the door and I stooped down to examine them. We both stared in amazement for several minutes without speaking.

"Only I sleep like the dead," he added, straightening up again, "and so heard nothing, I suppose."

We traced the paw-marks from the mouth of his tent in a direct line across to the girl's, but nowhere else about the camp was there a sign of the strange visitor. The deer, dog, or whatever it was that had twice favored us with a visit in the night, had confined its attentions to these two tents. And, after all, there was really nothing out of the way about these visits of an unknown animal, for although our own island was destitute of life, we were in the heart of a wilderness, and the mainland and larger islands must be swarming with all kinds of four-footed creatures, and no very prolonged swimming was necessary to reach us. In any other country it would not have caused a moment's interest, interest of the kind we felt, that is. In our Canadian camps the bears were for ever grunting about among the provision bags at night, porcupines scratching unceasingly, and chipmunks scuttling over everything.

"My daughter is overtired, and that's the truth of it," explained Maloney presently when he rejoined us and had examined in turn the other paw-marks. "She's been overdoing it lately, and camp life, you know, always means a great excitement to her. It's natural enough, if we take no notice she'll be all right." He paused to borrow my tobacco pouch and fill his pipe, and the blundering way he filled it and spilled the precious weed on the ground visibly belied the calm of his easy language. "You might take her out for a bit of fishing, Hubbard, like a good chap. She's hardly up to the long day in the cutter. Show her some of the other islands in your canoe, perhaps. Eh?"

And by lunchtime the cloud had passed away as suddenly, and as suspiciously, as it had come.

But in the canoe, on our way home, having till then purposely ignored the subject uppermost in our minds, she suddenly spoke to me in a way that again touched the note of sinister alarm—the note that kept on sounding and sounding until finally John Silence came with his great vibrating presence and relieved it. Yes, and even after he came, too, for a while.

"I'm ashamed to ask it," she said abruptly, as she steered me home, her sleeves rolled up, her hair blowing in the wind, "and ashamed of my silly tears too, because I really can't make out what caused them, but, Mr. Hubbard, I want you to promise me not to go off for your long expeditions, just yet. I beg it of you." She was so in earnest that she forgot the canoe, and the wind caught it sideways and made us roll dangerously. "I have tried hard not to ask this," she added, bringing the canoe round again, "but I simply can't help myself."

It was a good deal to ask, and I suppose my hesitation was plain, for she went on before I could reply, and her beseeching expression and intensity of manner impressed me very forcibly.

"For another two weeks only—"

"Mr. Sangree leaves in a fortnight," I said, seeing at once what she was driving at, but wondering if it was best to encourage her or not.

"If I knew you were to be on the island till then," she said, her face alternately pale and blushing, and her voice trembling a little, "I should feel so much happier."

I looked at her steadily, waiting for her to finish.

"And safer," she added almost in a whisper, "especially at night, I mean."

"Safer, Joan?" I repeated, thinking I had never seen her eyes so soft and tender. She nodded her head, keeping her gaze fixed on my face.

It was really difficult to refuse, whatever my thoughts and judgment may have been, and somehow I understood that she spoke with good reason, though for the life of me I could not have put it into words.

"Happier, and safer," she said gravely, the canoe giving a dangerous lurch as she leaned forward in her seat to catch my answer. Perhaps, after all, the wisest way was to grant her request and make light of it, easing her anxiety without too much encouraging its cause.

"All right, Joan, you queer creature, I promise," and the instant look of relief in her face, and the smile that came back like sunlight to her eyes, made me feel that, unknown to myself and the world, I was capable of considerable sacrifice after all.

"But, you know, there's nothing to be afraid of," I added sharply, and she looked up in my face with the smile women use when they know we are talking idly, yet do not wish to tell us so.

"You don't feel afraid, I know," she observed quietly.

"Of course not. Why should I?"

"So, if you will just humour me this once I, I will never ask anything foolish of you again as long as I live," she said gratefully.

"You have my promise," was all I could find to say.

She headed the nose of the canoe for the lagoon lying a quarter of a mile ahead, and paddled swiftly, but a minute or two later she paused again and stared hard at me with the dripping paddle across the thwarts.

"You've not heard anything at night yourself, have you?" she asked.

"I never hear anything at night," I replied shortly, "from the moment I lie down till the moment I get up."

"That dismal howling, for instance," she went on, determined to get it out, "far away at first and then getting closer, and stopping just outside the camp?"

"Certainly not."

"Because, sometimes I think I almost dreamed it."

"Most likely you did," was my unsympathetic response.

"And you don't think father has heard it either, then?"

"No. He would have told me if he had."

This seemed to relieve her mind a little. "I know mother hasn't," she added, as if speaking to herself, "for she hears nothing, ever."

It was two nights after this conversation that I woke out of deep sleep and heard sounds of screaming. The voice was really horrible, breaking the peace and silence with its shrill clamour. In less than ten seconds I was half dressed and out of my tent. The screaming had stopped abruptly, but I knew the general direction, and ran as fast as the darkness would allow over to the women's quarters, and on getting close I heard sounds of suppressed weeping. It was Joan's voice. And just as I came up I saw Mrs. Maloney, marvellously attired, fumbling with a lantern. Other voices became audible in the same moment behind me, and Timothy Maloney arrived, breathless, less than half dressed, and carrying another lantern that had gone out on the way from being banged against a tree. Dawn was just breaking, and a chill wind blew in from the sea. Heavy black clouds drove low overhead.

The scene of confusion may be better imagined than described. Questions in frightened voices filled the air against this background of suppressed weeping. Briefly, Joan's silk tent had been torn, and the girl was in a state bordering upon hysterics. Somewhat reassured by our noisy presence, however, for she was plucky at heart, she pulled herself together and tried to explain what had happened, and her broken words, told there on the edge of night and morning upon this wild island ridge, were oddly thrilling and distressingly convincing.

"Something touched me and I woke," she said simply, but in a voice still hushed and broken with the terror of it, "something pushing against the tent. I felt it through the canvas. There was the same sniffing and scratching as before, and I felt the tent give a little as when wind shakes it. I heard breathing, very loud, very heavy breathing, and then came a sudden great tearing blow, and the canvas ripped open close to my face."

She had instantly dashed out through the open flap and screamed at the top of her voice, thinking the creature had actually got into the tent. But nothing was visible, she declared, and she heard not the faintest sound of an animal making off under cover of the darkness. The brief account seemed to exercise a paralysing effect upon us all as we listened to it. I can see the dishevelled group to this day, the wind blowing the women's hair, and Maloney craning his head forward to listen, and his wife, open-mouthed and gasping, leaning against a pine tree.

"Come over to the stockade and we'll get the fire going," I said, "that's the first thing," for we were all shaking with the cold in our scanty garments. And at that moment Sangree arrived wrapped in a blanket and carrying his gun. He was still drunken with sleep.

"The dog again," Maloney explained briefly, forestalling his questions, "been at Joan's tent. Torn it, by Gad! this time. It's time we did something." He went on mumbling confusedly to himself.

Sangree gripped his gun and looked about swiftly in the darkness. I saw his eyes aflame in the glare of the flickering lanterns. He made a movement as though to start out and hunt—and kill. Then his glance fell on the girl crouching on the ground, her face hidden in her hands, and there leaped into his features an expression of savage anger that transformed them. He could have faced a dozen lions with a walking stick at that moment, and again I liked him for the strength of his anger, his self-control, and his hopeless devotion.

But I stopped him going off on a blind and useless chase.

"Come and help me start the fire, Sangree," I said, anxious also to relieve the girl of our presence, and a few minutes later the ashes, still growing from the night's fire, had kindled the fresh wood, and there was a blaze that warmed us well while it also lit up the surrounding trees within a radius of twenty yards.

"I heard nothing," he whispered. "What in the world do you think it is? It surely can't be only a dog!"

"We'll find that out later," I said, as the others came up to the grateful warmth. "The first thing is to make as big a fire as we can."

Joan was calmer now, and her mother had put on some warmer, and less miraculous, garments. And while they stood talking in low voices Maloney and I slipped off to examine the tent. There was little enough to see, but that little was unmistakable. Some animal had scratched up the ground at the head of the tent, and with a great blow of a powerful paw, a paw clearly provided with good claws, had struck the silk and torn it open. There was a hole large enough to pass a fist and arm through.

"It can't be far away," Maloney said excitedly. "We'll organise a hunt at once, this very minute."

We hurried back to the fire, Maloney talking boisterously about his proposed hunt. "There's nothing like prompt action to dispel alarm," he whispered in my ear, and then turned to the rest of us.

"We'll hunt the island from end to end at once," he said, with excitement. "That's what we'll do. The beast can't be far away. And the Bo'sun's Mate and Joan must come too, because they can't be left alone. Hubbard, you take the right shore, and you, Sangree, the left, and I'll go in the middle with the women. In this way we can stretch clean across the ridge, and nothing bigger than a rabbit can possibly escape us." He was extraordinarily excited, I thought. Anything affecting Joan, of course, stirred him prodigiously. "Get your guns and we'll start the drive at once," he cried. He lit another lantern and handed one each to his wife and Joan, and while I ran to fetch my gun I heard him singing to himself with the excitement of it all.

Meanwhile the dawn had come on quickly. It made the flickering lanterns look pale. The wind, too, was rising, and I heard the trees moaning overhead and the waves breaking with increasing clamour on the shore. In the lagoon the boat dipped and splashed, and the sparks from the fire were carried aloft in a stream and scattered far and wide.

We made our way to the extreme end of the island, measured our distances carefully, and then began to advance. None of us spoke. Sangree and I, with cocked guns, watched the shore lines, and all within easy touch and speaking distance. It was a slow and blundering drive, and there were many false alarms, but after the best part of half an hour we stood on the farther end, having made the complete tour, and without putting up so much as a squirrel. Certainly there was no living creature on that island but ourselves.

"I know what it is!" cried Maloney, looking out over the dim expanse of grey sea, and speaking with the air of a man making a discovery. "It's a dog from one of the farms on the larger islands." He pointed seawards where the archipelago thickened. "And it's escaped and turned wild. Our fires and voices attracted it, and it's probably half starved as well as savage, poor brute!"

No one said anything in reply, and he began to sing again very low to himself.

The point where we stood, a huddled, shivering group, faced the wider channels that led to the open sea and Finland. The grey dawn had broken in earnest at last, and we could see the racing waves with their angry crests of white. The surrounding islands showed up as dark masses in the distance, and in the east, almost as Maloney spoke, the sun came up with a rush in a stormy and magnificent sky of red and gold. Against this splashed and gorgeous background black clouds, shaped like fantastic and legendary animals, filed past swiftly in a tearing stream, and to this day I have only to close my eyes to see again that vivid and hurrying procession in the air. All about us the pines made black splashes against the sky. It was an angry sunrise. Rain, indeed, had already begun to fall in big drops.

We turned, as by a common instinct, and, without speech, made our way back slowly to the stockade, Maloney humming snatches of his songs, Sangree in front with his gun, prepared to shoot at a moment's notice, and the women floundering in the rear with myself and the extinguished lanterns.

Yet it was only a dog!

Really, it was most singular when one came to reflect soberly upon it all. Events, say the occultists, have souls, or at least that agglomerate life due to the emotions and thoughts of all concerned in them, so that cities, and even whole countries, have great astral shapes which may become visible to the eye of vision, and certainly here, the soul of this drive, this vain, blundering, futile drive, stood somewhere between ourselves and laughed.

All of us heard that laugh, and all of us tried hard to smother the sound, or at least to ignore it. Every one talked at once, loudly, and with exaggerated decision, obviously trying to say something plausible against heavy odds, striving to explain naturally that an animal might so easily conceal itself from us, or swim away before we had time to light upon its trail. For we all spoke of that "trail" as though it really existed, and we had more to go upon than the mere marks of paws about the tents of Joan and the Canadian. Indeed, but for these, and the torn tent, I think it would, of course, have been possible to ignore the existence of this beast intruder altogether.

And it was here, under this angry dawn, as we stood in the shelter of the stockade from the pouring rain, weary yet so strangely excited, it was here, out of this confusion of voices and explanations, that, very stealthily, the ghost of something horrible slipped in and stood among us. It made all our explanations seem childish and untrue. The false relation was instantly exposed. Eyes exchanged quick, anxious glances, questioning, expressive of dismay. There was a sense of wonder, of poignant distress, and of trepidation. Alarm stood waiting at our elbows. We shivered.

Then, suddenly, as we looked into each other's faces, came the long, unwelcome pause in which this new arrival established itself in our hearts.

And, without further speech, or attempt at explanation, Maloney moved off abruptly to mix the porridge for an early breakfast, Sangree to clean the fish, myself to chop wood and tend the fire, Joan and her mother to change their wet garments, and, most significant of all, to prepare her mother's tent for its future complement of two.

Each went to his duty, but hurriedly, awkwardly, silently, and this new arrival, this shape of terror and distress stalked, viewless, by the side of each.

"If only I could have traced that dog," I think was the thought in the minds of all.

But in camp, where every one realizes how important the individual contribution is to the comfort and well-being of all, the mind speedily recovers tone and pulls itself together.

During the day, a day of heavy and ceaseless rain, we kept more or less to our tents, and though there were signs of mysterious conferences between the three members of the Maloney family, I think that most of us slept a good deal and stayed alone with his thoughts. Certainly I did, because when Maloney came to say that his wife invited us all to a special "tea" in her tent, he had to shake me awake before I realized that he was there at all.

And by supper time we were more or less even-minded again, and almost jolly. I only noticed that there was an undercurrent of what is best described as "jumpiness," and that the merest snapping of a twig, or plop of a fish in the lagoon, was sufficient to make us start and look over our shoulders. Pauses were rare in our talk, and the fire was never for one instant allowed to get low. The wind and rain had ceased, but the dripping of the branches still kept up an excellent imitation of a downpour. In particular, Maloney was vigilant and alert, telling us a series of tales in which the wholesome humorous element was especially strong. He lingered, too, behind with me after Sangree had gone to bed, and while I mixed myself a glass of hot Swedish punch, he did a thing I had never known him do before—he mixed one for himself, and then asked me to light him over to his tent. We said nothing on the way, but I felt that he was glad of my companionship.

I returned alone to the stockade, and for a long time after that kept the fire blazing, and sat up smoking and thinking. I hardly knew why, but sleep was far from me for one thing, and for another, an idea was taking form in my mind that required the comfort of tobacco and a bright fire for its growth. I lay against a corner of the stockade seat, listening to the wind whispering and to the ceaseless drip-drip of the trees. The night, otherwise, was very still, and the sea quiet as a lake. I remember that I was conscious, peculiarly conscious, of this host of desolate islands crowding about us in the darkness, and that we were the one little spot of humanity in a rather wonderful kind of wilderness.

But this, I think, was the only symptom that came to warn me of highly strung nerves, and it certainly was not sufficiently alarming to destroy my peace of mind. One thing, however, did come to disturb my peace, for just as I finally made ready to go, and had kicked the embers of the fire into a last effort, I fancied I saw, peering at me round the farther end of the stockade wall, a dark and shadowy mass that might have been, that strongly resembled, in fact, the body of a large animal. Two glowing eyes shone for an instant in the middle of it. But the next second I saw that it was merely a projecting mass of moss and lichen in the wall of our stockade, and the eyes were a couple of wandering sparks from the dying ashes I had kicked. It was easy enough, too, to imagine I saw an animal moving here and there between the trees, as I picked my way stealthily to my tent. Of course, the shadows tricked me.

And though it was after one o'clock, Maloney's light was still burning, for I saw his tent shining white among the pines.

It was, however, in the short space between consciousness and sleep, that time when the body is low and the voices of the submerged region tell sometimes true, that the idea which had been all this while maturing reached the point of an actual decision, and I suddenly realized that I had resolved to send word to Dr. Silence. For, with a sudden wonder that I had hitherto been so blind, the unwelcome conviction dawned upon me all at once that some dreadful thing was lurking about us on this island, and that the safety of at least one of us was threatened by something monstrous and unclean that was too horrible to contemplate. And, again remembering those last words of his as the train moved out of the platform, I understood that Dr. Silence would hold himself in readiness to come.

"Unless you should send for me sooner," he had said.

I found myself suddenly wide awake. It is impossible to say what woke me, but it was no gradual process, seeing that I jumped from deep sleep to absolute alertness in a single instant. I had evidently slept for an hour and more, for the night had cleared, stars crowded the sky, and a pallid half-moon just sinking into the sea threw a spectral light between the trees.

I went outside to sniff the air, and stood upright. A curious impression that something was astir in the Camp came over me, and when I glanced across at Sangree's tent, some twenty feet away, I saw that it was moving. He too, then, was awake and restless, for I saw the canvas sides bulge this way and that as he moved within.

The flap pushed forward. He was coming out, like myself, to sniff the air, and I was not surprised, for its sweetness after the rain was intoxicating. And he came on all fours, just as I had done. I saw a head thrust round the edge of the tent.

And then I saw that it was not Sangree at all. It was an animal. And the same instant I realized something else too—it was the animal, and its whole presentment for some unaccountable reason, was unutterably malefic.

A cry I was quite unable to suppress escaped me, and the creature turned on the instant and stared at me with baleful eyes. I could have dropped on the spot, for the strength all ran out of my body with a rush. Something about it touched in me the living terror that grips and paralyses. If the mind requires but the tenth of a second to form an impression, I must have stood there stockstill for several seconds while I seized the ropes for support and stared. Many and vivid impressions flashed through my mind, but not one of them resulted in action, because I was in instant dread that the beast any moment would leap in my direction and be upon me. Instead, however, after what seemed a vast period, it slowly turned its eyes from my face, uttered a low whining sound, and came out altogether into the open.

Then, for the first time, I saw it in its entirety and noted two things. It was about the size of a large dog, but at the same time it was utterly unlike any animal that I had ever seen. Also, that the quality that had impressed me first as being malefic was really only its singular and original strangeness. Foolish as it may sound, and impossible as it is for me to adduce proof, I can only say that the animal seemed to me then to be—not real.

But all this passed through my mind in a flash, almost subconsciously, and before I had time to check my impressions, or even properly verify them, I made an involuntary movement, catching the tight rope in my hand so that it twanged like a banjo string, and in that instant the creature turned the corner of Sangree's tent and was gone into the darkness.

Then, of course, my senses in some measure returned to me, and I realized only one thing: it had been inside his tent!

I dashed out, reached the door in half a dozen strides, and looked in. The Canadian, thank God! lay upon his bed of branches. His arm was stretched outside, across the blankets, the fist tightly clenched, and the body had an appearance of unusual rigidity that was alarming. On his face there was an expression of effort, almost of painful effort, so far as the uncertain light permitted me to see, and his sleep seemed to be very profound. He looked, I thought, so stiff, so unnaturally stiff, and in some indefinable way, too, he looked smaller, shrunken.

I called to him to wake, but called many times in vain. Then I decided to shake him, and had already moved forward to do so vigorously when there came a sound of footsteps padding softly behind me, and I felt a stream of hot breath burn my neck as I stooped. I turned sharply. The tent door was darkened and something silently swept in. I felt a rough and shaggy body push past me, and knew that the animal had returned. It seemed to leap forward between me and Sangree—in fact, to leap upon Sangree, for its dark body hid him momentarily from view, and in that moment my soul turned sick and coward with a horror that rose from the very dregs and depths of life, and gripped my existence at its central source.

The creature seemed somehow to melt away into him, almost as though it belonged to him and were a part of himself, but in the same instant, that instant of extraordinary confusion and terror in my mind, it seemed to pass over and behind him, and, in some utterly unaccountable fashion, it was gone. And the

Canadian woke and sat up with a start.

"Quick! You fool," I cried, in my excitement, "the beast has been in your tent, here at your very throat while you sleep like the dead. Up, man! Get your gun! Only this second it disappeared over there behind your head. Quick, or Joan—"

And somehow the fact that he was there, wide-awake now, to corroborate me, brought the additional conviction to my own mind that this was no animal, but some perplexing and dreadful form of life that drew upon my deeper knowledge, that much reading had perhaps assented to, but that had never yet come within actual range of my senses.

He was up in a flash, and out. He was trembling, and very white. We searched hurriedly, feverishly, but found only the traces of paw-marks passing from the door of his own tent across the moss to the women's. And the sight of the tracks about Mrs. Maloney's tent, where Joan now slept, set him in a perfect fury.

"Do you know what it is, Hubbard, this beast?" he hissed under his breath at me. "It's a damned wolf, that's what it is—a wolf lost among the islands, and starving to death, desperate. So help me God, I believe it's that!"

He talked a lot of rubbish in his excitement. He declared he would sleep by day and sit up every night until he killed it. Again his rage touched my admiration, but I got him away before he made enough noise to wake the whole camp.

"I have a better plan than that," I said, watching his face closely. "I don't think this is anything we can deal with. I'm going to send for the only man I know who can help. We'll go to Waxholm this very morning and get a telegram through."

Sangree stared at me with a curious expression as the fury died out of his face and a new look of alarm took its place.

"John Silence," I said, "will know—"

"You think it's something—of that sort?" he stammered.

"I am sure of it."

There was a moment's pause. "That's worse, far worse than

anything material," he said, turning visibly paler. He looked from my face to the sky, and then added with sudden resolution, "Come, the wind's rising. Let's get off at once. From there you can telephone to Stockholm and get a telegram sent without delay."

I sent him down to get the boat ready, and seized the opportunity myself to run and wake Maloney. He was sleeping very lightly, and sprang up the moment I put my head inside his tent. I told him briefly what I had seen, and he showed so little surprise that I caught myself wondering for the first time whether he himself had seen more going on than he had deemed wise to communicate to the rest of us.

He agreed to my plan without a moment's hesitation, and my last words to him were to let his wife and daughter think that the great psychic doctor was coming merely as a chance visitor, and not with any professional interest.

So, with frying pan, provisions, and blankets aboard, Sangree and I sailed out of the lagoon fifteen minutes later, and headed with a good breeze for the direction of Waxholm and the borders of civilisation.

IV

Although nothing John Silence did ever took me, properly speaking, by surprise, it was certainly unexpected to find a letter from Stockholm waiting for me. "I have finished my Hungary business," he wrote, "and am here for ten days. Do not hesitate to send if you need me. If you telephone any morning from Waxholm I can catch the afternoon steamer."

My years of intercourse with him were full of "coincidences" of this description, and although he never sought to explain them by claiming any magical system of communication with my mind, I have never doubted that there actually existed some secret telepathic method by which he knew my circumstances and gauged the degree of my need. And that this power was independent of time in the sense that it saw into the future, always seemed to me equally apparent.

Sangree was as much relieved as I was, and within an hour of sunset that very evening we met him on the arrival of the little coasting steamer, and carried him off in the dinghy to the camp we had prepared on a neighbouring island, meaning to start for home early next morning.

"Now," he said, when supper was over and we were smoking round the fire, "let me hear your story." He glanced from one to the other, smiling.

"You tell it, Mr. Hubbard," Sangree interrupted abruptly, and went off a little way to wash the dishes, yet not so far as to be out of earshot. And while he splashed with the hot water, and scraped the tin plates with sand and moss, my voice, unbroken by a single question from Dr. Silence, ran on for the next half-hour with the best account I could give of what had happened.

My listener lay on the other side of the fire, his face half hidden by a big sombrero. Sometimes he glanced up questioningly when a point needed elaboration, but he uttered no single word till I had reached the end, and his manner all through the recital was grave and attentive. Overhead, the wash of the wind in the pine branches filled in the pauses, the darkness settled down over the sea, and the stars came out in thousands, and by the time I finished the moon had risen to flood the scene with silver. Yet, by his face and eyes, I knew quite well that the doctor was listening to something he had expected to hear, even if he had not actually anticipated all the details.

"You did well to send for me," he said very low, with a significant glance at me when I finished, "very well," and for one swift second his eye took in Sangree, "for what we have to deal with here is nothing more than a werewolf, rare enough, I am glad to say, but often very sad, and sometimes very terrible."

I jumped as though I had been shot, but the next second was

heartily ashamed of my want of control, for this brief remark, confirming as it did my own worst suspicions, did more to convince me of the gravity of the adventure than any number of questions or explanations. It seemed to draw close the circle about us, shutting a door somewhere that locked us in with the animal and the horror, and turning the key. Whatever it was had now to be faced and dealt with.

"No one has been actually injured so far?" he asked aloud, but in a matter-of-fact tone that lent reality to grim possibilities.

"Good heavens, no!" cried the Canadian, throwing down his dishcloths and coming forward into the circle of firelight. "Surely there can be no question of this poor starved beast injuring anybody, can there?"

His hair straggled untidily over his forehead, and there was a gleam in his eyes that was not all reflection from the fire. His words made me turn sharply. We all laughed a little short, forced laugh.

"I trust not, indeed," Dr. Silence said quietly. "But what makes you think the creature is starved?" He asked the question with his eyes straight on the other's face. The prompt question explained to me why I had started, and I waited with just a tremor of excitement for the reply.

Sangree hesitated a moment, as though the question took him by surprise. But he met the doctor's gaze unflinchingly across the fire, and with complete honesty.

"Really," he faltered, with a little shrug of the shoulders, "I can hardly tell you. The phrase seemed to come out of its own accord. I have felt from the beginning that it was in pain and... starved, though why I felt this never occurred to me till you asked."

"You really know very little about it, then?" said the other, with a sudden gentleness in his voice.

"No more than that," Sangree replied, looking at him with a puzzled expression that was unmistakably genuine. "In fact, nothing at all, really," he added, by way of further explanation.

"I am glad of that," I heard the doctor murmur under his breath, but so low that I only just caught the words, and Sangree missed them altogether, as evidently he was meant to do.

"And now," he cried, getting on his feet and shaking himself with a characteristic gesture, as though to shake out the horror and the mystery, "let us leave the problem till tomorrow and enjoy this wind and sea and stars. I've been living lately in the atmosphere of many people, and feel that I want to wash and be clean. I propose a swim and then bed. Who'll second me?" And two minutes later we were all diving from the boat into cool, deep water, that reflected a thousand moons as the waves broke away from us in countless ripples.

We slept in blankets under the open sky, Sangree and I taking the outside places, and were up before sunrise to catch the dawn wind. Helped by this early start we were half-way home by noon, and then the wind shifted to a few points behind us so that we fairly ran. In and out among a thousand islands, down narrow channels where we lost the wind, out into open spaces where we had to take in a reef, racing along under a hot and cloudless sky, we flew through the very heart of the bewildering and lonely scenery.

"A real wilderness," cried Dr. Silence from his seat in the bows where he held the jib sheet. His hat was off, his hair tumbled in the wind, and his lean brown face gave him the touch of an Oriental. Presently he changed places with Sangree, and came down to talk with me by the tiller.

"A wonderful region, all this world of islands," he said, waving his hand to the scenery rushing past us, "but doesn't it strike you there's something lacking?"

"It... hard," I answered, after a moment's reflection. "It has a superficial, glittering prettiness, without..." I hesitated to find the word I wanted.

John Silence nodded his head with approval.

"Exactly," he said. "The picturesqueness of stage scenery that is not real, not alive. It's like a landscape by a clever painter, yet without true imagination. Soulless—that's the word you wanted."

"Something like that," I answered, watching the gusts of wind on the sails. "Not dead so much, as without soul. That's it."

"Of course," he went on, in a voice calculated, it seemed to me, not to reach our companion in the bows, "to live long in a place like this, long and alone, might bring about a strange result in some men."

I suddenly realized he was talking with a purpose and pricked up my ears.

"There's no life here. These islands are mere dead rocks pushed up from below the sea—not living land, and there's nothing really alive on them. Even the sea, this tideless, brackish sea, neither salt water nor fresh, is dead. It's all a pretty image of life without the real heart and soul of life. To a man with too strong desires who came here and lived close to nature, strange things might happen."

"Let her out a bit," I shouted to Sangree, who was coming aft. "The wind's gusty and we've got hardly any ballast."

He went back to the bows, and Dr. Silence continued.

"Here, I mean, a long sojourn would lead to deterioration, to degeneration. The place is utterly unsoftened by human influences, by any humanising associations of history, good or bad. This landscape has never awakened into life. It's still dreaming in its primitive sleep."

"In time," I put in, "you mean a man living here might become brutal?"

"The passions would run wild, selfishness become supreme, the instincts coarsen and turn savage probably."

"But—"

"In other places just as wild, parts of Italy for instance, where there are other moderating influences, it could not happen. The character might grow wild, savage too in a sense, but with a human wildness one could understand and deal with. But here, in a hard place like this, it might be otherwise." He spoke slowly, weighing his words carefully.

I looked at him with many questions in my eyes, and a precautionary cry to Sangree to stay in the fore part of the boat, out of earshot.

"First of all there would come callousness to pain, and indifference to the rights of others. Then the soul would turn savage, not from passionate human causes, or with enthusiasm, but by deadening down into a kind of cold, primitive, emotionless savagery, by turning, like the landscape, soulless."

"And a man with strong desires, you say, might change?"

"Without being aware of it, yes. He might turn savage, his instincts and desires turn animal. And if," he lowered his voice and turned for a moment towards the bows, and then continued in his most weighty manner, "owing to delicate health or other predisposing causes, his Double, you know what I mean, of course, his etheric Body of Desire, or astral body, as some term it, that part in which the emotions, passions and desires reside, if this, I say, were for some constitutional reason loosely joined to his physical organism, there might well take place an occasional projection—"

Sangree came aft with a sudden rush, his face aflame, but whether with wind or sun, or with what he had heard, I cannot say. In my surprise I let the tiller slip and the cutter gave a great plunge as she came sharply into the wind and flung us all together in a heap on the bottom. Sangree said nothing, but while he scrambled up and made the jib sheet fast my companion found a moment to add to his unfinished sentence the words, too low for any ear but mine, "Entirely unknown to himself, however."

We righted the boat and laughed, and then Sangree produced the map and explained exactly where we were. Far away on the horizon, across an open stretch of water, lay a blue cluster of islands with our crescent-shaped home among them and the safe anchorage of the lagoon. An hour with this wind would get us there comfortably, and while Dr. Silence and Sangree fell into conversation, I sat and pondered over the strange suggestions that had just been put into my mind concerning the "Double," and the possible form it might assume when dissociated temporarily from the physical body.

The whole way home these two chatted, and John Silence was as gentle and sympathetic as a woman. I did not hear much of their talk, for the wind grew occasionally to the force of a hurricane and the sails and tiller absorbed my attention, but I could see that Sangree was pleased and happy, and was pouring out intimate revelations to his companion in the way that most people did, when John Silence wished them to do so.

But it was quite suddenly, while I sat all intent upon wind and sails, that the true meaning of Sangree's remark about the animal flared up in me with its full import. For his admission that he knew it was in pain and starved was in reality nothing more or less than a revelation of his deeper self. It was in the nature of a confession. He was speaking of something that he knew positively, something that was beyond question or argument, something that had to do directly with himself. "Poor starved beast" he had called it in words that had "come out of their own accord," and there had not been the slightest evidence of any desire to conceal or explain away. He had spoken instinctively, from his heart, and as though about his own self.

And half an hour before sunset we raced through the narrow opening of the lagoon and saw the smoke of the dinner-fire blowing here and there among the trees, and the figures of Joan and the Bo'sun's Mate running down to meet us at the landing-stage.

V

Everything changed from the moment John Silence set foot on that island. It was like the effect produced by calling in some big doctor, some great arbiter of life and death, for consultation. The sense of gravity increased a hundredfold. Even inanimate objects took upon themselves a subtle alteration, for the setting of the adventure, this deserted bit of sea with its hundreds of uninhabited islands, somehow turned sombre. An element that was mysterious, and in a sense disheartening, crept unbidden into the severity of grey rock and dark pine forest and took the sparkle from the sunshine and the sea.

I, at least, was keenly aware of the change, for my whole being shifted, as it were, a degree higher, becoming keyed up and alert. The figures from the background of the stage moved forward a little into the light, nearer to the inevitable action. In a word this man's arrival intensified the whole affair.

And, looking back down the years to the time when all this happened, it is clear to me that he had a pretty sharp idea of the meaning of it from the very beginning. How much he knew beforehand by his strange divining powers, it is impossible to say, but from the moment he came upon the scene and caught within himself the note of what was going on amongst us, he undoubtedly held the true solution of the puzzle and had no need to ask questions. And this certitude it was that set him in such an atmosphere of power and made us all look to him instinctively, for he took no tentative steps, made no false moves, and while the rest of us floundered he moved straight to the climax. He was indeed a true diviner of souls.

I can now read into his behaviour a good deal that puzzled me at the time, for though I had dimly guessed the solution, I had no idea how he would deal with it. And the conversations I can reproduce almost verbatim, for, according to my invariable habit, I kept full notes of all he said.

To Mrs. Maloney, foolish and dazed, to Joan, alarmed, yet plucky, and to the clergyman, moved by his daughter's distress below his usual shallow emotions, he gave the best possible treatment in the best possible way, yet all so easily and simply as to make it appear naturally spontaneous. For he dominated the Bo'sun's Mate, taking the measure of her ignorance with infinite patience. He keyed up Joan, stirring her courage and interest to the highest point for her own safety, and the Reverend Timothy he soothed and comforted, while obtaining his implicit obedience, by taking him into his confidence, and leading him gradually to a comprehension of the issue that was bound to follow.

And Sangree, here his wisdom was most wisely calculated, he neglected outwardly because inwardly he was the object of his unceasing and most concentrated attention. Under the guise of apparent indifference his mind kept the Canadian under constant observation.

There was a restless feeling in the camp that evening and none of us lingered round the fire after supper as usual. Sangree and I busied ourselves with patching up the torn tent for our guest and with finding heavy stones to hold the ropes, for Dr. Silence insisted on having it pitched on the highest point of the island ridge, just where it was most rocky and there was no earth for pegs. The place, moreover, was midway between the men's and women's tents, and, of course, commanded the most comprehensive view of the camp.

"So that if your dog comes," he said simply, "I may be able to catch him as he passes across."

The wind had gone down with the sun and an unusual warmth lay over the island that made sleep heavy, and in the morning we assembled at a late breakfast, rubbing our eyes and yawning. The cool north wind had given way to the warm southern air that sometimes came up with haze and moisture across the Baltic, bringing with it the relaxing sensations that produced enervation and listlessness.

And this may have been the reason why at first I failed to notice that anything unusual was about, and why I was less alert than normally, for it was not till after breakfast that the silence of our little party struck me and I discovered that Joan had not yet put in an appearance. And then, in a flash, the last heaviness of sleep vanished and I saw that Maloney was white and troubled and his wife could not hold a plate without trembling.

A desire to ask questions was stopped in me by a swift glance from Dr. Silence, and I suddenly understood in some vague way that they were waiting till Sangree should have gone. How this idea came to me I cannot determine, but the soundness of the intuition was soon proved, for the moment he moved off to his tent, Maloney looked up at me and began to speak in a low voice.

"You slept through it all," he half whispered.

"Through what?" I asked, suddenly thrilled with the knowledge that something dreadful had happened.

"We didn't wake you for fear of getting the whole camp up," he went on, meaning, by the camp, I supposed, Sangree. "It was just before dawn when the screams woke me."

"The dog again?" I asked, with a curious sinking of the heart.

"Got right into the tent," he went on, speaking passionately but very low, "and woke my wife by scrambling all over her. Then she realized that Joan was struggling beside her. And, by God! The beast had torn her arm—scratched all down the arm she was, and bleeding."

"Joan injured?" I gasped.

"Merely scratched, this time," put in John Silence, speaking for the first time, "suffering more from shock and fright than actual wounds."

"Isn't it a mercy the doctor was here?" said Mrs. Maloney, looking as if she would never know calmness again. "I think we should both have been killed."

"It has been a most merciful escape," Maloney said, his pulpit voice struggling with his emotion. "But, of course, we cannot risk another. We must strike camp and get away at once."

"Only poor Mr. Sangree must not know what has happened. He is so attached to Joan and would be so terribly upset," added the Bo'sun's Mate distractedly, looking all about in her terror.

"It is perhaps advisable that Mr. Sangree should not know what has occurred," Dr. Silence said with quiet authority, "but I think, for the safety of all concerned, it will be better not to leave the island just now." He spoke with great decision and Maloney looked up and followed his words closely.

"If you will agree to stay here a few days longer, I have no doubt we can put an end to the attentions of your strange visitor, and incidentally have the opportunity of observing a most singular and interesting phenomenon."

"What!" gasped Mrs. Maloney, "A phenomenon? You mean that you know what it is?"

"I am quite certain I know what it is," he replied very low, for we heard the footsteps of Sangree approaching, "though I am not so certain yet as to the best means of dealing with it. But in any case it is not wise to leave precipitately."

"Oh, Timothy, does he think it's a devil?" cried the Bo'sun's Mate in a voice that even the Canadian must have heard.

"In my opinion," continued John Silence, looking across at me and the clergyman, "it is a case of modern lycanthropy with other complications that may—" He left the sentence unfinished, for Mrs. Maloney got up with a jump and fled to her tent fearful she might hear a worse thing, and at that moment Sangree turned the corner of the stockade and came into view.

"There are footmarks all round the mouth of my tent," he said with excitement. "The animal has been here again in the night. Dr. Silence, you really must come and see them for yourself. They're as plain on the moss as tracks in snow."

But later in the day, while Sangree went off in the canoe to fish the pools near the larger islands, and Joan still lay, bandaged and resting, in her tent, Dr. Silence called me and the tutor and proposed a walk to the granite slabs at the far end. Mrs. Maloney sat on a stump near her daughter, and busied herself energetically with alternate nursing and painting.

"We'll leave you in charge," the doctor said with a smile that was meant to be encouraging, "and when you want us for lunch, or anything, the megaphone will always bring us back in time."

For, though the very air was charged with strange emotions, every one talked quietly and naturally as with a definite desire to counteract unnecessary excitement.

"I'll keep watch," said the plucky Bo'sun's Mate, "and meanwhile I find comfort in my work." She was busy with the sketch she had begun on the day after our arrival. "For even a tree," she added proudly, pointing to her little easel, "is a symbol of the divine, and the thought makes me feel safer." We glanced for a moment at a daub which was more like the symptom of a disease than a symbol of the divine, and then took the path round the lagoon.

At the far end we made a little fire and lay round it in the shadow of a big boulder. Maloney stopped his humming suddenly and turned to his companion.

"And what do you make of it all?" he asked abruptly.

"In the first place," replied John Silence, making himself comfortable against the rock, "it is of human origin, this animal. It is undoubted lycanthropy."

His words had the effect precisely of a bombshell. Maloney listened as though he had been struck.

"You puzzle me utterly," he said, sitting up closer and staring at him.

"Perhaps," replied the other, "but if you'll listen to me for a few moments you may be less puzzled at the end, or more. It depends how much you know. Let me go further and say that you have underestimated, or miscalculated, the effect of this primitive wild life upon all of you."

"In what way?" asked the clergyman, bristling a trifle.

"It is strong medicine for any town-dweller, and for some of you it has been too strong. One of you has gone wild." He uttered these last words with great emphasis.

"Gone savage," he added, looking from one to the other.

Neither of us found anything to reply.

"To say that the brute has awakened in a man is not a mere metaphor always," he went on presently.

"Of course not!"

"But, in the sense I mean, may have a very literal and terrible significance," pursued Dr. Silence. "Ancient instincts that no one dreamed of, least of all their possessor, may leap forth—"

"Atavism can hardly explain a roaming animal with teeth and claws and sanguinary instincts," interrupted Maloney with impatience.

"The term is of your own choice," continued the doctor equably, "not mine, and it is a good example of a word that indicates a result while it conceals the process, but the explanation of this beast that haunts your island and attacks your daughter is of far deeper significance than mere atavistic tendencies, or throwing back to animal origin, which I suppose is the thought in your mind."

"You spoke just now of lycanthropy," said Maloney, looking bewildered and anxious to keep to plain facts evidently. "I think I have come across the word, but really, really, it can have no actual significance today, can it? These superstitions of mediaeval times can hardly—"

He looked round at me with his jolly red face, and the expression of astonishment and dismay on it would have made me shout with laughter at any other time. Laughter, however, was never farther from my mind than at this moment when I listened to Dr. Silence as he carefully suggested to the clergyman the very explanation that had gradually been forcing itself upon my own mind.

"However mediaeval ideas may have exaggerated the idea is

not of much importance to us now," he said quietly, "when we are face to face with a modern example of what, I take it, has always been a profound fact. For the moment let us leave the name of any one in particular out of the matter and consider certain possibilities."

We all agreed with that at any rate. There was no need to speak of Sangree, or of any one else, until we knew a little more.

"The fundamental fact in this most curious case," he went on, "is that the 'Double' of a man—"

"You mean the astral body? I've heard of that, of course," broke in Maloney with a snort of triumph.

"No doubt," said the other, smiling, "no doubt you have. That this Double, or fluidic body of a man, as I was saying, has the power under certain conditions of projecting itself and becoming visible to others. Certain training will accomplish this, and certain drugs likewise. Illnesses, too, that ravage the body may produce temporarily the result that death produces permanently, and let loose this counterpart of a human being and render it visible to the sight of others.

"Every one, of course, knows this more or less today, but it is not so generally known, and probably believed by none who have not witnessed it, that this fluidic body can, under certain conditions, assume other forms than human, and that such other forms may be determined by the dominating thought and wish of the owner. For this Double, or astral body as you call it, is really the seat of the passions, emotions and desires in the psychical economy. It is the Passion Body, and, in projecting itself, it can often assume a form that gives expression to the overmastering desire that moulds it, for it is composed of such tenuous matter that it lends itself readily to the moulding by thought and wish."

"I follow you perfectly," said Maloney, looking as if he would much rather be chopping firewood elsewhere and singing.

"And there are some persons so constituted," the doctor went on with increasing seriousness, "that the fluid body in them is but loosely associated with the physical, persons of poor health as a rule, yet often of strong desires and passions, and in these persons it is easy for the Double to dissociate itself during deep sleep from their system, and, driven forth by some consuming desire, to assume an animal form and seek the fulfilment of that desire."

There, in broad daylight, I saw Maloney deliberately creep closer to the fire and heap the wood on. We gathered in to the heat, and to each other, and listened to Dr. Silence's voice as it mingled with the swish and whirr of the wind about us, and the falling of the little waves.

"For instance, to take a concrete example," he resumed, "suppose some young man, with the delicate constitution I have spoken of, forms an overpowering attachment to a young woman, yet perceives that it is not welcomed, and is man enough to repress its outward manifestations. In such a case, supposing his Double be easily projected, the very repression of his love in the daytime would add to the intense force of his desire when released in deep sleep from the control of his will, and his fluidic body might issue forth in monstrous or animal shape and become actually visible to others. And, if his devotion were dog-like in its fidelity, yet concealing the fires of a fierce passion beneath, it might well assume the form of a creature that seemed to be half dog, half wolf—"

"A werewolf, you mean?" cried Maloney, pale to the lips as he listened.

John Silence held up a restraining hand. "A werewolf," he said, "is a true psychical fact of profound significance, however absurdly it may have been exaggerated by the imaginations of a superstitious peasantry in the days of unenlightenment, for a werewolf is nothing but the savage, and possibly sanguinary, instincts of a passionate man scouring the world in his fluidic body, his passion body, his body of desire. As in the case at hand, he may not know it—"

"It is not necessarily deliberate, then?" Maloney put in quickly, with relief.

"It is hardly ever deliberate. It is the desires released in sleep from the control of the will finding a vent. In all savage races it has been recognised and dreaded, this phenomenon styled 'Wehr Wolf,' but today it is rare. And it is becoming rarer still, for the world grows tame and civilised, emotions have become refined, desires lukewarm, and few men have savagery enough left in them to generate impulses of such intense force, and certainly not to project them in animal form."

"By Gad!" exclaimed the clergyman breathlessly, and with increasing excitement, "then I feel I must tell you, what has been given to me in confidence, that Sangree has in him an admixture of savage blood, by ancestry—"

"Let us stick to our supposition of a man as described," the doctor stopped him calmly, "and let us imagine that he has in him this admixture of savage blood, and further, that he is wholly unaware of his dreadful physical and psychical infirmity, and that he suddenly finds himself leading the primitive life together with the object of his desires, with the result that the strain of the untamed wild-man in his blood—"

"Berserker, for instance," from Maloney.

"Yes, perfectly," agreed the doctor, "the result, I say, that this savage strain in him is awakened and leaps into passionate life. What then?"

He looked hard at Timothy Maloney, and the clergyman looked hard at him.

"The wild life such as you lead here on this island, for instance, might quickly awaken his savage instincts, his buried instincts, and with profoundly disquieting results."

"You mean his Subtle Body, as you call it, might issue forth automatically in deep sleep and seek the object of its desire?" I said, coming to Maloney's aid, who was finding it more and more difficult to get words.

"Precisely, yet the desire of the man remaining utterly unmalefic, pure and wholesome in every sense."

"Ah!" I heard the clergyman gasp.

"The lover's desire for union run wild, run savage, tearing its way out in primitive, untamed fashion, I mean," continued the doctor, striving to make himself clear to a mind bounded by conventional thought and knowledge, "for the desire to possess, remember, may easily become importunate, and, embodied in this animal form of the Subtle Body which acts as its vehicle, may go forth to tear in pieces all that obstructs, to reach to the very heart of the loved object and seize it. Au fond, it is nothing more than the aspiration for union, as I said, the splendid and perfectly clean desire to absorb utterly into itself..."

He paused a moment and looked into Maloney's eyes.

"...to bathe in the very heart's blood of the one desired," he added with grave emphasis.

The fire spurted and crackled and made me start, but Maloney found relief in a genuine shudder, and I saw him turn his head and look about him from the sea to the trees. The wind dropped just at that moment and the doctor's words rang sharply through the stillness.

"Then it might even kill?" stammered the clergyman presently in a hushed voice, and with a little forced laugh by way of protest that sounded quite ghastly.

"In the last resort it might kill," repeated Dr. Silence. Then, after another pause, during which he was clearly debating how much or how little it was wise to give to his audience, he continued. "And if the Double does not succeed in getting back to its physical body, that physical body would wake an imbecile, an idiot, or perhaps never wake at all."

Maloney sat up and found his tongue.

"You mean that if this fluid animal thing, or whatever it is, should be prevented getting back, the man might never wake again?" he asked, with shaking voice.

"He might be dead," replied the other calmly. The tremor of a positive sensation shivered in the air about us.

"Then isn't that the best way to cure the fool, the brute?" thundered the clergyman, half rising to his feet.

"Certainly it would be an easy and undiscoverable form of murder," was the stern reply, spoken as calmly as though it were a remark about the weather.

Maloney collapsed visibly, and I gathered the wood over the fire and coaxed up a blaze.

"The greater part of the man's life, of his vital forces, goes out with this Double," Dr. Silence resumed, after a moment's consideration, "and a considerable portion of the actual material of his physical body. So the physical body that remains behind is depleted, not only of force, but of matter. You would see it small, shrunken, dropped together, just like the body of a materialising medium at a seance. Moreover, any mark or injury inflicted upon this Double will be found exactly reproduced by the phenomenon of repercussion upon the shrunken physical body lying in its trance—"

"An injury inflicted upon the one you say would be reproduced also on the other?" repeated Maloney, his excitement growing again.

"Undoubtedly," replied the other quietly, "for there exists all the time a continuous connection between the physical body and the Double, a connection of matter, though of exceedingly attenuated, possibly of etheric, matter. The wound travels, so to speak, from one to the other, and if this connection were broken the result would be death."

"Death," repeated Maloney to himself, "death!" He looked anxiously at our faces, his thoughts evidently beginning to clear.

"And this solidity?" he asked presently, after a general pause, "this tearing of tents and flesh, this howling, and the marks of paws? You mean that the Double...?"

"Has sufficient material drawn from the depleted body to produce physical results? Certainly!" the doctor took him up. "Although to explain at this moment such problems as the passage of matter through matter would be as difficult as to explain how the thought of a mother can actually break the bones of the child unborn."

Dr. Silence pointed out to sea, and Maloney, looking wildly about him, turned with a violent start. I saw a canoe, with Sangree in the stern-seat, slowly coming into view round the farther point. His hat was off, and his tanned face for the first time appeared to me, to us all, I think, as though it were the face of some one else. He looked like a wild man. Then he stood up in the canoe to make a cast with the rod. I recalled the expression of his face as I had seen it once or twice, notably on that occasion of the evening prayer, and an involuntary shudder ran down my spine.

At that very instant he turned and saw us where we lay, and his face broke into a smile, so that his teeth showed white in the sun. He looked in his element, and exceedingly attractive. He called out something about his fish, and soon after passed out of sight into the lagoon.

For a time none of us said a word.

"And the cure?" ventured Maloney at length.

"Is not to quench this savage force," replied Dr. Silence, "but to steer it better, and to provide other outlets. This is the solution of all these problems of accumulated force, for this force is the raw material of usefulness, and should be increased and cherished, not by separating it from the body by death, but by raising it to higher channels. The best and quickest cure of all," he went on, speaking very gently and with a hand upon the clergyman's arm, "is to lead it towards its object, provided that object is not unalterably hostile, to let it find rest where—"

He stopped abruptly, and the eyes of the two men met in a single glance of comprehension.

266

"Joan?" Maloney exclaimed, under his breath.

"Joan!" replied John Silence.

We all went to bed early. The day had been unusually warm, and after sunset a curious hush descended on the island. Nothing was audible but that faint, ghostly singing which is inseparable from a pinewood even on the stillest day—a low, searching sound, as though the wind had hair and trailed it o'er the world.

With the sudden cooling of the atmosphere a sea fog began to form. It appeared in isolated patches over the water, and then these patches slid together and a white wall advanced upon us. Not a breath of air stirred. The firs stood like flat metal outlines, the sea became as oil. The whole scene lay as though held motionless by some huge weight in the air, and the flames from our fire, the largest we had ever made, rose upwards, straight as a church steeple.

As I followed the rest of our party tent-wards, having kicked the embers of the fire into safety, the advance guard of the fog was creeping slowly among the trees, like white arms feeling their way. Mingled with the smoke was the odour of moss and soil and bark, and the peculiar flavour of the Baltic, half salt, half brackish, like the smell of an estuary at low water.

It is difficult to say why it seemed to me that this deep stillness masked an intense activity. Perhaps in every mood lies the suggestion of its opposite, so that I became aware of the contrast of furious energy, for it was like moving through the deep pause before a thunderstorm, and I trod gently lest by breaking a twig or moving a stone I might set the whole scene into some sort of tumultuous movement. Actually, no doubt, it was nothing more than a result of overstrung nerves.

There was no more question of undressing and going to bed than there was of undressing and going to bathe. Some sense in me was alert and expectant. I sat in my tent and waited. And at the end of half an hour or so my waiting was justified, for the canvas suddenly shivered, and someone tripped over the ropes that held it to the earth. John Silence came in.

The effect of his quiet entry was singular and prophetic. It was just as though the energy lying behind all this stillness had pressed forward to the edge of action. This, no doubt, was merely the quickening of my own mind, and had no other justification, for the presence of John Silence always suggested the near possibility of vigorous action, and as a matter of fact, he came in with nothing more than a nod and a significant gesture.

He sat down on a corner of my ground-sheet, and I pushed the blanket over so that he could cover his legs. He drew the flap of the tent after him and settled down, but hardly had he done so when the canvas shook a second time, and in blundered Maloney.

"Sitting in the dark?" he said self-consciously, pushing his head inside, and hanging up his lantern on the ridge-pole nail. "I just looked in for a smoke. I suppose—"

He glanced round, caught the eye of Dr. Silence, and stopped. He put his pipe back into his pocket and began to hum softly— that underbreath humming of a nondescript melody I knew so well and had come to hate.

Dr. Silence leaned forward, opened the lantern and blew the light out. "Speak low," he said, "and don't strike matches. Listen for sounds and movements about the camp, and be ready to follow me at a moment's notice." There was light enough to distinguish our faces easily, and I saw Maloney glance again hurriedly at both of us.

"Is the camp asleep?" the doctor asked presently, whispering.

"Sangree is," replied the clergyman, in a voice equally low. "I can't answer for the women. I think they're sitting up."

"That's for the best." And then he added, "I wish the fog would thin a bit and let the moon through. Later we may want it."

"It is lifting now, I think," Maloney whispered back. "It's

over the tops of the trees already."

I cannot say what it was in this commonplace exchange of remarks that thrilled. Probably Maloney's swift acquiescence in the doctor's mood had something to do with it, for his quick obedience certainly impressed me a good deal. But, even without that slight evidence, it was clear that each recognised the gravity of the occasion, and understood that sleep was impossible and sentry duty was the order of the night.

"Report to me," repeated John Silence once again, "the least sound, and do nothing precipitately."

He shifted across to the mouth of the tent and raised the flap, fastening it against the pole so that he could see out. Maloney stopped humming and began to force the breath through his teeth with a kind of faint hissing, treating us to a medley of church hymns and popular songs of the day.

Then the tent trembled as though someone had touched it.

"That's the wind rising," whispered the clergyman, and pulled the flap open as far as it would go. A waft of cold damp air entered and made us shiver, and with it came a sound of the sea as the first wave washed its way softly along the shores.

"It's got round to the north," he added, and following his voice came a long-drawn whisper that rose from the whole island as the trees sent forth a sighing response. "The fog'll move a bit now. I can make out a lane across the sea already."

"Hush!" said Dr. Silence, for Maloney's voice had risen above a whisper, and we settled down again to another long period of watching and waiting, broken only by the occasional rubbing of shoulders against the canvas as we shifted our positions, and the increasing noise of waves on the outer coast-line of the island. And over all whirred the murmur of wind sweeping the tops of the trees like a great harp, and the faint tapping on the tent as drops fell from the branches with a sharp pinging sound.

We had sat for something over an hour in this way, and Maloney and I were finding it increasingly hard to keep awake, when suddenly Dr. Silence rose to his feet and peered out. The next minute he was gone.

Relieved of the dominating presence, the clergyman thrust his face close into mine. "I don't much care for this waiting game," he whispered, "but Silence wouldn't hear of my sitting up with the others. He said it would prevent anything happening if I did."

"He knows," I answered shortly.

"No doubt in the world about that," he whispered back. "It's this 'Double' business, as he calls it, or else it's obsession as the Bible describes it. But it's bad, whichever it is, and I've got my Winchester outside ready cocked, and I brought this too." He shoved a pocket Bible under my nose. At one time in his life it had been his inseparable companion.

"One's useless and the other's dangerous," I replied under my breath, conscious of a keen desire to laugh, and leaving him to choose. "Safety lies in following our leader—"

"I'm not thinking of myself," he interrupted sharply, "only, if anything happens to Joan tonight I'm going to shoot first, and pray afterwards!"

Maloney put the book back into his hip-pocket, and peered out of the doorway. "What is he up to now, in the devil's name, I wonder," he added, "going round Sangree's tent and making gestures. How weird he looks disappearing in and out of the fog."

"Just trust him and wait," I said quickly, for the doctor was already on his way back. "Remember, he has the knowledge, and knows what he's about. I've been with him through worse cases than this."

Maloney moved back as Dr. Silence darkened the doorway and stooped to enter.

"His sleep is very deep," he whispered, seating himself by the door again. "He's in a cataleptic condition, and the Double may be released any minute now. But I've taken steps to imprison it in the tent, and it can't get out till I permit it. Be on the watch for signs of movement." Then he looked hard at Maloney. "But no violence, or shooting, remember, Mr. Maloney, unless you want a murder on your hands. Anything done to the Double acts by repercussion upon the physical body. You had better take out the cartridges at once."

His voice was stern. The clergyman went out, and I heard him emptying the magazine of his rifle. When he returned he sat nearer the door than before, and from that moment until we left the tent he never once took his eyes from the figure of Dr. Silence, silhouetted there against sky and canvas.

And, meanwhile, the wind came steadily over the sea and opened the mist into lanes and clearings, driving it about like a living thing.

It must have been well after midnight when a low booming sound drew my attention, but at first the sense of hearing was so strained that it was impossible exactly to locate it, and I imagined it was the thunder of big guns far out at sea carried to us by the rising wind. Then Maloney, catching hold of my arm and leaning forward, somehow brought the true relation, and I realized the next second that it was only a few feet away.

"Sangree's tent," he exclaimed in a loud and startled whisper.

I craned my head round the corner, but at first the effect of the fog was so confusing that every patch of white driving about before the wind looked like a moving tent and it was some seconds before I discovered the one patch that held steady. Then I saw that it was shaking all over, and the sides, flapping as much as the tightness of the ropes allowed, were the cause of the booming sound we had heard. Something alive was tearing frantically about inside, banging against the stretched canvas in a way that made me think of a great moth dashing against the walls and ceiling of a room. The tent bulged and rocked.

"It's trying to get out, by Jupiter!" muttered the clergyman, rising to his feet and turning to the side where the unloaded rifle lay. I sprang up too, hardly knowing what purpose was in my mind, but anxious to be prepared for anything. John Silence, however, was before us both, and his figure slipped past and blocked the doorway of the tent. And there was some quality in his voice next minute when he began to speak that brought our minds instantly to a state of calm obedience.

"First, the women's tent," he said low, looking sharply at Maloney, "and if I need your help, I'll call."

The clergyman needed no second bidding. He dived past me and was out in a moment. He was labouring evidently under intense excitement. I watched him picking his way silently over the slippery ground, giving the moving tent a wide berth, and presently disappearing among the floating shapes of fog.

Dr. Silence turned to me. "You heard those footsteps about half an hour ago?" he asked significantly.

"I heard nothing."

"They were extraordinarily soft, almost the soundless tread of a wild creature. But now, follow me closely," he added, "for we must waste no time if I am to save this poor man from his affliction and lead his werewolf Double to its rest. And, unless I am much mistaken," he peered at me through the darkness, whispering with the utmost distinctness, "Joan and Sangree are absolutely made for each other. And I think she knows it too, just as well as he does."

My head swam a little as I listened, but at the same time something cleared in my brain and I saw that he was right. Yet it was all so weird and incredible, so remote from the commonplace facts of life as commonplace people know them, and more than once it flashed upon me that the whole scene, people, words, tents, and all the rest of it, were delusions created by the intense excitement of my own mind somehow, and that suddenly the sea-fog would clear off and the world become normal again.

The cold air from the sea stung our cheeks sharply as we left the close atmosphere of the little crowded tent. The sighing of the trees, the waves breaking below on the rocks, and the lines and patches of mist driving about us seemed to create the momentary illusion that the whole island had broken loose and was floating out to sea like a mighty raft.

The doctor moved just ahead of me, quickly and silently. He was making straight for the Canadian's tent where the sides still boomed and shook as the creature of sinister life raced and tore about impatiently within. A little distance from the door he paused and held up a hand to stop me. We were, perhaps, a dozen feet away.

"Before I release it, you shall see for yourself," he said, "that the reality of the werewolf is beyond all question. The matter of which it is composed is, of course, exceedingly attenuated, but you are partially clairvoyant, and even if it is not dense enough for normal sight you will see something."

He added a little more I could not catch. The fact was that the curiously strong vibrating atmosphere surrounding his person somewhat confused my senses. It was the result, of course, of his intense concentration of mind and forces, and pervaded the entire camp and all the persons in it. And as I watched the canvas shake and heard it boom and flap I heartily welcomed it. For it was also protective.

At the back of Sangree's tent stood a thin group of pine trees, but in front and at the sides the ground was comparatively clear. The flap was wide open and any ordinary animal would have been out and away without the least trouble. Dr. Silence led me up to within a few feet, evidently careful not to advance beyond a certain limit, and then stooped down and signalled to me to do the same. And looking over his shoulder I saw the interior lit faintly by the spectral light reflected from the fog, and the dim blot upon the balsam boughs and blankets signifying Sangree, while over him, and round him, and up and down him, flew the dark mass of "something" on four legs, with pointed muzzle and sharp ears plainly visible against the tent sides, and the occasional gleam of fiery eyes and white fangs.

I held my breath and kept utterly still, inwardly and outwardly, for fear, I suppose, that the creature would become conscious of my presence, but the distress I felt went far deeper than the mere sense of personal safety, or the fact of watching something so incredibly active and real. I became keenly aware of the dreadful psychic calamity it involved. The realisation that Sangree lay confined in that narrow space with this species of monstrous projection of himself, that he was wrapped there in the cataleptic sleep, all unconscious that this thing was masquerading with his own life and energies, added a distressing touch of horror to the scene. In all the cases of John Silence, and they were many and often terrible, no other psychic affliction has ever, before or since, impressed me so convincingly with the pathetic impermanence of the human personality, with its fluid nature, and with the alarming possibilities of its transformations.

"Come," he whispered, after we had watched for some minutes the frantic efforts to escape from the circle of thought and will that held it prisoner, "come a little farther away while I release it."

We moved back a dozen yards or so. It was like a scene in some impossible play, or in some ghastly and oppressive nightmare from which I should presently awake to find the blankets all heaped up upon my chest.

By some method undoubtedly mental, but which, in my confusion and excitement, I failed to understand, the doctor accomplished his purpose, and the next minute I heard him say sharply under his breath, "It's out! Now watch!"

At this very moment a sudden gust from the sea blew aside the mist, so that a lane opened to the sky, and the moon, ghastly and unnatural as the effect of stage limelight, dropped down in a momentary gleam upon the door of Sangree's tent, and I perceived that something had moved forward from the interior darkness and stood clearly defined upon the threshold. And, at the same moment, the tent ceased its shuddering and held still.

There, in the doorway, stood an animal, with neck and muzzle thrust forward, its head poking into the night, its whole body poised in that attitude of intense rigidity that precedes the spring into freedom, the running leap of attack. It seemed to be about the size of a calf, leaner than a mastiff, yet more squat than a wolf, and I can swear that I saw the fur ridged sharply upon its back. Then its upper lip slowly lifted, and I saw the whiteness of its teeth.

Surely no human being ever stared as hard as I did in those next few minutes. Yet, the harder I stared the clearer appeared the amazing and monstrous apparition. For, after all, it was Sangree, and yet it was not Sangree. It was the head and face of an animal, and yet it was the face of Sangree: the face of a wild dog, a wolf, and yet his face. The eyes were sharper, narrower, more fiery, yet they were his eyes, his eyes run wild. The teeth were longer, whiter, more pointed, yet they were his teeth, his teeth grown cruel. The expression was flaming, terrible, exultant—yet it was his expression carried to the border of savagery—his expression as I had already surprised it more than once, only dominant now, fully released from human constraint, with the mad yearning of a hungry and importunate soul. It was the soul of Sangree, the long suppressed, deeply loving Sangree, expressed in its single and intense desire, pure utterly and utterly wonderful.

Yet, at the same time, came the feeling that it was all an illusion. I suddenly remembered the extraordinary changes the human face can undergo in circular insanity, when it changes from melancholia to elation, and I recalled the effect of hascheesh, which shows the human countenance in the form of the bird or animal to which in character it most approximates, and for a moment I attributed this mingling of Sangree's face with a wolf to some kind of similar delusion of the senses. I was mad, deluded, dreaming! The excitement of the day, and this dim light of stars and bewildering mist combined to trick me. I had been amazingly imposed upon by some false wizardry of the senses. It was all absurd and fantastic. It would pass.

And then, sounding across this sea of mental confusion like a bell through a fog, came the voice of John Silence bringing me back to a consciousness of the reality of it all.

"Sangree, in his Double!"

And when I looked again more calmly, I plainly saw that it was indeed the face of the Canadian, but his face turned animal, yet mingled with the brute expression a curiously pathetic look like the soul seen sometimes in the yearning eyes of a dog, the face of an animal shot with vivid streaks of the human.

The doctor called to him softly under his breath, "Sangree! Sangree, you poor afflicted creature! Do you know me? Can you understand what it is you're doing in your 'Body of Desire'?"

For the first time since its appearance the creature moved. Its ears twitched and it shifted the weight of its body on to the hind legs. Then, lifting its head and muzzle to the sky, it opened its long jaws and gave vent to a dismal and prolonged howling.

But, when I heard that howling rise to heaven, the breath caught and strangled in my throat and it seemed that my heart missed a beat, for, though the sound was entirely animal, it was at the same time entirely human.

"The savage blood!" whispered John Silence, when I caught his arm for support, "the ancestral cry."

And that poignant, beseeching cry, that broken human voice, mingling with the savage howl of the brute beast, pierced straight to my very heart and touched there something that no music, no voice, passionate or tender, of man, woman or child has ever stirred before or since for one second into life. It echoed away among the fog and the trees and lost itself somewhere out over the hidden sea. And some part of myself, something that was far more than the mere act of intense listening, went out with it, and for several minutes I lost consciousness of my surroundings and felt utterly absorbed in the pain of another stricken fellow-creature.

Again the voice of John Silence recalled me to myself.

"Hark!" he said aloud. "Hark!"

His tone galvanised me afresh. We stood listening side by side.

Far across the island, faintly sounding through the trees and brushwood, came a similar, answering cry. Shrill, yet wonderfully musical, shaking the heart with a singular wild sweetness that defies description, we heard it rise and fall upon the night air.

"It's across the lagoon," Dr. Silence cried, but this time in full tones that paid no tribute to caution. "It's Joan! She's answering him!"

Again the wonderful cry rose and fell, and that same instant the animal lowered its head, and, muzzle to earth, set off on a swift easy canter that took it off into the mist and out of our sight like a thing of wind and vision.

The doctor made a quick dash to the door of Sangree's tent, and, following close at his heels, I peered in and caught a momentary glimpse of the small, shrunken body lying upon the branches but half covered by the blankets—the cage from which most of the life, and not a little of the actual corporeal substance, had escaped into that other form of life and energy, the body of passion and desire.

By another of those swift, incalculable processes which at this stage of my apprenticeship I failed often to grasp, Dr. Silence reclosed the circle about the tent and body.

"Now it cannot return till I permit it," he said, and the next second was off at full speed into the woods, with myself close behind him. I had already had some experience of my companion's ability to run swiftly through a dense wood, and I now had the further proof of his power almost to see in the dark. For, once we left the open space about the tents, the trees seemed to absorb all the remaining vestiges of light, and I understood that special sensibility that is said to develop in the blind—the sense of obstacles.

And twice as we ran we heard the sound of that dismal howling drawing nearer and nearer to the answering faint cry from the point of the island whither we were going.

Then, suddenly, the trees fell away, and we emerged, hot and breathless, upon the rocky point where the granite slabs ran bare into the sea. It was like passing into the clearness of open day. And there, sharply defined against sea and sky, stood the figure of a human being. It was Joan.

I at once saw that there was something about her appearance that was singular and unusual, but it was only when we had moved quite close that I recognised what caused it. For while the lips wore a smile that lit the whole face with a happiness I had never seen there before, the eyes themselves were fixed in a steady, sightless stare as though they were lifeless and made of glass.

I made an impulsive forward movement, but Dr. Silence instantly dragged me back.

"No," he cried, "don't wake her!"

"What do you mean?" I replied aloud, struggling in his grasp.

"She's asleep. It's somnambulistic. The shock might injure her permanently."

I turned and peered closely into his face. He was absolutely calm. I began to understand a little more, catching, I suppose, something of his strong thinking.

"Walking in her sleep, you mean?"

He nodded. "She's on her way to meet him. From the very beginning he must have drawn her—irresistibly."

"But the torn tent and the wounded flesh?"

"When she did not sleep deep enough to enter the somnambulistic trance he missed her. He went instinctively and in all innocence to seek her out, with the result, of course, that she woke and was terrified—"

"Then in their heart of hearts they love?" I asked finally.

John Silence smiled his inscrutable smile. "Profoundly," he

answered, "and as simply as only primitive souls can love. If only they both come to realize it in their normal waking states his Double will cease these nocturnal excursions. He will be cured, and at rest."

The words had hardly left his lips when there was a sound of rustling branches on our left, and the very next instant the dense brushwood parted where it was darkest and out rushed the swift form of an animal at full gallop. The noise of feet was scarcely audible, but in that utter stillness I heard the heavy panting breath and caught the swish of the low bushes against its sides. It went straight towards Joan, and as it went the girl lifted her head and turned to meet it. And the same instant a canoe that had been creeping silently and unobserved round the inner shore of the lagoon, emerged from the shadows and defined itself upon the water with a figure at the middle thwart. It was Maloney.

It was only afterwards I realized that we were invisible to him where we stood against the dark background of trees. The figures of Joan and the animal he saw plainly, but not Dr. Silence and myself standing just beyond them. He stood up in the canoe and pointed with his right arm. I saw something gleam in his hand.

"Stand aside, Joan girl, or you'll get hit," he shouted, his voice ringing horribly through the deep stillness, and the same instant a pistol-shot cracked out with a burst of flame and smoke, and the figure of the animal, with one tremendous leap into the air, fell back in the shadows and disappeared like a shape of night and fog. Instantly, then, Joan opened her eyes, looked in a dazed fashion about her, and pressing both hands against her heart, fell with a sharp cry into my arms that were just in time to catch her.

And an answering cry sounded across the lagoon—thin, wailing, piteous. It came from Sangree's tent.

"Fool!" cried Dr. Silence, "you've wounded him!" and before we could move or realize quite what it meant, he was in the canoe and half-way across the lagoon.

Some kind of similar abuse came in a torrent from my lips,

too, though I cannot remember the actual words, as I cursed the man for his disobedience and tried to make the girl comfortable on the ground. But the clergyman was more practical. He was spreading his coat over her and dashing water on her face.

"It's not Joan I've killed at any rate," I heard him mutter as she turned and opened her eyes and smiled faintly up in his face. "I swear the bullet went straight."

Joan stared at him. She was still dazed and bewildered, and still imagined herself with the companion of her trance. The strange lucidity of the somnambulist still hung over her brain and mind, though outwardly she appeared troubled and confused.

"Where has he gone to? He disappeared so suddenly, crying that he was hurt," she asked, looking at her father as though she did not recognise him. "And if they've done anything to him, they have done it to me too, for he is more to me than—"

Her words grew vaguer and vaguer as she returned slowly to her normal waking state, and now she stopped altogether, as though suddenly aware that she had been surprised into telling secrets. But all the way back, as we carried her carefully through the trees, the girl smiled and murmured Sangree's name and asked if he was injured, until it finally became clear to me that the wild soul of the one had called to the wild soul of the other and in the secret depths of their beings the call had been heard and understood. John Silence was right. In the abyss of her heart, too deep at first for recognition, the girl loved him, and had loved him from the very beginning. Once her normal waking consciousness recognised the fact they would leap together like twin flames, and his affliction would be at an end, his intense desire would be satisfied, he would be cured.

And in Sangree's tent Dr. Silence and I sat up for the remainder of the night—this wonderful and haunted night that had shown us such strange glimpses of a new heaven and a new hell, for the Canadian tossed upon his balsam boughs with high fever in his blood, and upon each cheek a dark and curious contusion showed, throbbing with severe pain although the skin was not broken and there was no outward and visible sign of blood.

"Maloney shot straight, you see," whispered Dr. Silence to me after the clergyman had gone to his tent, and had put Joan to sleep beside her mother, who, by the way, had never once awakened. "The bullet must have passed clean through the face, for both cheeks are stained. He'll wear these marks all his life—smaller, but always there. They're the most curious scars in the world, these scars transferred by repercussion from an injured Double. They'll remain visible until just before his death, and then with the withdrawal of the subtle body they will disappear finally."

His words mingled in my dazed mind with the sighs of the troubled sleeper and the crying of the wind about the tent. Nothing seemed to paralyse my powers of realisation so much as these twin stains of mysterious significance upon the face before me.

It was odd, too, how speedily and easily the camp resigned itself again to sleep and quietness, as though a stage curtain had suddenly dropped down upon the action and concealed it, and nothing contributed so vividly to the feeling that I had been a spectator of some kind of visionary drama as the dramatic nature of the change in the girl's attitude.

Yet, as a matter of fact, the change had not been so sudden and revolutionary as appeared. Underneath, in those remoter regions of consciousness where the emotions, unknown to their owners, do secretly mature, and owe thence their abrupt revelation to some abrupt psychological climax, there can be no doubt that Joan's love for the Canadian had been growing steadily and irresistibly all the time. It had now rushed to the surface so that she recognised it. That was all.

And it has always seemed to me that the presence of John Silence, so potent, so quietly efficacious, produced an effect, if one may say so, of a psychic forcing-house, and hastened incalculably the bringing together of these two "wild" lovers. In that sudden awakening had occurred the very psychological climax required to reveal the passionate emotion accumulated below. The deeper knowledge had leaped across and transferred itself to her ordinary consciousness, and in that shock the collision of the personalities had shaken them to the depths and shown her the truth beyond all possibility of doubt.

"He's sleeping quietly now," the doctor said, interrupting my reflections. "If you will watch alone for a bit I'll go to Maloney's tent and help him to arrange his thoughts." He smiled in anticipation of that "arrangement." "He'll never quite understand how a wound on the Double can transfer itself to the physical body, but at least I can persuade him that the less he talks and 'explains' tomorrow, the sooner the forces will run their natural course now to peace and quietness."

He went away softly, and with the removal of his presence Sangree, sleeping heavily, turned over and groaned with the pain of his broken head.

And it was in the still hour just before the dawn, when all the islands were hushed, the wind and sea still dreaming, and the stars visible through clearing mists, that a figure crept silently over the ridge and reached the door of the tent where I dozed beside the sufferer, before I was aware of its presence. The flap was cautiously lifted a few inches and in looked—Joan.

That same instant Sangree woke and sat up on his bed of branches. He recognised her before I could say a word, and uttered a low cry. It was pain and joy mingled, and this time all human. And the girl too was no longer walking in her sleep, but fully aware of what she was doing. I was only just able to prevent him springing from his blankets.

"Joan, Joan!" he cried, and in a flash she answered him, "I'm here. I'm with you always now," and had pushed past me into the tent and flung herself upon his breast.

"I knew you would come to me in the end," I heard him whisper.

"It was all too big for me to understand at first," she murmured, "and for a long time I was frightened."

"But not now!" he cried louder. "You don't feel afraid now of, of anything that's in me."

"I fear nothing," she cried, "nothing, nothing!"

I led her outside again. She looked steadily into my face with eyes shining and her whole being transformed. In some intuitive way, surviving probably from the somnambulism, she knew or guessed as much as I knew.

"You must talk tomorrow with John Silence," I said gently, leading her towards her own tent. "He understands everything."

I left her at the door, and as I went back softly to take up my place of sentry again with the Canadian, I saw the first streaks of dawn lighting up the far rim of the sea behind the distant islands.

And, as though to emphasize the eternal closeness of comedy to tragedy, two small details rose out of the scene and impressed me so vividly that I remember them to this very day. For in the tent where I had just left Joan, all aquiver with her new happiness, there rose plainly to my ears the grotesque sounds of the Bo'sun's Mate heavily snoring, oblivious of all things in heaven or hell, and from Maloney's tent, so still was the night, where I looked across and saw the lantern's glow, there came to me, through the trees, the monotonous rising and falling of a human voice that was beyond question the sound of a man praying to his God.

Gabriel-Ernest

by Saki

"There is a wild beast in your woods," said the artist Cunningham, as he was being driven to the station. It was the only remark he had made during the drive, but as Van Cheele had talked incessantly his companion's silence had not been noticeable.

"A stray fox or two and some resident weasels. Nothing more formidable," said Van Cheele. The artist said nothing.

"What did you mean about a wild beast?" said Van Cheele later, when they were on the platform.

"Nothing. My imagination. Here is the train," said Cunningham.

That afternoon Van Cheele went for one of his frequent rambles through his woodland property. He had a stuffed bittern in his study, and knew the names of quite a number of wild flowers, so his aunt had possibly some justification in describing him as a great naturalist. At any rate, he was a great walker. It was his custom to take mental notes of everything he saw during his walks, not so much for the purpose of assisting contemporary science as to provide topics for conversation afterwards. When the bluebells began to show themselves in flower he made a point of informing every one of the fact. The season of the year might have warned his hearers of the likelihood of such an occurrence, but at least they felt that he was being absolutely frank with them.

What Van Cheele saw on this particular afternoon was, however, something far removed from his ordinary range of experience. On a shelf of smooth stone overhanging a deep pool in the hollow of an oak coppice a boy of about sixteen lay asprawl, drying his wet brown limbs luxuriously in the sun. His wet hair, parted by a recent dive, lay close to his head, and his light-brown eyes, so light that there was an almost tigerish gleam in them, were turned towards Van Cheele with a certain lazy watchfulness. It was an unexpected apparition, and Van Cheele found himself engaged in the novel process of thinking before he spoke. Where on earth could this wild-looking boy hail from? The miller's wife had lost a child some two months ago, supposed to have been swept away by the mill-race, but that had been a mere baby, not a half-grown lad.

"What are you doing there?" he demanded.

"Obviously, sunning myself," replied the boy.

"Where do you live?"

"Here, in these woods."

"You can't live in the woods," said Van Cheele.

"They are very nice woods," said the boy, with a touch of patronage in his voice.

"But where do you sleep at night?"

"I don't sleep at night, that's my busiest time."

Van Cheele began to have an irritated feeling that he was grappling with a problem that was eluding him.

"What do you feed on?" he asked.

"Flesh," said the boy, and he pronounced the word with slow relish, as though he were tasting it.

"Flesh! What flesh?"

"Since it interests you, rabbits, wild-fowl, hares, poultry, lambs in their season, children when I can get any. They're usually too well locked in at night, when I do most of my hunting. It's quite two months since I tasted child-flesh."

Ignoring the chaffing nature of the last remark Van Cheele tried to draw the boy on the subject of possible poaching operations.

"You're talking rather through your hat when you speak of feeding on hares." (Considering the nature of the boy's toilet the simile was hardly an apt one.) "Our hillside hares aren't easily caught."

"At night I hunt on four feet," was the somewhat cryptic response.

"I suppose you mean that you hunt with a dog?" hazarded Van Cheele.

The boy rolled slowly over on to his back, and laughed a weird low laugh, that was pleasantly like a chuckle and disagreeably like a snarl.

"I don't fancy any dog would be very anxious for my company, especially at night."

Van Cheele began to feel that there was something positively uncanny about the strange-eyed, strange-tongued youngster.

"I can't have you staying in these woods," he declared authoritatively.

"I fancy you'd rather have me here than in your house," said the boy.

The prospect of this wild, nude animal in Van Cheele's primly ordered house was certainly an alarming one.

"If you don't go. I shall have to make you," said Van Cheele.

The boy turned like a flash, plunged into the pool, and in a moment had flung his wet and glistening body half-way up the bank where Van Cheele was standing. In an otter the movement would not have been remarkable, in a boy Van Cheele found it sufficiently startling. His foot slipped as he made an involuntarily backward movement, and he found himself almost prostrate on the slippery weed-grown bank, with those tigerish yellow eyes not very far from his own. Almost instinctively he half raised his hand to his throat. The boy laughed again, a laugh in which the snarl had nearly driven out the chuckle, and then, with another of his astonishing lightning movements, plunged out of view into a yielding tangle of weed and fern.

"What an extraordinary wild animal!" said Van Cheele as he picked himself up. And then he recalled Cunningham's remark "There is a wild beast in your woods."

Walking slowly homeward, Van Cheele began to turn over in his mind various local occurrences which might be traceable to the existence of this astonishing young savage.

Something had been thinning the game in the woods lately, poultry had been missing from the farms, hares were growing unaccountably scarcer, and complaints had reached him of lambs being carried off bodily from the hills. Was it possible that this wild boy was really hunting the countryside in company with some clever poacher dogs? He had spoken of hunting "four-footed" by night, but then, again, he had hinted strangely at no dog caring to come near him, "especially at night." It was certainly puzzling. And then, as Van Cheele ran his mind over the various depredations that had been committed during the last month or two, he came suddenly to a dead stop, alike in his walk and his speculations. The child missing from the mill two months ago—the accepted theory was that it had tumbled into the mill-race and been swept away, but the mother had always declared she had heard a shriek on the hill side of the house, in the opposite direction from the water. It was unthinkable, of course, but he wished that the boy had not made that uncanny remark about child-flesh eaten two months ago. Such dreadful things should not be said even in fun.

Van Cheele, contrary to his usual wont, did not feel disposed to be communicative about his discovery in the wood. His position as a parish councillor and justice of the peace seemed somehow compromised by the fact that he was harbouring a personality of such doubtful repute on his property. There was even a possibility that a heavy bill of damages for raided lambs and poultry might be laid at his door. At dinner that night he was quite unusually silent.

"Where's your voice gone to?" said his aunt. "One would

think you had seen a wolf."

Van Cheele, who was not familiar with the old saying, thought the remark rather foolish. If he had seen a wolf on his property his tongue would have been extraordinarily busy with the subject.

At breakfast next morning Van Cheele was conscious that his feeling of uneasiness regarding yesterday's episode had not wholly disappeared, and he resolved to go by train to the neighbouring cathedral town, hunt up Cunningham, and learn from him what he had really seen that had prompted the remark about a wild beast in the woods. With this resolution taken, his usual cheerfulness partially returned, and he hummed a bright little melody as he sauntered to the morning-room for his customary cigarette. As he entered the room the melody made way abruptly for a pious invocation. Gracefully asprawl on the ottoman, in an attitude of almost exaggerated repose, was the boy of the woods. He was drier than when Van Cheele had last seen him, but no other alteration was noticeable in his toilet.

"How dare you come here?" asked Van Cheele furiously.

"You told me I was not to stay in the woods," said the boy calmly.

"But not to come here. Supposing my aunt should see you!"

And with a view to minimising that catastrophe, Van Cheele hastily obscured as much of his unwelcome guest as possible under the folds of a Morning Post. At that moment his aunt entered the room.

"This is a poor boy who has lost his way—and lost his memory. He doesn't know who he is or where he comes from," explained Van Cheele desperately, glancing apprehensively at the waif's face to see whether he was going to add inconvenient candour to his other savage propensities.

Miss Van Cheele was enormously interested.

"Perhaps his underlinen is marked," she suggested.

"He seems to have lost most of that, too," said Van Cheele,

making frantic little grabs at the Morning Post to keep it in its place.

A naked homeless child appealed to Miss Van Cheele as warmly as a stray kitten or derelict puppy would have done.

"We must do all we can for him," she decided, and in a very short time a messenger, dispatched to the rectory, where a page-boy was kept, had returned with a suit of pantry clothes, and the necessary accessories of shirt, shoes, collar, etc. Clothed, clean, and groomed, the boy lost none of his uncanniness in Van Cheele's eyes, but his aunt found him sweet.

"We must call him something till we know who he really is," she said. "Gabriel-Ernest, I think. Those are nice suitable names."

Van Cheele agreed, but he privately doubted whether they were being grafted on to a nice suitable child. His misgivings were not diminished by the fact that his staid and elderly spaniel had bolted out of the house at the first incoming of the boy, and now obstinately remained shivering and yapping at the farther end of the orchard, while the canary, usually as vocally industrious as Van Cheele himself, had put itself on an allowance of frightened cheeps. More than ever he was resolved to consult Cunningham without loss of time.

As he drove off to the station his aunt was arranging that Gabriel-Ernest should help her to entertain the infant members of her Sunday-school class at tea that afternoon.

Cunningham was not at first disposed to be communicative.

"My mother died of some brain trouble," he explained, "so you will understand why I am averse to dwelling on anything of an impossibly fantastic nature that I may see or think that I have seen."

"But what did you see?" persisted Van Cheele.

"What I thought I saw was something so extraordinary that no really sane man could dignify it with the credit of having actually happened. I was standing, the last evening I was with you, half-hidden in the hedge-growth by the orchard gate, watching the dying glow of the sunset. Suddenly I became aware of a naked boy, a bather from some neighbouring pool, I took him to be, who was standing out on the bare hillside also watching the sunset. His pose was so suggestive of some wild faun of Pagan myth that I instantly wanted to engage him as a model, and in another moment I think I should have hailed him. But just then the sun dipped out of view, and all the orange and pink slid out of the landscape, leaving it cold and grey. And at the same moment an astounding thing happened—the boy vanished too!"

"What! Vanished away into nothing?" asked Van Cheele excitedly.

"No, that is the dreadful part of it," answered the artist. "On the open hillside where the boy had been standing a second ago, stood a large wolf, blackish in colour, with gleaming fangs and cruel, yellow eyes. You may think—"

But Van Cheele did not stop for anything as futile as thought. Already he was tearing at top speed towards the station. He dismissed the idea of a telegram. "Gabriel-Ernest is a werewolf" was a hopelessly inadequate effort at conveying the situation, and his aunt would think it was a code message to which he had omitted to give her the key. His one hope was that he might reach home before sundown. The cab which he chartered at the other end of the railway journey bore him with what seemed exasperating slowness along the country roads, which were pink and mauve with the flush of the sinking sun. His aunt was putting away some unfinished jams and cake when he arrived.

"Where is Gabriel-Ernest?" he almost screamed.

"He is taking the little Toop child home," said his aunt. "It was getting so late, I thought it wasn't safe to let it go back alone. What a lovely sunset, isn't it?"

But Van Cheele, although not oblivious of the glow in the western sky, did not stay to discuss its beauties. At a speed for which he was scarcely geared he raced along the narrow lane that led to the home of the Toops. On one side ran the swift current of the mill-stream, on the other rose the stretch of bare hillside. A dwindling rim of red sun showed still on the skyline, and the next turning must bring him in view of the ill-assorted couple he was pursuing. Then the colour went suddenly out of things, and a grey light settled itself with a quick shiver over the landscape. Van Cheele heard a shrill wail of fear, and stopped running.

Nothing was ever seen again of the Toop child or Gabriel-Ernest, but the latter's discarded garments were found lying in the road so it was assumed that the child had fallen into the water, and that the boy had stripped and jumped in, in a vain endeavour to save it. Van Cheele and some workmen who were near by at the time testified to having heard a child scream loudly just near the spot where the clothes were found. Mrs. Toop, who had eleven other children, was decently resigned to her bereavement, but Miss Van Cheele sincerely mourned her lost foundling. It was on her initiative that a memorial brass was put up in the parish church to "Gabriel-Ernest, an unknown boy, who bravely sacrificed his life for another."

Van Cheele gave way to his aunt in most things, but he flatly refused to subscribe to the Gabriel-Ernest memorial.

THE WEREWOLF

by Eugene Field

IN THE REIGN of Egbert the Saxon there dwelt in Britain a maiden named Yseult, who was beloved of all, both for her goodness and for her beauty. But, though many a youth came wooing her, she loved Harold only, and to him she plighted her troth.

Among the other youth of whom Yseult was beloved was Alfred, and he was sore angered that Yseult showed favor to Harold, so that one day Alfred said to Harold: "Is it right that old Siegfried should come from his grave and have Yseult to wife?" Then added he, "Prithee, good sir, why do you turn so white when I speak your grandsire's name?"

Then Harold asked, "What know you of Siegfried that you taunt me? What memory of him should vex me now?"

"We know and we know," retorted Alfred. "There are some tales told us by our grandmas we have not forgot."

So ever after that Alfred's words and Alfred's bitter smile haunted Harold by day and night.

Harold's grandsire, Siegfried the Teuton, had been a man of cruel violence. The legend said that a curse rested upon him, and that at certain times he was possessed of an evil spirit that wreaked its fury on mankind. But Siegfried had been dead full many years, and there was naught to mind the world of him save the legend and a cunning-wrought spear which he had from Brunehilde, the witch. This spear was such a weapon that it never lost its brightness, nor had its point been blunted. It hung in Harold's chamber, and it was the marvel among weapons of that time.

Yseult knew that Alfred loved her, but she did not know of the bitter words which Alfred had spoken to Harold. Her love for Harold was perfect in its trust and gentleness. But Alfred had hit the truth: the curse of old Siegfried was upon Harold—slumbering a century, it had awakened in the blood of the grandson, and Harold knew the curse that was upon him, and it was this that seemed to stand between him and Yseult. But love is stronger than all else, and Harold loved.

Harold did not tell Yseult of the curse that was upon him, for he feared that she would not love him if she knew. Whensoever he felt the fire of the curse burning in his veins he would say to her, "Tomorrow I hunt the wild boar in the uttermost forest," or, "Next week I go stag-stalking among the distant northern hills." Even so it was that he ever made good excuse for his absence, and Yseult thought no evil things, for she was trustful; ay, though he went many times away and was long gone, Yseult suspected no wrong. So none beheld Harold when the curse was upon him in its violence.

Alfred alone bethought himself of evil things. "'Tis passing strange," quoth he, "that ever and anon this gallant lover should quit our company and betake himself whither none knoweth. In sooth 'twill be well to have an eye on old Siegfried's grandson."

Harold knew that Alfred watched him zealously, and he was tormented by a constant fear that Alfred would discover the curse that was on him, but what gave him greater anguish was the fear that mayhap at some moment when he was in Yseult's presence, the curse would seize upon him and cause him to do great evil unto her, whereby she would be destroyed or her love for him would be undone forever. So Harold lived in terror, feeling that his love was hopeless, yet knowing not how to combat it.

Now, it befell in those times that the country round about was ravaged of a werewolf, a creature that was feared by all men howe'er so valorous. This werewolf was by day a man, but by night a wolf given to ravage and to slaughter, and having a charmed life against which no human agency availed aught. Wheresoever he went he attacked and devoured mankind, spreading terror and desolation round about, and the dream-readers said that the earth would not be freed from the werewolf until some man offered himself a voluntary sacrifice to the monster's rage.

Now, although Harold was known far and wide as a mighty huntsman, he had never set forth to hunt the werewolf, and, strange enow, the werewolf never ravaged the domain while Harold was therein. Whereat Alfred marvelled much, and oftentimes he said, "Our Harold is a wondrous huntsman. Who is like unto him in stalking the timid doe and in crippling the fleeing boar? But how passing well doth he time his absence from the haunts of the werewolf. Such valor beseemeth our young Siegfried."

Which being brought to Harold his heart flamed with anger, but he made no answer, lest he should betray the truth he feared.

It happened so about that time that Yseult said to Harold, "Wilt thou go with me tomorrow even to the feast in the sacred grove?"

"That can I not do," answered Harold. "I am privily summoned hence to Normandy upon a mission of which I shall some time tell thee. And I pray thee, on thy love for me, go not to the feast in the sacred grove without me."

"What say'st thou?" cried Yseult. "Shall I not go to the feast of Ste. Aelfreda? My father would be sore displeased were I not there with the other maidens. 'Twere greatest pity that I should despite his love thus."

"But do not, I beseech thee," Harold implored. "Go not to the feast of Ste. Aelfreda in the sacred grove! And thou would thus love me, go not—see, thou my life, on my two knees I ask it!"

"How pale thou art," said Yseult, "and trembling."

"Go not to the sacred grove upon the morrow night," he begged.

Yseult marvelled at his acts and at his speech. Then, for the first time, she thought him to be jealous, whereat she secretly rejoiced (being a woman).

"Ah," quoth she, "thou dost doubt my love," but when she saw a look of pain come on his face she added, as if she repented of the words she had spoken, "or dost thou fear the werewolf?"

Then Harold answered, fixing his eyes on hers, "Thou hast said it. It is the werewolf that I fear."

"Why dost thou look at me so strangely, Harold?" cried Yseult. "By the cruel light in thine eyes one might almost take thee to be the werewolf!"

"Come hither, sit beside me," said Harold tremblingly, "and I will tell thee why I fear to have thee go to the feast of Ste. Aelfreda tomorrow evening. Hear what I dreamed last night. I dreamed I was the werewolf—do not shudder, dear love, for 'twas only a dream.

"A grizzled old man stood at my bedside and strove to pluck my soul from my bosom.

"'What would'st thou?' I cried.

"'Thy soul is mine,' he said, 'thou shalt live out my curse. Give me thy soul, hold back thy hands, give me thy soul, I say.'

"'Thy curse shall not be upon me,' I cried. 'What have I done that thy curse should rest upon me? Thou shalt not have my soul.'

"'For my offence shalt thou suffer, and in my curse thou shalt endure hell. It is so decreed.'

"So spake the old man, and he strove with me, and he prevailed against me, and he plucked my soul from my bosom, and he said, 'Go, search and kill' and, and lo, I was a wolf upon the moor.

"The dry grass crackled beneath my tread. The darkness of the night was heavy and it oppressed me. Strange horrors tortured my soul, and it groaned and groaned, gaoled in that wolfish body. The wind whispered to me, with its myriad voices it spake to me and said, 'Go, search and kill.' And above these voices sounded the hideous laughter of an old man. I fled the moor, whither I knew not, nor knew I what motive lashed me on.

"I came to a river and I plunged in. A burning thirst consumed me, and I lapped the waters of the river. They were waves of flame, and they flashed around me and hissed, and what they said was, 'Go, search and kill,' and I heard the old man's laughter again.

"A forest lay before me with its gloomy thickets and its sombre shadows, with its ravens, its vampires, its serpents, its reptiles, and all its hideous brood of night. I darted among its thorns and crouched amid the leaves, the nettles, and the brambles. The owls hooted at me and the thorns pierced my flesh. 'Go, search and kill,' said everything. The hares sprang from my pathway. The other beasts ran bellowing away, every form of life shrieked in my ears—the curse was on me—I was the werewolf.

"On, on I went with the fleetness of the wind, and my soul groaned in its wolfish prison, and the winds and the waters and the trees bade me, 'Go, search and kill, thou accursed brute. Go, search and kill.'

"Nowhere was there pity for the wolf. What mercy, thus, should I, the werewolf, show? The curse was on me and it filled me with a hunger and a thirst for blood. Skulking on my way within myself I cried, 'Let me have blood, oh, let me have human blood, that this wrath may be appeased, that this curse may be removed.'

"At last I came to the sacred grove. Sombre loomed the poplars, the oaks frowned upon me. Before me stood an old man—'twas he, grizzled and taunting, whose curse I bore. He feared me not. All other living things fled before me, but the old man feared me not. A maiden stood beside him. She did not see me, for she was blind.

"Kill, kill,' cried the old man, and he pointed at the girl beside him.

"Hell raged within me. The curse impelled me. I sprang at her throat. I heard the old man's laughter once more, and then—then I awoke, trembling, cold, horrified."

Scarce was this dream told when Alfred strode that way.

"Now, by'r Lady," quoth he, "I bethink me never to have seen a sorrier twain."

Then Yseult told him of Harold's going away and how that Harold had besought her not to venture to the feast of Ste. Aelfreda in the sacred grove.

"These fears are childish," cried Alfred boastfully. "And thou sufferest me, sweet lady, I will bear thee company to the feast, and a score of my lusty yeomen with their good yew-bows and honest spears, they shall attend me. There be no werewolf, I trow, will chance about with us."

Whereat Yseult laughed merrily, and Harold said, "'Tis well, thou shalt go to the sacred grove, and may my love and Heaven's grace forefend all evil."

Then Harold went to his abode, and he fetched old Siegfried's spear back unto Yseult, and he gave it into her two hands, saying, "Take this spear with thee to the feast tomorrow night. It is old Siegfried's spear, possessing mighty virtue and marvellous."

And Harold took Yseult to his heart and blessed her, and he kissed her upon her brow and upon her lips, saying, "Farewell, oh, my beloved. How wilt thou love me when thou know'st my sacrifice. Farewell, farewell forever, oh, alder-liefest mine."

So Harold went his way, and Yseult was lost in wonderment.

On the morrow night came Yseult to the sacred grove wherein the feast was spread, and she bore old Siegfried's spear with her in her girdle. Alfred attended her, and a score of lusty yeomen were with him. In the grove there was great merriment, and with singing and dancing and games withal did the honest folk celebrate the feast of the fair Ste. Aelfreda.

But suddenly a mighty tumult arose, and there were cries of "The werewolf!" "The werewolf!" Terror seized upon all—stout hearts were frozen with fear. Out from the further forest rushed the werewolf, wood wroth, bellowing hoarsely, gnashing his fangs and tossing hither and thither the yellow foam from his snapping jaws. He sought Yseult straight, as if an evil power drew him to the spot where she stood. But Yseult was not afeared. Like a marble statue she stood and saw the werewolf's coming. The yeomen, dropping their torches and casting aside their bows, had fled. Alfred alone abided there to do the monster battle.

At the approaching wolf he hurled his heavy lance, but as it struck the werewolf's bristling back the weapon was all to-shivered.

Then the werewolf, fixing his eyes upon Yseult, skulked for a moment in the shadow of the yews and thinking then of Harold's words, Yseult plucked old Siegfried's spear from her girdle, raised it on high, and with the strength of despair sent it hurtling through the air.

The werewolf saw the shining weapon, and a cry burst from his gaping throat, a cry of human agony. And Yseult saw in the werewolf's eyes the eyes of some one she had seen and known, but 'twas for an instant only, and then the eyes were no longer human, but wolfish in their ferocity. A supernatural force seemed to speed the spear in its flight. With fearful precision the weapon smote home and buried itself by half its length in the werewolf's shaggy breast just above the heart, and then, with a monstrous sigh—as if he yielded up his life without regret—the werewolf fell dead in the shadow of the yews.

Then, ah, then in very truth there was great joy, and loud were the acclaims, while, beautiful in her trembling pallor, Yseult was led unto her home, where the people set about to give great feast to do her homage, for the werewolf was dead, and she it was that had slain him.

But Yseult cried out: "Go, search for Harold! Go, bring him to me. Nor eat, nor sleep till he be found."

"Good my lady," quoth Alfred, "how can that be, since he hath betaken himself to Normandy?"

"I care not where he be," she cried. "My heart stands still until I look into his eyes again."

"Surely he hath not gone to Normandy," outspake Hubert. "This very eventide I saw him enter his abode."

They hastened thither, a vast company. His chamber door was barred.

"Harold, Harold, come forth!" they cried, as they beat upon the door, but no answer came to their calls and knockings. Afeared, they battered down the door, and when it fell they saw that Harold lay upon his bed.

"He sleeps," said one. "See, he holds a portrait in his hand, and it is her portrait. How fair he is and how tranquilly he sleeps."

But no, Harold was not asleep. His face was calm and beautiful, as if he dreamed of his beloved, but his raiment was red with the blood that streamed from a wound in his breast—a gaping, ghastly spear wound just above his heart.

Running Wolf

by *Algernon Blackwood*

T**HE MAN WHO ENJOYS** an adventure outside the general experience of the race, and imparts it to others, must not be surprised if he is taken for either a liar or a fool, as Malcolm Hyde, hotel clerk on a holiday, discovered in due course. Nor is "enjoy" the right word to use in describing his emotions. The word he chose was probably "survive."

When he first set eyes on Medicine Lake he was struck by its still, sparkling beauty, lying there in the vast Canadian backwoods, next by its extreme loneliness, and, lastly—a good deal later, this—by its combination of beauty, loneliness, and singular atmosphere, due to the fact that it was the scene of his adventure.

"It's fairly stiff with big fish," said Morton of the Montreal Sporting Club. "Spend your holiday there, up Mattawa way, some fifteen miles west of Stony Creek. You'll have it all to your-self except for an old Indian who's got a shack there. Camp on the east side—if you'll take a tip from me." He then talked for half an hour about the wonderful sport, yet he was not other-wise very communicative, and did not suffer questions gladly, Hyde noticed. Nor had he stayed there very long himself. If it was such a paradise as Morton, its discoverer and the most expe-rienced rod in the province, claimed, why had he himself spent only three days there?

"Ran short of grub," was the explanation offered, but to an-other friend he had mentioned briefly, "flies," and to a third, so Hyde learned later, he gave the excuse that his half-breed "took sick," necessitating a quick return to civilization.

Hyde, however, cared little for the explanations. His interest in these came later. "Stiff with fish" was the phrase he liked. He took the Canadian Pacific train to Mattawa, laid in his outfit at Stony Creek, and set off thence for the fifteen-mile canoe trip without a care in the world.

Travelling light, the portages did not trouble him. The water was swift and easy, the rapids negotiable. Everything came his way, as the saying is. Occasionally he saw big fish making for the deeper pools, and was sorely tempted to stop, but he resisted. He pushed on between the immense world of forests that stretched for hundreds of miles, known to deer, bear, moose, and wolf, but strange to any echo of human tread, a deserted and primeval wilderness. The autumn day was calm, the water sang and sparkled, the blue sky hung cloudless over all, ablaze with light. Toward evening he passed an old beaver-dam, rounded a little point, and had his first sight of Medicine Lake. He lifted his dripping paddle; the canoe shot with silent glide into calm water. He gave an exclamation of delight, for the loveliness caught his breath away.

Though primarily a sportsman, he was not insensible to beauty. The lake formed a crescent, perhaps four miles long, its width between a mile and half a mile. The slanting gold of sunset flooded it. No wind stirred its crystal surface. Here it had lain since the American Indian's god first made it. Here it would lie until he dried it up again. Towering spruce and hemlock trooped to its very edge, majestic cedars leaned down as if to drink, crimson sumachs shone in fiery patches, and maples gleamed orange and red beyond belief. The air was like wine, with the silence of a dream.

It was here the natives formerly "made medicine," with all the wild ritual and tribal ceremony of an ancient day. But it was of Morton, rather than of Indians, that Hyde thought. If this lonely, hidden paradise was really stiff with big fish, he owed a lot to Morton for the information. Peace invaded him, but the excitement of the hunter lay below.

He looked about him with quick, practised eye for a camping place before the sun sank below the forests and the half-lights came. The Indian's shack, lying in full sunshine on the eastern shore, he found at once, but the trees lay too thick about it for comfort, nor did he wish to be so close to its inhabitant. Upon the opposite side, however, an ideal clearing offered. This lay already in shadow, the huge forest darkening it toward evening, but the open space attracted. He paddled over quickly and examined it. The ground was hard and dry, he found, and a little brook ran tinkling down one side of it into the lake. This outfall, too, would be a good fishing spot. Also it was sheltered. A few low willows marked the mouth.

An experienced camper soon makes up his mind. It was a perfect site, and some charred logs, with traces of former fires, proved that he was not the first to think so. Hyde was delighted. Then, suddenly, disappointment came to tinge his pleasure. His kit was landed, and preparations for putting up the tent were begun, when he recalled a detail that excitement had so far kept in the background of his mind—Morton's advice. But not Morton's only, for the storekeeper at Stony Creek had reinforced it. The big fellow with straggling moustache and stooping shoulders, dressed in shirt and trousers, had handed him out a final sentence with the bacon, flour, condensed milk, and sugar. He had repeated Morton's half-forgotten words:

"Put yer tent on the east shore. I should," he had said at parting.

He remembered Morton, too, apparently. "A shortish fellow, brown as an Indian and fairly smelling of the woods. Travelling with Jake, the half-breed." That assuredly was Morton. "Didn't stay long, now, did he?" he added in a reflective tone.

"Going Windy Lake way, are yer? Or Ten Mile Water, maybe?" he had first inquired of Hyde.

"Medicine Lake."

"Is that so?" the man said, as though he doubted it for some obscure reason. He pulled at his ragged moustache a moment. "Is that so, now?" he repeated. And the final words followed him down-stream after a considerable pause, the advice about the best shore on which to put his tent.

All this now suddenly flashed back upon Hyde's mind with a tinge of disappointment and annoyance, for when two experienced men agreed, their opinion was not to be lightly disregarded. He wished he had asked the storekeeper for more details. He looked about him, he reflected, he hesitated. His ideal camping ground lay certainly on the forbidden shore. What in the world, he pondered, could be the objection to it?

But the light was fading. He must decide quickly one way or the other. After staring at his unpacked dunnage and the tent, already half erected, he made up his mind with a muttered expression that consigned both Morton and the storekeeper to less pleasant places. "They must have some reason," he growled to himself, "fellows like that usually know what they're talking about. I guess I'd better shift over to the other side, for tonight, at any rate."

He glanced across the water before actually reloading. No smoke rose from the Indian's shack. He had seen no sign of a canoe. The man, he decided, was away. Reluctantly, then, he left the good camping ground and paddled across the lake, and half an hour later his tent was up, firewood collected, and two small trout were already caught for supper. But the bigger fish, he knew, lay waiting for him on the other side by the little outfall, and he fell asleep at length on his bed of balsam boughs, annoyed and disappointed, yet wondering how a mere sentence could have persuaded him so easily against his own better judgment. He slept like the dead. The sun was well up before he stirred.

But his morning mood was a very different one. The brilliant light, the peace, the intoxicating air, all this was too exhilarating for the mind to harbour foolish fancies, and he marvelled that he could have been so weak the night before. No hesitation lay in him anywhere. He struck camp immediately after breakfast, paddled back across the strip of shining water, and quickly settled in upon the forbidden shore, as he now called it, with a contemptuous grin. And the more he saw of the spot, the better he liked it. There was plenty of wood, running water to drink, an open space about the tent, and there were no flies. The fishing, moreover, was magnificent. Morton's description was fully justified, and "stiff with big fish" for once was not an exaggeration.

The useless hours of the early afternoon he passed dozing in the sun, or wandering through the underbrush beyond the camp. He found no sign of anything unusual. He bathed in a cool, deep pool. He revelled in the lonely little paradise. Lonely it certainly was, but the loneliness was part of its charm. The stillness, the peace, the isolation of this beautiful backwoods lake delighted him. The silence was divine. He was entirely satisfied.

After a brew of tea, he strolled toward evening along the shore, looking for the first sign of a rising fish. A faint ripple on the water, with the lengthening shadows, made good conditions. Plop followed plop, as the big fellows rose, snatched at their food, and vanished into the depths. He hurried back. Ten minutes later he had taken his rods and was gliding cautiously in the canoe through the quiet water.

So good was the sport, indeed, and so quickly did the big trout pile up in the bottom of the canoe that, despite the growing lateness, he found it hard to tear himself away. "One more," he said, "and then I really will go." He landed that "one more," and was in act of taking it off the hook, when the deep silence of the evening was curiously disturbed. He became abruptly aware that someone watched him. A pair of eyes, it seemed, were fixed upon him from some point in the surrounding shadows.

Thus, at least, he interpreted the odd disturbance in his happy mood, for thus he felt it. The feeling stole over him without the slightest warning. He was not alone. The slippery big trout dropped from his fingers. He sat motionless, and stared about him.

Nothing stirred. The ripple on the lake had died away, there was no wind, the forest lay a single purple mass of shadow. The yellow sky, fast fading, threw reflections that troubled the eye and made distances uncertain. But there was no sound, no movement, he saw no figure anywhere. Yet he knew that someone watched him, and a wave of quite unreasoning terror gripped him. The nose of the canoe was against the bank. In a moment, and instinctively, he shoved it off and paddled into deeper water. The watcher, it came to him also instinctively, was quite close to him upon that bank. But where? And who? Was it the Indian?

Here, in deeper water, and some twenty yards from the shore, he paused and strained both sight and hearing to find some possible clue. He felt half ashamed, now that the first strange feeling passed a little. But the certainty remained. Absurd as it was, he felt positive that someone watched him with concentrated and intent regard. Every fibre in his being told him so, and though he could discover no figure, no new outline on the shore, he could even have sworn in which clump of willow bushes the hidden person crouched and stared. His attention seemed drawn to that particular clump.

The water dripped slowly from his paddle, now lying across the thwarts. There was no other sound. The canvas of his tent gleamed dimly. A star or two were out. He waited. Nothing happened.

Then, as suddenly as it had come, the feeling passed, and he knew that the person who had been watching him intently had gone. It was as if a current had been turned off, the normal world flowed back, the landscape emptied as if someone had left a room. The disagreeable feeling left him at the same time, so that he instantly turned the canoe in to the shore again, landed, and, paddle in hand, went over to examine the clump of willows he had singled out as the place of concealment. There was no one there, of course, nor any trace of recent human occupancy. No leaves, no branches stirred, nor was a single twig displaced. His keen and practised sight detected no sign of tracks upon the ground. Yet, for all that, he felt positive that a little time ago someone had crouched among these very leaves and watched him. He remained absolutely convinced of it. The watcher, whether Indian, hunter, stray lumberman, or wandering half-breed, had now withdrawn, a search was useless, and dusk was falling. He returned to his little camp, more disturbed perhaps than he cared to acknowledge. He cooked his supper, hung up his catch on a string, so that no prowling animal could get at it during the night, and prepared to make himself comfortable until bedtime. Unconsciously, he built a bigger fire than usual, and found himself peering over his pipe into the deep shadows beyond the firelight, straining his ears to catch the slightest sound. He remained generally on the alert in a way that was new to him.

A man under such conditions and in such a place need not know discomfort until the sense of loneliness strikes him as too vivid a reality. Loneliness in a backwoods camp brings charm, pleasure, and a happy sense of calm until, and unless, it comes too near. It should remain an ingredient only among other conditions. It should not be directly, vividly noticed. Once it has crept within short range, however, it may easily cross the narrow line between comfort and discomfort, and darkness is an undesirable time for the transition. A curious dread may easily follow—the dread lest the loneliness suddenly be disturbed, and the solitary human feel himself open to attack.

For Hyde, now, this transition had been already accomplished. The too intimate sense of his loneliness had shifted abruptly into the worse condition of no longer being quite alone. It was an awkward moment, and the hotel clerk realized his position exactly. He did not quite like it. He sat there, with his back to the blazing logs, a very visible object in the light, while all about him the darkness of the forest lay like an impenetrable wall. He could not see a foot beyond the small circle of his campfire. The silence about him was like the silence of the dead. No leaf rustled, no wave lapped. He himself sat motionless as a log.

Then again he became suddenly aware that the person who watched him had returned, and that same intent and concentrated gaze as before was fixed upon him where he lay. There was no warning, he heard no stealthy tread or snapping of dry twigs, yet the owner of those steady eyes was very close to him, probably not a dozen feet away. This sense of proximity was overwhelming.

It is unquestionable that a shiver ran down his spine. This time, moreover, he felt positive that the man crouched just beyond the firelight, the distance he himself could see being nicely calculated, and straight in front of him. For some minutes he sat without stirring a single muscle, yet with each muscle ready and alert, straining his eyes in vain to pierce the darkness, but only succeeding in dazzling his sight with the reflected light. Then, as he shifted his position slowly, cautiously, to obtain another angle of vision, his heart gave two big thumps against his ribs and the hair seemed to rise on his scalp with the sense of cold that shot horribly up his spine. In the darkness facing him he saw two small and greenish circles that were certainly a pair of eyes, yet not the eyes of Indian, hunter, or of any human being. It was a pair of animal eyes that stared so fixedly at him out of the night. And this certainly had an immediate and natural effect upon him.

For, at the menace of those eyes, the fears of millions of long dead hunters since the dawn of time woke in him. Hotel clerk though he was, heredity surged through him in an automatic wave of instinct. His hand groped for a weapon. His fingers fell on the iron head of his small camp axe, and at once he was himself again. Confidence returned, the vague, superstitious dread was gone. This was a bear or wolf that smelt his catch and came to steal it. With beings of that sort he knew instinctively how to deal, yet admitting, by this very instinct, that his original dread had been of quite another kind.

"I'll damned quick find out what it is," he exclaimed aloud, and snatching a burning brand from the fire, he hurled it with good aim straight at the eyes of the beast before him.

The bit of pitch-pine fell in a shower of sparks that lit the dry grass this side of the animal, flared up a moment, then died quickly down again. But in that instant of bright illumination he saw clearly what his unwelcome visitor was. A big timber wolf sat on its hindquarters, staring steadily at him through the firelight. He saw its legs and shoulders, he saw its hair, he saw also the big hemlock trunks lit up behind it, and the willow scrub on each side. It formed a vivid, clear-cut picture shown in clear detail by the momentary blaze. To his amazement, however, the wolf did not turn and bolt away from the burning log, but withdrew a few yards only, and sat there again on its haunches, staring, staring as before. Heavens, how it stared! He "shoo-ed" it, but without effect. It did not budge. He did not waste another good log on it, for his fear was dissipated now. A timber wolf was a timber wolf, and it might sit there as long as it pleased, provided it did not try to steal his catch. No alarm was in him anymore. He knew that wolves were harmless in the summer and autumn, and even when "packed" in the winter, they would attack a man only when suffering desperate hunger. So he lay and watched the beast, threw bits of stick in its direction, even talked to it, wondering only that it never moved. "You can stay there forever, if you like," he remarked to it aloud, "for you cannot get at my fish, and the rest of the grub I shall take into the tent with me!"

The creature blinked its bright green eyes, but made no move.

Why, then, if his fear was gone, did he think of certain things as he rolled himself in the Hudson Bay blankets before going to sleep? The immobility of the animal was strange, its refusal to turn and bolt was still stranger. Never before had he known a wild creature that was not afraid of fire. Why did it sit and watch him, as with purpose in its dreadful eyes? How had he felt its presence earlier and instantly? A timber wolf, especially a solitary timber wolf, was a timid thing, yet this one feared neither man nor fire. Now, as he lay there wrapped in his blankets inside the cosy tent, it sat outside beneath the stars, beside the fading embers, the wind chilly in its fur, the ground cooling beneath its planted paws, watching him, steadily watching him, perhaps until the dawn.

It was unusual, it was strange. Having neither imagination nor tradition, he called upon no store of racial visions. Matter of fact, a hotel clerk on a fishing holiday, he lay there in his blankets, merely wondering and puzzled. A timber wolf was a timber wolf and nothing more. Yet this timber wolf—the idea haunted him—was different. In a word, the deeper part of his original uneasiness remained. He tossed about, he shivered sometimes in his broken sleep. He did not go out to see, but he woke early and unrefreshed.

Again, with the sunshine and the morning wind, however, the incident of the night before was forgotten, almost unreal. His hunting zeal was uppermost. The tea and fish were delicious, his pipe had never tasted so good, the glory of this lonely lake amid primeval forests went to his head a little. He was a hunter before the Lord, and nothing else. He tried the edge of the lake, and in the excitement of playing a big fish, knew suddenly that it, the wolf, was there. He paused with the rod, exactly as if struck. He looked about him, he looked in a definite direction. The brilliant sunshine made every smallest detail clear and sharp—boulders of granite, burned stems, crimson sumach, pebbles along the shore in neat, separate detail—without revealing where the watcher hid. Then, his sight wandering farther inshore among the tangled undergrowth, he suddenly picked up the familiar, half-expected outline. The wolf was lying behind a granite boulder, so that only the head, the muzzle, and the eyes were visible. It merged in its background. Had he not known it was a wolf, he could never have separated it from the landscape. The eyes shone in the sunlight.

There it lay. He looked straight at it. Their eyes, in fact, actually met full and square. "Great Scott!" he exclaimed aloud, "why, it's like looking at a human being!" From that moment, unwittingly, he established a singular personal relation with the beast. And what followed confirmed this undesirable impression, for the animal rose instantly and came down in leisurely fashion to the shore, where it stood looking back at him. It stood and stared into his eyes like some great wild dog, so that he was aware of a new and almost incredible sensation—that it courted recognition.

"Well! well!" he exclaimed again, relieving his feelings by addressing it aloud, "if this doesn't beat everything I ever saw! What d'you want, anyway?"

He examined it now more carefully. He had never seen a wolf so big before. It was a tremendous beast, a nasty customer to tackle, he reflected, if it ever came to that. It stood there absolutely fearless and full of confidence. In the clear sunlight he took in every detail of it—a huge, shaggy, lean-flanked timber wolf, its wicked eyes staring straight into his own, almost with a kind of purpose in them. He saw its great jaws, its teeth, and its tongue, hung out, dropping saliva a little. And yet the idea of its savagery, its fierceness, was very little in him.

He was amazed and puzzled beyond belief. He wished the Indian would come back. He did not understand this strange behaviour in an animal. Its eyes, the odd expression in them, gave him a queer, unusual, difficult feeling. Had his nerves gone wrong, he almost wondered.

The beast stood on the shore and looked at him. He wished for the first time that he had brought a rifle. With a resounding smack he brought his paddle down flat upon the water, using all his strength, till the echoes rang as from a pistol-shot that was audible from one end of the lake to the other. The wolf never stirred. He shouted, but the beast remained unmoved. He blinked his eyes, speaking as to a dog, a domestic animal, a creature accustomed to human ways. It blinked its eyes in return.

At length, increasing his distance from the shore, he continued fishing, and the excitement of the marvellous sport held his attention—his surface attention, at any rate. At times he almost forgot the attendant beast, yet whenever he looked up, he saw it there. And worse, when he slowly paddled home again, he observed it trotting along the shore as though to keep him company. Crossing a little bay, he spurted, hoping to reach the other point before his undesired and undesirable attendant. Instantly the brute broke into that rapid, tireless lope that, except on ice, can run down anything on four legs in the woods. When he reached the distant point, the wolf was waiting for him. He raised his paddle from the water, pausing a moment for reflection, for this very close attention—there were dusk and night yet to come—he certainly did not relish. His camp was near. He had to land. He felt uncomfortable even in the sunshine of broad day, when, to his keen relief, about half a mile from the tent, he saw the creature suddenly stop and sit down in the open. He waited a moment, then paddled on. It did not follow. There was no attempt to move, it merely sat and watched him. After a few hundred yards, he looked back. It was still sitting where he left it. And the absurd, yet significant, feeling came to him that the beast divined his thought, his anxiety, his dread, and was now showing him, as well as it could, that it entertained no hostile feeling and did not meditate attack.

He turned the canoe toward the shore, he landed. He cooked his supper in the dusk, the animal made no sign. Not far away it certainly lay and watched, but it did not advance. And to Hyde, observant now in a new way, came one sharp, vivid reminder of the strange atmosphere into which his commonplace personality had strayed. He suddenly recalled that his relations with the beast, already established, had progressed distinctly a stage further. This startled him, yet without the accompanying alarm he must certainly have felt twenty-four hours before. He had an understanding with the wolf. He was aware of friendly thoughts toward it. He even went so far as to set out a few big fish on the spot where he had first seen it sitting the previous night. "If he comes," he thought, "he is welcome to them. I've got plenty, anyway." He thought of it now as "he."

Yet the wolf made no appearance until he was in the act of entering his tent a good deal later. It was close on ten o'clock, whereas nine was his hour, and late at that, for turning in. He had, therefore, unconsciously been waiting for him. Then, as he was closing the flap, he saw the eyes close to where he had placed the fish. He waited, hiding himself, and expecting to hear sounds of munching jaws, but all was silence. Only the eyes glowed steadily out of the background of pitch darkness. He closed the flap. He had no slightest fear. In ten minutes he was sound asleep.

He could not have slept very long, for when he woke up he could see the shine of a faint red light through the canvas, and the fire had not died down completely. He rose and cautiously peeped out. The air was very cold. He saw his breath. But he also saw the wolf, for it had come in, and was sitting by the dying embers, not two yards away from where he crouched behind the flap. And this time, at these very close quarters, there was something in the attitude of the big wild thing that caught his attention with a vivid thrill of startled surprise and a sudden shock of cold that held him spellbound. He stared, unable to believe his eyes, for the wolf's attitude conveyed to him something familiar that at first he was unable to explain. Its pose reached him in the terms of another thing with which he was entirely at home. What was it? Did his senses betray him? Was he still asleep and dreaming?

Then, suddenly, with a start of uncanny recognition, he

knew. Its attitude was that of a dog. Having found the clue, his mind then made an awful leap. For it was, after all, no dog its appearance aped, but something nearer to himself, and more familiar still. Good heavens! It sat there with the pose, the attitude, the gesture in repose of something almost human. And then, with a second shock of biting wonder, it came to him like a revelation. The wolf sat beside that campfire as a man might sit.

Before he could weigh his extraordinary discovery, before he could examine it in detail or with care, the animal, sitting in this ghastly fashion, seemed to feel his eyes fixed on it. It slowly turned and looked him in the face, and for the first time Hyde felt a full-blooded, superstitious fear flood through his entire being. He seemed transfixed with that nameless terror that is said to attack human beings who suddenly face the dead, finding themselves bereft of speech and movement. This moment of paralysis certainly occurred. Its passing, however, was as singular as its advent. For almost at once he was aware of something beyond and above this mockery of human attitude and pose, something that ran along unaccustomed nerves and reached his feeling, even perhaps his heart. The revulsion was extraordinary, its result still more extraordinary and unexpected. Yet the fact remains. He was aware of another thing that had the effect of stilling his terror as soon as it was born. He was aware of appeal, silent, half expressed, yet vastly pathetic. He saw in the savage eyes a beseeching, even a yearning, expression that changed his mood as by magic from dread to natural sympathy. The great grey brute, symbol of cruel ferocity, sat there beside his dying fire and appealed for help.

This gulf betwixt animal and human seemed in that instant bridged. It was, of course, incredible. Hyde, sleep still possibly clinging to his inner being with the shades and half shapes of dream yet about his soul, acknowledged, how he knew not, the amazing fact. He found himself nodding to the brute in half consent, and instantly, without more ado, the lean grey shape rose like a wraith and trotted off swiftly, but with stealthy tread, into the background of the night.

When Hyde woke in the morning his first impression was that he must have dreamed the entire incident. His practical nature asserted itself. There was a bite in the fresh autumn air, the bright sun allowed no half lights anywhere. He felt brisk in mind and body. Reviewing what had happened, he came to the conclusion that it was utterly vain to speculate. No possible explanation of the animal's behaviour occurred to him. He was dealing with something entirely outside his experience. His fear, however, had completely left him. The odd sense of friendliness remained. The beast had a definite purpose, and he himself was included in that purpose. His sympathy held good.

But with the sympathy there was also an intense curiosity. "If it shows itself again," he told himself, "I'll go up close and find out what it wants." The fish laid out the night before had not been touched.

It must have been a full hour after breakfast when he next saw the brute. It was standing on the edge of the clearing, looking at him in the way now become familiar. Hyde immediately picked up his axe and advanced toward it boldly, keeping his eyes fixed straight upon its own. There was nervousness in him, but kept well under. Nothing betrayed it. Step by step he drew nearer until some ten yards separated them. The wolf had not stirred a muscle as yet. Its jaws hung open, its eyes observed him intently. It allowed him to approach without a sign of what its mood might be. Then, with these ten yards between them, it turned abruptly and moved slowly off, looking back first over one shoulder and then over the other, exactly as a dog might do, to see if he was following.

A singular journey it was they then made together, animal and man. The trees surrounded them at once, for they left the lake behind them, entering the tangled bush beyond. The beast, Hyde noticed, obviously picked the easiest track for him to follow, for obstacles that meant nothing to the four-legged expert, yet were difficult for a man, were carefully avoided with an almost uncanny skill, while yet the general direction was accurately kept. Occasionally there were windfalls to be surmounted, but though the wolf bounded over these with ease, it was always waiting for the man on the other side after he had laboriously climbed over. Deeper and deeper into the heart of the lonely forest they penetrated in this singular fashion, cutting across the arc of the lake's crescent, it seemed to Hyde, for after two miles or so, he recognized the big rocky bluff that overhung the water at its northern end. This outstanding bluff he had seen from his camp, one side of it falling sheer into the water. It was probably the spot, he imagined, where the Indians held their medicine-making ceremonies, for it stood out in isolated fashion, and its top formed a private plateau not easy of access. And it was here, close to a big spruce at the foot of the bluff upon the forest side, that the wolf stopped suddenly and for the first time since its appearance gave audible expression to its feelings. It sat down on its haunches, lifted its muzzle with open jaws, and gave vent to a subdued and long-drawn howl that was more like the wail of a dog than the fierce barking cry associated with a wolf.

By this time Hyde had lost not only fear, but caution too, nor, oddly enough, did this warning howl revive a sign of unwelcome emotion in him. In that curious sound he detected the same message that the eyes conveyed—appeal for help. He paused, nevertheless, a little startled, and while the wolf sat waiting for him, he looked about him quickly. There was young timber here. It had once been a small clearing, evidently. Axe and fire had done their work, but there was evidence to an experienced eye that it was Indians and not white men who had once been busy here. Some part of the medicine ritual, doubtless, took place in the little clearing, thought the man, as he advanced again towards his patient leader. The end of their queer journey, he felt, was close at hand.

He had not taken two steps before the animal got up and moved very slowly in the direction of some low bushes that formed a clump just beyond. It entered these, first looking back to make sure that its companion watched. The bushes hid it. A moment later it emerged again. Twice it performed this pantomime, each time, as it reappeared, standing still and staring at the man with as distinct an expression of appeal in the eyes as an animal may compass, probably. Its excitement, meanwhile, certainly increased, and this excitement was, with equal certainty, communicated to the man. Hyde made up his mind quickly. Gripping his axe tightly, and ready to use it at the first hint of malice, he moved slowly nearer to the bushes, wondering with something of a tremor what would happen.

If he expected to be startled, his expectation was at once fulfilled, but it was the behaviour of the beast that made him jump. It positively frisked about him like a happy dog. It frisked for joy. Its excitement was intense, yet from its open mouth no sound was audible. With a sudden leap, then, it bounded past him into the clump of bushes, against whose very edge he stood, and began scraping vigorously at the ground. Hyde stood and stared, amazement and interest now banishing all his nervousness, even when the beast, in its violent scraping, actually touched his body with its own. He had, perhaps, the feeling that he was in a dream, one of those fantastic dreams in which things may happen without involving an adequate surprise, for otherwise the manner of scraping and scratching at the ground must have seemed an impossible phenomenon. No wolf, no dog certainly, used its paws in the way those paws were working. Hyde had the odd, distressing sensation that it was hands, not paws, he watched. And yet, somehow, the natural, adequate surprise he should have felt was absent. The strange action seemed not entirely unnatural. In his heart some deep hidden spring of sympathy and pity stirred instead. He was aware of pathos.

The wolf stopped in its task and looked up into his face.

Hyde acted without hesitation then. Afterwards he was wholly at a loss to explain his own conduct. It seemed he knew what to do, divined what was asked, expected of him. Between his mind and the dumb desire yearning through the savage animal there was intelligent and intelligible communication. He cut a stake and sharpened it, for the stones would blunt his axe-edge. He entered the clump of bushes to complete the digging his four-legged companion had begun. And while he worked, though he did not forget the close proximity of the wolf, he paid no attention to it. Often his back was turned as he stooped over the laborious clearing away of the hard earth. No uneasiness or sense of danger was in him any more. The wolf sat outside the clump and watched the operations. Its concentrated attention, its patience, its intense eagerness, the gentleness and docility of the grey, fierce, and probably hungry brute, its obvious pleasure and satisfaction, too, at having won the human to its mysterious purpose—these were colours in the strange picture that Hyde thought of later when dealing with the human herd in his hotel again. At the moment he was aware chiefly of pathos and affection. The whole business was, of course, not to be believed, but that discovery came later, too, when telling it to others.

The digging continued for fully half an hour before his labour was rewarded by the discovery of a small whitish object. He picked it up and examined it—the finger-bone of a man. Other discoveries then followed quickly and in quantity. The cache was laid bare. He collected nearly the complete skeleton. The skull, however, he found last, and might not have found at all but for the guidance of his strangely alert companion. It lay some few yards away from the central hole now dug, and the wolf stood nuzzling the ground with its nose before Hyde understood that he was meant to dig exactly in that spot for it. Between the beast's very paws his stake struck hard upon it. He scraped the earth from the bone and examined it carefully. It was perfect, save for the fact that some wild animal had gnawed it, the teeth-marks being still plainly visible. Close beside it lay the rusty iron head of a tomahawk. This and the smallness of the bones confirmed him in his judgment that it was the skeleton not of a white man, but of an Indian.

During the excitement of the discovery of the bones one by one, and finally of the skull, but, more especially, during the period of intense interest while Hyde was examining them, he had paid little, if any, attention to the wolf. He was aware that it sat and watched him, never moving its keen eyes for a single moment from the actual operations, but of sign or movement it made none at all. He knew that it was pleased and satisfied, he knew also that he had now fulfilled its purpose in a great measure. The further intuition that now came to him, derived, he felt positive, from his companion's dumb desire, was perhaps the cream of the entire experience to him. Gathering the bones together in his coat, he carried them, together with the tomahawk, to the foot of the big spruce where the animal had first stopped. His leg actually touched the creature's muzzle as he passed. It turned its head to watch, but did not follow, nor did it move a muscle while he prepared the platform of boughs upon which he then laid the poor worn bones of an Indian who had been killed, doubtless, in sudden attack or ambush, and to whose remains had been denied the last grace of proper tribal burial. He wrapped the bones in bark. He laid the tomahawk beside the skull. He lit the circular fire round the pyre, and the blue smoke rose upward into the clear bright sunshine of the Canadian autumn morning till it was lost among the mighty trees far overhead.

In the moment before actually lighting the little fire he had turned to note what his companion did. It sat five yards away, he saw, gazing intently, and one of its front paws was raised a little from the ground. It made no sign of any kind. He finished the work, becoming so absorbed in it that he had eyes for nothing but the tending and guarding of his careful ceremonial fire. It was only when the platform of boughs collapsed, laying their charred burden gently on the fragrant earth among the soft wood ashes, that he turned again, as though to show the wolf what he had done, and seek, perhaps, some look of satisfaction in its curiously expressive eyes. But the place he searched was empty. The wolf had gone.

He did not see it again. It gave no sign of its presence anywhere; he was not watched. He fished as before, wandered through the bush about his camp, sat smoking round his fire after dark, and slept peacefully in his cosy little tent. He was not disturbed. No howl was ever audible in the distant forest, no twig snapped beneath a stealthy tread, he saw no eyes. The wolf that behaved like a man had gone forever.

It was the day before he left that Hyde, noticing smoke rising from the shack across the lake, paddled over to exchange a word or two with the Indian, who had evidently now returned. The Indian came down to meet him as he landed, but it was soon plain that he spoke very little English. He emitted the familiar grunts at first, then bit by bit Hyde stirred his limited vocabulary into action. The net result, however, was slight enough, though it was certainly direct:

"You camp there?" the man asked, pointing to the other side.

"Yes."

"Wolf come?"

"Yes."

"You see wolf?"

"Yes."

The Indian stared at him fixedly a moment, a keen, wondering look upon his coppery, creased face.

"You 'fraid wolf?" he asked after a moment's pause.

"No," replied Hyde, truthfully. He knew it was useless to ask questions of his own, though he was eager for information. The other would have told him nothing. It was sheer luck that the man had touched on the subject at all, and Hyde realized that his own best role was merely to answer, but to ask no questions. Then, suddenly, the Indian became comparatively voluble. There was awe in his voice and manner.

"Him no wolf. Him big medicine wolf. Him spirit wolf."

Whereupon he drank the tea the other had brewed for him, closed his lips tightly, and said no more. His outline was discernible on the shore, rigid and motionless, an hour later, when Hyde's canoe turned the corner of the lake three miles away, and landed to make the portages up the first rapid of his homeward stream.

It was Morton who, after some persuasion, supplied further details of what he called the legend. Some hundred years before, the tribe that lived in the territory beyond the lake began their annual medicine-making ceremonies on the big rocky bluff at the northern end, but no medicine could be made. The spirits, declared the chief medicine man, would not answer. They were offended. An investigation followed. It was discovered that a young brave had recently killed a wolf, a thing strictly forbidden, since the wolf was the totem animal of the tribe. To make matters worse, the name of the guilty man was Running Wolf. The offence being unpardonable, the man was cursed and driven from the tribe:

"Go out. Wander alone among the woods, and if we see you we slay you. Your bones shall be scattered in the forest, and your spirit shall not enter the Happy Hunting Grounds till one of another race shall find and bury them."

"Which meant," explained Morton laconically, his only comment on the story, "probably forever."

TARNHELM

by Hugh Walpole

I

I WAS, I SUPPOSE, at that time a peculiar child, peculiar a little by nature, but also because I had spent so much of my young life in the company of people very much older than myself.

After the events that I am now going to relate, some quite indelible mark was set on me. I became then, and have always been since, one of those persons, otherwise insignificant, who have decided, without possibility of change, about certain questions.

Some things, doubted by most of the world, are for these people true and beyond argument. This certainty of theirs gives them a kind of stamp, as though they lived so much in their imagination as to have very little assurance as to what is fact and what fiction. This 'oddness' of theirs puts them apart. If now, at the age of fifty, I am a man with very few friends, very much alone, it is because, if you like, my Uncle Robert died in a strange manner forty years ago and I was a witness of his death.

I have never until now given any account of the strange proceedings that occurred at Faildyke Hall on the evening of Christmas Eve in the year 1890. The incidents of that evening are still remembered very clearly by one or two people, and a kind of legend of my Uncle Robert's death has been carried on into the younger generation. But no one still alive was a witness of them as I was, and I feel it is time that I set them down upon paper.

I write them down without comment. I extenuate nothing, I disguise nothing. I am not, I hope, in any way a vindictive man, but my brief meeting with my Uncle Robert and the circum-stances of his death gave my life, even at that early age, a twist difficult for me very readily to forgive.

As to the so-called supernatural element in my story, every-one must judge for himself about that. We deride or we accept according to our natures. If we are built of a certain solid practi-cal material the probability is that no evidence, however definite, however first-hand, will convince us. If dreams are our daily portion, one dream more or less will scarcely shake our sense of reality.

However, to my story.

My father and mother were in India from my eighth to my thirteenth years. I did not see them, except on two occasions when they visited England. I was an only child, loved dearly by both my parents, who, however, loved one another yet more. They were an exceedingly sentimental couple of the old-fash-ioned kind. My father was in the Indian Civil Service, and wrote poetry. He even had his epic, Tantalus: A Poem in Four Cantos, published at his own expense.

This, added to the fact that my mother had been considered an invalid before he married her, made my parents feel that they bore a very close resemblance to the Brownings, and my father even had a pet name for my mother that sounded curiously like the famous and hideous 'Ba.'

I was a delicate child, was sent to Mr. Ferguson's Private Academy at the tender age of eight, and spent my holidays as the rather unwanted guest of various relations.

"Unwanted" because I was, I imagine, a difficult child to understand. I had an old grandmother who lived at Folkestone, two aunts, who shared a little house in Kensington, an aunt, uncle and a brood of cousins inhabiting Cheltenham, and two uncles who lived in Cumberland. All these relations, except the two uncles, had their proper share of me and for none of them had I any great affection.

Children were not studied in those days as they are now. I was thin, pale and bespectacled, aching for affection but not knowing at all how to obtain it, outwardly undemonstrative but inwardly emotional and sensitive, playing games, because of my poor sight, very badly, reading a great deal more than was good for me, and telling myself stories all day and part of every night.

All of my relations tired of me, I fancy, in turn, and at last it was decided that my uncles in Cumberland must do their share. These two were my father's brothers, the eldest of a long family of which he was the youngest. My Uncle Robert, I understood, was nearly seventy, my Uncle Constance some five years younger. I remember always thinking that Constance was a funny name for a man.

My Uncle Robert was the owner of Faildyke Hall, a country house between the lake of Wastwater and the little town of Seascale on the sea coast. Uncle Constance had lived with Uncle Robert for many years. It was decided, after some family correspondence, that the Christmas of this year, 1890, should be spent by me at Faildyke Hall.

I was at this time just eleven years old, thin and skinny, with a bulging forehead, large spectacles and a nervous, shy manner. I always set out, I remember, on any new adventures with mingled emotions of terror and anticipation. Maybe this time the miracle would occur: I should discover a friend or a fortune, should cover myself with glory in some unexpected way, be at last what I always longed to be, a hero.

I was glad that I was not going to any of my other relations for Christmas, and especially not to my cousins at Cheltenham, who teased and persecuted me and were never free of ear-splitting noises. What I wanted most in life was to be allowed to read in peace. I understood that at Faildyke there was a glorious library.

My aunt saw me into the train. I had been presented by my uncle with one of the most gory of Harrison Ainsworth's romances, The Lancashire Witches, and I had five bars of chocolate cream, so that that journey was as blissfully happy as any experience could be to me at that time. I was permitted to read in peace, and I had just then little more to ask of life.

Nevertheless, as the train puffed its way north, this new country began to force itself on my attention. I had never before been in the North of England, and I was not prepared for the sudden sense of space and freshness that I received.

The naked, unsystematic hills, the freshness of the wind on which the birds seemed to be carried with especial glee, the stone walls that ran like grey ribbons about the moors, and, above all, the vast expanse of sky upon whose surface clouds swam, raced, eddied and extended as I had never anywhere witnessed.

I sat, lost and absorbed, at my carriage window, and when at last, long after dark had fallen, I heard 'Seascale' called by the porter, I was still staring in a sort of romantic dream. When I stepped out onto the little narrow platform and was greeted by the salt tang of the sea wind my first real introduction to the North Country may be said to have been completed. I am writing now in another part of that same Cumberland country, and beyond my window the line of the fell runs strong and bare against the sky, while below it the Lake lies, a fragment of silver glass at the feet of Skiddaw.

It may be that my sense of the deep mystery of this country had its origin in this same strange story that I am now relating. But again perhaps not, for I believe that that first evening arrival at Seascale worked some change in me, so that since then none of the world's beauties—from the crimson waters of Kashmir to the rough glories of our own Cornish coast—can rival for me the sharp, peaty winds and strong, resilient turf of the Cumberland hills.

That was a magical drive in the pony-trap to Faildyke that evening. It was bitterly cold, but I did not seem to mind it. Everything was magical to me.

From the first I could see the great slow hump of Black Combe jet against the frothy clouds of the winter night, and I could hear the sea breaking and the soft rustle of the bare twigs in the hedgerows.

I made, too, the friend of my life that night, for it was Bob Armstrong who was driving the trap. He has often told me since (for although he is a slow man of few words he likes to repeat the things that seem to him worth while) that I struck him as 'pitifully lost' that evening on the Seascale platform. I looked, I don't doubt, pinched and cold enough. In any case it was a lucky appearance for me, for I won Armstrong's heart there and then, and he, once he gave it, could never bear to take it back again.

He, on his side, seemed to me gigantic that night. He had, I believe, one of the broadest chests in the world: it was a curse to him, he said, because no ready-made shirts would ever suit him.

I sat in close to him because of the cold. He was very warm, and I could feel his heart beating like a steady clock inside his rough coat. It beat for me that night, and it has beaten for me, I'm glad to say, ever since.

In truth, as things turned out, I needed a friend. I was nearly asleep and stiff all over my little body when I was handed down from the trap and at once led into what seemed to me an immense hall crowded with the staring heads of slaughtered animals and smelling of straw.

I was so sadly weary that my uncles, when I met them in a vast billiard-room in which a great fire roared in a stone fireplace like a demon, seemed to me to be double.

In any case, what an odd pair they were! My Uncle Robert was a little man with grey untidy hair and little sharp eyes hooded by two of the bushiest eyebrows known to humanity. He wore (I remember as though it were yesterday) shabby country clothes of a faded green colour, and he had on one finger a ring with a thick red stone.

Another thing that I noticed at once when he kissed me (I

detested to be kissed by anybody) was a faint scent that he had, connected at once in my mind with the caraway-seeds that there are in seed-cake. I noticed, too, that his teeth were discoloured and yellow.

My Uncle Constance I liked at once. He was fat, round, friendly and clean. Rather a dandy was Uncle Constance. He wore a flower in his buttonhole and his linen was snowy white in contrast with his brother's.

I noticed one thing, though, at that very first meeting, and that was that before he spoke to me and put his fat arm around my shoulder he seemed to look towards his brother as though for permission. You may say that it was unusual for a boy of my age to notice so much, but in fact I noticed everything at that time. Years and laziness, alas, have slackened my observation.

II

I had a horrible dream that night. It woke me screaming, and brought Bob Armstrong in to quiet me.

My room was large, like all the other rooms that I had seen, and empty, with a great expanse of floor and a stone fireplace like the one in the billiard-room. It was, I afterwards found, next to the servants' quarters. Armstrong's room was next to mine, and Mrs. Spender's, the housekeeper's, beyond his.

Armstrong was then, and is yet, a bachelor. He used to tell me that he loved so many women that he never could bring his mind to choose any one of them. And now he has been too long my personal bodyguard and is too lazily used to my ways to change his condition. He is, moreover, seventy years of age.

Well, what I saw in my dream was this. They had lit a fire for me (and it was necessary; the room was of an icy coldness) and I dreamt that I awoke to see the flames rise to a last vigour before they died away. In the brilliance of that illumination I was conscious that something was moving in the room. I heard the movement for some little while before I saw anything.

I sat up, my heart hammering, and then to my horror discerned, slinking against the farther wall, the evillest-looking yellow mongrel of a dog that you can fancy.

I find it difficult, I have always found it difficult, to describe exactly the horror of that yellow dog. It lay partly in its colour, which was vile, partly in its mean and bony body, but for the most part in its evil head—flat, with sharp little eyes and jagged yellow teeth.

As I looked at it, it bared those teeth at me and then began to creep, with an indescribably loathsome action, in the direction of my bed. I was at first stiffened with terror. Then, as it neared the bed, its little eyes fixed upon me and its teeth bared, I screamed again and again.

The next I knew was that Armstrong was sitting on my bed, his strong arm about my trembling little body. All I could say over and over was, "The Dog! the Dog! the Dog!"

He soothed me as though he had been my mother.

"See, there's no dog there! There's no one but me! There's no one but me!"

I continued to tremble, so he got into bed with me, held me close to him, and it was in his comforting arms that I fell asleep.

III

In the morning I woke to a fresh breeze and a shining sun and the chrysanthemums, orange, crimson and dun, blowing against the grey stone wall beyond the sloping lawns. So I forgot about my dream. I only knew that I loved Bob Armstrong better than anyone else on earth.

Everyone during the next days was very kind to me. I was so deeply excited by this country, so new to me, that at first I could think of nothing else. Bob Armstrong was Cumbrian from the top of his flaxen head to the thick nails under his boots, and, in grunts and monosyllables, as was his way, he gave me the colour of the ground.

There was romance everywhere: smugglers stealing in and out of Drigg and Seascale, the ancient Cross in Gosforth church-yard, Ravenglass, with all its seabirds, once a port of splendour.

Muncaster Castle and Broughton and black Wastwater with the grim Screes, Black Combe, upon whose broad back the shadows were always dancing, even the little station at Seascale, naked to the sea-winds, at whose bookstalls I bought a publication entitled the Weekly Telegraph that contained, week by week, installments of the most thrilling story in the world.

Everywhere romance—the cows moving along the sandy lanes, the sea thundering along the Drigg beach, Gable and Scafell pulling their cloud-caps about their heads, the slow voices of the Cumbrian farmers calling their animals, the little tinkling bell of the Gosforth church—everywhere romance and beauty.

Soon, though, as I became better accustomed to the country, the people immediately around me began to occupy my attention, stimulate my restless curiosity, and especially my two uncles. They were, in fact, queer enough.

Faildyke Hall itself was not queer, only very ugly. It had been built about 1830, I should imagine, a square white building, like a thick-set, rather conceited woman with a very plain face. The rooms were large, the passages innumerable, and everything covered with a very hideous whitewash. Against this whitewash hung old photographs yellowed with age, and faded, bad water-colours. The furniture was strong and ugly.

One romantic feature, though, there was, and that was the little Grey Tower where my Uncle Robert lived. This Tower was at the end of the garden and looked out over a sloping field to the Scafell group beyond Wastwater. It had been built hundreds of years ago as a defence against the Scots. Robert had had his study and bedroom there for many years and it was his domain. No one was allowed to enter it, save his old servant Hucking, a bent, wizened, grubby little man who spoke to no one and, so they said in the kitchen, managed to go through life without sleeping. He looked after my Uncle Robert, cleaned his rooms, and was supposed to clean his clothes.

I, being both an inquisitive and romantic-minded boy, was soon as eagerly excited about this Tower as was Bluebeard's wife about the forbidden room. Bob told me that whatever I did I was never to set foot inside.

And then I discovered another thing—that Armstrong hated, feared and was proud of my Uncle Robert. He was proud of him because he was head of the family, and because, so he said, he was the cleverest old man in the world.

"Nothing he can't seemingly do," said Bob, "but he don't like you to watch him at it."

All this only increased my longing to see the inside of the Tower, although I couldn't be said to be fond of my Uncle Robert either.

It would be hard to say that I disliked him during those first days. He was quite kindly to me when he met me, and at mealtimes, when I sat with my two uncles at the long table in the big, bare, whitewashed dining room, he was always anxious to see that I had plenty to eat. But I never liked him. It was perhaps because he wasn't clean. Children are sensitive to those things. Perhaps I didn't like the fusty, seed-caky smell that he carried about with him.

Then there came the day when he invited me into the Grey Tower and told me about Tarnhelm.

Pale slanting shadows of sunlight fell across the chrysanthemums and the grey stone walls, the long fields and the dusky hills. I was playing by myself by the little stream that ran beyond the rose garden, when Uncle Robert came up behind me in the soundless way he had, and, tweaking me by the ear, asked me whether I would like to come with him inside his Tower. I was, of course, eager enough, but I was frightened too, especially when I saw Hucking's moth-eaten old countenance peering at us from one of the narrow slits that pretended to be windows.

However, in we went, my hand in Uncle Robert's hot dry one. There wasn't, in reality, so very much to see when you were inside—all untidy and musty, with cobwebs over the doorways and old pieces of rusty iron and empty boxes in the corners, and the long table in Uncle Robert's study covered with a thousand things—books with the covers hanging on them, sticky green bottles, a looking-glass, a pair of scales, a globe, a cage with mice in it, a statue of a naked woman, an hour-glass, everything old and stained and dusty.

However, Uncle Robert made me sit down close to him, and told me many interesting stories. Among others the story about Tarnhelm.

Tarnhelm was something that you put over your head, and its magic turned you into any animal that you wished to be. Uncle Robert told me the story of a god called Wotan, and how he teased the dwarf who possessed Tarnhelm by saying that he couldn't turn himself into a mouse or some such animal, and the dwarf, his pride wounded, turned himself into a mouse, which the god easily captured and so stole Tarnhelm.

On the table, among all the litter, was a grey skull-cap.

"That's my Tarnhelm," said Uncle Robert, laughing. "Like to see me put it on?"

But I was suddenly frightened, terribly frightened. The sight of Uncle Robert made me feel quite ill. The room began to run round and round. The white mice in the cage twittered. It was stuffy in that room, enough to turn any boy sick.

IV

That was the moment, I think, when Uncle Robert stretched out his hand towards his grey skull-cap, after that I was never happy again in Faildyke Hall. That action of his, simple and apparently friendly though it was, seemed to open my eyes to a number of things.

We were now within ten days of Christmas. The thought of Christmas had then—and, to tell the truth, still has—a most happy effect on me. There is the beautiful story, the geniality and kindliness, still, in spite of modern pessimists, much happiness and goodwill. Even now I yet enjoy giving presents and receiving them, then it was an ecstasy to me, the look of the parcel, the paper, the string, the exquisite surprise.

Therefore I had been anticipating Christmas eagerly. I had been promised a trip into Whitehaven for present-buying, and there was to be a tree and a dance for the Gosforth villagers. Then after my visit to Uncle Robert's Tower, all my happiness of anticipation vanished. As the days went on and my observation of one thing and another developed, I would, I think, have run away back to my aunts in Kensington, had it not been for Bob Armstrong.

It was, in fact, Armstrong who started me on that voyage of observation that ended so horribly, for when he had heard that Uncle Robert had taken me inside his Tower his anger was fearful. I had never before seen him angry. Now his great body shook, and he caught me and held me until I cried out.

He wanted me to promise that I would never go inside there again. What? Not even with Uncle Robert? No, most especially not with Uncle Robert, and then, dropping his voice and looking around him to be sure that there was no one listening, he began to curse Uncle Robert. This amazed me, because loyalty to his masters was one of Bob's great laws. I can see us now, standing on the stable cobbles in the falling white dusk while the horses stamped in their stalls, and the little sharp stars appeared one after another glittering between the driving clouds.

"I'll not stay," I heard him say to himself. "I'll be like the rest. I'll not be staying. To bring a child into it..."

From that moment he seemed to have me very specially in

his charge. Even when I could not see him I felt that his kindly eye was upon me, and this sense of the necessity that I should be guarded made me yet more uneasy and distressed.

The next thing that I observed was that the servants were all fresh, had been there not more than a month or two. Then, only a week before Christmas, the housekeeper departed. Uncle Constance seemed greatly upset at these occurrences. Uncle Robert did not seem in the least affected by them.

I come now to my Uncle Constance. At this distance of time it is strange with what clarity I still can see him—his stoutness, his shining cleanliness, his dandyism, the flower in his buttonhole, his little brilliantly shod feet, his thin, rather feminine voice. He would have been kind to me, I think, had he dared, but something kept him back. And what that something was I soon discovered. It was fear of my Uncle Robert.

It did not take me a day to discover that he was utterly subject to his brother. He said nothing without looking to see how Uncle Robert took it, suggested no plan until he first had assurance from his brother, was terrified beyond anything that I had before witnessed in a human being at any sign of irritation in my uncle.

I discovered after this that Uncle Robert enjoyed greatly to play on his brother's fears. I did not understand enough of their life to realize what were the weapons that Robert used, but that they were sharp and piercing I was neither too young nor too ignorant to perceive.

Such was our situation, then, a week before Christmas. The weather had become very wild, with a great wind. All nature seemed in an uproar. I could fancy when I lay in my bed at night and heard the shouting in my chimney that I could catch the crash of the waves upon the beach, see the black waters of Wastwater cream and curdle under the Screes. I would lie awake and long for Bob Armstrong, the strength of his arm and the warmth of his breast, but I considered myself too grown a boy to make any appeal.

I remember that now almost minute by minute my fears increased. What gave them force and power, who can say? I was much alone, I had now a great terror of my uncle, the weather was wild, the rooms of the house large and desolate, the servants mysterious, the walls of the passages lit always with an unnatural glimmer because of their white colour, and although Armstrong had watch over me he was busy in his affairs and could not always be with me.

I grew to fear and dislike my Uncle Robert more and more. Hatred and fear of him seemed to be everywhere and yet he was always soft-voiced and kindly. Then, a few days before Christmas, occurred the event that was to turn my terror into panic.

I had been reading in the library Mrs. Radcliffe's Romance of the Forest, an old book long forgotten, worthy of revival. The library was a fine room run to seed, bookcases from floor to ceiling, the windows small and dark, holes in the old faded carpet. A lamp burnt at a distant table. One stood on a little shelf at my side.

Something, I know not what, made me look up. What I saw then can even now stamp my heart in its recollection. By the library door, not moving, staring across the room's length at me, was a yellow dog.

I will not attempt to describe all the pitiful fear and mad freezing terror that caught and held me. My main thought, I fancy, was that that other vision on my first night in the place had not been a dream. I was not asleep now. The book in which I had been reading had fallen to the floor, the lamps shed their glow, I could hear the ivy tapping on the pane. No, this was reality.

The dog lifted a long, horrible leg and scratched itself. Then very slowly and silently across the carpet it came towards me.

I could not scream, I could not move, I waited. The animal was even more evil than it had seemed before, with its flat head, its narrow eyes, its yellow fangs. It came steadily in my direction, stopped once to scratch itself again, then was almost at my chair.

It looked at me, bared its fangs, but now as though it grinned at me, then passed on. After it was gone there was a thick fœtid scent in the air, the scent of caraway-seed.

V

I think now on looking back that it was remarkable enough that I, a pale, nervous child who trembled at every sound, should have met the situation as I did. I said nothing about the dog to any living soul, not even to Bob Armstrong. I hid my fears, and fears of a beastly and sickening kind they were, too, within my breast. I had the intelligence to perceive, and how I caught in the air the awareness of this I can't, at this distance, understand, that I was playing my little part in the climax to something that had been piling up, for many a month, like the clouds over Gable.

Understand that I offer from first to last in this no kind of explanation. There is possibly, and to this day I cannot quite be sure, nothing to explain. My Uncle Robert died simply, but you shall hear.

What was beyond any doubt or question was that it was after my seeing the dog in the library that Uncle Robert changed so strangely in his behaviour to me. That may have been the merest coincidence. I only know that as one grows older one calls things coincidence more and more seldom.

In any case, that same night at dinner Uncle Robert seemed twenty years older. He was bent, shrivelled, would not eat, snarled at anyone who spoke to him and especially avoided even looking at me. It was a painful meal, and it was after it, when Uncle Constance and I were sitting alone in the old yellow-papered drawing-room—a room with two ticking clocks for ever racing one another—that the most extraordinary thing occurred. Uncle Constance and I were playing draughts. The only sounds were the roaring of the wind down the chimney, the hiss and splutter of the fire, the silly ticking of the clocks. Suddenly

Uncle Constance put down the piece that he was about to move and began to cry.

To a child it is always a terrible thing to see a grown-up person cry, and even to this day to hear a man cry is very distressing to me. I was moved desperately by poor Uncle Constance, who sat there, his head in his white plump hands, all his stout body shaking. I ran over to him and he clutched me and held me as though he would never let me go. He sobbed incoherent words about protecting me, caring for me… seeing that that monster…

At the word I remember that I too began to tremble. I asked my uncle what monster, but he could only continue to murmur incoherently about hate and not having the pluck, and if only he had the courage…

Then, recovering a little, he began to ask me questions. Where had I been? Had I been into his brother's Tower? Had I seen anything that frightened me? If I did would I at once tell him? And then he muttered that he would never have allowed me to come had he known that it would go as far as this, that it would be better if I went away that night, and that if he were not afraid… Then he began to tremble again and to look at the door, and I trembled too. He held me in his arms, then we thought that there was a sound and we listened, our heads up, our two hearts hammering. But it was only the clocks ticking and the wind shrieking as though it would tear the house to pieces.

That night, however, when Bob Armstrong came up to bed he found me sheltering there. I whispered to him that I was frightened. I put my arms around his neck and begged him not to send me away. He promised me that I should not leave him and I slept all night in the protection of his strength.

How, though, can I give any true picture of the fear that pursued me now? For I knew from what both Armstrong and Uncle Constance had said that there was real danger, that it was no hysterical fancy of mine or ill-digested dream. It made it worse that Uncle Robert was now no more seen. He was sick. He kept within his Tower, cared for by his old wizened manservant. And so, being nowhere, he was everywhere. I stayed with Armstrong when I could, but a kind of pride prevented me from clinging like a girl to his coat.

A deathly silence seemed to fall about the place. No one laughed or sang, no dog barked, no bird sang. Two days before Christmas an iron frost came to grip the land. The fields were rigid, the sky itself seemed to be frozen grey, and under the olive cloud Scafell and Gable were black.

Christmas Eve came.

On that morning, I remember, I was trying to draw, some childish picture of one of Mrs. Radcliffe's scenes, when the double doors unfolded and Uncle Robert stood there. He stood there, bent, shrivelled, his long, grey locks falling over his collar, his bushy eyebrows thrust forward. He wore his old green suit and on his finger gleamed his heavy red ring. I was frightened, of course, but also I was touched with pity. He looked so old, so frail, so small in this large empty house.

I sprang up. "Uncle Robert," I asked timidly, "are you better?"

He bent still lower until he was almost on his hands and feet, then he looked up at me, and his yellow teeth were bared, almost as an animal snarls. Then the doors closed again.

The slow, stealthy, grey afternoon came at last. I walked with Armstrong to Gosforth village on some business that he had. We said no word of any matter at the Hall. I told him, he has reminded me, of how fond I was of him and that I wanted to be with him always, and he answered that perhaps it might be so, little knowing how true that prophecy was to stand. Like all children I had a great capacity for forgetting the atmosphere that I was not at that moment in, and I walked beside Bob along the frozen roads, with some of my fears surrendered.

But not for long. It was dark when I came into the long, yellow drawing room. I could hear the bells of Gosforth church pealing as I passed from the ante-room.

A moment later there came a shrill, terrified cry: "Who's that? Who is it?"

It was Uncle Constance, who was standing in front of the yellow silk window curtains, staring at the dusk. I went over to him and he held me close to him.

"Listen!" he whispered. "What can you hear?"

The double doors through which I had come were half open. At first I could hear nothing but the clocks, the very faint rumble of a cart on the frozen road. There was no wind.

My uncle's fingers gripped my shoulder. "Listen!" he said again. And now I heard. On the stone passage beyond the drawing room was the patter of an animal's feet. Uncle Constance and I looked at one another. In that exchanged glance we confessed that our secret was the same. We knew what we should see.

A moment later it was there, standing in the double doorway, crouching a little and staring at us with a hatred that was mad and sick—the hatred of a sick animal crazy with unhappiness, but loathing us more than its own misery.

Slowly it came towards us, and to my reeling fancy all the room seemed to stink of caraway-seed.

"Keep back! Keep away!" my uncle screamed.

I became oddly in my turn the protector.

"It shan't touch you! It shan't touch you, uncle!" I called.

But the animal came on.

It stayed for a moment near a little round table that contained a composition of dead waxen fruit under a glass dome. It stayed here, its nose down, smelling the ground. Then, looking up at us, it came on again.

Oh God! Even now as I write after all these years it is with me again, the flat skull, the cringing body in its evil colour and that loathsome smell. It slobbered a little at its jaw. It bared its fangs.

Then I screamed, hid my face in my uncle's breast and saw that he held, in his trembling hand, a thick, heavy, old-fashioned revolver.

Then he cried out, "Go back, Robert... Go back!"

The animal came on. He fired. The detonation shook the room. The dog turned and, blood dripping from its throat, crawled across the floor.

By the door it halted, turned and looked at us. Then it disappeared into the other room.

My uncle had flung down his revolver. He was crying, sniffling. He kept stroking my forehead, murmuring words.

At last, clinging to one another, we followed the splotches of blood, across the carpet, beside the door, through the doorway.

Huddled against a chair in the outer sitting room, one leg twisted under him, was my Uncle Robert, shot through the throat.

On the floor, by his side, was a grey skull-cap.

THE WEREWOLF HOWLS

by Clifford Ball

Twilight had come upon the slopes of the vineyards, and a gentle, caressing breeze drifted through the open casement to stir into further disorder the papers upon the desk where Monsieur Etienne Delacroix was diligently applying himself. He raised his leonine head, the hair of which had in his later years turned to gray, and stared vacantly from beneath bushy brows at the formation of a wind-driven cloud as if he thought that the passive elements of the heavens could, if they so desired, aid him in some momentous decision.

There was a light but firm tap on the door which led to the hall of the château. Monsieur Delacroix blinked as his thoughts were dispersed and, in some haste, gathered various documents together and thrust them into the maw of a large envelope before bidding the knocker to enter.

Pierre, his eldest son, came quietly into the room. The father felt a touch of the pride he could never quite subdue when Pierre approached, for he had a great faith in his son's probity, as well as an admiration for the straight carriage and clear eye he, at his own age, could no longer achieve. Of late he had been resting a great many matters pertaining to the management of the Château Doré and the business of its vineyards, which supported the estate, on the broad shoulders poised before him.

But Etienne Delacroix had been born in a strict household and his habits fashioned in a stern school, and was the lineal descendant of ancestors who had planted their peasant's feet, reverently but independently, deep into the soil of France, so visible emotions were to him a betrayal of weakness. There was no trace of the deep regard he felt for his son evident when he addressed the younger man.

"Where are your brothers? Did I not ask you to return with them?"

"They are here, Father. I entered first, to be certain that you were ready to receive us."

"Bid them enter."

Jacques and François came in to stand with their elder brother and were careful to remain a few inches in his rear; he was the acknowledged spokesman. Their greetings were spoken simultaneously, Jacques' voice breaking off on a high note which caused him obvious embarrassment, for he was adolescent. Together, thought Monsieur Delacroix, they represented three important steps in his life, three payments on account to posterity. He was glad his issue had all been males. Since the early death of his wife he had neither cared for any woman nor taken interest in anything feminine.

"I have here, my son, some papers of importance," he announced, addressing Pierre. "As you observe, I am placing them here where you may easily obtain them in the event of my absence." Suiting the action to the word, he removed the bulky envelope to a drawer in the desk and turned its key, allowing the tiny piece of metal to remain in its lock. "I am growing older," his fierce, challenging eyes swept the trio as if he dared a possible contradiction, "and it is best that you are aware of these accounts, which are relative to the business of the château,"

"Non, non!" chorused all three. "You are as young as ever, papa!"

"Sacre blue! Do you name me a liar, my children? Attend, Pierre!"

"Yes, papa."

"I have work for you this night."

The elder son's forehead wrinkled. "But the work, it is over.

Our tasks are completed. The workers have been checked, the last cart is in the shed—"

"This is a special task, one which requires the utmost diligence of you all. It is of the wolf."

"The werewolf!" exclaimed Jacques, crossing himself.

THE OTHER BROTHERS remained silent, but mingled expressions of wonder and dislike passed across their features. Ever since the coming of the wolf the topic of its depredations had been an unwelcome one in the household of the Château Doré.

"Mon Dieu, Jacques!" exploded the head of the house. "Have you, too, been listening to the old wives' tales? Must you be such an imbecile, and I your father? Rubbish! There can be no werewolves. Has not the most excellent Father Cromecq flouted such stories ten thousand times? It is a common wolf, a large one, true, but nevertheless a common mongrel, a beast from the distant mountain. Of its ferocity we are unfortunately well aware, so it must be dispatched with the utmost alacrity."

"But, the workers say, papa, that there have been no wolves in the fields for more than a hundred—"

"Peste! The ever verbose workers! The animal is patently a vagrant, a stray beast driven from the mountains by the lash of its hunger. And I, Etienne Delacroix, have pronounced that it must die!"

The father passed a heavy hand across his forehead, for he was weary from his unaccustomed labor over the accounts. His hands trembled slightly, the result of an old nervous disorder. The fingers were thick, and blunt from the hardy toil of earlier years. The blue veins were still corded from the strength which he had once possessed.

"It is well," said Pierre in his own level tones. "Since the wolf came upon and destroyed poor little Marguerite D'Estourie, tearing her throat to shreds, and the gendarmes who almost cornered it were unable to slap it because they could not shoot straight, and it persists in—"

"It slashed the shoulder of old Gavroche who is so feeble he cannot walk without two canes!" interrupted François, excitedly.

"—ravaging our ewes," concluded the single-minded Pierre, who was not to be side-tracked once he had chosen his way, whether in speech or action. "The damage to our flocks has been great, papa. It is just that we should take action, since the police have failed. I have thought this wolf strange, too, although I place no faith in demons. If it but seeks food, why must it slay so wantonly and feed so little? It is indeed like a great, gray demon in appearance. Twice have I viewed it, leaping across the meadows in the moonlight, its long, gray legs hurling it an unbelievable distance at every bound. And Marie Polydore, of the kitchens, found its tracks only yesterday at the very gates of the château!"

"I have been told," revealed Jacques, flinging his hands about in adolescent earnestness, "that the wolf is the beast-soul of one who has been stricken by the moon-demons. By day he is as other men, but by night, though he has the qualities of a saint he cannot help himself. Perhaps he is one with whom we walk and talk, little guessing his dreadful affliction."

"Silence!" roared Monsieur Delacroix. One of his clenched fists struck the desk a powerful blow and the sons were immediately quieted. "Must I listen to the ranting and raving and driveling of fools and imbeciles? Am I not still the master of the Château Doré? I will tend to the accursed matter as I have always, will I not? I have always seen to the welfare of the dwellers in the shadow of the Château Doré! And with the help of the good God I shall continue to do so, until the last drop of my blood has dried away from my bones. You comprehend?"

In a quieter tone, after the enforced silence, he continued: "I have given orders to both the foreman and Monsieur the mayor that this night, the night of the full moon by which we may detect the marauder, all the people of the vineyards and of the town beyond must remain behind locked windows and barred doors. If they have obeyed my orders—and may the good God look after those who have not—they are even now secure in the safety of their respective homes. Let me discover but one demented idiot peeking from behind his shutter and I promise you he shall have cause to remember his disobedience!"

PIERRE NODDED without speaking, knowing he was being instructed to punish a possible, but improbable, offender.

"Now, we are four intelligent men, I trust," said Monsieur Delacroix, pretending not to notice the glow of pleasure which suffused Jacques' features at being included in their number. "We are the Delacroixs, which is sufficient. And as leaders we must, from time to time, grant certain concessions to the inferior mentalities of the unfortunate who dwell in ignorance, so I have this day promised the good foremen, who petitioned me regarding the activities of this wolf, to perform certain things. They firmly believe the gray wolf is a demon, an inhuman atrocity visited upon us by the Evil One. And also, according to their ancient but childish witch lore, that it may only be destroyed by a silver weapon."

Monsieur Delacroix reached beneath his chair and drew forth a small, but apparently heavy, sack. Upending it on the surface of the desk, he scattered in every direction a double dozen glittering cylindrical objects.

"Bullets!" exclaimed Jacques.

"Silver bullets!" amended Pierre.

"Yes, my son. Bullets of silver which I molded myself in the cellars, and which I have shown to the men, with the promise that they will be put to use."

"Expensive weapons," commented the thrifty François.

"It is the poor peasant's belief. If we slew this wolf with mere lead or iron they would still be frightened of their own shadows and consequently worthless at their work, as they have been for the past month. Here are the guns. Tonight you will go forth, my sons, and slay this fabulous werewolf, and cast its carcass upon the cart-load of dry wood I have had piled by the vineyard road, and burn it until there is nothing left but the ash, for all to see and know."

"Yes, papa," Assented Pierre and François as one, but the boy Jacques cried: "What? So fine a skin? I would like it for the wall of my room! These who have seen the wolf say its pelt is like silver shaded into gray—"

"Jacques!" Etienne Delacroix's anger flooded his face with a great surge of red and bulging veins, and Pierre and François were stricken with awe at the sight of their father's wrath.

"If you do not burn this beast as I say, immediately after slaying it, I will forget you are my son, and almost a man! I will—"

His own temper choked him into incoherency.

"I crave your pardon, father," begged Jacques, humbled and alarmed. "I forgot myself."

"We will obey, papa, as always," said François, quickly, and Pierre gravely nodded.

"The moon will soon be up," said Monsieur Delacroix, after a short silence. The room had grown dark while they talked. Receiving a wordless signal from his father, Pierre struck a match and lit the blackened lamp on the desk. With the startling transition, as light leaped forth to dispel the murky shadows of the room, Pierre came near to exclaiming aloud at sight of the haggard lines in his father's face. For the first time in his life he realized that what his parent had said earlier in the evening about aging was not spoken jocularly, not the repeated jest Monsieur Delacroix had always allowed himself, but the truth. His father was old.

"You had better go," said Etienne Delacroix, as his keen eyes caught the fleeting expression on his son's face. His fingers drummed a muffled tattoo upon the fine edge of his desk, the only sign of his nervous condition that he could not entirely control. "Monsieur the Mayor's opinion is that the wolf is stronger when the moon is full. But it is mine that tonight it walls be easier to discover."

THE THREE turned to the door, but as they reached the threshold Monsieur Delacroix beckoned to the eldest. "An instant, Pierre. I speak to you alone."

The young man closed the door on his brothers' backs and returned to the desk, his steady eyes directed at his father.

Monsieur Delacroix, for the moment, seemed to have forgotten what he intended to say. His head was bowed on his chest and the long locks of his ashen hair had fallen forward over his brow. Suddenly he sat erect, as if it took an immense effort of his will to perform the simple action, and again Pierre was startled to perceive the emotions which twisted his father's features.

It was the first time he had ever seen tenderness there, or beheld love in the eyes he had sometimes, in secret, thought a little cruel.

"Have you a pocket crucifix, my son?"

"In my room."

"Take it with you tonight. And, you will stay close to Jacques, will you not?" His voice was hoarse with unaccustomed anxiety. "He is young, confident, and careless. I would not wish to endanger your good mother's last child."

Pierre was amazed. It had been fifteen years since he had last heard his father mention his mother.

"You have been a good son, Pierre. Obey me now. Do not let the three of you separate, for I hear this beast is a savage one and unafraid even of armed men. Take care of yourself, and see to your brothers."

"Will you remain in the château for safety, papa? You are not armed."

"I am armed by my faith in the good God and the walls of

Château Doré. When you have lit the fire under the wolf's body, I will be there."

He lowered the leonine head once more, and Pierre, not without another curious look, departed.

For a long while Monsieur Delacroix sat immobile, his elbows resting on the padded arras of the chair, the palms of his hands pressing into his cheeks. Then he abruptly arose and, approaching the open casement, drew the curtains wide. Outside, the long, rolling slopes fell away toward a dim horizon already blanketed by the dragons of night, whose tiny, flickering eyes were winking into view one by one in the dark void above. Hurrying cloudlets scurried in little groups across the sky.

Lamps were being lit in the jumble of cottages that were the abodes of Monsieur Delacroix's workmen, but at the moment the sky was illuminated better than the earth, for the gathering darkness seemed to ding like an animate thing to the fields and meadows, and stretch ebony claws across the ribbon of the roadway.

It was time for the moon to rise.

Monsieur Delacroix turned away from the casement and with swift, certain steps went to the door, opening it. The hall was still, but from the direction of the dining room there came a clatter of dishes as the servants cleared the table. Quickly, with an unusual alacrity for a man of his years, he silently traversed the floor of the huge hall and passed through its outer portals. A narrow gravel lane led him along the side of the château until he reached the building's extreme corner, where he abandoned it to strike off across the closely clipped sward in the direction of a small clump of beech trees.

The night was warm and peaceful, with no threat of rain. A teasing zephyr tugged at the thick locks on his uncovered head. From somewhere near his feet came the chirp of a cricket.

In the grove it was darker until he came to its center, wending through and past the entangled thickets like one who had traveled the same path many times, and found the small glade that opened beneath the stars. Here there was more light again but no breeze at all. In the center of the glade was an oblong, grassy mound, and at one end of it a white stone, and on the stone the name of his wife.

M ONSIEUR DELACROIX STOOD for an instant beside the grave with lowered head, and then he sank to his knees and began to pray.

In the east the sky began to brighten as though some torch-bearing giant drew near, walking with great strides beyond the edge of the earth. The stars struggled feebly against the superior illumination, but their strength diminished as a narrow band of encroaching yellow fire appeared on the rim of the world.

With its arrival the low monotone of prayer was checked, to continue afterward with what seemed to be some difficulty. Monsieur Delacroix's throat was choked, either with grief for the unchangeable past or an indefinable apprehension for the inevitable future. His breath came in struggling gasps and tiny beads of perspiration formed on his face and hands. His prayers became mumbled, jerky utterances, holding no recognizable phrases of speech. Whispers, and they ceased altogether.

A small dark cloud danced across a far-off mountain top, slid furtively over the border of the land, and for a minute erased the yellow gleam from the horizon. Then, as if in terror, shaken by its own temerity, it fled frantically into oblivion, and the great golden platter of the full moon issued from behind the darkness it had left to deluge the landscape with a ceaseless shower of illusive atoms, tiny motes that danced the pathways of space.

Monsieur Delacroix gave a low cry like a child in pain. His agonized eyes were fixed on the backs of his two hands as he held them pressed against the dew-dampened sward. His fingers had begun to stiffen and curl at their tips. He could see the long, coarse hairs sprouting from the pores of his flesh, as he had many times within the past month since the night he had fallen asleep by the grave of his wife and slept throughout the night under the baleful beams of the moon.

He flung back his head, whimpering because of the terrible pressure he could feel upon his skull, and its shape appeared to alter so that it seemed curiously elongated. His eyes were bloodshot, and as they sank into their sockets his lips began to twitch over the fangs in his mouth.

The three brothers, crouching nervously in the shadows of the vineyards, started violently.

Jacques, the younger, almost lost his grasp on the gun with the silver bullets which his father had given him.

From somewhere nearby there had arisen a great volume of sound, swirling and twisting and climbing to shatter itself into a hundred echoes against the vault of the heavens, rushing and dipping and sinking into the cores of all living hearts and the very souls of men—the hunting-cry of the werewolf.

www.ingramcontent.com/pod-product-compliance
Lightning Source LLC
Chambersburg PA
CBHW061045190726
48286CB00006B/1620